In Grace's Time

Kathie Giorgio

ISBN: 978-1-61296-897-1
PUBLISHED BY BLACK ROSE WRITING
www.blackrosewriting.com

Printed in the United States of America
Suggested Retail Price (SRP) $20.95

In Grace's Time is printed in Adobe Garamond Pro

The ride continues in a new direction. Thanks to all who encouraged me to hold on tight through the loop-de-loops and corkscrews. I do it all for you.

In Grace's Time

The night I lost you someone pointed me towards the *Five Stages of Grief.*
Go that way, they said, it's easy, like learning to climb stairs after the
amputation.
And so I climbed.

-excerpt from The Five Stages Of Grief
Linda Pastan

CHAPTER ONE
Grace

Grace used to have three children. Now she had two. Two remaining children, like the sad remainders she used to find when she did division in grade school. And this did divide the family; four of them, Nick, Grace, Mary and JJ, here, from the one over there. Paul. The answer to another math problem. Three take away one equals two. Mary and JJ, the remainders. Paul, the one taken away.

Division. Subtraction. The worst possible math.

In math, though, the number that was subtracted disappeared. The one taken away was magically gone from the page, from the chalkboard, from the calculator. Just like that. But for Grace, while Paul was out of her sight, the loss of him was always there, as opaque and wretched as a pen blot on the page. The ink couldn't be erased. It was steady. Never-ending. It knocked her not only from her feet, but from her mind, her body, her heart, even from the rest of her family. All because of a math problem. All because of The Moment.

The Moment where life becomes death. In the case of a child, a life that deserved to be a life with every definition that afforded, was taken away. Grace bore witness to The Moment. She watched it happen, without knowing she was watching it at all.

Grace wondered if all women who saw their children die relived it over and over again, forever and ever. It was such an odd thing, a horrible thing, pairing reliving with death. For Grace, that awful copulation happened with no warning. Was it the same for mothers who dealt with diagnoses, who dealt with times in ICUs, in ERs, who had at least five minutes to prepare, as it was for the woman who had no time to prepare at all? Who didn't know to shout, to say no, to run out and, with the full force of her body, impossibly stop what was about to happen? There was no time for grief to build, but instead, it impacted her just as death was impacted on her son, all at once, a preposterous force, erupting Grace's life and Paul's into millions of pieces. Grace was a million pieces still, six months later. Paul was just gone.

On that day, Grace thought she was only watching as her child graciously, but grumpily played hide and seek with his little brother, who was really too old for such a game. They were both ignored by their older sister who refused to play at all, but also refused to leave, leaning against the A-frame of the old swingset. Grace looked out the kitchen window while she drank her afternoon cup of coffee and held one of three Oreo cookies. She watched her boy climb a tree. Watched him disappear into the leaves.

And then Grace knew, in that exact moment as his hand popped out of the canopy. Paul reached out for the next branch which wasn't there and she saw instead that his fingers were going to touch a power line. Grace's eyes went immediately into blink against a blinding light so profound, so brilliant, it far surpassed her expectations of who Paul might be when he grew up. And then Grace watched him fall, like the negative of a photograph, her eyes diminished to black and white from the flash. Her middle boy. Paul. Fifteen years old. Not a boy, really. Not a man either. On the cusp.

But from that day onward, her boy. He would never grow into anything or anyone else.

Even as Grace ran out of the house, she knew he was dead. She didn't even reach for the phone. It was her neighbors who called 911.

Grace sat at the base of the tree and pulled the husk of her son into her lap. She could hear her daughter and younger son screaming, crying, she felt their arms around her neck. But she only looked at Paul's face. Already, the color leached. No pink cheeks, no bright eyes, brighter smile. Before the paramedics even got there, Grace did what no mother should ever have to do.

She closed her son's eyes.

Now, Grace stood at the sink and stared at that same tree. The season was blending into fall and the leaves were starting to color. When Paul was small, he used to collect the red and orange leaves like a dandelion bouquet and present them to her. He never brought her dandelions. Other mothers spoke of those sunshine bouquets, but Grace only knew them through her older child, her daughter, Mary, and through her younger son, JJ. For Paul, tucked in the middle, two years after Mary, three years before JJ, a bouquet for Mom meant leaves. Autumn leaves. She loved them.

But she hated this tree. And she couldn't stand to look at it for one more minute. She set down her coffee mug and dug in the junk drawer for the hammer and a small plastic box of nails. Then she closed the curtains. They were the type called Priscillas, something she always wondered about, who this Priscilla was who would have curtains named after her. What a strange way to be immortalized. The curtains were for decoration mostly, pulled to the side of the window like a girl's pigtails and held back with ruffled ties. Grace undid the ties and spread the curtains across the window. The edges lay flat on the sill. Carefully, efficiently, Grace took the hammer and pounded twenty nails, sealing the sill and the curtains together. Then, to make sure the curtains didn't separate in any way, didn't let in a single glimpse of leaf or bark or branch, she pulled out the stapler. The sound of the staples' bite wasn't as satisfying as the hammer, but it worked. The window was encased in cloth against the outside. Against what Grace saw, over and over, forever and ever, when she looked there.

Grace admired the cheery yellow and white gingham. She'd chosen the curtains, these Priscillas, when she and Nick first moved there, with just Mary sixteen years ago. That morning, they signed the papers on the house, one-year old Mary wriggling and protesting on Grace's lap, then they got married in the afternoon, and returned to their new home that night. The first weekend in their house was their honeymoon, and on their honeymoon, they conceived Paul. Grace visualized Priscillas at her kitchen window that evening, the first evening she looked out at the tree. Nick looked out the window too, tucked himself behind Grace with his arms around her waist, his lips pressed against her neck, a conception about to occur.

A conception that Grace still thought of as a gift. She'd just turned thirty-eight years old when she gave birth to Mary, another gift, Grace's first gift, after years of trying to conceive. She was still thirty-eight when her first husband, Steven, left, after he discovered that fatherhood wasn't at all what he imagined and that being married to a mother wasn't what he imagined either. Grace was thirty-nine when she married Nick. At forty, she birthed Paul, an age when she never expected to be a mother again. And then JJ, a stunning surprise at forty-three. Forty-three years old, and the mother of three children. Two completely unexpected.

And now almost fifty-six, and the mother of two children. Or was it three? Two remaining. One taken. An unexpected child now unexpectedly gone.

Grace traced her finger down the stapled seam of the curtains, feeling cloth, then metal, cloth, then metal, thin strips of cold in the soft. The curtains always reminded Grace of her mother. Her mother loved Priscillas too. She had them in her own kitchen. They were close to the only traditional, conventional thing in her mother's house. Grace didn't know of anyone else whose mother looked into crystal balls, collected nativity sets, buttered spiders for good luck. But when it came to curtains, Grace and her mother loved tradition; they loved gingham Priscillas. Grace's mother's were blue and white, bright, she said, as the summer sky. Grace's were the yellow of sunshine.

On some days, Grace couldn't bear to see the blue sky or the sun or cheerful squares of gingham. On this day, she couldn't stand to see that tree. She wondered about combinations, about timing, about the emptiness of days that used to be full.

Paul died six months ago, before this day of hammering curtains. Grace's mother, six months before that. Cancer.

Turning her back on the window, Grace put her mug into the dishwasher and looked around. There were things she should do. She'd done so little for six months. She tried to feel determined.

It was time. Her husband told her so every day. And on this day, he'd told her by writing it in the dust on their bedroom dresser. *It's time, Grace.* Grace got the message, as gentle as it was.

She just wasn't sure what it was time for. She slouched for a moment in the new dim of her kitchen. But then she straightened. She knew what she could do. She could go visit her mother in the bank vault.

****

Grace tried to visit once a month, usually on a Thursday, and a glance at a calendar confirmed that's what this day was. Another glance, directed at the clock, told her she had plenty of time before the kids got home from school. Most days, her children, her remaining children, three minus one equals two, found her still in bed when they arrived home. Mary came home from the school where Grace used to teach. She taught high school English for thirty years and she thought she'd be there until she retired. But then there was Paul's death in April and Grace was unable to finish the year. When the fall came, five months later, and the kids returned to school, she found she couldn't. She could barely get out of bed.

Nick tried to convince her to go. He said it would help her to get back into a routine. But on the first day of school, after Grace watched two children instead of three go out the door, she went back to bed, fully clothed. To Nick, each day she stayed away made it easier to not return. To Grace, she stayed away each day because it was so hard. She didn't even tell Nick when the ultimatum came reluctantly from the school. Grace resigned.

There was just no way to predict when her energy would wane and when it would return and when it simply seemed like Grace would never move again.

Grace wondered about her grief. Was it going the wrong way? It only seemed to get larger. Sometimes, Grace felt like her entire life was framed by those two graves, appearing one right after the other. Her mother's and Paul's. Sometimes, when her mind's eye dodged between those two repetitive graves, she felt that the only thing left to her was her own grave, her own body, covered in layers of dirt. And, when she really thought about it, when she allowed her mind to admit it, she knew that was what she wanted.

But there were two other children. Remaining children. There were Mary and JJ. Their arms were still around her neck, their cries in her ears. And there was Nick too. A husband. The father of her dead child, the father of her youngest. And Mary's stepfather, the only father she'd ever really known.

Because of the graves, there was no need to go to the bank vault, Grace knew that. She knew it wasn't typical, not conventional, just like her mother wasn't conventional. Grace could go to the cemetery, the way anybody else would. She did go there sometimes to sit between her mother's headstone and the one next door. Her father's. Her mother believed that a neglected grave was a disgrace, so Grace always left flowers, proof that the graves weren't ignored. Roses for her mother. Whatever was on sale for her father. Her father was practical, and he would have liked that.

There was no disgrace. Not there. Not for them.

But then there was Paul. And his grave, over a hill and three rows down. It was decorated and visited, but not by Grace. She told herself her mother, while disapproving, would also understand why she just couldn't go there yet. "Grace," her mother would say. Her voice would have that tone that somehow combined remonstrance and consolation. Grace would only have to nod and answer, "I know, Mom," for her mother's voice to soften further and melt and she'd pat Grace's hand and nod too and say, "It's okay, Gracie. In your time."

Grace didn't know when her time was. And she didn't know if it would ever be. Though Nick kept insisting it was now. "It's time, Grace," he would say, and lay his hand on her shoulder. Sometimes he planted a kiss on her forehead. "It's time." He wrote it in the dust.

Grace wondered for what.

That morning, on this Thursday, after nailing the Priscillas shut, Grace managed to make the bed she shared with her husband and load the breakfast dishes into the dishwasher before she left for the bank. Her remaining children were at school and her husband was at work. The cat stretched black and white tuxedo in a basket of laundry, left out so that Grace would remember to do it. At least three days ago.

Grace patted the cat on her way out the door, as was her custom, and her mother's before her. Her mother considered cats lucky, friends of the spirits and spells and superstitions she so enjoyed and collected in her life. She instructed Grace to always pat a cat before leaving the house so the spirits would come alert by the purr and watch over things until the family's return. Grace's cat was named TheCat, and he yawned and fell back asleep, purring in family underwear.

The bank was a five-minute drive away. In the year since Grace's mother's death, the same bank teller always escorted Grace to the vault and performed the key ritual with her. The teller, Sheri, studied Grace every time over dark round glasses, and Grace wondered what the purpose of the glasses was, since she never seemed to look through them. Sheri's nametag was always pinned in a straight line, like a ruler, on her lapel. Maybe the glasses were for that.

Grace greeted Sheri, then held up her key and waggled it. "I would like to see safety deposit box number eighty-one please."

Sheri studied Grace over her glasses as if she never saw her before. Then she nodded and they went into the vault together, Sheri's key ring jangling, Grace's lone key pressed against her palm. Grace looked around and was relieved when nobody else was there. Visiting her mother was difficult when there was a crowd. Other people came in carrying calculators, rustling papers, but Grace just came for conversation.

Grace and Sheri stood side by side in front of the wall of boxes, their keys at the ready. Grace always felt like they were about to set a prisoner free. Sheri started the ritual by inserting her key into box number eighty-one, twisting it, then stepping back. Every move the woman made was sharp with precision. Grace's key took its turn, she always felt sloppily in comparison, and then she pulled the box safely into her arms. Rescuing the prisoner. Freeing her mother. She went to a privacy room, listening to Sheri's shoes as they clicked away.

And then there was only Grace, her mother, and the box, filled with the things that only Grace knew about. Things that were for Grace alone. Secrets.

There was a pendant. It was a long black wooden face, a tiny sibling to the stones of Easter Island, dangling from a slim silver chain. Her mother said it was her personal guardian spirit and she wore it every day. Grace had instructions that upon her mother's death, she was to take the pendant from her mother's body and then clasp it around her own neck. Grace's mother wanted her spirit's energy to transfer to Grace. Grace did remove the pendant, before her mother's body cooled, before her last breath had time to escape the room, but she didn't put the chain around her neck. She knew it was a gift from her mother. But it didn't yet feel like the time to wear it herself.

Time again. Time for what? For when she could follow instructions exactly? For when she could stay out of bed for an entire day? For when she could no longer disgrace a grave? Nick said it was time.

For what?

Grace's mother believed strongly in her spirits, like this little black face, and spells. When Grace was thirteen years old, her mother hung dollar bills in the attic because she said the spirits would touch them and make the family rich. But the dollars kept disappearing instead of doubling. Grace's mother burned incense and left offerings like sandwich bologna and olive loaf. The spirits liked preservatives, she said, it kept them grounded. But still the dollars vanished, and the lunchmeat too. Finally, she rubbed the bills with peppermint extract. Then she traced the icy-fresh smell to her husband's wallet. He was always thrifty and he said it was a waste to hang dollar bills in the attic, even if they were supposed to double their worth. It was silly, he said, and Grace remembered that. She remembered the look on her mother's face. Dollars were never hung again.

But here, in the safety deposit box, there were dollars with the pendant. The amount made Grace nervous. She counted it every time she visited, just to make sure it was all still there. Twenty-two thousand, three-hundred and twelve dollars. Her mother gave it to her the morning she entered hospice. It was why the safety deposit box existed even before her mother didn't. The cash came first; the pendant joined it after the death.

When Grace's mother gave her the money, she said, "Gracie, this is for you," and piled neat bundles of bills in Grace's lap. She'd tied them with brightly colored ribbon, as if she was braiding hair, the way she used to braid Grace's, the way Grace used to braid Mary's. "Hold out your hand," she said, and then placed a shiny quarter, two dimes, a nickel, and three pennies onto Grace's palm. "That's what it came out to," she said.

"Okay..." Grace said. She never did find out what "it" was, where it came from.

"Put the change in a special spot in your purse. You never know when you're going to need some change, and usually when you do, you never have any."

Grace did as she was told, and the shiny coins were in a special zippered section of her purse even now. The coins were definitely real, but at first, Grace thought the dollars were fake. Another spell of sorts. Maybe fake money tied in ribbon and stacked in piles would bring real money, in a way the peppermint dollar bills in the attic didn't. But when she picked some of them up, she felt their thickness and their recognizable quality. She looked at her mother, dumbfounded. "How much is this?" she asked. "Where is it from?"

Her mother shrugged. "It's a lot and it's from me. This money is for you and you alone, Grace. A gift just for you."

Grace dropped the bills, then reached across to grasp her mother's hands. "Mom, you know I appreciate this," she said. "But you have medical bills to pay, and now hospice—"

"You're not listening, Grace. I want you to put this somewhere where no one else can find it and where you can get to it quickly if necessary. A safety deposit box in only your name." She looked at Grace levelly, no waver, no tremor, no tears. There was just Grace's mother there, in that glance. Not the woman who'd been pain-ridden for months now. Cancer, for that moment, took a step away and left behind the woman Grace knew so well. Grace was so glad to see her. "I don't want Nick to know about it."

Grace was dumbfounded again. Her mother liked Nick. She hadn't liked Grace's first husband, Steven, but Nick was always hugged, fed, and praised.

Her mother looked at Grace and smiled. "Sometimes a woman finds herself wanting to be away for a while, Gracie. To escape. And she can't because there's a husband, there are children. There are always responsibilities, and I know you take your responsibilities very seriously. So this is your very own, no one else's. Just for you. Should you ever need to escape. I want to know that you have it. I've saved it just for you, for this reason."

Grace remembered the peppermint bills in her father's wallet and the look on her mother's face when her father said her mother's special spell was silly. There was nothing silly here.

Grace didn't know what to say. It felt underhanded to not let Nick know about the money, and it felt a bit worse to not use it to make her mother as comfortable as possible in her last days. But, her mother insisted, this was about her comfort. She needed Grace to have this. Grace never liked saying no to her mother and so she took the money and chose a bank five minutes away from home. She figured if she ever needed to escape, she'd want to get away quickly.

A month later, her mother died and the pendant settled into the safety deposit box instead of around Grace's neck. She had a huge estate sale, selling her mother's spirit- and spell-laden collections and then the house itself to cover the final expenses. The small amount left over, she put into accounts for the kids, for their college education.

When Paul died, she closed his account. She split the amount in two and deposited it into Mary's and JJ's college funds. She cried during the whole transaction. It was at the family bank, not the one with her mother's safety deposit box. Grace wished Selma was there. Selma would have only stared at her. The teller at the family bank offered tissue after tissue and kept patting Grace's hand which trembled as she signed the necessary paperwork.

But that pendant, Grace held onto. It became her mother, and she began to talk to it every month. The graves, she visited every other month or so.

Tucked safely in the privacy room, Grace gently rubbed the pendant's black wooden face with her thumb. "Hi, Mom," she said. She raised it to her lips for just a moment, kissing the smoothness that was not her mother's face. But it was; it was the closest thing Grace had and so she kissed it.

And then she filled her mother in. She talked about the children, the remaining children, how Mary was sullen and withdrawn, JJ deliberately perky and bright, driven to lift the family up, push them along. Like his father. Grace heard her own voice and still, a year later, missed the sound of her mother's responses. The give and take of the easy conversation that was a lifetime long until her mother's life ended. And then Grace's voice hitched. And stopped. It was time to talk about Paul. The missing child. The dead child. Unexpected.

Was he with her mother?

Grace just didn't know. She didn't know what she believed. But she knew what she wanted to. Some days, the only way Grace got through was picturing her mother and son, their heads bowed together, talking in that special lifelong conversation that Grace used to share with her mother. And the lifelong conversation which was cut short with her son. Now, she hoped they spoke to each other.

"I haven't been to Paul's grave yet, Mom," she said quietly. "I've tried, but I just can't do it." She closed her eyes for a moment, barricading tears. And then she felt her mother. She felt the sigh that she knew would come, and there was her hand, patting Grace's, and she felt the air move with her nod. Grace gripped her mother's invisible fingers. "It's not neglected though, JJ sees to that. He's talking about making Halloween decorations. When school started, he found

Paul's backpack. He stuffed it with some notebooks, a pencil box, and some brand new pencils and pens. He even found an eraser in the shape of a rocket ship. He strapped the backpack over Paul's headstone." Grace stopped and thought of that blue denim backpack, slung over the shoulders of a gravestone, getting wet in the rain, maybe covered by leaves. Leaves that wouldn't be gathered into a bouquet. "JJ doesn't go alone," she said. "Nick goes with him. Sometimes Mary. But, well, not me." Grace felt the sigh again. "I'll get there, I promise, Mom," she said. "I know you think he needs his mother. I'll go. I will. In my time," Grace said, and she heard her mother's voice in her own.

Her time. "In your time, Gracie." She just couldn't imagine it ever being her time again. But she didn't tell her mother that. She didn't tell Nick either.

Grace placed the pendant in the middle of the neatly stacked piles of beribboned bills. "I should get going," she said. She almost stood up, but then stopped and picked up the pendant one more time, feeling its chain slip cold between her fingers. "I miss you, Mom." She swiftly kissed the wooden face, then returned it to the box. "Nick would say hi if he knew you were here. So would the kids. They miss you too." She hesitated, then touched the pendant with one finger. "Is Paul with you? Does Paul miss you, or does he have you for company?" Her throat began to close. "Does he miss me? Please, Mom," she said. "If he's there, if you're there, please take care of each other." She closed the box, returned it to its slot, and locked it tightly.

As Grace walked out of the bank, she nodded and waved at Sheri, stiff behind her teller's window. Sheri looked over her glasses at Grace like she never saw her before.

Next door to the bank, there was a doll museum and shop called The Nursery. Grace always stopped for just a minute to look in the window. The dolls seemed to smile, wink, live in the sunshine behind the glass and Grace thought about holding them and brushing their hair.

There was only one thing Grace didn't like about her magical mother. There was only one thing that confounded Grace. Grace's mother never allowed dolls in the house. That made the child Grace, and even the adult Grace, want one with an appetite that surpassed obsession. Christmas after Christmas, birthday after birthday, the child Grace topped her gift lists with all sorts of dolls. In the sixties, dolls were just beginning to come incredibly alive and the Sears Christmas Catalog was filled with talkers, wetters, walkers, and criers. Grace wanted them all and begged for them every chance she got. She kept the catalog year-round, until the next one came out. But her mother always said no.

Whenever Grace asked her mother why she didn't like dolls, and she asked often, her mother only said that she had a promise to keep. She never explained this, and she never said to who, and sometimes, Grace worked herself past her reticence over the expression on her mother's face and asked for more. *Why? What promise? Why can't I have a doll?* Grace's mother sealed her lips and lowered her eyes and turned away. Grace sometimes offered an apology for the badgering that clearly hurt her mother. But other times, she didn't. Other times, she was just too angry.

She was a little girl. She should have a doll. All little girls had dolls. Grace just wanted to hold one and care for it, have it be her very own.

Grace's childhood best friend, Sarah Ann, lived right across the street. She owned even more than dolls; she had carriages, beds, bottles, and wardrobes. When Sarah Ann and Grace played, they had to play outside in their yards or in Grace's room. Grace's mother wouldn't let her inside Sarah Ann's house, because she knew that once Grace disappeared behind that door, she would lunge for the dolls. Of course she would. But Grace never had the opportunity. Even when Sarah Ann came over for sleepovers, she wasn't allowed to bring a favorite doll to sleep with. She brought a teddy bear.

Grace knew all of this. She tried all of the tricks. And her mother foiled her every time.

Once, Grace heard her mother talking with Sarah Ann's mother. Sarah Ann's mother said, "Diana, why can't Gracie play with dolls? She's a *girl*." In Sarah Ann's mother's voice, Grace heard her own befuddled curiosity.

There was a silence. Then Grace's mother said, "Grace has plenty of other toys."

Which of course was no answer and brought no satisfaction at all.

Grace's mother wasn't conventional. But in this case, Grace wished and wished for a mother who did things like other mothers.

Only once was there a doll in Grace's bed, but it wasn't from a store or a catalog. It was a cornhusk doll made by a gypsy Grace and her mother met at the farmer's market, held every Saturday from May through October. This woman read Tarot and made strange-smelling teas that caused Grace to wrinkle her nose and slap both hands over her mouth. Grace's mother was concerned that Grace was clumsy; she was always tripping over her own feet or falling down the stairs. Her mother wanted her to live up to her name, to glide even when just walking to the bathroom. The gypsy woman made the doll and instructed Grace to sleep with it. The doll's cornsilk grace, she said, would rub off during the night. It was made from the truest corn, grown in Iowa, she said, and Grace saw her mother light up. To Grace, corn was what you bought at the county fair; its husk was stripped back, it was dipped in a huge vat of butter, and then you sprinkled it with salt until it sparkled like the night sky. How could corn not be true when it grew from the ground, whether that ground was in Iowa or Wisconsin or any place on the face of the earth?

Dolls weren't made from corn. Corn wasn't in the Sears Catalog.

Climbing into her bed that night, the cornhusk doll on the pillow next to her, Grace thought of her father calling her mother silly, and Grace wanted to call her mother that as well. But she didn't.

Instead, she shredded the doll and left it in a pile under her pillow. When Grace returned to bed the next evening, every golden corn strip was gone. Her mother never mentioned that doll again.

After leaving the bank vault and Sheri, Grace stopped as usual by The Nursery and looked in its window. To her surprise, it was empty. There was a box, draped with what looked like black velvet, and some leaves and gourds were scattered near the glass. Disappointed, Grace was just beginning to leave when a man appeared in the window. He was carrying a doll.

He placed her on the box and the sun fell inside and lit her hair. Set upright, her eyes popped open and their bright blue flew directly into Grace's gaze. Grace saw the doll's smile and in her smile, she remembered the picture in the catalogs, the commercials on television. This was Chatty Cathy, and she graced the cover of the catalog when Grace was four or five years old. She was a wonder. She had a magical string that, when pulled, gave her the gift of speech. Grace tore her picture from the catalog and kept it for years, but she never held her nor touched her nor heard her voice. She topped Grace's gift lists long after her popularity was over and the little girl population moved on to ogling dolls with even higher performance skills.

The man in the window maneuvered Cathy's arms gently into a blue corduroy coat. On her head, he perched a matching hat. He raised one of her hands so she seemed to be waving and he hung a small red purse over her shoulder. Then he walked away.

Grace stepped a little closer, moving off the sidewalk and into the grass. She flattened her fingers on the glass. She wondered how Cathy would feel if she held her hand.

The man reappeared. The sun caught his glasses. He raised a brush to the doll's hair and then he saw Grace. He looked at her for a moment, brush upraised, and then he smiled. Grace smiled back, but then walked quickly away. She felt silly, being caught at the window with her hand pressed against it, staring at a doll. Grace was a grown woman. She could hear her father again, telling her mother that she was silly.

But this man, the doll man, smiled. It was a nice smile. At the corner of the bank building, Grace looked over her shoulder.

The man stood on the steps of The Nursery, watching her. He waved, or possibly beckoned, Grace couldn't tell for sure.

She moved around the corner to her car. Leaning against it, she tucked her hands in her pockets and raised her face to the waning summer sunshine.

Grace wondered how Cathy's skin felt, how her hair felt. Soft? Silky? Did she feel real? Grace wondered how Cathy's voice sounded when the magical ring was pulled. She could feel it fitting like jewelry around the first knuckle of her finger.

What would Cathy say?

The man's smile was nice.

Grace climbed into her car. Maybe, she thought, when she came back next month for the next visit to her mother, she would go inside The Nursery. Maybe she would touch Cathy. Maybe she would hear her voice.

If Chatty Cathy was still in the window, the next time it was a Thursday when Grace found some energy.

Her mother would say no. Grace knew that.

But Grace was grown now, wasn't she. And her mother was in her grave.

There was no remaining mother.

****

By the time the kids got home from school, Grace had the laundry loaded in the washing machine and the dishwasher door closed. She wished she'd dusted. At the very least, Nick's message on the bedroom dresser should have been wiped away, but there was the visit to the bank vault and the children came home and soon Grace had to start dinner.

Mary and JJ walked in one behind the other, Mary in the lead, as usual. She dropped her backpack on the floor by her favorite reading chair in the living room and JJ set his next to Grace, who was waiting for them on the couch. She smiled at him. "How was your day?" she asked.

"Pretty good." He gave Grace a one-armed hug before sitting down next to

19

her.

Mary was rubbing her knuckles and Grace saw a red flag. "And your day?" Grace asked.

"His day wasn't good either," Mary said. "He just doesn't want to tell you."

JJ glanced quickly at her. "You shouldn't tell either, Mary. You know what Dad said." They looked at each other, Mary rubbing her knuckles more slowly now as she considered.

"What did Dad say?" Nick said a lot of things, but Grace couldn't think of anything he'd told her that would keep the kids from talking about their days.

JJ flipped through a pile of newspapers on the coffee table. Grace tried to remember how long it was since she threw some away. "That we're not supposed to tell you," JJ said.

"Tell me what?"

Mary sat on the floor. Grace admired the way she could just fold her legs so boneless and easy and end up in a sit as if she'd always been there. TheCat walked in and rolled around her thin hips. "Dad says that with Grandma dying last year and then Paul, you're not quite right and that's why the house looks like this. We can't keep up with everything without you, and right now, you can't do much of anything."

"Mary," JJ warned.

TheCat climbed into her lap. "We're not supposed to worry you about stuff. So you can start pulling yourself together. Dad says it's time."

And there it was. Even the kids, the remaining kids, thought it was time. Grace looked around. She'd been so proud just a few minutes ago of getting done what she had. The dishwasher door. The laundry. Yes, there was the message in the dust, but she wasn't without accomplishment. She got things done today.

But in the view of the living room, that suddenly didn't seem like enough. Besides the newspapers, there were empty soda cans, half-closed potato chip bags, DVD cases, books. Jackets, which hadn't been worn for weeks. Dishes that never made it to the kitchen. Dishes she hadn't even noticed were missing. There was a fork on the floor, right next to Mary's knee.

But still. There was Nick. And Mary. And JJ. Grace folded her arms. They had hands too, didn't they? They had feet. Couldn't keep up without her? Why couldn't they? And she was doing some things. Look at what she'd done today. She was not without accomplishment.

It's time, Grace.

Grace could hear Nick. He wasn't mean; he was patient. And reasonable. And sometimes, Grace hated reasonable. She hated reasonable right this very minute.

Time for what? To clean up the house? To visit the grave? To stop crying every single day as if she had a constant reservoir of tears that filled from some unknown place where Paul was? Where her mother was? Where their heads were together in conversation that Grace so wanted to hear. A conversation she started and that she was unable to finish. Because they were gone. Her son, unexpectedly. Her mother, expectedly, but in the most horrible way.

In your time, Gracie, her mother would say. It wasn't Grace's time. She didn't know if it would ever be.

She looked at JJ who shrugged and sat back, putting his feet on the coffee table. Some of the newspapers scattered to the floor, joining others from earlier feet, earlier shrugs. Yes, the kids had hands. Yes, they had feet. But at twelve and seventeen years old, the house wasn't their responsibility. *Without you, we can't keep up.* "So what kind of stuff happened today that you shouldn't tell me?"

Mary's hand slid down TheCat's back and then up the slim tail. "There was a guy bugging JJ after school, when I stopped to pick him up. I took care of it," she said.

Grace looked again at her daughter's red knuckles. "What did you do?"

Mary quickly covered her telltale hand with the other. "Mom, this guy was yelling, telling everyone that Paul blew up like a firecracker."

Grace froze. She saw the flash. She saw it again.

"Lit up," JJ said. "He said lit up, not blew up."

Grace thought of firecrackers and their light and noise. There was a flash when Paul touched the wire. A blinding flash, bigger than anything Grace ever saw. Bigger than lightning, than an explosion, than fireworks. And a noise, a bang, when he fell.

A firecracker. Paul was a firecracker. And Grace was frozen in hell.

She looked at JJ. "What did you say to this boy?"

"Nothing." He kicked at more papers. "Because Paul did sort of die like a firecracker." He echoed Grace's thoughts. "Didn't he? The guy was sorta right."

"No, he wasn't!" TheCat was dumped as Mary flowed to her feet just as easily as when she sat. "It wasn't like that at all! Firecrackers go off on purpose. Paul was an accident." Her fists were clenched and Grace studied the skinned knuckles. The firecracker boy definitely got the worst end of this fight.

Grace took a breath, shook her head. "Kids shouldn't be saying stuff like that," she said to JJ. "The next time someone says something mean about Paul, tell him it's not nice to talk about and then walk away." Grace turned to Mary. "And you…don't hit."

The moment hung in the air. Neither child looked at her.

Grace felt her shoulders drop. "Please," she said. "You are always to tell me what happens at school. I want to know. I want to hear." They looked at each other again, and Grace knew they were weighing the two directives. Dad's "Don't tell your mother." Mom's "I'm okay, tell me."

How many times were her two children, her remaining children, going to be placed in a spot they shouldn't have to be in?

How many times was she?

But then they nodded.

Grace grabbed their hands and pulled them to the kitchen. "Get yourselves a snack," she said. She watched as JJ stuck his head in the pantry and Mary stuck her head in the fridge.

Then Grace went back to bed. Just for a while. Just for a break. She had two hours before Nick came home.

She was already in the kitchen when Nick pulled in the driveway. She received her peck on the cheek, and then they stood at the counter together while Nick sorted through the mail. Nick placed his hand on the small of Grace's back. It was a gesture, a pressure she loved. So different from some of Nick's other pressures. But all of them, she knew, were offered with love. She never doubted Nick's motivations.

"How was your day?" he asked.

"Okay. How about you?" Grace got some chicken breasts from the fridge and washed them, preparing them for a quick breaded baking in the oven.

"Pretty good." He looked at the chicken. "Chicken for dinner?"

"Yes. I thought with rice."

"Sounds good. I'll say hi to the kids." He left the room and Grace watched him go. She thought about her visit with her mother in the bank vault and she realized she hadn't told her mother anything about Nick. She thought about how he told the kids not to say anything to her.

TheCat appeared and pressed his back against Grace's legs. She felt the stiffness, the softness, heard her husband's voice, her kids', the tinny theme song of a video game. She tried to take it in, to let it encompass her the way it always did, always, since there were the five of them. The five. But there was a voice still missing, there was an empty space in the air of this house that she felt for the last six months. And right then, as she listened for him, as she tried to hear Paul's voice in the mix, the boy-voice breaking at times with the man he was supposed to become, Grace realized she was waiting for the impossible. That gap was never going to close. There was no way on this earth to fill it. Because Paul was no longer on this earth.

She dropped the chicken and to Grace, the splat it made was deafening. TheCat thought so too, leaping straight up in the air. But then, nose twitching, he went over to investigate the white and so very raw meat.

Grace let him. Even though it was their dinner. Even though it was raw and would likely make TheCat sick and he would create a mess. Which someone would have to clean up. Someone who wasn't Grace, because she would likely be back up in bed, her eyes tightly closed in order to fling herself into sleep, or staring blankly at the ceiling. But none of it mattered. Not then.

Because Grace was thinking about escape. Just leaving this house, these people, that cat, the ruined chicken, and that killer tree. The tree that killed Paul. The tree behind the nailed and curtained window, the yellow and white gingham Pricillas, that her husband had yet to notice, and that she would have to explain. Standing there, Grace thought about getting away from Paul too, from her forever dead son, from his never-to-end absence. Unexpected.

Nothing was as it should be.

Looking down at her hands, Grace remembered the black wooden face of her mother's pendant as she held it in her palms, let the chain slide through her fingers. She remembered it dangling around her mother's neck and for a moment, just that moment, she closed her eyes and saw it around her own neck too.

If her mother's spirit infused through Grace, if an escape propelled her forward, she wondered if she could survive this. If she could move beyond putting one foot in front of the other. Putting one foot in front of the other sometimes with a break in bed between steps. A long break. This wasn't survival. This wasn't living. It was inertia.

But then Grace heard JJ's laugh and Mary's grunt of dismissal as she tried to ignore him. The sounds there and gone as quickly as losing at Hide and Seek. As quickly as clinging to a tree, and then being blown out of it with a light so bright, your mother had to blink away your last breath.

TheCat gagged and Grace blinked now, then swooped down to snatch up the cold and clammy chewed-on chicken breasts. With a bang, she threw them into the disposal, turned it on, let the motor chew and grind.

There had to be supper. She had to feed her family. Grace took her responsibilities very seriously. Just as her mother said.

But because of that, there was cash in the safety deposit box too. For an escape. Should she ever want to be away.

She never thought she would want that.

But she never thought she would be the mother of a dead boy. Of a boy who lit her life still, but in such a different way than when he filled the gap in this house.

Grace turned to the freezer and dug out two pizzas. They would do. They would have to. Nick would raise an eyebrow and she would have to offer an explanation. There was always just so much to explain.

****

Late that night, after the kids went to bed, Grace sat at the kitchen table, the overhead the only light on in the first floor of the house. She'd made it this far, intent on checking the school notes on the fridge to see if she was forgetting anything for the next day. But when she walked into the room and saw all the notes dangling from the fridge door, it seemed the only thing she could do was sit down.

She could hear Nick upstairs, unmaking their bed, putting on his flannel pajama pants and t-shirt. She wasn't surprised when he came looking for her. He always needed to know where she was now.

He sat in a chair next to her. "Are you tired, hon?" he asked.

She nodded. It was another new habit of his. Since Paul's death, Nick was always asking if she was tired and she always said yes.

"Are you hungry or thirsty or anything?"

Sitting back, Grace considered. "I'm both, actually. Hungry and thirsty."

And she was. She could feel the emptiness in her stomach, the ache of dry in her throat. Hunger and thirst surprised her. It was like that a lot since Paul died; days would pass when she couldn't remember eating a thing. Then a hunger would descend like a voracious cloud and she couldn't eat enough. Even so, Grace couldn't say how much weight she'd lost. She refused to get on a scale anymore. As if a number on a dial could somehow measure what she really lost.

What she lost was one-hundred and forty pounds of fifteen-year old boy. A five foot, eight inch boy. She knew, because Paul had a well exam just before his death. They'd both marveled over his weight and height. It seemed so

24

substantial. He was the size of an adult.

But he was her boy. Her unexpected gift.

The weight loss, and the refusal to weigh herself, made Nick want to take care of Grace all the more. Was she tired? Yes. Was she hungry? Sometimes. But the caretaking Grace missed was the I love you's, the Come to bed's. The kisses down the back of the neck, the arms reaching around. Hugging her waist. Cupping her breasts.

That all stopped with Paul's death too. Everything stopped, it seemed.

And while she missed it, while she missed the intimacy of marriage, the closeness of her husband, Grace knew the conundrum that if Nick came to her right then, if he stood and went to the back of the chair instead of to the pantry, if he planted his lips down her neck in the way she loved so well, if he slid a hand in between the buttons of her blouse, Grace would scream. She would hunch her shoulders, snap her arms across her chest, drop her head to the table. Because the only touch she wanted was her boy's.

Her boy's hand. In hers. Just like it was when he was small, before he became the size of an adult.

Though that day in the doctor's office, when they walked out, Paul slid his hand in hers again. Just for the walk from the door to the car. Neither of them said anything. But when Grace squeezed, Paul squeezed back, and Grace thought she could die of happiness right there. Her substantial boy would still hold her hand. And then he couldn't anymore.

She held him in her arms when he was dead. That wasn't the last touch that she wanted. There needed to be at least one more.

Nick stood up and looked in the pantry. "We've got a box of those microwave brownies. Why don't you go on up and get ready for bed? I'll make these and some decaf coffee and bring them up for us."

Grace smiled. Snacks in bed were a normal thing, a familiar thing, and she loved sharing those last moments before bed with Nick. Brownies and coffee in bed sounded decadent, even though it was decaf. Because her stomach didn't shudder in repulsion, because she actually looked forward to it, the world seemed to make sense tonight.

She ran up the steps and looked in on the kids. Mary, as usual, was completely uncovered. Grace long since gave up wrapping her daughter in blankets and the footie pajamas she used to resort to were a thing of the past. Teenagers, Mary informed her, did not wear footie pajamas even in the middle of the coldest Wisconsin winter. She was spread-eagled on the bed, and despite being seventeen years old, despite being a senior in high school, despite not wearing footie pajamas, her Pinky ragdoll was pressed under her cheek. Mary slept with this old pink ragdoll every night since she was two weeks old. Grace found it at a rummage sale. Pulling Pinky out, she touched the doll against Mary's palm. She clenched the doll instantly, pulling it to her stomach and rolling her whole body around it. Like a mother around a fetus. Grace remembered the sweet infant mouth that used to suck on Pinky's arms and legs.

Grace looked at that aged doll and thought again of Chatty Cathy. Mary had a doll, something Grace herself never had. Grace's mother hated Pinky. When Grace's mother visited, Grace had to search the house afterwards for the pink gingham ragdoll, to try to calm her wailing child. Pinky was on top of a bookshelf. Behind the couch. Tucked behind a plant. To her mother's credit, she never took Pinky outside of the house or put her in the trash. But it was hard to give credit when a little girl was wailing. When Mary was old enough, she joined the searches too. And eventually, when Grandma came around, Mary knew to hide the doll in her closet.

But they never once spoke about it. Not once. Not Grace and her daughter. Not Grace and her mother.

Grace didn't like remembering the times she was angry with her mother. Now she touched Mary's hair, ran her fingers down its length. She did so in stealth; since Paul's death, Mary didn't often allow herself to be touched. The sullen withdrawal into her own private grief grieved Grace further. Nick explained it away as normal adolescence. Grace knew it was more. But she was so stunned, beyond stunned, by her own grief, her own loss, she found herself unable to help, even when she knew her child was in distress. Both of her children were. Her remaining children.

When Grace was deep down honest, when she thought the things that she would never say out loud and that she thought so swiftly, they were barely a buzz, Grace knew she was a bit resentful of her children's grief. The loss of a brother, she thought, just for the splittest of seconds, couldn't be anywhere near as hard as the loss of a son.

Grace pulled her hand from Mary's hair. She suddenly felt that she didn't have the right to touch her own daughter.

Crossing over to JJ's room, Grace found him buried in his lower bunk. She dug through a quilt, two blankets, and a sheet before she found his face and sweat-plastered hair. After pulling the quilt off the bed and heaving it to the other side of the room, far out of reach of sleeping hands, Grace tucked the rest around JJ's shoulders and patted his overheated cheek.

Then she straightened and carefully rested her arm on the empty bunk above. Paul's bunk. She didn't look at it. But she felt it. It felt so cold after JJ's warm body.

JJ steadfastly refused to debunk the beds. It was the only steadfast part of this forward-thinking boy, the only part that refused to move ahead. He said he couldn't sleep without his roof, the bottom of Paul's bunk. Most of Paul's things were gone, packed away in a corner of the basement, except for this bed, his bedspread, and a poster of the solar system that hung near his pillow. Grace refused to look at any of it, but she tucked the bedspread in more tightly, which really wasn't possible, but going through the motions felt good. She thought about whispering goodnight to the missing Paul, but she didn't, and then she left the room.

In her bedroom, the bedside lamps were turned on low. Grace's side of the electric blanket was set on high and the bed felt comfortably body-heated when she slipped in. Her electric blanket was always turned on since Paul's death; she just couldn't get warm. She had to nudge TheCat to make room for her feet. He purred peacefully and came to rest on her lap.

"No brownies for you," she told him. "Especially after the raw chicken. Naughty cat."

TheCat appeared in the rain gutter soon after Grace married Nick. Mary was still a toddler and Grace was pregnant with Paul, though she didn't know it yet. TheCat washed up one night after a downpour. He was tiny and Grace fed him out of a baby bottle. She remembered holding the tiny kitten like a newborn, his back curved into her elbow, the tiniest paws on the bottle, toddler Mary sitting on the arm of the chair, stroking the kitten's ears, and all of them closing their eyes with contentment.

While Grace's mother loved cats, she was horrified when she heard Grace wanted to give the kitten a name. Her mother said that animals didn't need names, they were above names, and that cats in particular were on a very high rung of the spiritual ladder. To name a cat was demeaning; it would anger the cat and it would anger the spirits. Grace tried to explain that little Mary just wanted to name her kitty and Grace really didn't think the cat would mind. Grace's mother only glared. "You need to teach children, Gracie," she said.

So the cat came to be called TheCat. It was a compromise, one that both she and her mother could live with, one that could be talked about and not hidden away in a closet. From her mother's stories and botched spells and bizarre superstitions, Grace figured most spirits probably had a sense of humor anyway, so she would be forgiven.

Nick came in with a loaded tray of brownies and two steaming mugs. Getting into bed, he put the tray between them, their hips bolstering and steadying their snack. For that moment, Grace allowed herself to relish; all was chocolate and steam and warmth. Normal. Familiar. TheCat purred.

Between bites, Nick said, "The kids told me what happened after school today."

And then the normal was gone.

"You mean the firecracker thing?"

"Yes." He licked his fingers, then held her hand. "I wish the kids wouldn't bother you with that type of thing."

"They told me you wouldn't want me to know."

Nick glanced at her. "I thought it would be better for you. That it would help. You know…not being reminded. You have enough to deal with."

Grace picked up another brownie and wondered how anything could help. She thought of the stapled and nailed curtains in the kitchen. Not being reminded, being reminded, it all hurt. "It's okay, really, Nick." She chewed and savored the chocolate. "Though I have been feeling a bit…overwhelmed, maybe? That might be the right word." She thought of that moment before dinner, the splat of the chicken breasts, the gagging of TheCat. The moment when she stood and thought of escape. "Like maybe I need to get away for a while." That didn't sound so bad. Escape sounded like she was running, ducking, covering. But getting away? Not so bad.

He took the last brownie, then placed the tray on the floor. "Don't you think," he said slowly, "that it would be better for you to take it easy now? It's not time for a family vacation, it would feel wrong. Let's wait until things get normal again."

Normal was exactly what Grace was trying for. But suddenly, Grace felt like she was surrounded with lunacy. Lunacy of her own. Of her family's. The sheer lunacy of the word normal. The incomprehensible lunacy of a boy unexpectedly gone, just like that.

"That's never going to happen, Nick. You know that. That upper bunk is always going to be empty. My mother's house will always have strangers in it. I can't return to normal. There is no normal anymore. Normal's gone. It died." TheCat's eyes slitted at her, but in a pleasant way, almost a smile. Grace was tempted to shove him off the bed. How could he smile? Paul loved TheCat.

Didn't TheCat miss him? She took another deep breath. "And I wasn't thinking of a family vacation, I was talking about only me."

Nick was silent for a moment, then he slipped out of the bed. He stacked the mugs on the tray. She listened to the clink and the clatter as he placed them on the dresser. Probably right over his message, written in the dust.

Grace wasn't keeping up.

We can't keep up with everything without you, and right now, you can't do much of anything.

Nick got back into the bed and carefully kissed Grace's cheek. Not the back of her neck. Not her mouth. "I think," he said in a whisper, "it's best that you stay here, Grace. You haven't even been able to return to work."

Grace turned off her light and so did Nick and she breathed in the darkness. The remaining warmth of the coffee, brownies, and the electric blanket dragged her toward sleep.

But Nick wasn't done. "Grace?" she heard him say from a great distance. "What happened with the curtains downstairs? The ones over the sink. Did you do that?"

The Priscillas. "Yes," she said. "I just couldn't stand to look at that tree for one more minute."

She waited, but Nick didn't say anything at first. She felt herself drift again toward sleep. But then Nick said, "I took the curtains down. I put them in the trash. Grace, the kids just can't see something like that."

With a shriek, Grace was up, the cat was on the floor, the covers were thrown back. Grace ran down the hall and down the stairs and came to a stop in front of the kitchen sink. The window was open again, more than open, it was bare, just glass and wooden frame. The outside was there, right there, and Grace saw the tree, silhouetted against the night sky. Its branches were darker than dark and they were bare and they reached up as if trying to snatch something. Grace saw the flash of her son's life all over again, the flash of her son's death, of The Moment, and she shrieked again and leaned forward, powering her head into the glass. The impact left her with stars.

"Grace!" Nick grabbed her from behind, not gently at all, not like he used to at all, and pulled her away. "Stop that!" He hauled her over to the kitchen table and dumped her in the chair, the same chair where she sat just a little bit before. He sat next to her. He glanced at the ceiling, toward the children sleeping on the second floor.

"Why did you take down the curtains?" Grace consciously toned down her voice. But she couldn't control the tremor. "I fixed the problem. I didn't want to see the tree and I fixed the problem, and now you just ruined it."

"That's not how you fix problems." Nick folded his hands and Grace could see him trying to be calm. She wondered why. Why did he always have to be calm? What was so calm about losing a son? "Imagine what Mary and JJ thought today, Grace, when they came in here after school and they saw a window with the curtains stapled and nailed."

Grace thought back. Mary's head in the fridge, JJ's in the pantry. "They didn't even notice."

"Well, I did. And they would have." Nick grabbed her hands. "I'll put up blinds, okay? I'll put them up this weekend. And then you can lower them until you want to look outside again."

Grace wanted to tell Nick that this weekend was impossibly far away and that if she had to look out that window any more, she wouldn't be able to come into this kitchen. But she could see the reasonable in Nick. And she could see the unreasonable in herself.

There was just no arguing. She let her head fall forward.

Nick took one of her hands, stroked her fingers. "Grace, don't you think it would help if you went back to work? I have, the kids have gone back to school. You're still here, and…well, you're still here."

Go back to work. Go back to school. Where Paul was supposed to be. She might have even had him in her classroom this year. If she went back to work, she would see the empty desk, even though he never sat in it. She'd know it was for him.

She knew everyone else in the family was back on track. She knew it, and she hated it. How could they just go on? Especially Nick. Especially Nick who also lost a son. How could the pattern of his day just continue as if an entire thread hadn't been knotted, knotted again, and ripped out, leaving an unmendable hole?

"Nick," she said. "I'll go back to work. Someday. But not to school. I resigned. They accepted."

Nick stared. His mouth hung open, shaped around words that wouldn't come.

Without a word and without a glance over her shoulder, Grace got up and returned to their bedroom. Her forehead was throbbing and she knew that she likely had a goose-egg there, poking out like the start of a horn. The kids would notice that too, and what would she say then?

Maybe she wouldn't say anything. Ever. Maybe she would just go silent.

But then the kids would notice that and Nick would remind her to be reasonable.

Grace's head spun with the impossibility and with responsibility.

She climbed into bed and dutifully closed her eyes. It took awhile, but eventually, Nick joined her. She could tell he was laying on his back when his voice was directed toward the ceiling. "I can't believe you didn't tell me."

Grace took a deep breath. Then she said softly, "I'm sorry. I knew you wouldn't be happy. So I just kept it to myself."

Eventually, he rolled over and spooned her. In his embrace, she felt his acceptance. But she couldn't help but wonder what his dusty message would be the next morning.

She was almost asleep when he asked, "Do you think you could wash a load of towels tomorrow? We're out of clean ones. I didn't get a chance to throw in a load tonight; I was helping the kids with their homework."

A vision of the stiff towels Grace knew were lining the basement banister appeared behind her closed eyelids. Those towels had been there for weeks, they hung there without life, without hope, and she felt her eyes moisten. Why did even the towels have to look dead? Grace opened her eyes to let the tears out, the same tears that ran down her cheeks yesterday and the day before and the day before that, that ran now into her skin, and were absorbed to reappear the next day. And the next and the next and the next. "I'll try," she whispered back.

"Of course you will," he said gently. "One day at a time, remember."

One day at a time. One foot after the other. Survival that left Grace nowhere. Except in a world that would forever be without her son. Without her mother. A place where towels died. Where loading the dishwasher was exhausting. A place where an evening seemed destined to end in balance, but then flew off kilter in a spattering of stars that weren't in the night sky.

Grace held on tight to the edge of her bed. She was afraid of falling off.

****

The washing machine hummed and Grace leaned gratefully against it. She managed to put about half of the bath towels into one load, and there was still a separate pile of hand towels and washcloths at her feet. She hoped she would remember to wash those too, and to put the first load in the dryer. Too many times in the past six months, she found a load already slumped, cold and stiff, around the agitator. She would stare into the machine and not even recognize the clothes there, not remember ever sorting them, tucking them in, adding detergent, hitting the start button. Sometimes, she wondered if someone else put them there and forgot.

But always, always, she knew it was her. Nobody else but her would forget and neglect. She did it. And then she didn't.

As she walked up the stairs, she kept her eyes on her feet and refused to look anywhere near the direction of the kitchen window. She put a mug of coffee in the microwave and stared at the declining numbers. It was the same mug from last night, left sitting on the counter even though Nick unloaded the dishes out of the dishwasher. He hadn't put the new dirty dishes in; those he left for her. Something she was supposed to be able to do. The kids' breakfast dishes were on the counter too. Nick also added a postscript to his dusty message on the dresser. First thing that morning, Grace read, "I know you can do it."

Do what? The laundry? The household chores? Go back to work? Get over her son's death? How does anyone get over their son's death? And why would she want to? Like Paul's death was just a lump of forgotten clothes around a washing machine agitator. Some things, Grace could, and would, forget. But Paul?

How could she?

The microwave beeped and Grace didn't know if she could lift her hand and open the door. Loading the towels took all of her energy and the overwhelm returned. Yesterday, the dishwasher door was too heavy. Today, it was the microwave. Maybe by tomorrow, she wouldn't be able to open any door at all.

Slowly, Grace turned toward the offending window. As if she was lifting weights, she raised her eyes to look out at the tree. It was there. Of course it was there. It would always be there. Just like Paul always wouldn't.

Maybe she should ask Nick to have the tree cut down. She blamed the tree. But maybe it wasn't the tree's fault.

Maybe it was her own, for not watching closely enough. For being a mother who would stand in the kitchen window, with a cup of coffee and an Oreo cookie, and not run or yell when she saw what was about to happen. For not knowing what was about to happen before it did. She should have known. She should have seen it coming.

Mothers were supposed to know. Grace's own mother always seemed to appear in that last gasp of moment before Grace hurt herself. Her mother would step into that space and Grace would be just fine.

Why wasn't Paul just fine?

Grace abruptly turned her back and returned to the microwave. She was reaching for the door when she remembered her visit to the bank vault the day before. Today, it was time to visit the graves.

And with that, the world made sense. She had something to do.

Her steps now deliberately purposeful, Grace gathered her purse and her keys. The cemetery was across town. There would be time enough to go there and back before the towels were ready for the dryer. Grace checked her wallet, making sure she had enough cash to stop at the florist. She remembered!

It was amazing how good that made her feel.

The cemetery was just across the street from the florist. For years, Grace's mother was after her to buy the plots next to hers and Grace's father's, but Grace just didn't want to think about death until she had to. By then, all the neighboring plots were occupied. It was Nick who chose Paul's spot over a hill and three rows down. Grace couldn't. Even when she had to, she just couldn't think about death. Not this one. Not her son. No mother thinks of death when it comes to their fifteen-year old. But then, maybe if she had, she would have had that moment to get in between Paul and the tree, Paul and the wire. The moment her mother saved Grace from so many times.

The moment Grace failed.

The drive didn't take long. Grace parked the car in the street and walked into the florist shop. Ann, the owner, looked up and smiled.

"Morning, Grace, how are you today?"

Grace never knew how to answer that question anymore. How are you supposed to be when your son has died? She used her fallback. "I'm okay," she said. She figured "okay" was pretty noncommittal. And it was all people generally wanted to know. No one wanted to know the truth when you'd lost a child.

"I've been watching for you, you're steady as clockwork." Ann came around the counter. "We've got some nice roses, lovely whites and yellows. They'd look real pretty with some fall leaves tucked around them."

Roses were always Grace's mother's favorite flower and Grace never bought her anything else. She chose a half-dozen roses, an even mix of the yellows and whites. Ann put green ferns around them, then padded the stems with crisp leaves. Grace glanced around the shop. "I'll be needing something for my father too," she said.

Ann laughed. "Your fiscally responsible father. Well, let's see. Daisies are on special. I could get you some of those."

"Special" and "on sale" were Grace's father's favorite words. Favorite flowers for her mother, favorite words for her father. "That'll be fine. Wrap them up, please." Grace walked over to look at a selection of birdbaths. There used to be one in her mother's back yard, a heavy one studded with shiny rocks. Like so many things, that birdbath was gone now. Grace hadn't been in her mother's backyard for a year, because it was no longer her mother's. The florist shop had some birdbaths that were similar and Grace let her fingers bump over the studded stones. But there were also birdbaths with little sculptures on their rims, squirrels, birds, and naked ladies dipping their slender feet. Grace remembered how Paul liked to watch birds. He liked anything that flew. She touched a stone dove, following the lines of its tail and spread wings. "Do they allow birdbaths in graveyards, Ann?" she asked.

The rustling behind her stopped. "I don't know, Grace," Ann said. "I've never heard of such a thing. I don't see anything wrong with it, I guess, though birds tend to be really messy. Feathers. Bird poop. Did your parents like birds?"

People tended to forget that third grave. Or avoid it. "I wasn't thinking of my parents."

She was thinking of Paul. And Paul loved birds. He loved anything that could take flight. Whether or not it breathed.

She loved Paul. When he breathed. And even now, when he didn't.

There was a pause, then the rustling resumed. When the work fell silent, Grace paid for the bouquets, then crossed the street to the cemetery. Leaves speckled the grass and Grace kicked at a few as she made her way to her parents' graves. Kneeling by her mother's headstone, Grace gently placed the roses in the flower holder. Leaning over, she gave her father his special daisies. After letting her hand rest on his grass for a moment, she stood up. She patted her parents' headstones one more time, then walked down the rows to the base of the hill.

If Grace climbed to the top, she knew she would see Paul's grave. She took a few steps. It wasn't a steep hill, and two or three more strides would bring her to the peak, but she stayed where she was and settled her hands in her pockets. Her clenched palms grew clammy. She listened to the summer whisper of the leaves still in the trees and the rustle of the ones that already fell. She thought again about cutting down the tree in the back yard, the tree that held Paul just before his death. That held him alive and just a few moments later, Grace held him dead.

It wasn't fair. A tree shouldn't get the last moments of Paul's life. A branch shouldn't catch his last breath.

Grace wondered if the denim backpack still hung on Paul's gravestone and if all of Paul's school supplies were still tucked inside. If they were gone, did it mean that someone stole them, or did it mean that Paul came, in the dark of the night, and swept them up to Heaven? And right now, even as she stood there, a few steps from the bottom of the hill, even as Mary and JJ were sitting in their desks at school, doing math or reading or social studies, was Paul at a heavenly desk? Was he learning the things he should have learned here?

Even though Grace's mother believed in spirits, and Grace believed in her mother, she wasn't sure she believed in Heaven. She particularly wasn't sure she believed in Heaven for fifteen-year old boys who should never have died in the first place.

Unexpected.

Of the three children, Paul was the best student. It wasn't fair, Grace realized again. It wasn't fair that his younger brother would surpass Paul's final grade and learn things that Paul wanted to know, hungered to know. It wasn't fair that his older sister would go on to college and Paul would never graduate high school. As the years passed, it would be like Paul shifted from being the middle child to the youngest. The remaining children would leave him in the dust. Ashes to ashes, dust to dust.

The dust on the dresser. *It's time. I know you can do it.*

Grace shook her head. Paul should be learning right here. He should be learning right now. He should be a sophomore in high school. He should be talking about Homecoming, ducking his head and ducking questions over whether or not he was going to ask a girl. Grace thought of his hand in hers the day they left the doctor, the answering squeeze, and she wondered what type of girl Paul would have picked for the dance. Whose hand would he have held? What girl would squeeze back?

Now he would never squeeze a hand. The last hand he squeezed was his mother's.

In her pockets, Grace clenched her fists even tighter.

It wasn't fair.

JJ was already talking about bringing Paul a pumpkin and maybe a trick or treat bag for Halloween, which was Paul's favorite holiday. In Grace's mind, she could see Paul's grave, but she remembered it as a brown patch surrounded by green. Nick told Grace, even though she didn't ask and didn't want to know, that the grass grew in well, that the grave didn't look new anymore. Paul fit in now, with all of the others.

Grace didn't want him to. He didn't belong there. He belonged at home.

She tried to picture his grave with a birdbath, one with a stone dove on its rim. Other birds would come and splash and rest on Paul's stone, then jitter through the grass. There would be leaves, red and gold, scattered about. Paul could gather them like he did every fall and bring them to Grace, and she would put them in a vase, the only one she ever used for this, dark brown, shot through with red, and she would set it on the fireplace mantel. They would both admire it.

Except she would stand there alone this year. Except the only way she would get a leaf bouquet was to gather it herself. Mary and JJ only brought her dandelion bouquets and they hadn't done that in years. Paul, last fall, when he was only fourteen years old, still brought her a leaf bouquet. He did it quietly, coming in after school one day, and Grace knew he gathered the leaves in their own yard, not on his way home. Not where his friends could see him. But he still gathered them, and he still gave them to her, and when she put them in their vase and then on the mantel, he stood by her side.

He held her hand coming out of the doctor's.

No more leaves. No more entwining fingers with the boy who was a gift. Who arrived unexpectedly. Who left unexpectedly.

Grace stepped backwards. And again. But before she reached the bottom of the hill, she waved her hand and called, "Hello, Paul! Mom's here!" Then she turned and ran from the cemetery.

That was enough. It would have to be. It took everything Grace had.

****

Back home, Grace immediately put the first load of towels into the dryer. Then the second load went into the washer and she walked back up the steps, a feeling of satisfaction and triumph relaxing her shoulders. She decided it was time for a reward, the cup of coffee she left in the microwave earlier and a treat before dusting Nick's two messages right off the dresser. She wondered where he would find to write next. The remaining smog on the bathroom mirror? A scattering of crumbs on the counter? Maybe a post-it note on the top envelope of a pile of unsorted mail.

For just a moment, Grace felt a flash of anger. She couldn't have said if the anger was for herself or for Nick. Grace's mother always said that anger was only useful if directed, and Grace didn't feel directed at all. So she tucked it away.

As she punched new numbers into the microwave, she noticed the blinking red light on the phone indicating voicemail. She started the microwave warming her coffee before she called in and entered the code. "You have one new message," the female recorded voice announced, and then Grace heard the principal from the high school. Where Grace used to teach. Where Mary was. Where Paul should have been.

"Grace, it's Jean Deets," she said. "Please call us as soon as you get in. This isn't an emergency, but we have a problem with Mary and we need to speak to you as soon as possible."

The school was on speed-dial, number three, still there from when it was Grace's workplace, before it became just Mary's school. Number one was Nick at work, two was still Grace's mother, although the number had been disconnected for almost a year. Four was the middle school. The microwave buzzed and Grace swore under her breath. The hot coffee would have to wait, along with her break.

"Waukesha North High School, may I help you?" asked the secretary.

"Hi, Bonnie, it's Grace. Jean called me."

"Hi, Grace. Hang on a sec."

There was a hum as the call was transferred and then the principal's warm voice spilled into Grace's ear. "Hello, Grace, how are you?"

"I was fine until you called. Principals never bring good news." Grace smiled. "What's up?"

"Well, your day isn't going to get much better. I have Mary sitting right outside my office. I need you to take her home for the rest of the day, and tomorrow as well. She can return on Monday."

Suspension? Grace swallowed hard. None of her children had ever been suspended. "What did she do?" Then she felt automatically guilty for assuming the worst, that it was a suspension and for assuming her daughter was to blame. It was possible that Mary was sick. That she was covered in bright red chicken pox. That she was horribly contagious. "Is she okay?"

"She's fine. From what I've been told, there was a fight between Mary and a girl in her art class over a painting Mary made. Mac Jorgensen's class, you know Mac, right?"

"Sure." He was a great teacher, a student favorite.

"He said the girls started fighting at the end of the class, as they were going out the door. Apparently, the girl took Mary's painting and refused to return it.

She kept tucking it behind her back. By the time Mac got there, Mary had the girl up against the wall and slamming the girl's head against it. She was totally out of control. Mac pulled Mary away. He saw it." There was a pause and Grace closed her eyes. "The girl was knocked unconscious, Grace. There was blood. You know the walls outside the art department; they're cinderblock. She had to be taken to the hospital. We're waiting for a report from her mother. There will at least be stitches. I'm hoping Mary didn't cause a concussion."

The girl might have a concussion, but it was Grace's head that spun. How to respond to something like this? She wanted to leap to Mary's defense, but could she? Why would Mary do such a thing? She understood and knew well Mary's possessiveness; once something was Mary's, it could only be Mary's, and so the girl stealing the painting would definitely cause a reaction. But to attack her?

Grace desperately wanted to blame it on the other girl.

And then, impossibly, she blamed it on Mary's dead brother.

For that second, for that breath, it was Paul's fault. If he hadn't climbed a tree, none of this would be happening. The day would be normal. The house would be clean. Grace would be in her classroom, helping her students get through "The Death of a Salesman". All three of the kids would be at school. Mary would be herself, but she wouldn't be withdrawn. She wouldn't be violent. She would be, as Nick declared, a normal teenager.

Grace knew this wasn't normal.

But Paul hadn't asked to die. He only asked for a good place to hide in a game he didn't even want to play.

Grace stared at the microwave which offered a nice warm cup of coffee for the second time that day. She pictured that mug steaming, fogging the window from the inside out. She wanted to sit down, to drink the coffee slowly and dunk an Oreo cookie into it. It was her favorite snack and she needed it right then. Right at that moment. She didn't want to be on the phone, talking about her daughter knocking another girl unconscious. Talking about her daughter who was supposed to have two brothers, not just one.

Did Mary still have two brothers?

Her remaining brother. Grace's remaining children. Did she have three children or two?

"Grace?"

She blinked. She had to handle this. "I'm sorry, Jean, I don't know what to say."

"I know. This is pretty extreme. I think Mary just got completely caught up in the heat of the moment." She paused. "Mary knows that the girl was taken away in an ambulance."

This was not something that seventeen-year old girls needed to know. Grace's daughter already had enough knowledge that she didn't need. She knew how it felt to lose a brother. To have him die right before her in what should have been a simple game. Hide. Seek. Find. And now she held the knowledge that she could really hurt someone. She could hurt someone badly. Ambulance-badly.

Grace looked at the refrigerator. The papers that overwhelmed her last night were still there; magnets holding notices and reminders and Mary's and JJ's graded papers and artwork. "The painting they were fighting over, did you see it?"

"Yes, I did. It's a picture of a girl dancing with a skeleton in a graveyard. The skeleton is wearing a blue backpack."

Grace felt her knees go weak. "I'll be right there," she said softly. After hanging up the phone, she grabbed her purse and headed for the door. Then she stopped and deliberately turned back. She opened the microwave. Holding the mug, she felt the black heat and thought of throwing the cup at the sink, watching it shatter, but she decided against it. Instead, she got three Oreos, sat down, and began her coffee break. It was a time for deep breathing.

Grace's time.

She considered calling Nick. She even reached for the phone. But then she remembered Nick's note on the dresser that morning. *I know you can do it!* It was there still. Right below *It's time.*

All she felt was tired. But she had to be able to do this.

Grace placed her empty mug in the dishwasher, then grabbed a paper towel and dampened it. She ran upstairs to her bedroom, and with one swipe, wiped out Nick's messages. The wet paper towel cut a swath through the dust, leaving one streak of clean wood shining through. It was enough. The messages were gone in such a way, it left a message of her own.

Leave me alone.

Grace went back downstairs, found TheCat and patted him, and left the house.

The school was only a couple of blocks away, but she drove. It just took a minute to pull into the parking lot, a minute Grace needed to try to calm herself down. As she moved through the lobby, Grace saw her daughter in front of the principal's office. Mary was slumped in her chair, her face in her hands. Her sandaled feet were twisted around the chair's metal legs and her painted toenails, black, looked like dots on dice against the white tiled floor. Her shoulders shuddered a little, but she was silent. As Grace walked to her, Mary looked up. The force of Mary's gaze, the sullen, the anger, the grief, the grief, the grief, guttered Grace to a stop.

And then those blue eyes filled and there was Grace's little girl. Grace ran the rest of the way and Mary was off the chair and they were wrapped in a hug. Though she was taller than Grace now, Mary's head rested on her mother's shoulder and Grace embraced harder than she had in all of Mary's seventeen years.

"Mom," Mary said. "Mom, I didn't mean to do it. I didn't. I'm so sorry!"

From inside the office, the receptionist called through the open door. "Hi, Grace," she said. "Come on in. I'm sure Jean is ready to see you. Mary, sit back down please. Your mother will be with you in a few minutes."

Mary crumpled into her chair. Her face returned to her hands.

Grace bent down. "I'm on your side, remember," she whispered into Mary's ear and she received the reward of a wan smile.

Behind the closed door of the principal's office, Jean motioned Grace into a chair. Grace sat back, trying to look relaxed and confident, though she wanted to perch on the edge. She wondered if this was worse than a suspension; maybe Mary was going to be expelled.

"I've been looking at Mary's file," Jean said. "This is new for her. She's always been assertive and confident, but well-behaved. She's never crossed over into violence."

"Yes, I know." Grace wondered if she should tell Jean about the firecracker boy from the day before, the red knuckles Mary tried to hide.

Jean folded her hands on her desk. "Grace, I'm sure Paul's death has been hard on her. Hard on all of you." She gave the softest, saddest smile. "I know it's been hard on you. We miss you here."

Grace nodded and forced her hands to unclench and rest on her knees. "Paul died six months ago," she said. "And six months before that, my mother died. It's been a difficult year."

Jean pursed her lips. "Have you ever considered counseling?"

Grace allowed one hand to curl back up. "You mean therapy?"

Jean nodded. "In a situation like this, Mary may be trying to deal with too much. And you all might be in such pain that you aren't always able to help each other. Here." She gave Grace a list. "These are therapists that we've worked with at this school. It could help, Grace. Not just Mary, but JJ too. Your whole family." She leaned forward. "It could help you."

Grace held the list between two fingers, then carefully balanced it on her lap. Mary isn't crazy, she thought. My family isn't crazy.

But she wasn't so sure about herself.

Jean set aside Mary's folder. Grace wondered where Paul's was. Did his folder get thrown away? Where did the folders of dead children go? It wouldn't make sense to archive it; there would never be anything to add to it.

No more progress reports. No more report cards.

Grace forced back tears. This was not about Paul. This was about Mary. Now was not the time nor the place.

Not Grace's time. She began to wonder about her place.

Jean handed over a stiff and heavy sheet of paper. "I think Mary might be having trouble letting go of Paul."

Grace stared, her breath held for a moment in surprise. "Why should she let him go?"

The principal just sat back. She nodded to the paper.

Grace looked and realized it was Mary's painting. As Jean described, a girl with ephemeral hair dancing with a skeleton. There was a blue backpack and gray gravestones. The only feature on either face was a smile. Bright smiles. Grace had no problem recognizing Mary and Paul. Recognizing who they used to be. Grace stood up. "So you want me to keep her home tomorrow?"

Jean nodded. "Just to give this a chance to blow over. She does need to be disciplined, you know. We have to have a formal suspension. Her behavior was not appropriate. It won't affect her graduation. She's on track for that."

"I understand." Grace hadn't even considered how this could affect graduation. That was so long from now. The end of the school year. Forever.

"Maybe tomorrow, you can take her to one of the therapist's. They can usually take new patients on short notice when there's an emergency recommendation from the school."

Grace folded the list and put it in her purse. The painting, she kept smooth. It was Mary's. She would return it to her and when they got home, it would be up to Mary where it went. Lately, she didn't want her work on the refrigerator. She hung it on the walls of her room. "I'll talk to her stepfather about it. We'll see. I suppose I should call the middle school; JJ will be expecting Mary to stop for him on her way home."

"That's okay, Grace. I'll call and ask one of the guidance counselors to talk to him before lunch so he knows not to wait." Jean stood up too and offered her hand.

Grace took it. "Thank you."

When Grace left the office. Mary did her amazing unjointed flow to her feet. Grace handed her the painting.

"You got it back!" she said.

"Yes, and you get a vacation from school until Monday."

"Really?" She looked delighted for a minute, then horrified. "I've been suspended?"

Grace nodded. She wondered if the other girl was going to be disciplined at all. She did steal the painting.

They went to the car and sat down. Grace listened to the click as Mary fastened her seatbelt. The painting rested in her lap. "So…" Grace said. Mary didn't respond. "So you knocked a girl out."

Mary's head dipped. "She stole my painting, Mom," she whispered.

"I know." Grace tapped the wheel. "Mary, Ms. Deets thinks maybe you should see a therapist."

Mary snapped her head back up. "Why? I don't want to do that. What would I talk about?"

"I don't know." Grace shook her head, then reached over and touched the skeleton. "Maybe about knocking girls unconscious. Maybe how you feel about Paul dying."

Mary snorted. "Really? That's not obvious?"

Grace had to agree. But Jean seemed to think it was time to let go. That they needed help letting go. Nick seemed to think it was time too.

Grace's mother said, "In your time, Gracie." Why was Grace's time different than everyone else's? Grace started the car. "But it might help you. I mean, look what happened yesterday. Look what happened today."

Mary looked out the window. "I didn't mean to hurt her, Mom," she said. "I only wanted my painting back. I thought she was going to rip it and then I got mad and madder and then I just couldn't stop. But when I realized what I was doing, I knew I did something really wrong. I'm sorry."

"I know, sweetie."

As they drove out of the parking lot, Mary took one of Grace's hands from the steering wheel. She held it in both of hers. Grace was immediately thrown back to the day she walked out of the doctor's office with Paul. They held hands. Now Mary held her hand. Her seventeen-year old daughter was holding on and squeezing as she did on the first day of kindergarten.

"Mom?" Mary said. Her voice was quiet and still. "That day? I told Paul to climb the tree."

Grace jumped and the car jerked. "What? What do you mean?"

"When JJ and Paul were playing hide-and-seek. I told Paul he should hide in the tree. Nobody ever hid there before. I told him he should climb way high, so that JJ wouldn't see him. Paul didn't want to, but he was running out of time, so he did. Then I guess he touched the wire. And fell. And died." Her grip numbed Grace's fingers. "It's my fault Paul died."

Grace's eyes blurred. Mary's fault? No. Whose fault was it? It wasn't Paul's. Grace knew he would never climb that tree, Paul just wasn't a climber. And it wasn't the tree's, how could it be the tree's, how could Grace ever think that? Grace should have stopped him, she should have, but how could she have known? Her mother would have known, if it was Grace climbing the tree.

Whose fault was it?

Grace knew the next thought that was coming, but she quickly inserted a substitute, the right thing, telling herself that it wasn't anyone's fault. She knew she should say it out loud, she urged her voice forward, she should tell Mary that it wasn't her fault, that she didn't send Paul to his death. Grace tried. She opened her mouth and she tried.

Mary leaned forward. "Mom?" she said, her voice high and full of tears. The sullen, the withdrawn, was gone. There was sad. Only sad. Grace's little girl was in the car.

"Oh, Mary, it's not..." Grace said and shoved at the words. They were as heavy as the dresser in her room, the dresser where her husband reminded her to dust, told her it was time, told her she could do it, the words that were gone now. But these words, the words Grace knew she should say, the words that would release Mary from any guilt, from the guilt she must have been feeling for six months now, stopped, banging against the backs of her teeth. Looking away, Grace said, "It's about time for lunch. How about a treat at McDonald's?"

Mary let go of Grace's hand.

Grace felt the loss, felt the warmth from Mary's skin falling away. Leaving Grace empty-handed.

These days, Grace always felt empty-handed.

Mary looked back out the window and Grace knew she wasn't going to be able to say the words. Those words that would have saved her daughter. Her little girl. One of her remaining children. First, Grace wasn't able to save her son. Now, she couldn't save Mary. All she had to do was speak. And she couldn't even do that.

"In your time, Gracie," her mother said.

Grace was out of time. For what, she wasn't sure. But there was just nothing left at all.

****

Grace watched and waited with Mary and JJ as Nick carefully arranged his coffee cup in the saucer so that the handle met his fingers exactly when he rested his elbow on the table. He could lift and lower his cup in this way without ever moving his arm, without ever uncurling his fingers from the graceful handle. He was a cup and saucer type of man; Grace preferred mugs. They held more, and she didn't mind wiping away the ring, when she remembered to do it. Most of the time now, she forgot and the kitchen table, the dining room table, the endtables and coffee table in the living room, her bedside table, all had a cheerful collection of rings. At least, Grace found it cheerful. It was like her décor was newly polka-dotted. But Nick didn't see it that way. She looked down now at her side of the table, which was glittered with interlocking rings. Glittered, her perception; littered in his.

"All right," Nick said. "To sum up. Mary gave a girl a concussion. The principal thinks Mary is out of control and that she needs a therapist." He traced the cup's handle with the tip of his finger. Everyone's eyes followed it, Grace noticed. She used to feel that same finger trace a line down her spine. She didn't have to wonder how long it had been since she last felt it.

Six months. Before then, she felt it a few times in the six months when it was only her mother that was dead. Not her son too.

Grace touched Mary's hands, folded seriously on the table. Mary never sat with folded hands. "I really don't know that therapy is necessary. This girl stole Mary's painting. Mary was provoked." Grace looked at her daughter and smiled. It wasn't returned, Mary's eyes were still glued on her step-father's tracing finger. "It's not like Mary's done this sort of thing before." She saw both Nick and JJ glance at Mary's knuckles, no longer red, but still skinned. "Much," Grace quickly added. "There's just been yesterday and today."

Nick twirled his cup and traced the handle with his left hand. His elbow on that side was perfectly placed too. "The principal is a professional, Grace. And she was your boss and friend. She's known Mary since she was in kindergarten. Maybe Mary does need help. This particular painting, and then the fight, is a sign of that. She can't seem to get on with her life. It's like she won't let Paul go."

There it was again. Grace sat up and so did Mary. Both kids turned to Grace. "Jean said that too. I don't understand this letting go thing. I don't think it's so bad to feel a connection with Paul. Even if he is dead."

Both of Nick's palms fell flat against the table and the kids jumped. "Grace, that's your mother talking again. Your mother with her spirits and oogie-boogie stuff."

Oogie-boogie stuff? "Maybe. But it's me talking too. I told Jean I didn't think it was necessary." She turned to Mary. "When Mary and I talked about it in the car, Mary wasn't even sure what she would talk about. Right?"

Mary quickly nodded, but Grace noticed her knuckles going white.

Nick sat back and sighed. "Well, let's at least try the counseling. If Mary doesn't like it or if she doesn't improve, we can always pull her out."

"I suppose." Grace studied Mary. She wondered why her daughter didn't protest being spoken about as if she wasn't in the room. Mary's expression didn't change toward approval or disapproval. It really hadn't changed much at all since their car ride this afternoon. After their lunch at McDonald's, where Mary only ate a few fries, she went up to her room and stayed there. She didn't even come down when JJ came home. When he went looking for her, he reported that he was told to just go away.

Nick looked at the kids. "All right, that's decided. Go on and start getting ready for bed."

Grace waited for Mary to protest, to say she didn't have to go to school tomorrow, but the girl said nothing and just left without a word.

JJ touched Grace's shoulder as he went by.

Nick got up to put his cup and saucer in the dishwasher. This meant the matter was settled, even between the two of them. Except it wasn't. Grace knew there was more that she had to tell him. There was Mary's confession in the car. There was Grace's response. Or her lack of one.

She looked at her mug, took a breath, then she pushed her words toward Nick's back. These words didn't stop at her teeth, the way they did earlier with Mary. They went right on through her lips and Grace wondered why some words were easier than others. "Mary told me today that it's her fault Paul died."

He turned quickly. "She said that?" He looked toward the window, but Grace knew he was looking straight through the wide open glass to the tree beyond. The view Grace saw every time she came in the kitchen now. Reminder after reminder after reminder, now window-framed like a favored painting on a wall. "I've read that kids often blame themselves for crises, like death or divorce, that sort of thing," he said. Since Paul's death, Nick developed an impressive library of self-help books. Grace often wondered just how many answers he thought he would find. She looked at them one afternoon, paging through this book on grief, that book on loss. She didn't find any answers. She just found more sadness.

Nick sat down again. "But I never thought of Mary as the self-blaming type. JJ maybe, but not Mary."

"She said she wasn't playing that day, but she told Paul to climb the tree and hide. And then he touched the wire." Grace watched Nick, saw him knot his eyebrows together. Nick wasn't home on the day of the accident, but Grace knew that this didn't keep him from seeing it. Grace knew the reality of it, she saw it, second by second, a playback that would never go away. Nick had his own nightmare, his own private version of Paul's outreached hand, his jerk and fall. But then Nick's eyes widened and Grace knew that this time, he was also seeing Mary watching from down below. His step-daughter. The girl he thought of as his own.

"God," Nick said. "Grace, what did you say to her?"

It was like he knew she wouldn't have handled it well. It was like he knew she blew it.

"Nothing. I didn't know what to say, so I took her to lunch at McDonald's." Grace grabbed her mug with both hands to brace herself. She thought of Mary that afternoon, saying she did something really wrong. But so did Grace. Grace knew absolutely that she did something really wrong too. She couldn't look at Nick's face. But she heard the scrape of his chair as he pushed it back and rose from the table.

"You didn't tell her it wasn't her fault? You didn't say it was okay?"

Grace shook her head. But it didn't seem like enough. Nick expected more. A voice. An explanation. "No." It was all she could give him.

"Jesus." He yanked himself away and walked over to the sink. Leaning against it, he stared out the window again.

Grace wished for the nailed Priscillas. She wished she could rip that imagined painting right off the wall.

"Grace, why didn't you tell her it wasn't her fault?" Nick's voice was soft, she could hear him flattening his yell. "She would have cried, gotten it out of her system. Now she's got her mother's blame to live with too."

"I didn't say I blamed her."

Nick turned around. Grace had always heard of people going pale and she supposed, in this situation, she expected that of Nick. But he wasn't pale. His face was purple. His face was never purple.

Grace fought the urge to scoot back her own chair and run. "Nick, how could I tell her it was okay? Maybe it was her fault, maybe Paul wouldn't have climbed the tree if she didn't tell him to. They never hid there before, she told me that herself, it was all her idea. She said Paul didn't want to climb the tree, but when she told him to, he did."

"Jesus Christ, Grace!" His voice grew louder and Grace glanced quickly upstairs where their children were preparing for bed. "It doesn't matter who told him to climb the tree. What matters is that we have a girl who is blaming herself for her brother's death. We can't bring Paul back. But there's still Mary."

"Mary hasn't gone anywhere," Grace said. She clamped her lips for a moment to keep the next words, "She's still alive," from coming out. She knew it would sound like blame. "She will be all right. She just needs some time." Immediately, Grace wanted those words back. They weren't the right ones either. It was Grace that was supposed to have time. *It's time, Grace. In your time, Gracie.*

Grace just couldn't wrap her head around anyone else's time. She couldn't. She didn't even understand her own.

Nick sat down and grabbed her hands. "Grace, maybe you should see this therapist too."

Grace sighed and pulled away. "No, Nick." She stood up and brought the mug to the sink. She rinsed it out for longer than necessary, letting the warm water run over fingers that she thought would never be warm again. Just like Paul's. Just like her mother's. Like Nick, she stared out the window. It was falling night, and the tree was black against a hard deepening sky.

"Grace, look at this house," Nick said from behind her. "Look at you. It's a mess. You're a mess. You've got to let them both go, Paul and your mother."

And that was when it went beyond too much. Grace threw her mug into the sink with both hands and she heard it shatter. She spun around and flapped her wet hands at Nick, throwing droplets in his face. It was the most violent thing she could think of to do. She wanted to hit him, but she knew that would be wrong. She'd already done one really wrong thing, she didn't want to do another. So she flapped until her hands were dry. "Why should I? I don't want to let go! I see Paul every day and every night, and that's just fine with me." He startled and Grace moaned. How could he be so stupid? "Don't you think I see Paul? When I make JJ's bed, I see Paul lying in the upper bunk. I see him playing video games, putting together his jigsaw puzzles, reading his books on planets. And yes, I know he's dead, but I can't look at the moon without seeing Paul. He's there, with the stars. Then at night, I dream of him. And my mother, Nick, my mother is everywhere. Even though she's not here anymore. I am not going to give that up! I shouldn't have to!" She stopped, held her hands still, then opened her arms up. "It's hard for me to live with and it hurts, but I don't think I could survive without seeing them in this way. I don't think I could survive, Nick."

Nick stood up very slowly, his shoulders drooping. "Then why won't you visit his grave, Grace?"

"Because I can't." Grace said it quickly, the same answer she always gave. The answer that didn't make any sense. Grace could see her son, hear his voice, even talk to him in her dreams. But she couldn't visit his grave. Nick folded his arms and Grace knew he expected an answer. Again. "I guess it's because I don't want to see him there, under the ground, under that rock. I want to see him here, with me. With us."

Moving toward her, Nick said, "Grace, your mother and Paul are dead. They're gone. They're never coming back and you have to let them go."

Grace pushed him away. She pushed him as hard as she knew he wanted her to push Paul and her mother. Far, far away. To heaven, to hell, to the dirt by their headstones. Just away. But she couldn't push them. That was wrong. That was really wrong. But the moment her hands hit Nick's chest, the moment she shoved her husband away, it felt right. It felt so right, Grace shook with it.

This money is yours, Grace. Should you ever find yourself wanting to be away.

Grace pushed Nick away. But it was herself that she wanted gone. Right there, right then, Grace felt like she couldn't stand to be in that house another minute. In that house where the phone rang and it was never her mother. In that house where Paul's chair at the table was stored out of sight in the garage, where his bed was empty, where his voice was absent, where she didn't even smell him anymore. If his smell could disappear, how long would it be before her visions of him disappeared too? His absence and his presence were so thickly entwined, her grief was ever present. But she just couldn't lose it.

Because then she would lose Paul. And her mother.

Nick stumbled backwards a few feet away. His face registered so much hurt, Grace wondered for a moment if she'd actually physically hurt him, if she'd hit a nerve. But then she knew she didn't. That's not what his face was showing.

She took a deep breath, a steadying breath. "My mother believed in a connection between the living and the dead," she said. "I'm not sure about that, but I know there's a connection between mother and son, daughter and mother. I can feel it, Nick. I can feel it even though they're not here. I do not have to let them go. And neither does Mary. Neither does JJ. If you can let them go, that's up to you. But I can't, and I don't think the children should be forced to either." Grace walked away, moving toward the stairs. "I'm getting ready for bed." She couldn't leave the house, not now, but she could leave the room.

"Grace."

She stopped with her back to him. Not another word, she thought. Not another word about Paul or my mother or I will explode. She closed her eyes, pictured his words hitting the back of his teeth, just as hers did this afternoon. If he told her to let Paul go one more time, she would catch those words in her own teeth, snatch them right out of the air. She would chew his words. She would bite them and spit them at his feet.

"Make the appointment for Mary. Or else I will."

"I'll make it." Those were the words she bit instead and then she left the room quickly, before he could tell her in that same threatening voice to make an appointment for herself.

Instead of running to her room, as she intended, Grace stopped at the top of the stairs. Tucked away in a corner of the landing, there was a curio cabinet, filled with knickknacks and figurines. On the second shelf, on the left, directly in the middle behind the pane of glass, there was something that Grace suddenly had to have. Carefully opening the door, she pulled out a small crystal ball from its three-legged gold stand.

Grace's mother gave her that ball on the day she married Nick and they moved into this house. Her mother said she captured some good spirits and put them inside of it to watch over Grace, her new marriage, and her new family. She told Grace that her first marriage was tormented by bad spirits and her mother wanted to make sure that never happened to her daughter again. The crystal ball was shiny and clear when Grace accepted it, and still warm from her mother's hands.

Grace warmed it now with her own. Then she carried it carefully to Mary's room.

The room was dark and Mary was spread-eagled in her bed again, Pinky crushed to her face. Grace sat down next to her hip and Mary thrashed, rolled, and curled around her without waking up from an angry sleep. Touching Mary's hair, Grace pulled the doll away, exposing her daughter's flushed cheeks, her fluttering eyelashes, to the cool of the room and the comfort of a mother's touch. Then Grace placed the crystal ball on the dresser, tucked neatly under the sole window. She tugged back the curtains. The streetlight coming in poured through the ball and refracted colors around the room. Violet, orange, and blue fell on Mary's face and chest. It seemed like a good sign.

"I guess it's you that needs some good spirits now," Grace whispered to her daughter. She kissed Mary's hot cheek and went to her own room.

For the rest of that evening, a time that Nick and Grace usually spent together, reading or watching television, they stayed apart. Grace could hear Nick watching the tv in the living room. It was tuned to the same show she had on in the bedroom. She took comfort that they were watching the show together, although on different sets and different places.

****

Grace worked her way down Jean's list until she found a therapist with an available hour that day. It amazed Grace how busy these therapists were...except for this one, they were booked solid for at least two weeks, and one said it would take about three months and suggested Grace call a hotline. Grace suddenly felt that she was surrounded, not only with her own unhappiness, but the unhappiness of others, of anyone that she might just pass on the street. It made her feel even sadder, but then she shook her head. She had to focus on her daughter's unhappiness. It had to come even before her own because children weren't supposed to be unhappy, apparently, even when their brothers died before their very eyes. Unhappiness was something to be fixed, dead brothers were something to be let go. And so Grace found this therapist.

His office was two doors down from the doll museum and Grace's mother at the bank vault. When Grace brought Mary into that office, she was relieved that the therapist wanted to see only Mary, once they were past introductions and general information; he said he'd spoken to the school and he would arrange a meeting with "the parents" after this initial appointment. Grace wasn't crazy about being referred to in this way; it wasn't even personal. Not Mary's mom and dad, not even Mary's parents. Just "the parents." But the school recommended this man and he was available now, and so Grace left Mary there, looking small and wary in one of the leather chairs with the therapist sitting directly opposite, and she went back outside, closing the door softly as she went.

For a moment, she was relieved at Jean's suggestion of a therapist. For a moment, Grace was relieved to leave her daughter's unhappiness in someone else's hands. And then she felt washed over with guilt and shame.

Grace walked slowly toward the doll museum. She hoped the man wouldn't be in the window again, watching for her, keeping an eye out. Grace could still see his face, just about ready to smile.

But the store window was empty. No man, no doll. Grace gawked for a moment at the velvet-covered box, the strewn leaves and gourds. Without the doll, it looked so barren. Who would have thought Chatty Cathy would have been sold so fast? But she was, someone else wanted her, just like when Grace was a child, and Grace's heart slammed against the window. It was one more loss. Grace remembered the way Cathy's hand reached up behind the glass, as if she was waving or reaching out, and how much Grace wanted to touch her. But she missed that opportunity. Again. And now Cathy was gone.

Grace found herself running up the steps and into the shop. It was the type of shop that should have ringing bells at the door, but there was no jingle. The door whispered shut behind her.

She caught sight of the man, standing at a counter and packing dolls into a cardboard box. Maybe he had Cathy there? Maybe he hadn't sold her yet? He looked surprised, then he smiled. "May I help you?" he asked.

Grace was breathing heavily and she swallowed before she spoke. "That doll you had in the window just the other day. Chatty Cathy. She's gone?"

The man gently set down a doll and then walked toward Grace. His eyes behind round glasses were very round too and they were the softest shade of gray. His shirt was opened three buttons down and the chest hair that curled up and out was silver. "I remember you," the man said quietly. He stopped a foot or so in front of Grace, putting his hands in his pockets, which jingled, the way the door was supposed to. "You were the one at the window, right at the window, just like a little girl run away from her mother. Your nose was pressed flat and you seemed to be trying to hold the doll's hand." He smiled again, but Grace could tell he wasn't making fun of her. "She's still here. I just pulled her out. Just a few minutes ago."

Grace tried to fight down her blush and the quaver she knew would be in her voice. "She's…quite a doll. I always wanted her when I was a little girl and I asked for her every Christmas and every birthday, but I never got her."

He motioned to the rear of the store. "Come back here." He led Grace just beyond the counter, where she saw row after row of shelves. Every available space in the shop was covered with dolls. There were smiling dolls, stoic dolls, dolls made of plastic and cloth and china. Some faces, Grace recognized, others she didn't, but she wanted to touch them all. Pat their hair, smooth their dresses, place a kiss on every cheek. Each and every one.

She also knew, without a doubt, that this was not a place her mother would approve of. But right now, surrounded as she was with all the playmates she ever wanted, Grace didn't care. So much of her life, Grace spent being a good girl. Now, the world around her threatened to fall, already fell, in fact, and Grace wanted to break the rules. She wanted to be with the dolls.

"Here," the man said, and he pulled Chatty Cathy from one of the shelves. She still wore her coat and hat, but the coat was unbuttoned and Grace could see her pink and white party dress. He held her out.

And with that, Grace took her in her arms. She held a doll for the very first time in her life. She did the one thing her mother forbade her to do in a place her mother wouldn't want her to be. She did the one thing she disliked about her mother, whom she loved.

Grace held the doll outright, her hands around the doll's waist. She wondered if she should hug her, cradle her, pull her to her chest like a child. Her weight, dangling there in midair, was delicious. Her hair caught the light and tumbled over Grace's wrists in a golden synthetic river. The eyes were blue, heavily lashed, and closed when Grace tilted her. Six freckles speckled her cheeks, three on each, forming two neat inhuman triangles, and her lips parted slightly to show two small white teeth. Grace searched under her hair for the magic string. Pulling it carefully, she heard Cathy's voice for the very first time.

"Please carry me," she said.

Grace laughed. The doll was perfect. "I would love to," Grace told her, and then she stuck her hand out at the man, who hovered close by. "I'm Grace," she said.

"Nice to meet you," the man said. "I'm Virgil."

Grace carried the doll to the counter. After standing her firmly on her white-shoed feet, Grace smoothed the golden hair. "Why did you take her from the window? She looked wonderful there. I'm sure she would have brought customers in for you." Grace looked at Virgil and smiled. "She brought me in."

Though Grace wasn't sure yet if she was a customer. How could she buy a doll?

But she'd already held her. She already broke the rule. It couldn't get any worse, could it?

And she had the money. But it was her mother's money.

"I'm closing the shop for a couple months," Virgil said. He touched the doll, twitching her skirt, tapping a shoe. "Every fall, I close for a while and travel around the country on a shopping trip. I go into towns and check out estate sales, flea markets, that kind of thing."

Grace glanced around. "I wondered where you got them all."

"I get a lot when I travel. Though plenty of people bring them in when they clean out their houses, or the houses of others. Those that have passed, mostly." He picked up a cardboard box and placed a doll inside. "I do a lot of business on eBay. These dolls are going to new homes, and I have to get them shipped before I leave in the morning."

"So you just travel around, looking for dolls?" Grace watched him tuck tissue, a soft papery blanket, delicately into the box. His fingers were long, his nails manicured.

"Yep. I don't even know where I'm going next. I just follow the roads, find names I like, new directions. I want to go into Iowa this time. Haven't gone that way for a few years." He sealed the box with tape that shrieked when he unrolled it. Grace flinched; she couldn't help but wonder if the doll was shrieking inside. "I check out the local newspapers wherever I go. I've seen a lot of the country that way. Brought home a lot of dolls too."

Grace touched Cathy's fingers, traced the way they curled into her plastic palm. "Virgil, do you remember a doll that came out about the same time as Cathy? She was supposed to be sick or hurt, and she came with a couple casts and crutches and spots that were supposed to be the measles or chicken pox." Grace studied Cathy's careful smile, the white teeth perfect and straight. "That doll always looked so sad." Chatty Cathy never looked sad.

"Maribel Get Well," he said instantly. "She's a winner, a Madame Alexander doll. Did you have one?"

"No." Grace didn't know how to tell this man who was surrounded by dolls that she was never allowed their company. She scanned the shelves, looking for those poor plastered limbs. "Do you have her here?"

"Not right now. I get one in from time to time. I'll watch out for her on my trip, if you'd like."

"Yes, please, I'd like that," she said. Grace reached for Cathy's string.

Cathy said, "I love you."

"I love you too," Grace told her. And she did. She'd waited for years to say that.

"So you didn't have Cathy or Maribel, yet you remember them both so well." Virgil picked up another box. "I would have guessed they were your childhood favorites."

Grace shook her head. "I didn't have them," she said. Then, when she felt Virgil's stare, she studied Cathy's blue eyes and said, "I didn't have any dolls. I wanted them, but I never had a one. I wanted Baby First Step, Cheerful Tearful, Baby Secret, Chrissy…I wanted them all."

"And you had none?" His voice rose; his hands stopped. "Were you poor? I'm so sorry, Grace."

"No, not at all. My mother just wouldn't let me." Grace felt the sudden and surprising burn of anger. It flared, and then it burned itself out. In that moment, surrounded by everything she ever wanted as a child, Grace found herself only wanting one thing. Her mother. She wanted her mother. And Paul too, of course.

She wanted her real child, not a plastic one. Grace suddenly wanted to push Cathy away. Just like she pushed Nick the night before. Was that what she had to do? Push everything away? And then she would get Paul back? Maybe if she gave up everything she ever wanted…

But she was supposed to let Paul go. That's why Mary was sitting in a therapist's office just a short distance away.

And Cathy was right here. Paul was in a grave. So was her mother. But her mother's money was just across the parking lot.

"Well." Virgil's voice was full of wonder. He placed another doll inside, tenderly touching her face. "What do you know about that," he said to the doll. "What do you know. I've never heard of such a thing. A mother not letting her little girl have dolls." He paused, then said again, "I'm so sorry, Grace." He said it the same way he had when he thought she was poor.

Grace touched Cathy, then picked her up again and held her tightly. She felt so solid. She felt so here.

Grace couldn't hold Paul anymore.

She remembered what it felt like to see the window of The Nursery so empty. Cathy, gone, just like her mother. Just like her son. And suddenly, right then, Grace's whole life seemed empty. For six months. For a year. For all the years that she'd never held a doll. "Virgil, how much is she?"

He seemed to think while he enclosed the other dolls in the box. "Coat and hat too?" he said finally. Grace nodded. "A hundred and twenty-five." He paused. "For you, a hundred."

Grace could smell Cathy's hair. Her arms creaked when they moved and so did her legs. "I need to run next door," Grace said. "Can you wait a moment? My bank is right there, I just have to get the money."

"Sure. Go ahead."

Grace put the doll down, tore herself away. "Don't sell her," she said. "Please."

He nodded solemnly. "Not to another soul, Grace," he said. "I promise."

Grace ran next door, her heart pounding. She had to wait in line, three people thick, before she got to Sheri. Sheri seemed surprised that Grace was there; she glanced down to her left and Grace saw a calendar. It hadn't been a month since her last visit, it was only a couple days. But she didn't have time to explain. As Sheri led Grace to the safety deposit boxes, she hated the unbroken rhythm of Sheri's shoes. Run! Grace thought. Can't you go faster, just this one day? This one time? They had their key ritual and then she left Grace with the box.

And with her mother. Her mother who hated dolls. In full view of Grace's sudden intentions.

Grace hesitated, but she pulled a hundred dollar bill from the pile. She started to close the lid. The black carved face of her mother's pendant stopped her. Like Nick the night before, the pendant, Grace's mother, demanded an explanation.

Grace sat down. "I'm going to buy this doll, Mother," she said. Her voice shook, but that was no longer unusual. Since Paul's death, Grace's voice shook a lot. "I know you don't approve. But you gave me the money to meet my needs. I need Chatty Cathy." Grace gripped the pendant face between her thumb and forefinger. "I need her, Mother," she repeated, and then, "I'm sorry. I have to."

The face felt warm. Everything felt warm. For a moment, Grace sat there and let the heat infuse her. She felt warmed from the inside out and she closed her eyes and let her mother wash over her like a new blanket purchased in the middle of a dark winter. Carefully, Grace unclasped the pendant, put it around her neck, and dropped it under her collar, next to her skin where it slid into her cleavage as if it belonged there. Then she looked at the piles of money.

Grace thought about her mother and needs and about getting away. She thought about pushing Nick and how right it felt, and how she stood in the middle of the kitchen, raw chicken breasts splatted on the floor, and thought about being away. She couldn't imagine leaving her family for long, but then she could never imagine buying a doll either. She tried before, but she always turned away empty-handed, her mother's reprimands loud in her ears.

Grace could never have imagined a life without her mother, though she knew, as the daughter, she was likely to end up in that space. And now, even though every day was empty of Paul, Grace still couldn't imagine a life without her son. How could anyone imagine a life without her child? How could anyone continue to live it?

Yet here Grace was now. And here was the money left by her mother. There were no reprimands. There were possibilities. She wore the black pendant that was her mother's favorite, that her mother wore every day, and that her mother left just for her. And then there was the money.

Grace dumped everything out of her purse, her unused makeup, coupons, her calculator and nail clippers. She saved her wallet, her checkbook, and her car keys. Then she crammed the money, all of it, into her purse, tucking it into corners and under every flap. The clasp barely closed. Looking at the leftover junk, Grace wondered what to do. Time was running out; Virgil had to leave. But it was Grace's time. Grace couldn't let it run out.

It's time, Grace. In your time, Gracie.

Grace scooped the mess up and dropped it into the safety deposit box. She could pick it up later, if she came back.

When she came back. Not if. For a moment, the warmth left Grace, and she shuddered.

Because she was going to buy a doll. And then she was going to leave.

But she would be back.

That first hundred dollar bill, Grace tucked into her jeans pocket. She didn't want to open her bulging purse in front of Virgil. She looked guiltily away from Sheri, feeling like she was stealing her own money, as she left the bank. She ran up the steps to The Nursery, relieved to find the door still unlocked and open, and waved the bill at Virgil. "I have it!" Grace called. "I want to take Cathy home."

Virgil stepped forward and presented Grace with Cathy. "She's all yours, Grace," he said. "Your first doll." He settled the doll back into her hands. "I feel so honored to be the one to bring her to you."

Grace didn't know what to do. It was like the first time Mary was placed in her arms, and suddenly, everything she imagined didn't seem like enough. She didn't know enough.

But she could learn. Even as an adult, Grace could learn to play with a doll.

She blushed and squirmed in her shoes. "Thank you so much," she said. "When do you leave for your trip?"

"Saturday," he said and then, "Tomorrow morning," as if she might not know.

"Have a wonderful time," she said.

"Thanks. I'll look for Maribel."

Grace left The Nursery and took a quick trip to her car to hide Cathy in the trunk. She wrapped her carefully in a blanket she kept there for emergencies. She didn't want Mary to see her. She didn't want to explain. Not to anyone.

That doll was Grace's and Grace's alone.

Clutching her purse tightly to her side, Grace went to collect her daughter. She wondered if in that one visit, Mary learned to let go. And then she wondered if Mary was going to have to let go again. Let go of her own mother.

Let go of Grace. Because it wasn't Paul that needed to be let go. It was Grace. Grace needed to be gone. And it would happen, Grace decided, tomorrow.

CHAPTER TWO
Virgil

Virgil watched Grace leave the store. She held the doll so stiffly. Most women cradled their dolls like infants, but Grace looked uncertain, as if she'd never held a doll before.

But then, there was no "as if". There'd never been a doll in Grace's life.

For Virgil, the sight of a woman with a doll was common, but something that still struck him as beautiful. Women with dolls, women with perpetual babies that would never grow up; it just seemed natural to him. It was natural for men too, but Virgil didn't see much of that in The Nursery. While boys were allowed to play with dolls now, without a second glance or a festering worry, men were still apart from it. Segregated from that bit of imagination that made a doll, privately, real.

Grace was an anomaly. Virgil never met a woman who wasn't allowed to play with dolls when she was a little girl. Every woman that came into his shop played with dolls as children, and they usually fit into one of two types. They were either looking to reconnect with a tossed-away doll from their past or for replacement parts for the favorite doll they still loved, or they were true collectors, coming in to find a bargain. One found treasure in the doll's companionship, the other in a doll's worth.

Virgil already knew which camp Grace fell into. He knew which camp he fell into as well, although the shelves and display cases of The Nursery declared him a collector. While Grace was the only woman he met who hadn't been allowed to play with dolls, Virgil was part of a vast legion of men his age that weren't allowed to play either, even though they wanted to.

Dolls kept Virgil company from early on, though originally, in secret. His older sister mothered an entire community, a new doll every birthday and every Christmas and she bought them with her allowance in between. Virgil constantly kidnapped them from her room. He liked the babies the best, the ones he could cradle and pretend to feed with a bottle. There were "Magic Bottles" then that made it look like the white fluid inside, the "milk", actually disappeared into the doll's mouth. By today's standards, primitive; but then, amazing. After a while, the bottle took on a sickly curdled look, but that didn't stop Virgil from feeding those babies as often as he could.

Virgil learned quickly to take care, to kidnap the dolls only when his father was at work, when his sister was occupied elsewhere, when his mother was busy. He also learned to keep his bedroom door securely closed. His play was always with one ear turned toward that closed door, listening for a footstep, particularly a heavy footstep, giving him time to quickly shove the doll under his bed or behind his back. His mother and sister knew, Virgil was well aware of that, and they chose to keep quiet, to ignore it, to allow Virgil his secret. He didn't flaunt his doll-playing in front of them and they didn't flaunt their acquiescence; they were a threesome of silent conspirators. Rebels at a time when boys played with trucks and threw balls.

Now, on days when a mother brought in her little boy to The Nursery, Virgil found himself overcome with envy. He so wished he had what the young boys had now. He often sat behind his counter, watching from the corner of his eye as the mother took her son around, patiently helping him to choose just the right doll. Sometimes, the mother was swollen with the next baby, and she clearly wanted to give her son the chance to have his own baby too.

Virgil longed for his own baby when he was a little boy. The stolen dolls were wonderful, but they weren't his own to sleep with at night, to take with him on outings. They always had to be returned, surreptitiously, to his sister. Sometimes, when his sister played in her room, Virgil would stand tight next to the wall and peer at her through the crack between the door's edge and the jamb. His sister always looked so happy, dressing, holding, feeding, singing to first this doll, then that; Virgil's arms would ache.

Now, when the mother in The Nursery brought her little boy up, a doll in his arms, Virgil carefully snipped the pricetag off without taking the doll away. He didn't even ask if they wanted a bag or a box. He knew the boy would want to hang on to that doll all the way home and then some. That doll would always be that boy's baby.

Virgil wondered what happened to that connection as the boy grew older. He'd yet to be in a man's house, other than his own, where a cherished doll sat on a shelf or a bed or a chair. Somewhere along the way, these boys grew into men who gave their dolls up. The women didn't. Or if they did, they eventually came in search of them again.

Virgil's father caught him with a doll only once. Virgil sank too deeply into play one day and didn't realize it was time for his father to come home, didn't hear the footstep in the hall, and suddenly, his door was open and his father was there. He was smiling, extending an invitation to go fishing the next day, and Virgil loved to fish with his father. But in his room, Virgil was swaddling a flannel blanket around a flaxen-haired doll. She was Virgil's favorite, a double of his sister's that she tossed away in favor of the newer one, given to her by a friend at a birthday party. Virgil treated the doll like an orphan, a diseased twin discarded on an iceberg to float into oblivion. He rescued her. He never knew her official name, and he never found her duplicate, but she had the softest head of hair he ever felt on a plastic doll. She wore a dress made of burlap with two big patches near the hem. Her eyes were gigantic, big brown saucers that took up most of her face. But the thing that caught him up, the thing that made this doll more precious to him than any of his sister's other dolls, was a teardrop. She had a clear plastic teardrop glued to one cheek. No matter what Virgil did, no matter how well he took care of her, that little baby cried and always required more. She wrenched Virgil's heart, twisted it into a loopy figure eight, and he loved her so much, that teardrop should have disappeared into a treasure trove of smiles.

The day his father caught Virgil in the company of this doll, she wept in his arms. When his father came into the room, Virgil held her tightly against his body. There was no time to hide her behind his back, to shove her under his bed.

"Virgil!" his father barked. "What are you doing?"

"Just playing," he said. He was six years old. "I'm a daddy like you. Like you, Daddy."

Something melted in his father's face then and he almost smiled. Virgil held the doll out to him, hoping his father wanted to hold her and nuzzle her like Virgil did. Instead, his father hollered for Virgil's sister and she came and took the baby away. She didn't look at Virgil as she did, but Virgil noticed that she carefully tucked the doll, with the blanket, under her arm. She didn't treat the doll as an unwanted orphan; she would take care of her until Virgil could have her again. He sat on his bed, his hands folded in his lap. It was one of those times when he knew he did something wrong, but he couldn't put his finger on what it was. He hung his head.

"Virgil," his father said. He sat down on the bed and took a deep breath.

"So you like to play with dolls. There's nothing wrong with that."

Relief and surprise washed over Virgil like the doll's flannel blanket. He leaned against his father. "I like that doll, Daddy," he said. "She cries, and I make her feel better."

"Virgil, she's a doll for girls, like your sister. See, there's dolls that girls play with and there's dolls, kind of, that boys play with. Let's go get you some of those."

"Yeah!" Virgil yelled, leaping to the floor and pumping his fist in the air. He couldn't imagine what made a boy doll different than ones that girls played with. He loved his orphan. But maybe the doll was a boy too! All of the dolls in his sister's room were girls, except for some of her Barbie dolls. Virgil pictured holding a little plastic boy in his arms and he yanked at his father to make him move faster. "Let's go, Daddy!"

His father laughed and called out to Virgil's mother that they were going to be gone for a while, doing guy stuff. For Virgil, going anywhere with his father was a treat all by itself. Virgil hardly ever saw him because he worked so much. His father was a tax accountant, something called a CPA, which were letters even though he worked with numbers.

On the way to the toy store that afternoon, Virgil sat in the front seat and thought about his boy doll. He pictured it, trying to figure out what would make it a boy. Maybe his hair would be darker and shorter or his eyes would be unlashed. Instead of a dress, he would wear blue overalls, like Virgil wore, with patches in the knees and seat instead of at the hem of a dress. Al, Virgil decided. When he got his boy baby, Virgil would name him Al. Little Al. They'd be Al and Virgil, Al and Daddy. Daddy Virgil, Virgil decided, so that his boy doll could call him Daddy without confusing him with Virgil's own daddy.

But once they got to the toy store, Virgil's father marched him right by the baby doll aisle. It was Aisle 8, as Virgil memorized from trips there with his mother and sister, whenever his sister saved enough money to buy a new doll. He grew used to standing there next to her, watching her point out that doll or this, hold that one, hug this one, and he wished with all his might it was him buying the doll. This time, he thought it would be, but he looked over his shoulder, seeing all those little fluttering eyes and outstretched arms as they walked past Aisle 8 and on to Aisle 14. Virgil never saw Aisle 14 before. It was filled with all sorts of plastic figures, some green, some tan. Army men, Virgil knew, military guys. They were tiny, they could fit in the palm of his hand, and they were muscled and carried weapons and wore camouflage. Even though they were smaller, they looked so much meaner than the Barbies.

They weren't dolls. Not at all. Virgil wanted a baby. He didn't see a baby here.

Virgil played with Army guys before, of course. His friends had them. They spit pretend machine gunfire out of their mouths, held the green and brown figures in front of them like weapons, shooting enemies, throwing men off cliffs, drowning them in oceans. All the enemies died. The Army guys always won. Virgil didn't like killing.

Virgil's father waved his hand up and down the whole aisle. "Pick some out, Virgil," he said. "Whichever ones you want. You can spend up to twenty-five dollars."

That was an enormous figure. But Virgil didn't want any.

"Daddy?" he said. "Can't I have some other kind of boy doll?"

His father scanned the shelves. "I think this is about all there is," he said. "There's some cowboys and Indians and stuff. Would you rather have those? Pick some out, Virgil."

"I want to look over here." Virgil grabbed his father's hand and pulled him to Aisle 8. As soon as his father saw where they were, he dug in his heels and hauled Virgil back to the Army guys.

"No, Virgil," he said. "Boys don't play with those kinds of dolls. Those are girl dolls. These are boy dolls. Boys play with these."

Virgil wanted to cry. How do you tell your father, whom you love, that you don't want warring, fighting, killer figures? Figures that aren't dolls at all? How do you tell him you want a baby doll that needs you, just like you need your own father? Virgil had his father in a toy store, the best combination of treats he would ever have in his life, and there was only Aisle 14 to choose from. Looking at the shelves, Virgil saw only plastic men who looked ready to slit someone's throat. Virgil liked the helicopters and the tanks, but he liked them better with no people inside.

His father kept waiting, so finally Virgil just closed his eyes and picked out batches and sets, an even number of green and brown, and one set of navy blue. Asking his dad for a tank and a helicopter seemed to make him happy; he lit up around his eyes and laughed. "You got it, Virgil!" he said, slapping Virgil on the shoulder. "Whatever you want."

But Virgil couldn't have whatever he wanted. He could only have what his father wanted. He could only have Aisle 14.

The next day, when his father came home, Virgil was playing in the living room. He'd found an old shoebox in his closet and he snuck a dishtowel from the kitchen. Carefully, as best he could, he was putting his Army guys down for a nap.

His father sat down on the floor next to Virgil. "What's going on here?" he asked. "Looks like a pretty big war. Is that the barracks?"

Virgil shook his head. "It's naptime, Daddy."

"Naptime?" His father wasn't even looking at him. He stared at the shoebox. "Where's the helicopter and the tank?"

"Upstairs. I played with them this morning. They're keen."

Virgil's dad just got up and left the room. Virgil sat back on his heels and looked at his sleeping Army guys. He had that feeling again, that he did something wrong. He went upstairs and thought about it for a while. He missed his sister's doll. He missed that baby girl. He imagined her in his sister's room, lying in a corner, that one tear on her cheek becoming more and more permanent, all because he wasn't there.

The plastic figures quickly ended up shoved in the shoebox in the back of Virgil's closet. He stole the baby doll out of his sister's room again. He didn't return her. He named her Josephine. He always made sure Josephine was tucked away under his bed by the earliest time his father might come home; four o'clock. Weekends, she just stayed under there, though sometimes Virgil stretched out on the floor, reading a book, while his hand crept under the bedspread until he clasped her plastic fingers.

But somehow, his father knew. Virgil overheard him once, when he was about eleven years old. He crept down the stairs, hoping to hear some of the Johnny Carson show without being discovered. Instead of hearing Johnny, he heard his father talking to his mother.

"There's just something wrong with that kid, Angie," he said. "I don't know what. But maybe if we call him by his middle name, it could be different. I've always been afraid that Virgil was a sissy name. I should never have agreed to let you name him."

"Don't be ridiculous, Frank," his mother said. "Virgil was a great Roman writer. Don't you remember from college? I read your old textbooks and I told you that's where I got the name from. He wrote about battles and monsters, dragons and centaurs. It's a wonderful name. I can't call Virgil Jerome. He's Virgil."

Virgil knew his parents had a bet over who could name the baby and his mother won. They guessed the day he would be born and she was right. Virgil came early by eight days. He was told his father chose a day that was a week after his due date. By a week after the due date, Virgil was home and firmly a part of his family, and he carried the name Virgil Jerome Purdy. It was on his birth certificate. His mother insisted that the bet be honored. Virgil never questioned any of that. It was just the way it was. His father, Virgil was told, wanted to name him Erik. With a K.

Virgil took a huge chance that night, pulling Josephine out from beneath his bed and cradling her until morning. He needed her so much just then. His father was right, there was something the matter. Virgil knew it too, the way he knew when he did something wrong. He just couldn't put his finger on it.

When Virgil left for college, he cleaned out his room, getting rid of things that were now too childish for a college man. He handed the Army guys, the helicopter and the tank to his mother, asking her to bring them to Goodwill when his father wasn't around. She nodded and turned away. Virgil debated about Josephine for a long time. He wanted her with him at college, but he knew what would happen if the other guys in the dorm saw her. By then, Virgil was suspicious of his difference, the very thing his father was so afraid of and that had nothing to do with playing with dolls. He was also aware of what could happen if his uncertainty was discovered, and a doll on his bed was like a red flag waving for attack. Virgil didn't know what his room would be like, he didn't know how easy it would be to hide the doll, how easy it would be for a nosy roommate to find her. So he made the difficult decision to keep Josephine at home, tucking her into another shoebox. He covered her gently with a soft flannel blanket, pretending her lashed eyes were tightly closed rather than staring mournfully up. He wished, not for the first time, that Josephine was a doll with sleeping blinking eyes. He put a Magic Bottle next to her. Then he put her on the highest shelf of the closet, as far back as he could reach, and covered her with more shoeboxes, filled with baseball cards that he wanted to save in case they were ever worth anything.

He felt foolish doing so. He was a grown man, as grown as eighteen years old can be, and he was tucking away a doll as if she was real. But while he felt foolish, he also felt better, thinking he was keeping her in a safe place. A place where she would wait for him.

But it wasn't safe at all. When Virgil came back home for his first visit, that particular shoebox was gone. The baseball cards were still there, but they were alone. Virgil knew he couldn't ask what happened to Josephine; he wasn't supposed to have her in the first place, even though by that point, he'd had her for years. He looked through his sister's room; she was already out on her own, graduated from college and in an apartment. Her dolls, the few she wanted to keep after she left for college, sat together in a sad and lonely bunch on her bookshelves. But Josephine wasn't there; not even her twin, the doll that was a birthday gift, was there. His sister told him once that she really didn't like the doll. "She's so pathetic," she said. "That damn tear."

Virgil wasn't happy either. He missed Josephine more than he missed his own parents, his own sister. Josephine was his family, his baby, the dearest to his heart.

And now he was surrounded by dolls at The Nursery. Dolls were his business. His sister lived in Minnesota with her two boys and a girl, and they all had dolls in their rooms that were presents from their Uncle Virgil. Virgil's mother was dead and his father still lived in the family home just outside of Chicago. He hadn't spoken to his father in years.

Virgil knew why his father didn't want him to play with Josephine. But he went ahead and grew into his father's nightmare anyway. And it had nothing to do with Josephine or with any of the dolls in Aisle 8. Virgil knew now, beyond any shadow of a doubt, that he would have still played with dolls even if he was born straight. But he wasn't. There were times when he was younger that he wished he could be who his father wanted him to be. But at sixty-five years old, Virgil finally just wanted to be himself.

The world rallied around the belief now that men like Virgil weren't dysfunctional, they weren't filled with "something's the matter." But for some, Virgil knew, there was still a murky level of disgust, and in his father, Virgil knew that disgust wasn't murky at all. While changes were underway and more and more states were legalizing gay marriage, Virgil still felt the need for his childhood secrecy. He never went anywhere hand in hand with another man. He never draped his arm around the waist of a man in public. It just would have made those around him uncomfortable, and it would have made some angry, and Virgil just wasn't ready for that kind of disclosure.

To his father, Virgil was unacceptable, and to Virgil, his father was unacceptable. So they lived their separate lives. Virgil assumed that if his father died, his sister would let him know.

While he appreciated all the rainbow goings-on in the news, Virgil didn't want who he was to be newsworthy. He wanted to just be comfortable with himself. He wasn't ever sure why his sexuality was anyone's business but his own. And whoever he was with. Who he wanted to be with.

And that would be Brad.

****

That night after Virgil met Grace for the first time, he looked around at all of the dolls before locking up The Nursery. He never thought he would go from a boyhood with one hidden doll to a shop filled to the brim. His degree was in accounting, just like his father, but on the day when he was coming home with his first paycheck from the bank where he was hired after graduation, he stopped at a rummage sale. There were dolls in a box, and on impulse, Virgil bought them all. It was his job and his money and he finally felt free to do what he wanted. The woman who took his money smiled and said, "Some little girl is going to love her daddy tonight."

Virgil stood there, those five dolls cradled in his arms, and he blurted, "They're not for a little girl. They're for me."

She blinked for a minute, but then she brightened. "Oh, you're a collector!" She dashed into her house and came back with a catalogue full of dolls and prices. Virgil sat there, drinking iced tea with this woman under a tree, the five dolls at his feet in their box, and they looked at the catalogue until long after the rummage sale closed.

For Virgil, that catalog was a paper bridge. It was a way he could own dolls and not have to worry about what the world thought. He was no longer a boy who liked something he shouldn't. He was a collector.

And then he made them his business.

Virgil went to a bookstore that night and bought himself one of those catalogues. He looked for Josephine and couldn't find her, but there were tons of other dolls and he wanted them all. Before long, in the privacy of his own apartment, he had shelves full, and then he began to get duplicates which he sold at a profit to other collectors so he could buy more dolls. When he started spending more time with the dolls than with his numbers at work, Virgil knew it was time for a new direction. So he took his knowledge of numbers, added some continuing education classes in business, and opened the shop. He called it The Nursery.

Looking around now, Virgil could remember where and when he bought each doll. He knew how much each cost, he knew what kind of profit he would make, and he knew what kind of shape the dolls were in when he got them. Some were naked, with snarled hair and whitened eyes that had to be cleaned with ammonia and water. Others were perfect, pristine, still unplayed with despite years passing since their manufacture, still strapped into their boxes or cases, their hair held down with a flimsy hairnet. A doll was worth more if it was in an unopened package, but Virgil still took them out. He released them from what he felt was a plastic and cardboard prison. He kept the boxes carefully stored in a back room, and when someone bought the doll, he presented the box too. Worth was important, but so was freedom and Virgil knew how important freedom could be. Good care was important as well; he brushed everyone's hair, made sure they were clean, set them up with other dolls on shelves and showcases, always making sure they were at least in pairs so they would never be lonely again.

Virgil knew that the expression on Grace's face when she first looked in the window at Chatty Cathy reflected the one on Virgil's own face whenever he purchased a doll. Every doll. Chatty Cathy filled an absence inside of Grace. Virgil knew that absence well. He still sought Josephine.

Virgil thought of himself as a matchmaker of sorts. He placed orphan doll-babies into new homes. Sometimes, like with Grace, the mothers needed the babies as much as the babies needed the mothers. Virgil liked this so much more than just selling to collectors. He loved putting families together.

With Grace and Cathy, he felt like he made the greatest match ever. He felt like he changed two lives. One was a plastic life, but Chatty Cathy deserved a mother that would keep her and love her forever. And Grace deserved Chatty Cathy. Every little girl deserved a doll. And every little boy too.

Virgil knew that now. He supposed he and Grace were a lot alike that way. They each had a parent who kept a child from what a son or daughter truly needed. He wondered why Grace's mother wouldn't let her play with dolls. Why would a mother do such a thing?

****

Virgil considered his one-bedroom apartment, tucked squarely and securely right above The Nursery, to be one of the best things about his life. He only had to walk downstairs to work and home was always just around the curve of a staircase. When he slept, he knew the hundreds of dolls in the shop slept as well, his floor and their ceiling the only thing between them. They were all in a safe home, a haven. The Nursery was better than an orphanage, better than a store. It was a home where the dolls were loved and where they could stay forever. Virgil would never throw a doll away, even if it spent years standing on one of his shelves.

Virgil kept his own favorites, the dolls that were not for sale, in his apartment. Ideal's Baby Boo slept or sat up in a small cradle in the corner of the living room. Every now and then, Virgil pulled the tiny pink pacifier out of her mouth to listen to her rhythmic wheezing cry. Another doll, Mattel's Baby First Step, stood proudly on her roller skates on one side of the entertainment center, while her sister, Mattel's Tippee Toes rode her plastic horse on the other. Pixie sat on Virgil's bedside table. Virgil found her at a flea market. She had no manufacturer mark on her, but he named her Pixie because of her perfect Y for a mouth and fine blonde plaits. Unfortunately, if the plaits were unbraided, they exposed a bald head; the doll was never meant to have free-flowing hair.

Certain things perturbed Virgil about the dolls and their makers. What sense did it make to put roller skates on a baby taking her first step? And why should a doll have to wear braids? Why couldn't her hair flow down her back? Other dolls made more sense. Boo cried when she lost her pacifier, the way any baby would. Tippee Toes, true to her name, rose high on her toes while riding a four-wheeled pink and yellow plastic horse, or she scooted along the floor on her tiny blue tricycle. In Virgil's mind, she was the most like a little girl and Boo was as much a baby as a molded piece of plastic could be.

Virgil's prize was Horman's Poor Pitiful Pearl. The rags-to-riches doll was the closest thing he could find to his childhood Josephine, and it was his best collector's guess that Josephine was actually a poor cousin of Pearl, basically a Poor Pitiful Pearl knock-off. Pearl lay in splendor on Virgil's bed. He found her dressed in playful rags in her original box at a flea market in Dickeyville, Wisconsin. Her hair was pulled back with a purposely torn red bandana and she looked at Virgil with huge brown eyes through the plastic window on her box. Her instructions explained that giving Pearl a loving home would magically change her from poor to rich. That was, of course, all that Virgil ever wanted to do, rescuing doll after doll after doll. So he bought her, freed her from the box and found a party dress inside, soft and silky and full of crinoline and lace. Pearl's hair, when released from the bandana, was a glorious platinum blonde and Virgil brushed it to perfection before crowning it with a pink silk bow. Even her feet looked better, taken out of ragged cloth shoes and then tucked into black patent leather slippers.

He thought of these chosen dolls as his children, his family. But he never stopped looking for Josephine. As a collector now, he knew that if she was a knock-off, she would be harder to find, and so far, that search proved futile. As a knock-off, the only person who would find her valuable was Virgil and she was just as likely to be thrown away into oblivion as put up for sale.

On the eve of his annual doll-hunting trip, after sending Grace on her way, Virgil looked at his special dolls while he packed his bags. The first few times he took this trip, he brought the dolls along. But now they were left at home. He knew they would be okay and it gave him someone to come home to. As he grew older, it became more and more important that someone be waiting for him when he came in the door.

Though he did wish he had someone there who breathed. Who hugged back. Who kissed him hello, goodnight, good morning. Who kissed him for no reason at all.

Virgil knew that Brad wanted to be Virgil's person at home, the greeter at the end of the day, the first person to say hello to in the morning. But Brad wasn't in Wisconsin, and he wasn't willing to move there. Brad wanted Virgil to move to him, to retire and leave everything behind, to move to Georgia to live the good life in the years they had left. Their relationship was ten years old now, ten years of seeing each other at least twice a year with numerous phone calls and sometimes surprise visits in between. Brad always came to see Virgil at Christmas, leaving behind his lush ripe Georgia valley to see some snow, and Virgil went there at the cusp of summer and fall, ending each of the doll-search jaunts at Brad's home, basking in the southern sunshine and his lover's smile. As if Brad could read Virgil's mind, the phone rang, and then there was his voice.

"Hello, sweetheart," he said, his voice as rich and thick as the sunshine that likely lit his porch earlier that day. "You'll be on the road tomorrow?"

"Yes, my love," Virgil answered. "I'm not sure what path I'll be taking, but you should find me at your door within the next few weeks."

"I can't wait," Brad said, and then he went into a long description of all the changes he made in his house since the last time Virgil saw it. Changes Virgil already knew about, because Brad talked about them as they were in process, including Virgil in the action as if he was a part of it. But now the changes were done, always in preparation for Virgil's visit, and always as if they were done for

Virgil himself, another enticement to make Georgia his home. Brad's voice took on a new tilt of excitement and expectation.

Virgil met Brad on the first of his trips to find dolls. Virgil ended up at a flea market in Macon. He was eating lunch when a man sat next to him at the picnic table. Their elbows bumped and he said, "Excuse me," and Virgil said, "No problem," and made room for him even though there was space across the table, on the bench on the opposite side. Virgil noticed the man wasn't carrying any bags or boxes, his hands only held his lunch, four hot dogs, two topped with relish, one with cheese, and one plain. Virgil was loaded down with six bags of dolls. It was a great flea market.

"Not finding anything good?" Virgil asked.

The man shrugged. "Not really here to buy," he said.

Virgil glanced at the paper boats holding the hot dogs. "Just here for the gourmet food?" This man was an oddity and it made Virgil a little uncomfortable. Eating lunch at a flea market, but not having any intention to buy? Bumping elbows with a stranger, sitting on the same side of a picnic bench with him, even though the opposite side was empty? Virgil knew by then about gay bars and movie houses, places he could go if he had a desire to meet someone. These were places where bumped elbows meant something. Did it mean something here too? But he was never picked up at a flea market before.

The man grinned and cocked his eyebrows, as if he knew what Virgil was thinking. "Hot dogs are damn good," he said. "I'd have a chili one, except their chili comes straight out of the can. I prefer homemade. Five-alarm." He wiped his hand on a napkin and then held it out to Virgil. "My name's Brad. I own a private dump just outside of town. The city pays me for the use of it, and they hire me to clean up after all these folks clear out. Vendors always leave unsellables behind. At least, the ones they've given up on."

So Virgil was talking with the dump man. He shook the outstretched hand, introduced himself, and looked at Brad more closely. His clothes were impeccable, his jeans so crisp, they had to be ironed. His hands were clean, even under the fingernails, and Virgil wondered just how he dug around in the garbage all day without getting dirty. Virgil found out later that Brad wore thick rubber gloves, going through them the way most people go through paper towels. He built a special dispenser right by his back door, and he pulled two new gloves out every time he went to work. He also wore mechanic's bright orange coveralls. During Virgil's visits, he loved sitting on the wraparound porch with a second cup of coffee in the morning, tracking the bright orange sunspot that was Brad cresting the hills of garbage. Virgil often dreamed of Brad wearing his coveralls. And fantasized about him without.

"What're you looking for?" Brad asked that first day, nudging Virgil's bags with his foot.

"Dolls," Virgil said. He knew the corners of Brad's mouth would twitch, and they did. "I run a small doll shop back home, selling to collectors."

Brad nodded. "And home is…"

"Wisconsin."

Brad whistled low between his teeth. "I get dolls all the time, out to the junkyard," he said.

Virgil had to stop eating. He pictured doll bodies, arms and legs and freckled noses sticking up through layers of trash bags and flat bicycle tires and rusted sump pumps. It made him feel sick. "Real dolls?" he asked. "Whole?"

Brad snorted. "Sure. People clean house, they don't know what to do with all that stuff. So they chuck it. Wanna see?"

It was definitely the most unusual bumped-elbow invitation turned proposition Virgil ever received. And it was the one that changed his life, that did what years of bar-humping was supposed to do. Virgil ending up staying the night at Brad's shack, after spending hours scrounging through the acreages of junk, a search that resulted in a full trunk and back seat of dolls. Brad's home was just a shack back then, but Brad showed Virgil his plans to use the trash to build himself a house. And he did. The house was two stories tall and completely finished and furnished with things Brad found in his morning excursions through the junk.

Now on the phone, Brad finished telling Virgil about the claw-footed tub he found and installed in the new guest bathroom. Those words, guest bathroom, made Virgil cringe. "What do you need a guest bathroom for?" he asked. "Just how many guests do you have?"

Brad's laugh was low and easy. "You're the most special guest I have, you know that, doll-baby. And you won't be staying in the guest room."

Virgil knew Brad sometimes had visitors during the year. He hated thinking of Brad lying cozy with another man. But what could Virgil say about it? How could he object? If Virgil stayed, if he moved in with Brad, if he made the commitment, then he could put a stop to it, Brad wouldn't have a need for anyone else. He said he went crazy thinking about Virgil, wanting Virgil to be there. Virgil said he went crazy too. He even brought home a pair of Brad's coveralls to sleep with, ones he wore the morning Virgil left one year, though

Virgil washed them before tucking them between his sheets. It was the closest thing to having Brad in bed. And it was the only thing in Virgil's bed when Brad wasn't visiting, other than dreams. Virgil seemed to find faithfulness easier than Brad did, this man who oozed southern sensuality, whose skin was warm to the touch and whose arms were both tender and firm.

Virgil only asked Brad once why he couldn't stay faithful, and Brad's face contorted a bit, in anger, Virgil thought at first, but then hurt, and then he smoothed himself out, smiled slow and lazy. "I ain't like that, dolly," he said. "It ain't that simple for me. Sleeping with your shirt isn't enough. I need you."

Virgil wondered, sometimes, if Brad's lack of faithfulness would disappear if he did make the commitment, though he knew in his heart of hearts that it would. While Brad's attention seemed splintered to Virgil, it was never splintered when they were together, whether in Wisconsin or Georgia. And Brad slipped talk of others into their conversations less and less in the last few years. Virgil didn't know if he just chose not to speak them, or if there really were less. He didn't think they'd dwindled to none. But he knew that Brad was as wrapped up in Virgil as Virgil was in him, and things were just right when they were together.

"I'll be there soon," Virgil said now.

"You comin' to stay this year, sweetheart?" Brad's voice deepened then and Virgil knew the answer he wanted to hear.

"I don't know, love," Virgil said. "We'll see." The answer Brad expected, but didn't want.

But Brad's response wasn't expected. "Virgil," he said. "I need an answer this year. I can't just keep going like this."

Virgil took a step backwards. "What do you mean?"

Brad's sigh was loud. "You know what I mean. We're not getting younger. And I don't want to get any older on my own. This time, Virgil, is it. We're either done at the end of this visit, or we become a pair." He paused. "Everything is different now. We can even get married, you know." He laughed. "Seems we've become legal. Our outlaw days are over."

Virgil was stunned. It was an ultimatum, but it was an ultimatum that was as fraught with pleasure as it was with danger. So he just nodded and told Brad he'd see him soon. Their goodbye was careful.

After they hung up, Virgil looked around his little apartment. He loved it here, it was everything he knew, and everything in it was a reflection of himself. From his niece's and nephews' photographs on the small fireplace mantel to the picture of Brad on the bedside table, it encompassed his whole life. During the Christmas visit, Virgil always put up a large tree and he hung two stockings at the fireplace. It was perfect until January, when he was alone again.

It was one thing to think about moving in with Brad. It was another to think about marriage. To Virgil, that felt like stepping out, loud and proud, in front of the whole world. And with Brad, that whole world would be Georgia. He'd heard the word faggot often enough around Brad's town. It was one scary thing to think about being two men living together there. It was another to think about stepping into a courthouse and getting married.

Again, Virgil wondered what business it was of the world's to know what he was doing behind closed doors.

But he always wanted to be part of a pair. A couple. Married, even when marriage was an impossibility.

Virgil looked around the room again, letting his eyes rest on his own special dolls. In Georiga, Virgil felt like a couple when Brad went out and rooted for garbage in the early morning after a hearty breakfast that Virgil cooked for him, and Virgil always had a big lunch ready for Brad by noon. Virgil cleaned all the dolls that Brad found, swaddled them or dressed them in clothes that were washed and hung out on a line to dry. Afternoons, the two men puttered around the house, and then shared another fine meal in the evening. Brad had a large assortment of porch swings and rockers on his big wraparound verandah, all of them found in various states of disrepair in the junkyard, all of them rescued and rehabilitated by Brad, just like Virgil rescued his dolls. Each night, Brad and Virgil chose a different place and a different seat to enjoy the stars. Virgil's favorite was a big wooden double rocker at the front of the house. Brad painted it bright purple and it glowed like the tail end of a sunset in the dark. Over the hills of garbage, the city lights created a halo that reminded Virgil there were people close by, and he was warm and embraced and alone with his lover. At night, during those two times of the year, there was a body next to his in bed and the face that turned to Virgil in the dark breathed warm air right before his mouth engulfed Virgil's in a kiss that left them both not wanting to sleep.

Brad would never move to Wisconsin. He hated the cold. But it was so hard for Virgil to think of moving to Georgia. Virgil was a midwestern boy, born and bred. The farthest he got from Chicago, his hometown, was Waukesha, Wisconsin, two hours north from his parents' home. The southern life was like molasses to Virgil. But he had to think beyond that, beyond leaving this state and this house. Virgil was getting older and he was living with hundreds of dolls. He loved the dolls, he really did, but there truly was one thing that Virgil wanted that the dolls could never provide. Virgil wanted something in his life that hugged him back. That hugged him back permanently, in a way that made Virgil know, without question, that that hug, that touch, the warm sound of his own name being called out, was always going to be there. It wasn't transient, the way nights coming home with someone from a bar used to be. It was solid, as solid as all the dolls on his shelves, but solid in a way that breathed, in a way that the dolls couldn't.

Virgil didn't feel alone, but he did feel lonely. He was surrounded by everything he loved. Except for a partner. Except for Brad. When Virgil held the dolls, their little arms reached up to his chin or pressed against his chest. They didn't circle him, grab him up in an embrace. They didn't hold Virgil tight. They didn't come up behind him while he cooked at the stove, they didn't wrap their arms around his waist and nuzzle his neck, murmuring sly promises and silly endearments. They didn't smell real.

And sometimes, real was just what Virgil wanted. Sometimes, plastic and cloth weren't enough. While he loved his dolls, while he loved his home and the way it was filled with his pretend family, Virgil wanted a partner. He wanted a spouse, a husband. He was in love, and he wanted to be with Brad.

But he didn't want the world to watch, no matter if they jeered or cheered.

CHAPTER THREE
Grace

As Grace ate supper with her family that night, she kept obsessing over three worries. Her mind popped to one, then the other, then the third. First, there was her purse, the one stuffed full with money. She hid it completely under her bed, pushing it until her arm couldn't reach any further.

Now she had to hope that no one went looking for her purse to pull out a dollar or two, needed for school lunches or spare change for the soda machine at work. She just couldn't take the chance that someone would find the twenty-two thousand, two-hundred and twelve dollars. Down one hundred from the original amount left to Grace, that bill handed over to Virgil that very afternoon. For the doll hidden away in Grace's trunk.

Who was Worry Number Two. Chatty Cathy. Grace hated thinking of her doll in the dark. But the doll would just have to wait. Grace just wasn't ready to explain about her yet.

Then there was Worry Number Three: Grace's mother's pendant, sitting smoothly next to her skin, tucked under her shirt. She hadn't had the time to pull it off, hide it away, but she also hadn't yet felt the inclination to. Now, at dinner, she was worried her family would notice, would see the puckered outline beneath her shirt and ask what it was. She wasn't ready to explain that either.

From one worry, to the next, to the next. Of course, there actually was a fourth worry, but Grace kept shoving that one away.

Worry Number Four: Just what the hell was Grace doing? What was she thinking?

Grace looked at her family gathered around the table. She managed to put together a meat loaf, baked a potato for each of them and opened a bag of salad and threw it into a bowl. There were several bottles of salad dressing in the fridge and Grace carefully checked the expiration dates and put the still-good ones on the table. She even warmed a loaf of French bread and now Nick layered his third piece with butter and smiled.

"Good dinner, Grace," he said.

Grace supposed it was. She could barely taste it. She noticed that JJ's chair was just a bit off-center across from Mary. Paul used to sit next to him and though Paul's chair was gone now and Nick kept shoving JJ's chair to the center, JJ automatically moved it to the side when he sat down. But his distance from the center was a little less with each passing month.

Grace hated that. The guest chair, most often used by Grace's mother, was gone into the garage as well. One chair hadn't been used for six months; the other, a year. Grace hated that too.

Nick pointed his bread at Mary. "So did you see the therapist today?" he asked.

Mary swallowed and nodded.

"What did you talk about?"

"Not much. Just stuff." She continued to look at her plate, scooping at her meat loaf.

"Like what?" Nick looked at Grace and rolled his eyes. She rolled hers back. It seemed like what he wanted her to do.

"He asked about my name, my age, who are the people in my family, do I like school, do I plan on going to college next year, where, and why did I knock out Amber Martin." Mary set down her fork and crossed her arms.

Amber Martin. So the girl had a name. The girl who stole Mary's painting. Grace wondered where Mary put it. She hadn't noticed it in Mary's bedroom the night before.

"So…what did you tell him?" Nick reached for his fourth piece of bread and Grace slid the butter back across the table. He could eat a whole loaf of French bread without stopping to think about it.

"I told him about Grandma dying and then about Paul, about how he died next, and how he died because of me." Her eyes remained level, looking at no one. Or maybe looking at the spot where Paul used to sit.

JJ's movements slammed to a stop so abruptly, his knife and fork flew from his hands and crashed against his plate to the floor. "Mary," he hissed. "We said we'd never—"

"I already told Mom," Mary said, but her eyes didn't shift to him at all.

Grace's eyes did. She stared at him. JJ knew about this? Aren't little brothers supposed to tattle? How could he keep something this enormous so secret?

Grace thought of her own secrets. Worry Number Four loomed large and she shoved it away.

"And I know you feel that way too, honey," Nick said quietly. "Mom told me."

Mary took Grace in, just for a moment, before she went back to looking at the air. In that moment, Grace was stabbed with the force of her own betrayal. She'd betrayed her daughter's trust.

Though maybe she already did. Maybe she betrayed that trust when she didn't tell Mary in the car yesterday afternoon that it was okay, that she didn't kill Paul.

But Mary did. Or at least, she instructed him to climb to a place where he would die.

Grace just didn't know what to say about that. She just didn't know.

Nick cleared his throat and said formally and clearly, "We all understand how you feel, Mary, but Paul's death isn't your fault. You didn't cause it."

Mary's head swung with JJ's and Grace's and they all looked at Nick. Grace could see the incredulity on the kids' faces and she could feel it on her own as well.

"It's not your fault," Nick repeated.

"Yes, it is," Mary said. "I told him to climb the tree."

"She did," JJ said. "I was there." His voice was strained. Grace wondered if he would break. If he would shatter. She wondered if she would shatter. She wondered if she already had.

Worry Number Four.

Nick looked at Grace. "It's not Mary's fault."

The kids' heads rotated in Grace's direction and Nick raised his eyebrows. Clearly, she was expected to echo.

Grace stopped wondering if she'd already shattered. She knew she did. She shattered the day she saw Paul fall. She shattered and scattered into a million pieces. Pieces she attempted to sweep together for her children.

Her remaining children. What mother could stand thinking of her own children that way? What mother could stand thinking of the child that wasn't remaining? The one that was lost? Taken away.

What was she supposed to call him? Her gone child? Her wiped off the face of the earth child? The child she was supposed to pretend never existed?

Grace wondered if it was possible to shatter more than once. Could pieces swept up be thrown with such force to the floor that they shattered again? Into dust?

Ashes to ashes, dust to dust.

Worry Number Four.

She shook her head and stood up. "Time for dessert, I guess," she said. As she walked by Nick, he grabbed her arm. Grace stopped. "It's apple pie, Nick," she said. "Mary and I picked it up from the bakery this afternoon. I'll put your piece in the microwave, I know you like it warm with your ice cream next to it." She yanked her arm away.

Grace could feel him staring as she sliced the pie. She considered if he would say something later, if he would shout. She doubted it. Nick never shouted. And he considered her fragile. She was fragile. She was shattered.

The kids watched her too. But then they both ate every bit of their pie, finding relief and escape in their dessert.

When supper was done, Nick loaded the dishwasher and Grace wiped off the table and the placemats while JJ settled down in front of a video game and Mary pretended not to watch from behind her book. Despite the familiarity, the sense of routine, Grace knew from the tension that this conversation was far from over. The tension was a new familiar. When the phone rang, she yelped, and that disrupted the routine too. Grace didn't yelp and the phone didn't usually ring after dinner.

Nick answered it, and Grace stood by the table and listened. As his dialogue continued, she noticed the kids suspended their playing and watching too, though their faces remained firmly fixed to the television screen.

"Okay," Nick said. "I agree. We'll be there in a few minutes." He hung up the phone. He took Grace's hand and led her to the couch. The kids turned to look at them. "Mary, that was Mrs. Martin, Amber's mother."

Mary looked away.

"Mrs. Martin says Amber is returning to school on Monday. She knows you'll be back then too. She thinks that you should apologize to Amber for what you did, before the two of you are together again in the art classroom. She talked with Ms. Deets, and Ms. Deets agreed."

What Mary did. Not a word about what Amber did. Grace rested a hand on Nick's knee. "Did her mother say Amber is going to apologize too?"

It was brief, but Grace saw a smile fly onto Mary's face. Grace knew she was just forgiven for the breach of trust.

Nick frowned. "Why does Amber need to apologize?"

"She stole my painting," Mary said softly. "She started it."

"Mrs. Martin and I didn't talk about that. In the light of things, what you did was much more serious, Mary. Let's just focus on that."

Grace didn't think that was fair. She and Mary exchanged glances. "Nick, that doesn't seem right," Grace said. "Amber shouldn't have taken the painting. Mary would never have hurt her if it wasn't to try and get the painting back."

Just like Paul wouldn't have died if Mary hadn't told him to climb the tree. It was the same thing, right? It made sense, right?

But it wasn't the same thing at all.

Nick sighed and stood up. "We're going over there, and Mary is going to apologize to Amber." He turned to JJ. "JJ, you can stay here by yourself for a bit, right?"

JJ looked relieved and quickly agreed. For a moment, Grace thought about volunteering to stay with him, but she figured she'd already pushed Nick's patience too far this evening. She shrugged at Mary. "Let's go, honey."

Mary stood up. The look on her face told Grace that the betrayal was back. Then, so slowly that Grace couldn't believe neither she nor Nick stopped her because it was obvious what she was going to do, Mary raised her book over her head, as far as her arm could reach, and then she fired it at the television screen.

The book was a hardcover. Mary never read paperbacks or e-books. She loved hardcover first editions. Grace loved her pickiness.

The sound when the screen cracked was like a gunshot. Or maybe like the sound when Paul touched the wire. Grace remembered that sound. It sounded the way a light that bright, that sudden, should.

JJ gasped, scrambled to his feet away from the shards and the sizzling of wires, and hurried to unplug the television. Mary stood there for a moment longer, then she turned without saying a word and walked away. Grace heard the sound of the back door closing, and then a muted slam of a car door. Grace and Nick just stared at what remained of the television.

"I can't believe she did that," Nick said. His voice was strung tight, yet it had a rubbery texture to it too, and Grace pictured a rubber band pulled between two fingers, then plucked like a banjo.

"I can believe it." Grace looked at her son, holding the tv cord like a leash. The cracks and pops disappeared and she sniffed. Nothing smelled like it was burning. "Amber should apologize too, Nick. She's a thief." She went to join her daughter in the car.

The drive to the Martin's house was silent.

Mrs. Martin answered the door and ushered them in to the living room.

Mr. Martin was there, and so was Amber. Grace studied her. She didn't look hurt, though there was a bruised set to her eyes. Mostly, Grace thought, she looked like a sneaky little girl that would steal another girl's very special picture. She had what Grace thought of as a pre-sneer set to her lips. It wouldn't take much for that sneer to become evident. Her facial muscles were ready for it. Grace tried, but failed, to stop the thought that Amber deserved what she got.

Grace and Nick stood behind Mary, each of them putting a hand on her shoulder, as she mumbled her apology. Grace could tell from the tilt of Mary's head that she didn't look directly at Amber. Amber folded her arms and said nothing, but when her father nudged her, she said, "Thanks."

There was nothing more. Grace waited for, and didn't receive, the apology from Amber. She thought about asking for it, but she knew that Nick would step in and speak over her. Instead, Grace, Nick and Mary pivoted like soldiers, marched out to the car, and went home.

JJ was in his room when they got there. The television's power cord was carefully coiled and held with a rubber band. JJ was in bed and asleep. She kissed his forehead and smoothed the blankets that didn't need smoothing.

Mary went to bed too, after Nick told her that she wouldn't receive another allowance until a new television was paid for. She nodded, then embraced Grace. This was a surprise and even more of a surprise was the smothered "I love you" against Grace's neck. There was so much Grace wanted to say, but the words got caught behind her teeth again.

Nick, after cleaning up the mess from the television, which included hauling the TV itself out to the curb, went up the steps without a glance at Grace. She heard their bedroom door click shut and then soft sounds from the television there. She thought of the night before, their separate vigils before separate televisions. There was only one television now. Maybe, she thought, this conversation was over. Maybe there would be quiet for a bit.

Grace needed quiet.

She sat on the couch and TheCat climbed into her lap. Only the lamp by her side was on; the rest of the house was in shadow. She couldn't remember the last time she sat alone in the living room at night. She thought about her purse, hidden under her bed, under where Nick rested right at this moment. She thought about the doll in her trunk. The pendant next to her skin.

Worry Number Four.

And she thought about Virgil. Grace imagined him driving from town to town, not looking at a map, discovering flea markets and rummage sales, rooting for dolls. He probably talked to himself the whole way. Because there was no one else.

Just like there was no one else in Grace's living room right then. There was no one for Grace to talk to, except herself.

Grace wondered what it would be like to drive for miles, looking for something that wasn't specific.

Worry Number Four. What the hell was she thinking?

Grace opened the drawer of the end table and pulled out a notebook and a pen, left there for scoring family card games. Grace propped the notebook on TheCat's back. She wrote the first letter to Mary.

Dear Mary,

I have decided to run away from home for a while. I need to get away just for a little bit, I don't know how long, and think about how I feel about things. Right now, I really really need time to think.

Anyway, in case you haven't noticed, there is a crystal ball on your dresser. It's from me and Grandma. Grandma gave it to me the night before I married Dad. She filled it with good spirits for our family and I thought you might like some good spirits on your side right now. Look at it often and think of me. I am always on your side.

I love you. See you soon.

Love,
Mom

One letter done. One step closer to something Grace never imagined doing, and didn't know now if she could. But she'd taken a step. Grace set down the pen, folded the paper and tucked it between her thigh and the arm of the chair. Putting it in writing like this made her suck her breath in. If she was putting this down, black ink, white paper, maybe she really would do this. Maybe her mother was right. Maybe she did find herself wanting to be away.

Maybe Worry Number Four was very, very real.

She started her second letter. Step Two.

To my JJ, my Jeffrey Joseph,

I'm going on a trip for a little while. I know you know how mixed up things have been here lately. I think I just need some fresh air and some time to think. I will miss you very much and I know it will be hard, but I really want to get better. I'm just not a very good mom right now and you and Mary need a very good mom.

I love you so much. I'm not leaving because I'm angry at you or Mary or Dad. You know how sometimes you lock yourself in your room for hours and when I ask you what you've been doing, you say, "Just thinking,"? Well, I need to lock myself up for a while too, and I can't lock myself up here because you all keep me from thinking. That didn't come out right. But I think you will know what I mean. You are such a smart boy.

I won't be gone long, sweetie. Be a good boy.

Love,
Mom

Grace folded this letter and tucked it next to Mary's. There was one more step to do. Well, two more, since she had to count actually stepping through the door, stepping out of her house with the intention of not coming back for a while. She took a breath and started on the last letter. The hardest, really, because she knew of the three people in her family, Nick would have the most difficult time understanding. Nick was the one who walked away that night without a glance. Nick would write in the dust on the dresser, "It's time, Grace, but not for this!"

She didn't even know what "this" was, though. How could she expect him to know? And there wasn't any more dust anyway. She cleaned it off, which was what he wanted her to do. But he wouldn't want her to do this.

Nick,

I'm not leaving you. I'm just taking a little break. Don't worry, I'm not using any of our money. I am fine. I just need some time and space to sort things out. I hope you will understand.

If it helps, there is a statue of St. Anthony in my underwear drawer. Mother gave it to me after Steven left. She said to hang him upside down in the front closet and he would make Steven come back. It didn't, as you know. But if you want, hang him in our closet. It will work this time because I promise you, and I promise St. Anthony, that I will be back.

St. Anthony didn't work back then because he knew that you were coming into my life. He knew that I needed to be with you. And I do. I just also need to be gone for a while. So much has happened. I can't get my head around it.

Don't worry. Take care of the kids and remember to feed TheCat.

Love you always,
Grace

Tomorrow was Saturday. If Grace left early, she would be gone before the kids or Nick woke up. She decided to leave the notes in the kids' rooms and on the dresser that she and Nick shared. The newly clean dresser. Nick's message to her was gone. Now hers to him would be there. This wouldn't be hard to do.

But it would be. It would be the hardest thing she'd ever done. If she did it.

Worry Number Four.

Grace closed her eyes and thought about sleep, about her bed upstairs with the mound of money underneath. She wondered if Nick was asleep, or if his lack of a glance changed and now he was ready to continue this conversation. She hoped not. It was no longer their conversation.

This was hers. It was Chatty Cathy's. And hopefully, it was Virgil's.

****

It was very early when Grace slipped out of bed. She didn't sleep much. The alarm couldn't be set because she didn't want Nick to wake up and ask why the alarm was set on a Saturday, so she just lifted her head every few minutes to check the time.

Nick was sleeping on his side. He always slept facing Grace. One arm curled under his pillow, the other wrapped around his stomach. Reaching carefully under the bed, Grace pulled out the purse. Her clothes were already waiting downstairs; she pulled them from the dryer and into a nondescript paper bag at the top of the basement steps last night, along with another set for later. For once, she was glad of her inability to get anything done. She'd started the laundry, gotten as far as the dryer, but never folded the clothes. A pair of underwear, socks, a bra, a shirt and jeans. She figured she could always buy more if necessary. She had money, money that was there just in case she ever wanted to be away. A part of being away was having clothes to wear.

When Grace's mother died and Grace had to clean out the house, she stood in her mother's closet and breathed in her scent. Her mother's body entered all those clothes and all the detergent in the world couldn't get her out. Grace stood there and inhaled and she was with her mother again.

She did the same with Paul. And then all the clothes, her mother's, Paul's, were gone.

Now she left the clothes in her closet for the kids and Nick. The scent would help them until she returned. She also left her toothbrush, her comb, all her toiletries. Grace believed that nobody ever left for good if their personal things were still on their bathroom sink, in their medicine cabinet, on their dresser. Her toothbrush and her deodorant would tell Mary and JJ and Nick even more than she could that she would be back.

Grace paused by the kids' doors for several minutes, but finally decided not to crack them open for one last look. She was afraid if she saw them, Mary with her crushed ragdoll, JJ under the empty bunk, they would change her mind. Grace suddenly felt that this was the most important decision of her life and she couldn't back out. Not even if she wanted to.

But she realized, as she took one step away, that she didn't want to back out. It was time.

Grace's time was now. Her need for escape was now. She was suddenly awash with gratitude and love for her mother, for her mother's thoughtfulness, for her ability to always give Grace what she needed.

Except for a doll, of course. But now, there was a doll in the trunk. Purchased with her escape money.

Grace tried not to consider what her mother would think of that.

In the kitchen, Grace put a handful of kibble in TheCat's bowl to keep him quiet. Then she dressed and rolled the bag shut. As an afterthought, she re-opened the bag and added a package of Oreos, a six-pack of bottled water, and two boxes of tissues. Then she slowly petted TheCat, feeling her fingers roll over his vertebrae and climb the length of his tail. He stood still for a change and his skin twitched. Grace was going to be gone for a while, she figured, and she needed all the luck she could get. She appreciated TheCat's still patience on this morning, so she kissed his nose. Grace had to kiss someone goodbye, and she realized it had to be someone that wouldn't ask her to stay. TheCat just sat in a spot of sunshine on the floor and purred as he watched her go. Grace felt it as a benediction.

The first order of this business of running away was releasing Chatty Cathy from the trunk. Grace whispered her apologies, then gently raised the doll until her eyes popped open. Grace smiled at Cathy's still face and raised her finger to pull the magic string, but then she stopped. There couldn't be any unusual noises. Closing the trunk carefully, she pushed until she heard it click. Then she curled Cathy into her arm, slung her heavy purse over her shoulder, and grasped the runaway bag with her free hand and headed down the street. She knew exactly where she was going.

Grace stopped only long enough to look at Paul's tree. She wished for the millionth time that a branch would have broken under her son as he climbed higher and higher. Then he never would have reached the electrical wires and he would have been alive as he fell. He would have landed on the ground with nothing more than a broken arm or leg, something that could be fixed and kept him settled firmly on the earth.

Grace remembered blaming the tree and she wondered if she could return to that judgement, blame the tree's inflexible limbs and its enduring strength, instead of her daughter and her spontaneous hide and seek instructions. But would Paul have ever thought of climbing that tree if Mary didn't suggest it?

No.

Paul was not a boy who took chances. He would have hidden in the usual places, ducked behind the garbage cans, crawled under a bush. He would have hidden, he would have been found, and he would be here. It was still Mary's fault, even though Grace would have given most anything to find a reason not to see it that way. Her logical mind, if her mind could be called logical since Paul's passing, just kept following its path like a mathematical equation. Mary telling Paul to climb the tree plus Paul climbing the tree and touching the wire equaled Paul dying. Mary started the equation.

It was the worst possible math.

Turning her back on the tree, Grace walked toward town.

The doll museum was lit up and there was a car parked outside. It was an old, old tank, a Chrysler Newport, and Grace walked around it in awe. Her father drove a car like that, big and handsome and impractical. Virgil's car was a rich tan, like coffee with cream, and the trim used to be white, but was now aged to beige. But the trim was the only part of the car that wasn't still bright and shiny. Virgil clearly kept his car pristine and despite it being a dinosaur, it shone as clean and new as any modern car waiting for sale in a dealership.

The door of the doll museum opened and Virgil came out. He was carrying a couple of suitcases and he was forced to put one down as he focused on locking his door. Grace watched as he checked the door once, stepped away, then checked the door again. When he turned around, he saw her.

"Grace!" he said. He walked, smiling, around the side of the car. "You're up awfully early, especially for a Saturday." His gaze dropped to the doll in Grace's arm and he stopped. He leaned against the car. "Is there a problem, Grace?" he asked softly. "With the doll? You don't want to return her?"

"Oh, no!" Grace tightened her arm around Cathy.

Virgil smiled again. He walked over and touched the doll's hair. "Let me hold her for a minute," he said.

Grace let her go. She immediately regretted it and rubbed her arms in the cool air. She was surprised at how quickly she felt bereft. And then she mentally shook herself. Bereft! She was bereft, but not because of a doll. What a word to use on a doll!

Virgil pulled the string. Cathy looked at him and said, "Will you play with me?" Laughing, he returned her. The weight of the doll in Grace's arm made everything feel okay again. "Well, what then?" he asked. He looked at the bag and the bulging purse. "What is it, Grace?"

It was the next step, the final step, finishing a cycle started last night with the letters to her family. Grace had to say what needed to be said. It was time. "I want to go with you."

He stared, then moved closer. Instead of touching the doll, his hand came to rest on Grace's shoulder. "With me?" he said.

"Yes, please." Grace turned Cathy around so they were both facing him. "Please, Virgil, I know you don't understand, but too many things have been happening lately. I need to go somewhere without a map and just look at the hills and talk to you and talk to myself too." She moved out from under his hand and placed Cathy on the hood of the car, though she held on to Cathy's outstretched fingers the way a mother would a child. "I want to sit and look at her and think about things with no interruptions, with no new problems barging in." She motioned toward The Nursery. "And I want to help you find dolls, lots of dolls. Especially Maribel Get Well." Virgil's eyes didn't move from her face and Grace had to look away. She brushed a speck of dust from Cathy's coat. "I don't even know what I'm saying, Virgil, which is why I need to go. I need some time to figure out what I'm saying. And you…well, you just sort of came along when I needed you." Grace didn't know exactly what she meant by that, but she didn't know what she meant so often now. She just knew she needed to be away, and she needed someone to take her there. It was time.

Virgil's hand touched Grace's hair this time, she felt his fingers catch in her curls. "Grace," he said quietly. "Don't you have a family?"

The words stabbed, even though Grace didn't think Virgil meant them as weapons. But yes, she did have a family. And yes, she was leaving them behind. "I have a husband and…two children." Three, she said to herself. I have three children. But one is a gone child.

They stood like that, the early morning sun around them, the car's trunk open, a doll on the hood.

"Why…" And then Virgil stopped. He left the rest of his obvious question dangling in the sunlit air and Grace wondered how to tell him. How to tell him that she'd lost a mother and a child, she'd lost a child in a horrible way. How to tell him that it was her daughter's fault and that fault made Grace's world go off kilter and that she knew she was off kilter too. "Oh, Virgil," she began, but then her throat closed. The familiar tears reappeared and Grace wondered if, like a crystal ball predicting bad fortune, they'd gone black.

Virgil grabbed Grace up in a hug. Her tears soaked in to the scratch of his denim shirt. Burrowing into his chest, she felt his ribs moving against hers.

"All right," he said. "I think company would be nice."

Grace heard the acceptance. She heard the questions too, knew that there was a lot that Virgil didn't say, didn't ask. But it didn't matter. He said yes. She was going away. It was the final step.

Worry Number Four.

Grace swept Cathy into her arms and pulled her string. Grace hoped she would say something momentous like "Let's go out into the world!" or "Look out, world, here we come!" but she only said, "Where are we going?"

Grace smiled at Virgil, then said to Cathy, "We're taking you on a trip."

When the car pulled away from the curb a few minutes later, Cathy was in the back with a seat belt around her tiny waist. Grace was in the front beside Virgil. Virgil had instructions to stop at the first available place outside of town for a cup of coffee, a bit of breakfast. Grace was thrilled when he complied. It felt like kismet. She'd never thought about what kismet would feel like before, but she knew, suddenly, that this was it.

She was also relieved that their path didn't take her past her house. Despite the sudden joy that left her trembling, she knew not all the trembles were from relief and happiness. If the car went by her house, the front door might open and her kids could be there, Nick behind them, looking for her, and she might throw the car door open and leap out. She might return before leaving to the tree in the back yard, the wide open curtainless kitchen window, the empty bunk, the unvisited grave, and Virgil and Cathy would roll on without her.

But it was best that she didn't. It was her time. Grace's time.

****

But the first part of Grace's time was much shorter than she expected. She'd pictured herself getting in the car and they would drive for hours. The scenery would change, depending on which direction they went, and Grace would admire it and she and Virgil would talk, and when it grew to night, they would pull over somewhere. She didn't let her mind extend to where. She wasn't even sure what to think about that yet.

But that wasn't what happened. They had coffee and doughnuts in a little shop just outside of Waukesha, and then, two hours later, Virgil pulled over at a gas station. They'd just passed a sign that identified where they were as St. Charles, Illinois.

Even though Virgil didn't pull up at a pump, Grace asked, "Do we need gas already? Man, this thing is a tank." She patted the seat.

Virgil shook his head. "No, we're fine. But this is our first stop. And I thought we should talk about a few things first."

Grace glanced at her watch. It was only ten o'clock. She was two hours from home. Two hours didn't feel very much like running away. What did? Five hours, Grace decided. Five hours meant it wasn't so easy to turn around and run back.

She didn't want to stop. She wanted to keep going.

"There's a flea market here," Virgil said. "The Kane County Flea Market. It's amazing. It actually started today, but Sunday is the best. A lot of vendors mark their stuff down to half off. They open early and close late. Imagine twelve thousand booths of stuff to dig through! Twelve thousand, Grace. A whole county fairgrounds!"

Grace swallowed. "Twelve thousand? That's a whole town!"

He laughed. "You bet it is, a whole town of people who love junk, who sell junk and buy junk. If you can't find it in Kane County, then it just doesn't exist."

Grace couldn't wrap her mind around a flea market that large. Why did Virgil have to go anywhere else? "Then maybe I'll find Maribel right away."

Virgil patted her knee. "Maybe," he said. "If not, there's plenty of other markets out there."

But if it's not here, it doesn't exist, Grace thought, but didn't say. "So if we're staying here, what do we do now?" Grace looked at her watch again. "What do we do with the rest of the day? Isn't it too early to check in anywhere? And it's too early for lunch – we just had breakfast."

"Well, first," Virgil swiveled in his seat, tilting his body toward her. "We need to talk, like I said."

Grace wondered if he was having second thoughts about her being there. What would she do if he told her he wanted her to go home? After all, he said everything existed at Kane County, and then he said it didn't. Maybe he said she could come, but now he'd say she couldn't. "About what?" She knew she could travel alone. She had enough money, though now she didn't have a car. She supposed she could rent one if Virgil didn't want her there anymore. Or she could buy a cheap used car, but that could take up a lot of her cash.

"Our sleeping arrangements."

Grace stared straight ahead. That was the place she hadn't allowed her mind to go to. What was proper etiquette when you ran away from your family on a doll-collecting journey with a man you'd just met the day before? Should they have separate hotel rooms? Maybe one of those with a door that connected them? Or should they pull off into a park somewhere and sleep in separate seats? Could Virgil afford hotels? The Nursery was in business a long time, he seemed to do well, but this old car wasn't a good sign that money was plentiful. Grace could afford to pay for a nice place, thanks to her mother, she could even do two rooms with no problem. But she didn't really want Virgil to know how much money she had. It was hard enough for Grace to think about, without him thinking about it too, and Grace knowing he was thinking about it.

And there was the obvious too. He was a man. She was a woman, though a married one. Was that going to matter?

She decided to hedge. You didn't get through two marriages, one that failed and one that lasted, at least so far, without learning how to hedge. "What do you think we should do?"

"I think a hotel room would be best." He paused, then reached over and patted her knee. "With two beds, of course. It would be cheaper for both of us if we shared a room and split the bill. Would you mind?"

Grace sighed. "I'd really like that, I don't want to be lonely." The moment she said that, she knew it was true. She needed to run away, she needed to be apart from her family, but she didn't want to be lonely. She was just as bad as Virgil with the inconsistencies, she decided. She straightened her back against the seat. "I can pay my own way, you know."

"I'm not worried." He sat back and stared out the window. "About that, though. About the…lonely."

Grace folded her hands.

"I just…well, I want you to know this from the get-go. Not that it matters. But it does. You know. A man and a woman traveling together." He shrugged and then sighed. "Oh, for Christ's sake. I'll just say it. I'm gay, Grace. So if there's a, you know, a problem with your husband, well, the answer isn't with me."

Grace felt relief release her shoulders. "Oh, but that's good, Virgil!" He looked at her. "No, I mean, you are my answer. You helped me to get out of there, to get away, and I needed that, but I didn't want to go alone. And here you are. And it's okay. Because I don't want that kind of involvement and neither do you and so there's not that kind of a problem."

He smiled. "Well, good. I guess. You're kind of confusing." He started the car again and they moved toward the center of St. Charles. "But a good kind of confusing, if there is such a thing." He nodded. "I don't think we need plushy hotels, like a big chain," he said. "Just something cozy with a shower and heat. I've stayed in a side-of-the-road motel that's just down the road here. I stop every year. It's very basic — not even a coffee pot or a microwave in the room, though they do have them in the lobby. I don't think we'll have a problem checking in early. Let's go see."

"Fine. Could we stop here first though?" Grace pointed at a Target. "I need to pick up a few things. I didn't bring very much with me."

"That's a good idea."

They pulled in and Virgil trailed Grace into the store. She picked out a small coffee pot and some soft flannel pajamas. There was no way she could face the morning without a fresh cup of coffee before she showered and dressed; going to the motel lobby in her pajamas and with bedhead was just not going to work. She also bought a small suitcase, a couple pairs of jeans and leggings, some casual shirts, packages of underwear and socks, new toiletries, some instant hot chocolate, coffee, and bags of potato chips and popcorn. "I thought we could have some hot chocolate tonight and popcorn in front of the t.v.," she said. Like a family, she thought. Virgil, Grace and Cathy. A gay doll salesman, a runaway wife, and an old talking doll.

But her family was at home. Her home. For a moment, Grace ached so hard, she couldn't breathe.

Virgil didn't seem to notice. "Sounds good," he said. At the checkout, he threw four candy bars onto the counter and then added a newspaper. "I buy a local paper wherever I go," he said. "I check out possible doll sales. Want ads, auctions, estate sales, that sort of thing." Before they left the store, they bought hot dogs and nachos at the food counter.

It didn't take long to find the roadside motel. It was long and well-lit and there were several cars parked outside the doorways. They were given room number eight.

Grace brought Cathy inside and set her on one of the beds. Virgil carried in her rolled-up sack and the bags from Target. Then he brought in his suitcase.

Grace pulled off Cathy's coat and hat and set up the little coffee pot by the sink. "Cups!" she called suddenly to Virgil. "We forgot about cups. What can we drink our coffee and hot chocolate in?" Since the room didn't offer a coffee pot or a microwave, the only cups they had were plastic, intended to be used with water and then thrown away.

He pulled his coat back on. "I'll go back to Target. They have mugs; I prefer that over Styrofoam anyway." He waved at her and was gone.

And for the first time since officially running away, Grace was alone. She sat on the bed and looked at her cell phone. Seventy-five text messages, twenty-five voicemails. And she wasn't even gone half a day yet.

After leaving that morning, it took all of a half hour before Grace's phone began to vibrate and light up like the atom bomb. Her phone trilled John Denver's "Rocky Mountain High", the song that signaled home even though she lived in Wisconsin, before Grace put it on silent. Then the phone began to gyrate with text messages and voicemails. Grace knew who they were from, every person in her family had a cell phone, but she didn't want to respond, and she didn't want to explain that to Virgil. She took her phone and stuffed it deep into the dollars in her purse. The money muffled the noise. For the first half of their two-hour trip, Grace talked. And talked. About anything that came to mind. Virgil seemed to keep up for a while, but then he drifted into a syncopation of "Uh-huhs". Grace wondered if he was sorry he agreed to let her tag along.

But as the time in the car passed and she got further from home, Grace felt a silence settling. She caught herself straining to hear something – vibrations from her phone? had they stopped? - and then she shook herself and looked out of the window. There was only the steady low rumble of the tires and Virgil's occasional hum. Grace felt unnerved.

Now the silence returned again and she was alone, sitting on one of the beds in a motel room in St. Charles, Illinois. When Grace looked at her phone, she found that there'd been nothing, no call, no text, for the last hour and a half. About the time Grace began to fall silent, so did her phone.

She considered reading the texts, listening to the voicemails. The ninety-minute silence likely meant that Nick crossed over from shocked to angry and that he'd imposed a ban on the kids phoning as well. But a part of Grace still hoped for the phone to sing, and for Nick's voice to fill her ear, saying, "It's okay, Grace, I understand, Grace." Even though she knew there was a limit to his patience.

From the lack of a glance the night before, and the conversation that was never finished, Grace thought she might have already surpassed that limit.

Grace turned on the television and set the volume on low. Sitting back on the bed with Cathy, she checked her phone for bars. An unfamiliar phone service ran its name across her little screen, but the bars were there, as was the connection to home. So she hit the number 1 – the speed dial to the landline in her house.

The phone rang only three times before it was picked up. Mary called out, "Hello?"

The sound of her daughter's voice made Grace's heart race. "Hi, sweetie," she said, fighting to keep her own voice from revealing her pulse.

"Mom. Hi." Mary sounded steady, but low.

Grace found herself not knowing what to say. "Where's Dad?" she asked. Nick's voice was in the background, getting louder, yelling, "Is that your mother?"

"He's coming," she said. Then she whispered hurriedly. "Look. I'm sorry. I'm so, so sorry. Please come back—" and here her voice jammed to a halt and Grace felt the impact against her ear.

"Mary," Grace said. "Mary." And her words stopped.

Mary's whisper changed. It wasn't an attempt to be quiet. Grace recognized it. It was the whisper of trying to squeeze words out of a clenched throat. "I'm sorry I told him to climb the tree. I should have thought it through. But you can't leave me here. You need to take me with you."

Grace's heart wrenched. "No, honey, no, I didn't—" she began, but then Nick was there, filling her ear with a mix of anger and fear. "Grace, is that you?"

"Yes, Nick." Grace wondered where Mary went, if she was standing there at Nick's shoulder or if she ran off to her room. Grace stared hard into the mirror, studying her face as she talked to her husband, a whole state away, but only two hours between them. She studied her face and wondered if she looked like a runaway wife.

"Where are you?"

"I'm in Illinois. In a motel room."

"How did you get there?"

Grace laughed. "In a car. What did you think, I walked?"

There was a pause. "You didn't take your car," he said slowly.

"I'm with a friend." Until that moment, Grace only thought about how to explain her absence to Nick. Her need to be away. Yet now there was Virgil and she had no idea how to explain him.

"Who?"

Grace shrugged. She could hear the doubt. She knew the words that Nick thought, possibly bit back – *You don't have any friends.* He was right. Her friends seemed to disappear, shoved away by the force of Grace's losses, one right after the other. Grace understood; you could talk to an adult who lost a mother, that wasn't abnormal, that wasn't unthinkable, but what did you say to someone who lost a child? What did you say to someone who experienced something that you couldn't possibly picture happening to you? There was nothing to say. "You don't know…him." Immediately, she wondered if she should have used Virgil's gender. "I just met him myself. He runs the doll museum in town."

Another pause. Grace could hear JJ's voice now, asking to talk to her. He was shushed, but he didn't leave the background and he began to grow strident. JJ was never strident.

"You left town with a man?" Nick's voice grew quiet and hard. Grace knew the expression his face held to go with that voice. By now, his eyebrows were so low, his eyes disappeared.

"No, not really," Grace said. "Not like you mean. For God's sake, Nick, he's a friend. And he's gay." Thank god for that, Grace thought. What would she have said if he wasn't?

What would she have done? She was so desperate to leave.

JJ's voice rose again, then stopped suddenly and she knew Nick just glared at him with those eyebrows. She closed her eyes. "I want you home," Nick said. "I want you home by tomorrow."

"No," Grace said. It was out of her mouth before she could even think it.

He was silent. Grace wondered if he was still there, if anyone was still there. It was like her whole family suddenly disappeared, sucked down by the O in her No. But Grace said it again.

"I said no, Nick. I'm going on a trip. I want to be on my own for a while."

"But you're not on your own. You're with…whoever he is."

The door opened and Virgil walked in, carrying another Target bag. "His name is Virgil Purdy," Grace said into the phone. Virgil looked instantly guilty.

"Virgil?" Nick almost choked. Then he began to wheedle. "Please, Grace, this can't be doing you any good. It's not doing us any good. Think of the kids. Come on home."

"It is doing me good. It's what I need to do. I'll be fine. I'd like to talk to JJ now, please."

Virgil opened the bag and displayed two large purple ceramic mugs with Lincoln's bust tattooed in white. Grace couldn't help but think Lincoln was never intended to be a coffee mug decoration. She almost giggled when she thought that with a face like Lincoln's, he shouldn't have decorated anything.

"I don't think you should talk to JJ, Grace," Nick said, his voice going suddenly smooth. "Maybe the kids should be off limits for a while. While you're gone. Until you come to your senses."

And Grace wondered if Nick just found the ploy that could bring her home.

JJ's voice rose in an uncharacteristic wail and Lincoln's bust disappeared in a haze of red. Grace surged to her feet. "Put him on the phone, Nick," she said. She had a new voice too. It was flat, but with the undertone of a monster engine. She sounded so calm, like she knew exactly what she was doing, but she also sounded restrained, like she was holding back a tremendous amount of horsepower. It surprised Grace, and apparently, it surprised Nick too and he respected it, because there was a pause and the wail stopped, then JJ came on.

"Hello, Mom," he said.

"Hi, honey." His voice sounded tiny now and Grace remembered before he even had words, when all he had were sounds, and he mewed like a kitten.

"I was surprised to get your letter," he said.

"I bet. Are you okay?"

"I guess so. Are you going to be gone for a long time?"

Grace heard the tears and she pictured his struggling face. She wondered if she'd seen tears on that face since the day of Paul's funeral. She didn't think so.

"No, sweetie, not long. Just a little while. For time to think, like I said in my letter."

"I know. I get it."

Grace was struck by his understanding. He got it. She wished more than anything he didn't. Her son shouldn't need to understand this. She wished there wasn't anything to get. "I'm glad you do, JJ. I really am. I promise I'll be back as soon as I can." She wondered about that "can." As soon as she could what? Get through the day? Not think about Paul?

Worry Number Four was back. What the hell was she doing?

"I'm going to go, JJ, okay? We'll talk again soon."

"Dad said he wants to talk some more."

"No, tell him I said goodbye. I love you, honey."

"Love you too, Mom," he said and the phone went dead and Grace could hear the difference between the silence of a sucked-away family and the silence of a boy who did as he was told, of a boy who got it, but was just stuck in the middle. Her cell rang almost immediately and Grace put it on silent before tucking it in her jeans pocket, where she could feel the returned insistence of its vibration.

Virgil sat down next to her. "Hard?" he asked.

She wiped her eyes and nose with her sleeve. It surprised her that she was crying. The motor car voice belied tears. "Even harder than I imagined," she said.

He put his arm around her. "You know, you really haven't told me why you wanted to go on this trip."

"Oh, Virgil," Grace said and all the reasons rammed right into her, slamming her spine into a curve. Her forehead almost touched her knees. "There's too much going on and I don't want to talk about it today, if that's okay. I don't even want to think about it. If I do, I know I'll be on the next bus home and I'll regret it for the rest of my life." She told the truth to herself as much as to Virgil. "This feels right. It feels right to me. It may not feel right for my husband, but it's right for me." She thought of her kids. She ached for them. She couldn't go home, but she ached for them.

More inconsistency.

"Okay then." Virgil stood and stretched. "Let's go out," he said. "Let's explore the downtown. It has a lot of neat little shops and there's an antique mall too. We can get a start on our doll hunt."

Grace began to stand, but then her body went weak. The thought of leaving the motel room felt foreign, as foreign as leaving her family early on a Saturday morning, running away with a bag of Oreos and a change of clothes. "Virgil, I think I want to stay here for now. You go on ahead. I might just take a nap. I didn't get much sleep last night."

Virgil nodded. "I bet you didn't." He collected his car keys, then hesitated. Without saying anything first, he bent over and kissed her on the top of her head. Then he said, "I hope that's okay. I just wanted to. You seemed to need something like that."

She smiled. "It's fine. Have fun. I'll be right here."

After Virgil left, Grace went into the bathroom to take a shower. She hadn't showered before leaving that morning, fearful that the sound of the water would wake someone up. Now, she stood under the spray for longer than usual, as it seemed the motel had an unending supply of hot water. She appreciated that. She needed it.

She heard the thought in her head, Worry Number Four grown into a voice that she didn't recognize. She knew it was there all along. It started the day before, when she took the money and the pendant from the safety deposit box. It started when she bought Cathy. And it started with the realization that, like her mother warned, she needed to be away. But this wasn't her mother's voice. Her mother would never be this judgmental.

What are you doing, Grace? Grace, what have you done?

Was it Grace's voice? Nick's?

She didn't know. She just didn't know.

CHAPTER FOUR
Virgil

It was years since Virgil was alone in a bedroom with a woman. In The Nursery, he was alone with women a lot, of course, but surrounded by the dolls, it didn't feel intimate at all. Now, at the end of a long and very surprising day, Virgil watched Grace sleep and fought a compulsion that surprised him further. He wanted to touch her hair, stroke her shoulders, pull the covers back and climb in, curl against her back, slip his arm around her waist to cup her breast. For the first time in years, he truly wanted to nuzzle a woman's neck.

A long and surprising day.

Despite being gay, he used to enjoy sleeping with women. He lost his virginity when he was fifteen years old with a red-haired girl named Amy in the last stall of the girls' bathroom by the gym in the basement of the high school. It was a wonderful, if awkward, initiation and Virgil slept with several women after that. There was so much quality there, the softness of their skin blending down into their fur, the moistness of a woman in heat. Virgil found himself wanting to drown, to plaster his body against hers, to completely mold their limbs together.

But then came the men. Because of the intensity there, Virgil refused to call himself bisexual, despite his soft and warm feelings for women. He felt comfort when he was with a woman; he felt truth when he was with a man. With Brad, he felt immersed in glorious and honest reality.

But studying Grace, seeing her face relaxed in sleep, her lips parted, her arms tight around her extra pillow, Virgil felt himself erect for a woman for the first time in years. There was something about Grace that called to him, that made him want to touch her and hold her, protect her and give her whatever pleasure he could. It was what drove him to say yes to her that morning, yes to a woman he barely knew to come on a trip that always ended with his lover in the middle of a junkyard in Georgia. Right now, Virgil wanted to remove that pillow from Grace's arms and replace it with himself, a warm, solid, real-life person.

It would be nice for us both, Virgil thought. Even though one of us is gay. Even though one of us is married.

Until the morning. It was amazing how the morning sun falling across a bed could chase away the loneliness that shadows brought the night before. Suddenly what was warm and right and fulfilling was awkward and wrong. Dishonest. Virgil knew that from many sunshine mornings.

But mornings with Brad were wonderful. There was never a shadow of loneliness to be chased away. The sunshine was warm, Southern, and right.

Grace was out of bounds in many ways. Virgil tried to focus his thoughts on dolls and on the trip. He concentrated on memories of the last visit with Brad, but his eyes kept opening to take in Grace. The curve of her beneath her blanket.

Women had the best hips!

Virgil rolled onto his back and stared at the ceiling.

The first time he made love to a man, Virgil met the truth. The suspicion was always there, but that first experience shot the suspicion out into the open and then embedded it full into his future. When he closed his eyes while touching a woman, his thoughts sometimes drifted to men he knew, to what they could do in bed. To what they could do to him.

That very first time with a man, Virgil was only twenty-one years old, six years older than when he lost his virginity to Amy in a high school restroom. He went to a gay bar and hated it. He hated the whole idea of it, but he didn't know where else to go. Where else could he meet someone, where else could he be sure that he was reading the cues correctly? He wanted to approach men before, but the fear held him back. Was that a friendly touch on the shoulder or a sensual hint? Was there meaning behind that wink as a joke was told? In the bar, Virgil knew what he was getting into. And he wanted to dip his toe in, check the water, and then get in deep if it felt as warm as he thought it would.

He was only there a half-hour before a man took him home. Virgil didn't know his name, but he knew the man was attractive, and when he came up behind Virgil on the barstool, his hands slid down Virgil's back to his buttocks and gave him shivers. When their clothes were off in his apartment, the man's first touch brought Virgil to orgasm. The man laughed and stroked more until Virgil was erect again, until Virgil could satisfy the man as well. At twenty-one, it didn't take long.

Men's bodies were so different. They were hard, not as moldable. Virgil didn't lose himself, he was aware of where he was and who he was with the whole time. Men were furry all over, and the patches of smooth soft skin were a surprise. When that first nameless man pushed himself into Virgil, Virgil felt something he could never feel with a woman. It hurt, that first time, and he felt so overwhelmed, he cried. When the man slid out of Virgil's body, Virgil heard himself whimper. It was like a part of himself fell away with that withdrawal.

Virgil didn't want to feel that way, but the feelings were there and now he knew the truth, the knowledge filling and quickening the beat of his heart. He was queer, he was gay, he was homosexual. In the dark of that stranger's apartment, Virgil's father's word came back to him too…he was a faggot. He was everything his father was afraid of when he saw Virgil playing with Josephine. In this nameless man's arms for just a few afterglow minutes, Virgil didn't care, but the streetlight hitting his face as he left made him want to duck for cover. He knew he would never be able to look his father in the eye again.

Much later came Brad and love. Sexual peak met raw encompassing emotion and Virgil gave in completely to the future that felt inevitable after that first meeting in a gay bar. Now, years later, here was Grace. And a very quiet attraction.

Virgil rolled again so he faced Grace and he gave himself permission to think of her. It wasn't really giving permission though. There was no stopping the thoughts on this night. He gave his thoughts full steam and he ran after them, wondering where they would go. He thought of her beneath him, of her soft voice calling his name. For Grace was soft, soft all over, from her name to her skin to her hair to the way she tilted her head toward her chest when she laughed. Virgil knew she would be like a feather mattress and in his mind, he sank into her and their bodies connected from neck to toe. They kissed so deeply, they lost their breath and didn't care.

Virgil gasped.

When he opened his eyes, he was spent. Grace still slept peacefully, her arms around her pillow. How child-like she looked, yet there were those woman curves shaping the blanket into gentle mountains and valleys. He wondered about his decision to bring Grace along on this particular trip, the trip he made every year, but this year's destination ended in ultimatum. If she wasn't sharing that motel room, Virgil's mind would be filled with images of Brad, of their reunion in his driveway, their joining in his bedroom.

Instead of dreaming about Brad and thinking about retiring and spending the rest of their lives together, instead of considering Brad's ultimatum, Virgil was fantasizing about a woman.

Shivering, he turned his back to Grace, pulling the covers up to his chin.

****

At the flea market the next day, Virgil and Grace went their separate ways. Grace was never at a flea market this big before, but despite its size, Virgil knew it like the back of his hand. He wanted to get going, to look for dolls tossed in piles on tables upon grass, tables upon gravel, tables lined up in open-air barns. Grace wanted to explore, to stop at every booth and Virgil knew if he stayed with her, he'd get impatient. He also wanted some space, some air and sunshine, knocking the visions from last night from his mind. He'd spent the day with a woman yesterday, a woman who spent the night in a bed so close to his, he could reach out an arm and run his fingers down the length of her, and he'd had breakfast with her that morning, the both of them sitting in pajamas until their first mugs of coffee were empty. It was domestic and exotic all at once, and now, in the air of the flea market, Virgil wanted to breathe in normal. He wanted to be alone, as he'd planned on being, as he always was when he was here. So they agreed on a meeting place, a big barn in the center of the fairgrounds, and Virgil told Grace they'd meet at noon for lunch. That gave him four hours of scavenging the tables and clearing his head.

The flea market at St. Charles was spectacular. There were vendors everywhere, selling from makeshift booths or straight out of trailers and trucks. Some rented space in the roofed sheds or air-conditioned buildings, but Virgil avoided those. Those vendors were likely to know the value of what they sold and to have an appropriate or jacked-up price. What Virgil looked for was someone who thought they were only selling beat-up unloved dolls. Dolls with no value. But Virgil knew the truth.

Virgil picked up a few dolls here and there and was almost ready to meet Grace when he saw the old metal bucket. It was filled to the rim with dolls, mostly naked. He knelt down beside it and browsed, taking some of the dolls out and laying them gently on the grass. They were modestly priced, all from around a buck to five dollars. It wasn't until he saw the little lavender one-piece romper that he knew he hit a find.

First came the lavender baby. A little further down, there was the blue. He carefully put them on the ground, but separated them so that it didn't look like they were a set. Yellow, pink, and green followed quickly. There were matching bonnets on their heads and little medallions around their necks, each engraved with their own special name. Emilie. Cecile. Yvonne. Marie. Annette. They were marked two-fifty apiece.

Twelve-fifty for the Madame Alexander Dionne Quintuplets dolls. They were all here, the set complete except for their box. Together, Virgil knew he could resell them for at least five-hundred dollars and possibly up to eight-hundred. They were in good shape, only their eyes were molded over. Cleaned with ammonia and water, their clothes washed and freshened, they'd be perfect.

Virgil put all of the dolls back into the bucket, glancing over at the vendor as he did so. He was careful to space the Quints; he didn't want to alert the vendor to this prize. Virgil stood up, hefted the bucket and said, "I'll give you ten bucks for all of them."

The man's eyes narrowed and he came over and squatted by the table. Virgil knew this stance well, it went back over generations, the men lowering themselves to the ground and haggling over everything from eggs to wood. Virgil hoped when he stood that the squat wouldn't appear, which would identify a vendor that didn't know all the cues and postures of barter. Hope diminishing a bit, Virgil put the bucket back on the ground and dropped into a squat too. The man ran his hands through the dolls, looking for what Virgil found so valuable. "Fifteen," he said finally. "Including the bucket."

Virgil swayed back on his heels and waited the appropriate amount of time. "Twelve," he said. "And you can keep the bucket."

"Thirteen." The vendor stood up. That was the signal Virgil was waiting for, letting him know that negotiations were at an end. He could take it or leave it. And he would certainly not leave the Dionne Quintuplets because of three extra dollars.

"Sold!" Virgil said and handed over the money. Waving off the offer for a bag, he tipped the bucket and poured the dolls into a canvas bag he carried over his shoulder, filled with his other purchases. Then, grinning, he headed off to meet Grace.

She was already by the barn. Her eyes looked wet and Virgil thought her cheeks were too pink, even after a morning in the sun. Virgil immediately put his arm around her and she leaned against him. "What is it?" he asked. "Did you think I wasn't coming for you?"

She shook her head. "No. It's silly, really, I just found this clock. This stupid, impractical, big, beautiful old clock. I can't take my mind off of it."

"A clock?" Virgil was surprised. He'd expected her to show up with an armful of dolls and doll accessories. But then, she'd only bought her first doll a couple days before. Maybe it took a while to shake off her mother's admonitions. "Where?"

Virgil followed her through the crowd to a table. He saw the clock long before they got there. It was regal, sitting surrounded by glass knick-knacks and coffee mugs. Its deep mahogany looked polished and the face glowed gold in the sun. Its pendulum was moving slowly, but steadily and Virgil just knew its voice would be a rich baritone.

They stopped in front of it. Grace gently touched the clock, using just the tips of her fingers. She opened the door and stroked its ornate face.

"See what I mean?" she said. "It's ridiculous. It would take up so much room. And it might break." She moved the minute hand to the top of the hour and they listened as it chimed ten times. "My mother loved clocks," she said softly.

Virgil wondered if this was a balancing act of sorts; she bought something her mother never told her to buy, and now she was considering buying something her mother loved. It made sense, even though the act of appeasement was for someone who was passed. At least, he thought so. Grace spoke of her mother in the past tense.

Virgil reached in and stopped the pendulum, carefully lifting it from its perch. "We can bring it into the hotels at night, set it up and let it run and chime. That will keep its innards going. And don't forget what kind of car I drive. It's practically as big as our hotel room." He smiled at Grace, watching her face light up to full beam. He called to the woman behind the table. "We'd like this clock. Could you box it, please?" As the woman wrapped the clock, Virgil realized he didn't even check the price, didn't attempt to barter. It didn't matter. Grace wanted the clock, and he wanted her to have it.

Grace peeked into his bag. "You found some dolls, Virgil?"

"Oh, yes." He rummaged through the pile. "I had a good morning, but there's something really special..." He pulled each of the quintuplets out, resting them in Grace's arms. "Do you know who these are?"

She shook her head.

Virgil took Emilie, holding her gently in his palm. "These five dolls are the Dionne Quintuplets, Grace. Remember them?"

Grace frowned, then nodded. "I remember reading about them. They were real people, right?" Grace handed the dolls back to Virgil so she could accept the clock and pay the seller. Then they walked toward the barn and their lunch.

"Oh, they were very real, five little Canadian girls born in 1934. The Madame Alexander line came out with these dolls soon after."

"So they're really old."

"Yes. And really valuable."

They almost had one foot inside the barn and Virgil was already smelling the rich scents of hamburgers and corn on the cob when Grace stopped short. Just outside the barn door, there was a booth filled with corn husk dolls.

The dolls were all sizes and dressed in dozens of costumes. They were obviously handmade by the large gypsy woman behind the table. She wore a turban on her head and a huge gold ring hung from her right ear. She obviously knew how to dress the part and work the crowd. When she smiled, Virgil saw she was missing one of her front teeth.

"Look, Virgil," Grace said and they walked to the table. She picked up one of the dolls.

Virgil picked up a corn husk too and examined it. Its dry leaves crinkled.

"These are beautiful," Grace said to the gypsy. "I had one once. My mother bought it for me."

Virgil looked at Grace in surprise.

Grace set the doll down. "It was the only time my mother allowed me to have a doll. I was supposed to sleep with it and it would make me graceful."

"Oh, that is one of these." The gypsy plucked a doll from the corner table and handed it to Grace. It wore no cloth costume; its clothes, like its body, were made entirely from corn husks.

Virgil touched Grace's elbow. "Do you still have it?"

"No, I hated it." She ran her fingers gently over the stiff skirt. "The only doll I could have and I hated it. I ripped it to pieces right after my mother put it in my bed."

"Your mother was mad," the gypsy said and nodded.

Grace frowned. "She never yelled at me," she said. "We never talked about it."

The gypsy nodded again. "Your mother was mad," she repeated.

The corners of Grace's lips turned down, but then she reached in her purse. "I'd like to buy this doll please," she said.

Another balancing act. Buy the forbidden doll, buy a clock that would have been beloved, buy a doll that was shredded.

"I'd like some too." Virgil picked out six of the dolls, dressed in various pinafores and aprons. "I know some collectors who will be interested," he told Grace.

While she wrapped them, the gypsy explained the spell behind each doll. Grace's was for the cultivation of grace and refinement. The two with aprons insured the growth of a happy household. The pinafores brought the preservation of innocence and the red gown created passion. When she said that, Virgil thought of the women who came to his shop. He picked out five more with the red gown.

The gypsy dipped in a small curtsy when she gave Grace her bag. "Your mother, she's not angry anymore," she said.

Balance.

Grace froze, but then she thanked her in a voice so soft, Virgil wasn't sure the gypsy heard. He slipped her an extra ten and she winked.

When they finally settled in the barn for their lunch, Virgil found himself grinning at Grace. She looked so happy, sitting there, the bag with the corn husk doll on her lap. The clock sat by her side. He remembered her saying the night before how this trip was right for her. And it was.

Virgil knew, sitting there, that it was right for him too. He wasn't sure how yet, and he wasn't sure how he was going to explain Grace to Brad, but Grace was just what Virgil needed.

****

That night in the motel, Virgil carefully washed all of the dolls, fourteen total, in the bathroom sink. Their clothes were stacked in a small pile to be bagged and packed away until they reached Brad's house and could use his washing machine and clothesline. When he stripped the Quints, he kept their little medals on in order to identify them for later re-dressing. They were completely identical without their clothes. The dolls with real hair received shampoos and those that were bald or who had molded hair were just scrubbed. Q-tips cleaned out the divots in their dimples and knuckles, lips and ears. Several of the blinking dolls needed their eyes cleaned with ammonia and water. It was an odd thing about the blinking dolls; their eyes tended to mold over if they weren't played with for a long time. Virgil found himself smiling as he restored each doll's bright eyes.

Carrying all fourteen dolls in his arms, he returned to the room. Grace was stretched out in the center of her bed, staring at the ceiling. Her eyes looked frozen and glazed, just like the dolls with painted-on eyes that never closed. "Grace?" he said sharply.

She blinked quickly and looked at him. He noticed Cathy was next to her, resting on the second pillow on the bed. The night before, Cathy remained in the hotel chair. The corn husk doll leaned against the lamp on the table between their beds.

Grace stood up and helped Virgil to seat the haired dolls on the dresser in front of the mirror. The other dolls lay on his bed. "I'm sorry," she said. "I get like that sometimes. I stare at the ceiling and sort of go to sleep with my eyes open." She laughed, but her laugh held no humor. Virgil frowned and plugged in his hair dryer.

"Won't their hair melt if you use that?" Grace asked.

Virgil shook his head. "Not if the dryer's on low or no heat. They'll be fine. It will help to get all the tangles out and it helps me to style their hair the way it originally was. Some of them haven't had their hair brushed in some time."

Grace sat quietly to watch. After a bit, she got her own brush and began to hesitantly, carefully brush Cathy's hair. "Like this?" she asked, her voice as soft as her strokes.

Virgil looked at her through the mirror. He realized this must be the first time she ever brushed a doll's hair. "Just like that. Just like with your kids, Grace," he said.

She smiled. Her strokes smoothed out, grew firmer. "Can I ask you a question, Virgil?"

"Sure," he said. The hair dryer was on low and provided a gentle, growling background.

"How do you know you're gay?"

Virgil startled. He wondered if she knew the thoughts that went through his mind the night before.

She didn't look at Virgil. "I mean…you don't seem gay to me. Beyond the doll thing, I mean." Then she slapped her hand over her mouth. "I'm sorry," she said behind her fingers. "I didn't mean that. It's not like if you're gay, you have to play with dolls. But…" She seemed to give up and leaned back on the bed. "I don't know what I mean."

"It's okay, Grace. Old stereotypes die hard." Virgil thought of his father. It wasn't the first time Virgil faced the question of how he knew; he used to ask himself the same thing. "I guess the fact that I like sex better with men than women gives me a pretty good clue," he said.

Grace laughed. "But when did you know for sure? Were you still a child?"

Virgil considered Grace for a moment, wondering where the question came from. Was Grace questioning her own sexuality? Was that why she ran away from home? Was she attracted to him and she picked up on his attraction to her? Or was she just curious? Or making conversation? "I don't know if there was a particular moment, an epiphany, when I was sure." There was that first time in the gay bar, but he had trouble calling that an epiphany. It was more of a verification. "I've heard of gay men who say they knew all their lives about their sexual orientation. It's like they never questioned it." Virgil shook his head. "I questioned it a lot." He thought of last night's reaction. "Sometimes I still do. And it always goes back to the same thing. I like men. I want to be with a man." He finished the first doll and moved on to the second. "I had the same best friend from the time I was a little boy until halfway through high school. His name was Victor. I think we got together because we both had weird names beginning with a V."

Grace set Cathy aside and carefully took the finished doll, gently straightened her legs, then put her on Virgil's bed with the others.

"Victor and I did things together, the things the psychology books say we're supposed to do," he said. "We peed on bushes, compared penis sizes, that kind of thing. Then we moved on to circle jerks, only we were the only guys in the circle." The next doll had hair that was supposed to flip up at the ends and Virgil carefully guided it in the right direction with the brush. "Eventually, Victor began bringing porno magazines to our circle. I didn't like them, but they kept Vic around, so I accepted it. But then he moved on to girls and he didn't come over as much. When we were together, he just sat around and told me all the things he did to girls when he went out on dates. I mean, I did stuff too. I went on dates. But I never seemed to get as much out of it as he did. I liked being with the girls, I really did, but I kept wondering what I was missing. Something was missing. But Victor was just so…" Virgil searched for the word. Savage came to his mind, but that wasn't it. While Victor was full of himself, he wasn't mean. He just seemed to grow bigger, right before Virgil's eyes, with the basic rightness of what he was doing. The physicality of it. The biology. "He was just so cocksure," Virgil ended. "Nothing was missing for him." His voice broke and he looked quickly at the doll. "I never felt lonelier or more like an outsider in my own life as I did then."

Virgil moved on down the line until all of the dolls lined up on his bedspread. The Dionne Quintuplets, who didn't have hair, stared at the ceiling like Grace did when he first came out of the bathroom. Their eyes didn't close and they looked vacant. Virgil wondered what Grace was seeing, when she didn't seem to be looking at anything at all.

Grace seemed to study the dolls, and from time to time, her fingers twitched. She wanted, Virgil realized, to play. That was what made her different. The women in The Nursery bought the dolls so they could look at them and remember. They displayed them in their houses as nostalgic prized possessions. But Grace didn't want that. She wanted to play. Dolls weren't nostalgia to her; they were what she wanted, but never had.

She didn't know how to play. He thought of her asking how to brush Cathy's hair.

He wondered how to teach an adult woman to mother a doll. A woman who had children, who knew how to mother. How do you play with an eternal child? A child that poses how you want her to, sits, stands, holds out her hands when you raise them to do so? Things were backwards for Grace. Shew was supposed to be with dolls first, then with her children. Instead, here she was, all grown up and stumped by a doll.

"Grace, how old are you?" he asked.

She startled. "I'm going to be fifty-six. Why?"

He shook his head. "I just wondered."

She returned to looking at the dolls. Cathy sat by her side. Her hair looked lovely.

Virgil began to prepare the dolls for travel. He brought plenty of cardboard boxes to store them in.

"So you've slept with a woman?" Grace asked.

So apparently, they weren't done with this topic yet. "Oh, sure. Lots of times." Their eyes met. "I liked it. Just not as much as when I'm with a man. It's different, Grace."

She nodded, then picked up the Quints. They sat stiffly and nakedly in her lap. "Have you ever found another Victor?"

Virgil got out his roll of bubble wrap and wrapped each doll in her own custom bubble blanket, stacking them in an empty box like bagged loaves of bread. Grace, he saw, flinched every time a doll became mummified. "There have been some," he said. "For the last ten years, I've been seeing a man who lives in Georgia. I usually see him on this trip, and at Christmas, he comes to visit me."

Grace sat up straighter. "Are we going to see him?"

Virgil looked hard at her. He wanted so much to get into her head, to see what she was thinking. He didn't tell her about the final destination before they left, and he wasn't sure it was fair to subject her to his longed-for reunion. But he couldn't imagine not ending up in Georgia. He had to go there. Brad was waiting.

Suddenly, Virgil wanted to tell Grace everything. He wanted to tell her that he was trying to decide if he wanted a permanent relationship with Brad, that he'd been given an outright ultimatum. He knew Brad's patience was wearing thin, and he knew that he himself was advancing in years and was running out of time to have the relationship that he so wanted. Virgil wanted to compare notes with Grace, to see how she felt about her husband, compare it to the way he felt about Brad. What made Grace commit to her husband? What made her leave him now? Virgil actually opened his mouth to start, but the words stuck somewhere near the base of his throat.

If he told her now that they were heading to Georgia, would she change her mind about coming? Would she go off on her own, or would she go back home?

Virgil didn't want Grace to go back home. He didn't know what he wanted, but he knew that. He wanted Grace there.

Busying himself again with the dolls, he said, "We'll see. Let's wait and see how things are going."

Grace set aside the Quints. She got up and put water into the little coffee pot and grabbed some potato chips too.

"What about you?" Virgil laughed nervously. He picked up the first of the Quints, Emilie, he saw by her tag, and rolled her in the plastic bubbles.

Grace grabbed the doll before he could put her in the box. "Virgil," she said, and then she pressed the doll to her chest. "Virgil, can the Quints stay out?"

He was surprised. He looked at her, the doll tucked in a hug, and she seemed almost stricken. "Well, sure," he said. "Of course, Grace."

"Can I dress them?"

Virgil didn't usually like putting clean dolls back in their dirty clothes, but he didn't want to say no. Finding the baggie, he handed it over. Grace unrolled Emilie, then set to dressing her and her sisters. Virgil directed her which color belonged to who. Her fingers stumbled with the tiny clothes.

Her adult fingers would likely stumble anyway, but Virgil knew they stumbled with an innocence. They stumbled with the never-learned ability to dress a stiff, inanimate object that in Grace's mind, if she was playing, if she was pretending, moved and wiggled under her grasp. Her tongue poked out between her lips as she worked.

Her smile when they were dressed was beatific.

Virgil wanted to applaud, but he held off. There was something fragile in this moment. He didn't want it to break. Too much attention would break it.

He waited until she sat back and then he picked up his question, as if their conversation wasn't interrupted. "As long as we're sharing slumber party secrets, tell me some yourself. When did you first notice boys?"

Grace sat back and looked at the dolls. Her expression was dreamy. "Not until late, I guess, compared to most girls. I remember my first boyfriend," she said. "His name was Mark. I thought he was heaven. He came over on Friday and Saturday nights and we watched television until my parents went to bed and then we fooled around. The night we finally did it, the night I finally said okay, we thought we were safe. Saturday Night Live was almost over, both of my parents should have been deep asleep. The moment we finished, Mark hadn't even rolled off of me yet, my mother came flying into the family room, banging a pot with a wooden spoon and screaming, 'Out, evil spirit, out!'"

Virgil sat back and laughed. "A pot? Evil spirit?"

Grace nodded. "My mother fancied herself a witch of sorts, I guess. She did these spells, weird spells, all the time. I never knew quite where she fit in with things. She wasn't Wiccan and she didn't have a cauldron in the back yard. She was just my mother. Well, Mark scooped up his clothes and ran from the house, my mother close behind, banging and yelling the whole way. He told me later he ran a half block buck-naked before my mother gave up. He hid behind some trees to get dressed." Grace laughed too. "For years, I had nightmares about boys running away from me, their butts gleaming in the moonlight, and my mother chasing them with her robe spread behind her like a cape."

The packing finished, Virgil folded the four flaps of the box lid closed. "So what did your mom do when she got home?"

Grace crossed the room and began making the hot chocolate. "Well, you know those weird spells?" Virgil nodded. "I got dressed while she was out chasing Mark, but she made me strip again. I had to lie down in the exact spot she found us in. Then she boiled some water and cooked some daisy petals, a rose, some bird feathers she found in the backyard, and garlic. After it cooled, she poured it into an empty salt shaker and she sprinkled it all over my body. She said it would return my innocence to me. But she said she would never restore my innocence again, that if I chose to be free and loose with my affections," Grace smiled, "her words, not mine, then I would just have to lay in my own juices. Um, also her words." Grace held out the potato chip bag. "Want some?"

"No thanks." Virgil reached behind her for the stash of candy. "So did it? Did the spell return your innocence?"

Grace thoughtfully chewed a potato chip. "In some ways, Virgil, I don't think it ever left. I think innocence has a lot more to it than just sex. There was just so much I didn't know. My mother taught me that hanging dollar bills in your attic was supposed to increase your wealth, but the rest of it? I just didn't know much. Not like the other kids."

Virgil nodded, wondered silently about dollar bills in the attic, about clanging pots and salt shaker potions, about not letting your little girl have dolls, and then accepted his mug. This new and intermittent silence was comfortable and he thought how he felt like he really knew Grace, like they lived a lifetime together, rather than just a couple days. The box of dolls rested between them. It was dark outside, the television was off, the clock lowed regularly from the dresser, and Cathy and the Quints slept with tightly shut and wide open eyes.

"Virgil," Grace said.

"What?" He looked at her over his mug. Her cheeks were pink from the steamy hot chocolate.

"I loved my mother. I really did. More than just about anybody, I think. I know she sounds crazy, but she was just everything to me. Well, everything until—"

Virgil wondered why she stopped. Everything until her husband came along? He patted her knee. "Of course you did," he said. "She was your mother. But why wouldn't she let you play with dolls?"

"I don't know." She shook her head. "I'll never know. She died a year ago."

It was what Virgil expected, but not with such heaviness in the words. Virgil knew that a parent's death could be hard, but still grieving a year later struck him as odd. Especially given that the mother who died was one who wouldn't let a little girl have a doll, and who also shouted about evil and chased boyfriends away by clattering on pots.

But the curtain that fell over Grace's face was beyond sad. Virgil couldn't bring himself to ask about it. Not yet. Her sadness shifted things and now he could feel the two short days that he'd known her. Despite their comfort, there'd been no lifetime.

Grace nudged the box between them with her foot. "Virgil, could you do me a favor?" she asked. "I know it sounds silly, but…would you please cut air holes in the box for those dolls?"

And that chased the gloom away. Virgil laughed out loud, started to scoff, but then he did as she asked. If she wanted to play that the dolls could breathe, then they would breathe. He was happy she was playing. As he cut each hole with his pocket knife, Grace's smile grew wider and her breath, like the dolls' she imagined, drew deeper. In that moment, Virgil saw how happy Grace could be. The shadows on her face disappeared and the young Grace bounded out, the child Grace who loved her mother, even though she didn't seem to Virgil to be a great mother at all. But seeing that heaviness lift made Virgil feel his own face mirroring the same joy. Handing Grace the box full of holes like the lid of a firefly jar, Virgil breathed with her. And with the dolls. He took the deepest breath he had in years.

CHAPTER FIVE
Grace

Before they moved on, Grace took a couple of photos of the hotel room with her cell phone, and then one of the outside as well. Grace wanted to remember it. She took a picture of Cathy and the Quints sitting on her bed too, but when she decided to send the photos via text to Mary and JJ, she left that one out. It was hard enough trying to explain why she was running away from home. It would be harder still to explain the dolls.

She didn't send the photos to Nick.

It was a school day, so she wasn't surprised when she didn't hear back from the kids. They weren't supposed to use their phones in school. Still, she wished they would sneak a peek, and an answer, anyway. She wondered how Mary was doing on her first day back after her suspension. She wondered if Amber had anything to say.

So Virgil and Grace left St. Charles after having breakfast at a roadside diner. As the morning sun warmed the car, Grace's stomach felt lazily full and she found her eyelids drooping. Virgil was very alert. He drummed his fingers on the wheel and hummed and occasionally whistled a few notes between his teeth. Then he started all over again with the humming and drumming. Before long, Grace found her foot tapping to his rhythm and she knew just when the whistle came in.

Grace glanced quickly into the backseat, checking that Cathy was still safely in her seatbelt. The Quints, the corn husk doll and Virgil's other finds were packed safely in the trunk. The clock rested securely in its box on the floor of the backseat. From time to time, a bump in the road caused it to bong, the sound rolling into the front seat like the contented toll of a church bell. Virgil smiled each time they heard it. "It's keeping us company," he said. "It's letting us know how happy it is that we bought it."

Saying things like that made Grace love Virgil right away. Her mother tucked feelings into inanimate objects too. So did Grace, though she'd learned to be quiet about it, once the kids grew past the age of pretending. Virgil wasn't quiet though, and she didn't have to be quiet with him.

Grace slid down in her seat, took off her shoes and put her socked feet on the dashboard. She heard the hum of the car, felt it vibrate along her spine, and she happily closed her eyes. She thought of her mother and of times when Grace, as a little girl, napped in the back seat, where Cathy was now. Grace and her parents used to travel a lot, especially in the summertime. Her mother was determined that Grace would see all of the fifty states and she did, except for Alaska and Hawaii. She still intended to see them someday since her mother felt it was so important.

For a moment, Grace held her breath. Maybe the money was for exactly that purpose – to go to the last two states and achieve her mother's goal. Not to go cruising cross country with a gay man and a trunk full of dolls. And a special doll in the back seat. A doll that her mother never wanted her to have.

Grace glanced again at Cathy. The doll's eyelids wobbled with the car's motion. Grace didn't want to see Alaska and Hawaii right now. She only wanted to be away. And that's what her mother said the money was for. She was doing what her mother wanted, even if she wasn't doing it in a way her mother would approve of.

Grace sighed and closed her eyes again. Virgil reached over and patted her knee. It was as familiar as coffee at her mother's. And this was only their third day. That familiarity was better than Alaska and Hawaii combined.

Grace's mother believed there was no greater education and no greater insurance than travel. The more spirits that were met and befriended, the more ethereal protection was offered. Grace's mother wanted Grace to be protected in all fifty states. Grace liked to think about that, a whole national network of spirits ready to come to her aid. It made her feel watched over and protected, even after her mother died. Even though Grace couldn't picture what a spirit might look like. She thought they might have wings.

Grace's mother made a point of buying something from every place they stayed on their vacations. Somewhere in the heart of every town was an old dusty, musty antique shop and that was where Grace and her mother headed as soon as they were settled. Her father snored in the hotel bed or sunned himself at the pool, and Grace and her mother searched for the store. Standing at the head of any Main Street anywhere, Grace's mother put her face in the air and breathed in as deeply as she could. Then she set off, like a drug dog on a bust, and Grace had to run to keep up with her. Her mother's nose always led them to the oldest antique shop in town.

Grace bet that Virgil could do the same thing, only with flea markets.

Her mother browsed in these antique stores, smiling and talking under her breath as she picked items up, dusted them with the hem of her blouse, patted them, and set them back down. A lucky few, those that touched her the most, she held to her chest in a brief embrace. She wanted to let all the items know that if she could, she would take the whole store home, take all the rusty garden tools, broken music boxes, and handless statues away from the dusty corners with no sunlight and little air.

She always found one special thing to bring back, to pack away in the suitcase. Grace knew the selection of only one was because of her father. Grace's mother would want the whole store; Grace's father would want nothing. They compromised with one, though the one expanded to include a store every place they stopped. It was a compromise that suited them both. Sometimes Grace's mother chose a trinket box, other times a figurine, but mostly, it was a clock or a Christmas nativity set.

Grace's mother loved clocks, she felt they were spirit-laden as they ticked away the timelessness of human lives, generation after generation. She talked often of a special friend she had, a friend who introduced her to clocks, long before she met Grace's father. And she meant introduced. Human face to clock face. Human heart to clock pendulum. "He thought they were real, Gracie," she said and she laid her hand on the closest clock's shoulder. They were in an antique store in Nebraska. "He said they breathed. He said their chimes were their voices." The first time Grace heard this, she was eight years old. Her mother had her lean her head against the glass door of the clock and listen. There was the heartbeat, Grace could hear it, as steady as her own. "See?" Grace's mother said. "James was right."

On that day, the day of the first storytelling about clocks, they bought the clock Grace leaned against. But when they brought it into the hotel and Grace exclaimed to her father about the clock's heart, he showed her the pendulum. He explained how it worked. Grace's mother shook her head and turned away. It was often like that with them. Some compromises didn't work, Grace thought now, though maybe a quietly turned back could be a compromise. The clock still came home, after all. It was hung in Grace's room.

After her mother died, Grace kept the clock, of course. It didn't hang in the bedroom she shared with Nick; he said he couldn't sleep through the chime.

But it was on the wall partway up the stairs and Grace, when she woke in the middle of the night, could hear it. And she heard it tick and chime throughout her day.

Compromise.

Because of compromise, and because of this man James, Grace's childhood home had many clocks, three per room, except in the bathrooms. Her mother felt that a room was safe if it bore a holy trinity of clocks. The bathrooms were excluded because Grace's mother worried that the humidity of running hot water would hurt them, and so only a broken clock resided in each of the three bathrooms. Besides the bathroom clocks, most worked, some didn't, but not for lack of trying. Grace's mother always attempted to have them repaired. She felt the spirits couldn't be happy if time wasn't passing. But she wouldn't throw them away if their time stopped. She told Grace, "Worth doesn't change with time or old age." She said James taught her that. Grace loved James, even though she never met him in person. She met him instead through her mother's voice, through the admiration that was there, and the love.

When each clock came home, Grace's mother hung it or set it in its place. Then she wound it and it moved forward with the time right where it left off. Very few of the clocks were actually on the correct time. This upset Grace's father and when the clocks would go off singly or together, belting out a chorus or singing a solo, his jaw clenched, his fists tightened, and he glared at his wristwatch. Grace's mother gave him the watch one Christmas, mostly as a joke, Grace suspected, but he loved it. It was an atomic watch, set to the atomic clock in Colorado. When he died, Grace's mother buried him with that watch so he would always know the exact time even in the hereafter. Grace's mother put her hand through her husband's hair, then whispered, "I'm sorry," so softly, Grace wasn't even sure she heard. She never knew what her mother was sorry for; she was certain it had to go deeper than a house filled with clocks chiming all different hours, deeper than a stop at an antique store in every town they came to. Deeper even than dollar bills hung in an attic. But she felt it wasn't her business; there was something intimate in the way her mother's hand touched her father's hair. Grace let it stay between husband and wife.

Grace's mother also loved Christmas. Her belief in spirits and spooks only seemed to deepen her belief in God and the Christ Child and all the Bible stories. She owned at least fifty nativity sets, made from all over the world. Every Christmas, crèches were placed in each room, even the bathrooms, and several were set up under the big Christmas tree in the living room.

Grace loved Christmas too, but not because of a love or a belief in God and the Christmas story. She loved all those little Christ Children, scattered throughout her house. They were dolls! Grace gathered them up and stole them away to her room where they took turns being cradled in her arms. Most of the little babies fit in the palm of her hand, but they were still babies and as close to a doll as Grace ever got. She crooned over them, her Christmas children, her own immaculate conception, until her mother noticed the empty mangers and came to collect them again. From Thanksgiving to the new year, Grace crept out of bed each night, located a baby, and slept with it the whole night through.

Grace wondered now if the nativity sets were packed up and away every January second so that Grace wouldn't have access to the Christ Children throughout the year. On January second, with her Christmas list requests unfulfilled yet again, Grace found herself newly barren.

There was a nativity set in her bedroom as well, but she couldn't sleep with that Christ baby. Grace's mother deliberately picked out a different type of crèche for Grace. She saw it on display in a used ceramics store in California. The figures weren't human, but symbols of what they were supposed to represent. In the manger lay a ceramic rainbow connected by a silver chain to a pot of gold. The clerk in the store told Grace's mother that the artisan who made the crèche believed people searched for Christ, and when they found him, it was like finding a new life, a new treasure. Just like the pot of gold at the end of the rainbow. But Grace just couldn't cuddle with a rainbow, even if it was attached to riches.

When Grace's mother died, all of the nativity sets were sold at the estate sale but one. Grace's favorite was made right in Waukesha by an artist at Brook Street Artisan's Village, over on Brook Street by the bus depot. The Bible characters in that set always looked so familiar to Grace, like the artist modeled it after people he saw on the streets around town, by Grace's children's school, by Grace's house, by the doll museum and the bank where her mother lived. But like her mother, Grace only brought it out at Christmas time.

The car hit a bump and the clock lowed in the backseat. Grace smiled and Virgil murmured, "Good company." She sat up and looked out of the window.

"Where are we?" she asked.

"Well…I decided to take a sort of scenic detour. We're going to a place I've never been before. I told you I wanted to go to Iowa, right?"

So this must be Iowa. "You did. Where are we going?"

Virgil nodded at the cornfields. "We're heading to a place called What

Cheer."

Grace immediately hated the name. What Cheer? As if any place could always be happy, could always be cheerful. Nobody ever died there? Nobody ever grieved or was sad? Grace shook her head. "I never heard of it."

"Most people haven't, I don't think." Virgil ran his hands around the big car's steering wheel, flexed his fingers, and then settled in at the nine and three spots. "They claim to have the largest flea market in the midwest."

"Larger than St. Charles?" Grace thought of the row after row, booth after booth, of vendors she saw the day before. "Virgil, I don't think I could take anything much bigger."

Virgil laughed and gave her the now familiar pat on the knee. "I don't think you have to worry, Grace. When I did some research, I found something in the small print." He let out a cackle, which startled Grace. Virgil was always so nice, but the cackle crossed the border from glee to something darker. "On the Monday after the flea market, a Monday like this one, they gather all of the unsold merchandize that the vendors don't want to take home. A guy there, who owns a barn and some acreage, makes a blanket offer, and then he buys all of it. He spends the rest of Monday setting up all of the unsold stuff in his barn and on Tuesday, he opens it to the public. Though he keeps it quiet and local." Virgil looked over and his eyes gleamed. "A lot of the stuff is sold cut rate. And we're going to see just how many dolls are left behind."

Left behind. Grace thought of her children and shuddered. "And how did you find this out? What small print?"

Virgil's gleam simmered and he blushed. The quiet Virgil returned. "Well...we're probably not supposed to know about this. In poking around, I found it in someone's blog. But hey, if we happen to be there..." He smacked the steering wheel and Grace worried he would cackle again.

"How long ago was this blog written?"

Virgil shrugged. "Two years."

Grace sat straight up. "Two years?" The car hit a bump and the clock lowed and Grace appreciated its exasperation. "This might not even be happening anymore! Two years?"

Virgil waved out the window. "Grace, you know what? I just decided, when I saw this, that I wasn't on any timeline. This is off my beaten path, but I thought, what the hell? I don't have anywhere to be at any one time. Do you?"

Grace shook her head. She had no idea where she was going or what she was doing. Though she had to admit, she kind of hoped Virgil did. It felt like someone needed to have a plan.

"Grace?" Virgil patted her knee. "I just thought this would be fun."

Fun was a word that hadn't been in Grace's vocabulary for six months. Actually, for a year. "Okay," she said. "It will be like a secret rescue mission. We'll gather up abandoned dolls and we'll bring them home."

Virgil laughed. It was warm today and he unwound his window and rested his arm on the edge. Grace dug in her purse, found a ponytail holder in a pocket and slung her hair back. Then she opened her window too.

The fresh air felt great. If she allowed herself to think it, even for just a second, Grace would admit that she felt great too. Right then, right there. She felt great, even though…

Six months.

She sat back and did her best to repress a big yawn, but failed. She couldn't get over how tired she felt. It was like running away sapped all of her energy. Or like running away allowed all of the grief she felt over the last year to surge over her all at once. Like the floodgates she'd built were gone, without her family holding them up. Forcing them up, she thought.

"We passed an interesting billboard a few miles back," Virgil said. "Looks like another one up ahead."

Grace looked and saw a billboard topped by a grinning cow, beckoning with its hoof. "COME SEE THE AMAZING FIVE-LEGGED COW AND TWO-HEADED CALF!" it said. "Oh!" Grace said. She sat up and dropped her feet to the floor.

When she was little, she always begged to see sights like these. Five-legged cows, four-eared dogs. Roadside zoos. Her father firmly refused because tourists went there, wearing plaid Bermuda shorts and black knee-high socks. Even when her father was a tourist, he didn't want to be one, and he never wore plaid Bermuda shorts. He did wear black socks, but under well-pressed slacks. Grace's mother looked at the billboards almost as wistfully as Grace did. Her mother thought these creatures might be jokes played by the spirits, intended to give everyone a good laugh. Or conversely, they could be major spiritual mistakes and the spirits would be angry if people took the time to see them, especially if they laughed. Spirits, Grace's mother said, had a good sense of humor, but they didn't like to be made fun of. They were embarrassed by their mistakes. Since she was uncertain if these roadside stops were good spiritual investments, her mother stood by her father and refused to let Grace see them. It was one compromise that Grace hated.

Now Grace turned to Virgil. "I've always wanted to stop at a place like that," she said.

He glanced sideways at her. "Me too. I've seen lots of signs like that on my trips and I'm always tempted. But I never wanted to go alone."

Grace reached for her shoes. "You're not alone now," she said. "And we're not on a timeline. Can we go?"

Virgil's fingers drummed once, then he glanced at his watch. "Sure, why not? What the hell, like I said before. What Cheer. Two-headed cows."

Grace tied her shoes quickly, then pointed out the cow exit to Virgil. He nodded and they followed the signs to the farm. It had a ticket booth by the entrance to its long driveway. A boy in overalls leaned out, chewing and popping his gum loudly. "You here to see the cow and calf?" he asked.

"Yes, two tickets, please," Virgil said.

The boy took the money. Grace memorized the amount and promised herself to pay Virgil back later. "Hold out your hands, please, fists up," the boy said and leaned into Virgil's window. He stamped a big red cow face on the backs of their hands. "Calf's not really a calf anymore, you know. He's a yearling. But my folks say we can't change the sign every year."

"At least it's still alive," Grace said. And she instantly felt the pang. Unlike Paul, she heard. Unlike your mother. Grace sat back. Her excitement fell away, the exact opposite of an adrenalin rush. Like the last row of tracks before a roller coaster came to a stop. She didn't want to stop.

She wondered if questions like these would always remain. Why was a two-headed calf still alive when her son was dead? Why was a five-legged cow alive when her mother was dead?

"Oh, yeah, they're alive, all right. Likes to eat too. Like they have two stomachs, though they don't. Two heads, but one stomach." Then he waved them on, making Grace feel like they were part of a huge crowd, though the Chrysler was the only car there.

A parking lot was laid out in gravel near the barn. As Grace got out of the car, she saw a woman coming from the house. She walked behind her apron, pulling it up to her face and rubbing. When she lowered it, Grace could see she was beaming. Her cheeks glistened and there was a red scarf in her hair.

"Hi," she said. "You here to see the cow and calf?"

"Yes, please," Virgil said. The excitement in his voice encouraged Grace's to reappear. She pushed her earlier questions behind her.

"My husband just let them out to pasture. Can I see your stamps?" They held out their hands and she examined them closely, raising their fists to nose-level. "Nice and neat," she said to Grace, patting her wrist. "He sometimes gets sloppy around lunch time." She led them to the back of the barn. The grass sloped down and all was green and fresh. Grace admired the white fence running the length of the field. Just over a little knoll, together under the shade of a tree, she could see the back ends of two cows, tails swinging in unison. The woman whistled and three heads came up.

The older cow ambled toward them first. Grace gaped at the fifth leg, dangling from the cow's belly, swinging into her udder. The extra leg was shorter than the other four and it seemed to be grasping for firm ground. It was withered, but clearly black and white and hooved. "Wow," Grace said. Virgil grabbed her hand with a sweaty palm.

The woman nodded proudly. She whistled again and the calf swung around, looking their way with both heads. When he or they walked forward, Virgil squeezed Grace's fingers tightly. It was a freak show, a real freak show. Both heads functioned. Four eyes looked this way and that and both mouths chewed cuds. The legs, the normal number, scrambled, going in all directions, but eventually, they or he made his or their way to the fence.

"It's like the legs get conflicting orders from two brains over how to walk," Virgil whispered.

The woman laughed quietly. "They've done real good. Mostly they manage to walk fine. Sometimes they wanna go different ways, then there's trouble." She scratched their heads, then produced an apple from her apron and fed the five-legged cow. "Wanna pet them? Go on ahead."

Grace patted the calf first, one hand on each head. Their twin tongues each licked one of Grace's wrists. Then she reached over their heads and scratched the back. The head on the left closed his eyes and arched his neck. Then he shook his ears and reached for some grass. As he took his first bite, the head on the right closed his eyes and arched his neck.

"They take turns with pleasure!" Grace said to Virgil and she laughed out loud. Compromise, she thought. Accepting two apples from the woman, Grace fed the boys.

"We have to be real careful how much we feed them," the woman said. "They both want to eat, but they only have one stomach. If we feed them too much, they can get the bloat. Then they're both miserable."

Virgil patted the five-legged cow and looked at the extra leg. "Does she mind it much?" he asked.

"Only when her udder's full," the woman said. "When the leg slaps her then, she gets kinda irritable. We milk her a lot, it helps. She's a good girl."

Grace looked at the cow's soft eyes and she suddenly wished the cow could use that fifth leg, that it gave her extra speed, extra agility, some superpower that other cows didn't have. Something other than a pain in the udder, a useless limb. "Is she the calf's mother?"

The woman nodded. "She is. I sometimes think that's why she didn't reject them. She understands."

The way a mother should, Grace thought. Her mind went to Mary and her eyes filled. A mother should accept.

Grace knew she was in the wrong. She knew that the minute she couldn't reassure Mary, when she couldn't get the words out that Paul's death wasn't Mary's fault. Even though Mary told him to hide in the tree. That was why Grace had to leave. She wasn't like this cow. The cow did the right thing. Grace didn't. She turned away and fought her tears.

"Well, thank you very much," Virgil said. He took Grace's hand and tucked it into his elbow.

"Yes, thank you," Grace said too.

"You're very welcome," the woman said. "If you want, you can visit our gift shop. We have lots of t-shirts with pictures of the cows. Bumper stickers too."

"No, thanks." Grace could tell the woman was disappointed, but she didn't need a t-shirt to remember this. Grace wasn't even sure she wanted to remember this. But looking around, she realized that the gift shop was probably the way this family earned their income. It wasn't that expensive to buy tickets. It certainly wouldn't take in enough to feed a family, especially one with a boy that sat in a ticket booth and worked hard to make neat stamps. Grace looked at Virgil. "You know what?" she said. "My kids might like a t-shirt. Let's go see what they have."

Grace didn't always do the wrong thing.

They both followed the woman up the path. As Grace looked through the selection, her heart hurt. The child who would have most appreciated these t-shirts was Paul. He was a big fan of the freaky, and of science too. If he was here, he would have been trying to figure out how the genetic accidents happened, how likely they were to happen, how likely it was that a five-legged cow would give birth to a two-headed calf, particularly if the father was a no-extra-parts bull. She wondered if she should buy one for him, if JJ would put it over the shoulders of his headstone for her. Grace picked out a shirt with the calf's picture for JJ and one of the cow for Mary. Then she chose an extra-large one for Paul with a picture of both cows on it. Paul himself wasn't an extra-large, but the shoulders of the headstone, she remembered, were wide. Virgil bought a bumper sticker for the Chrysler.

When they drove away, the boy waved from the ticket booth and Grace waved back, admiring the red cow on the back of her hand. "He did do a good job," she said to Virgil.

"He certainly did," Virgil said and reached across the steering wheel to show her his stamp.

Grace relaxed against her seat. She placed her hand on her knee and she watched the red cow as they drove down the freeway. She kept seeing the dangling leg and the two content heads. She kept seeing a mother who loved her children, no matter what.

Grace loved Mary. Of course she did.

But Paul was dead.

****

What Cheer, Iowa, didn't have a hotel, though it did have a bed and breakfast called the Time To Sleep Inn. Grace thought that was clever, but both she and Virgil thought a B & B would likely be too expensive. Grace also secretly thought that a B & B might be too social; she didn't feel like spending much time with anyone other than Virgil right now. It was odd; she felt like she needed the adventure and the away-time, but she also needed isolation and quiet.

They checked in to the chain hotel by the exit ramp of I-80. After unloading the car, they decided to drive back into What Cheer and take a look around. At the last minute, and on a whim, Grace retrieved Chatty Cathy and returned her to the back seat. When Virgil looked at her, she shrugged. "I guess I like her there," she said.

Virgil just smiled. And then he rebuckled the doll's seatbelt.

It didn't take long to realize the town had a theme to it, focusing around clocks. There was the Shop Around The Clock grocery store, the It's About Time gift shop, the Tick-Tock Quick-Stop Diner. "Let's go to dinner there tonight," Virgil suggested and Grace agreed. There didn't seem to be much else. She wondered what made the town decide to name their businesses after clocks. There was a large and beautiful clock tower, and the sight of it in this small town, surrounded by cornfields, made Virgil pull over. They rolled down their windows and waited the ten minutes to reach the top of the hour, just to hear it.

As four o'clock chimed around them, Virgil smiled and tapped the wheel in rhythm, but Grace was disappointed. It was tinny, not the lovely church bell sound she was expecting. Her mooing flea market clock sounded richer.

They drove toward the Time To Sleep Inn, and that's when Grace noticed what was just across the street. "Virgil!" she said. "Look at that! Stop!"

The big Chrysler skidded, and then Virgil pulled over to the side of the road. They both looked at the old Victorian house. A sign on the lawn declared it to be The Home For Wayward Clocks. Beneath, in small letters, it said, "A Clock Museum".

Virgil shut the car off. "Want to go see it?"

Grace thought of her mother, of the three clocks in every room but the bathrooms in her old house. She thought of the flea market clock, now sitting on the dresser of the new hotel. "Sure," she said. "If you don't mind. It's been a busy day already, what with the cows." She wondered if Virgil would have any interest, since the Home only held clocks, not dolls.

"I think it would be fun. One small business can always learn from another."

Grace cracked the back window for Cathy and felt silly for doing so. But she did it anyway.

There was a sign on the door to just come in, so Virgil escorted Grace through. As soon as they were in the entryway, Grace could hear them. The ticking of many, many clocks. It was an undercurrent, like the rush of a river. It wasn't intrusive, but it blended into her thoughts as easily as rain on the roof. She wished they'd gotten here earlier; they missed the top of the hour.

A woman stepped out of a room off to their right. "Hi," she said. "Welcome to the Home For Wayward Clocks."

While Virgil shook her hand, she introduced herself as Cooley, and Grace studied her. She didn't look like someone who would run a clock museum. Grace wasn't sure what a clock museum curator would look like, exactly, but she thought it would be someone older. She wondered if it was the word museum that made her think of old. Museums housed old things and it felt like their caretakers should be old too. This Cooley was young, maybe in her mid-thirties, and her gold curls fluttered around her shoulders like a corkscrew veil.

She listened as Cooley introduced them to the museum and explained all of the formalities. As she described her home and the best way to tour the clocks,

Grace felt a warmth as well as a caution. Cooley obviously loved the clocks, she wanted to share them, but she was worried about them at the same time. Grace couldn't help but recognize that feeling. The tone in Cooley's voice was the same as Grace's own every morning when she sent the kids off to school and told them to have a wonderful day, and that she loved them. And then she let them step out of the back door and out of her care, at least for a few hours.

Grace instantly liked Cooley.

When Virgil reached for his wallet, Grace quickly put her hand on his arm. "Let me pay this time, Virgil," she said. "You paid to see the cows."

"The cows?" Cooley asked. "Did you stop and see the five-legged cow and the two-headed calf?"

"We did!" Virgil said while Grace carefully opened her purse and covered it with one arm as she counted out the money. She decided to move a reasonable amount of it into her wallet later that night; digging into thousands out in public probably wasn't a good idea. She would tuck the rest into the small suitcase she bought at the Target, back in St. Charles. "You know them? They're about three hours away."

Cooley nodded. She smiled at Grace as she handed over the entrance fees. "I stopped there once on my way home from Chicago. The calf was about four months old then. He's —they're doing okay?"

Grace laughed. "I didn't know how to refer to them or him either."

They told Cooley of their visit and showed her their red cow stamps. Then she waved them on. "You're the only ones here right now. You don't need to hurry, though I do close at five. I'll be right here if you have any questions."

Grace nearly asked Cooley to come along with them, to supply them with what was clearly an abundance of knowledge, but also to supply them with company that knew the value of a visit to freak-show cows, to a museum filled only with clocks. But Virgil grabbed Grace's hand and led her away.

The deeper they got into the house, the more they marveled. There wasn't a wall, a table, or a shelf that didn't hold a clock. All of them were antiques; Grace couldn't find a one that needed batteries. The ticking was a constant, and at the quarter hour, as the clocks began to chime, Grace fell into a cascade of giggles. It was ridiculous, the sheer number of sounds that echoed through all the rooms, just to announce that fifteen minutes had passed, and would pass again. Grace's mother's house was filled with the cacophony of clocks too, but not like this. These clocks were set to the correct time and all of their voices, instead of going off at random, rose together in a grand noise. They sounded formal and they sounded like a riot, all at the same time.

Grandfather and grandmother clocks. Mantel and anniversary. And so many others that Grace couldn't name. Most ran, some didn't. Like Grace's mother, Cooley seemed to value even broken clocks. While none of the clocks here were for sale, Grace knew her mother would have loved this place. The clocks' energy flowed to the rooftop. Her mother would have felt it. Grace did.

When Grace explained that to Virgil, he said, "I hope they're filled with good spirits."

That made Grace stop. "I don't think my mother believed in bad spirits, Virgil." She looked around. She couldn't see a clock face anywhere near her that led her to believe it could be evil. Clocks were benevolent, she thought. They just wanted to remind you of the passing of time.

She thought of Paul, for whom time was frozen. Or forever gone. She thought of her mother. Quickly, she turned and went down a hallway.

They roamed from room to room and up and down the stairs through the half hour and the three-quarter. At three minutes to five, they returned to the entryway. Cooley stepped out to join them.

"Do you mind if we stay to hear them chime five o'clock?" Grace asked.

Cooley leaned against a table, tucked just inside the doorway. "That's not a problem," she said. "I'm glad you want to hear them."

While they waited, Grace picked out a couple postcards. She wished her mother was still alive, to see the pictures. She wished she'd known of this place before her mother's passing. Grace would have brought her here.

So much of Grace's life seemed to be about wishing now.

The grandmother clock in the hallway started the chorus. Her voice was a lovely tenor, and it was quickly joined in by the discordant songs of others. Despite the uprising of her sadness, Grace fell into giggles again. Virgil smiled. But Cooley closed her eyes and listened. Grace wondered if she did that four times every hour, all the day through. If she heard them in her sleep. If the clocks, like the rain at night, drifted into her dreams.

When the sound stopped, gentling into reverberations and then the ticking silence, Grace found her giggles transitioned to tears. She was embarrassed and turned away from Cooley and Virgil. "Thank you," she said over her shoulder, her words muffled by her sleeve as she wiped her eyes. "My mother would have loved this."

"Grace? Your mother?" Cooley asked.

Something in her voice, something soft and longing, made Grace turn despite her tears. "She died a year ago," she said. "She collected clocks too."

Cooley's hands were clasped at her waist like a girl in prayer, and in that moment, Grace could see who she was as that girl. A part of Grace, the part that held each of her children, yearned to hold Cooley too. But adult decorum held her back.

Cooley's expression swept from longing to sadness. "I'm sorry for your loss," she said. A formal statement, but Grace didn't doubt her sincerity.

Grace closed her fingers over her mother's Easter Island pendant and squeezed.

Just before leaving, Virgil asked Cooley about the post-flea market gathering in the barn. "Where is it exactly?"

Cooley seemed startled. "How do you know about that?"

Virgil smiled. "Well…it is the era of the internet, Cooley. It's hard to keep anything secret anymore."

Cooley shook her head. "Frank isn't going to be happy about that. The barn is just out of town, the opposite side of the freeway. You're planning on going? What are you looking for?"

Virgil tucked his hands in his pockets and rocked on his heels as he explained about The Nursery. Grace heard the same reverence and care in his voice that she heard earlier when Cooley talked about the Home For Wayward Clocks. That beloved child voice.

Cooley and Virgil didn't have the hollowness, though, that Grace's voice had when she spoke of Paul. She wondered if they'd ever lost anything. A doll. A clock. Were there people that they were missing?

She turned quickly away to wipe her face again. Then she had to return to their little triangle when Cooley spoke her name. "What would you be looking for in the barn, Grace?"

She shrugged. "I'm looking for a doll called Maribel Get Well. I always wanted her. But…I'm looking for everything, really. Or nothing. Depending on how you look at it." She felt ridiculous, but Cooley seemed to understand.

"Why don't you meet me here tomorrow morning?" she asked. "I was going to go anyway. I always see what Frank gathered for clocks. You can come as my guests. Then he won't be so upset that you found out his secret on the internet."

Virgil agreed enthusiastically and Grace found herself pleased that she would see Cooley again. They said their goodbyes and then they returned to the car.

Grace checked to make sure that Cathy was still there and still all right before she buckled herself in. When she looked back at the clock museum, she saw that the lights that brought a glow to the tall narrow windows on either side of the door were gone, likely turned off by Cooley after she escorted them out and as she finished her day. But the other windows, one by one, lit up with the evening's welcome and a sense of homecoming.

Grace wondered who was turning on the lights in her own house.

****

After dinner at the Tick-Tock Quick-Stop Diner, which had amazing meatloaf, mashed potatoes and homemade peach pie, they settled into the hotel. Grace checked her phone and found a text from JJ, exclaiming over her photo of last night's hotel. "Kewl!" he texted.

There was nothing from Mary.

Grace placed her second call home while Virgil was in the shower. She listened to the phone ring and she thought how different it sounded, further away, less familiar. For a moment, she was unreasonably afraid a stranger would answer, but it was JJ's voice that rolled into her ear.

"Hi, honey," she said.

He breathed in sharply and there was a distant voice asking a question. "It's for me!" JJ shouted. Then to Grace, "Hold on a minute."

Grace waited for and heard the click of the door. She knew JJ just locked himself in the coat closet. It was his favorite place when he took what he called his "personal private only-for-me, thank you," calls. He set up his old step-stool in there, once used to reach the bathroom sink while he brushed his teeth, and he sat on it behind the winter coats and talked so softly that the family only knew he was in there when the phone went missing from its cradle. Grace felt honored that she was one of his special calls, but then she wondered about the secrecy.

"JJ," she said when she could hear his steady breathing again. "What's going on? Why are we in the closet?"

"I wanted to talk to you by myself. Without Dad yelling questions. And Mary...without Mary being Mary. Just me," he said.

Grace smiled. Her third child, the tagalong, the second surprise after Paul's happy unplanned conception, often faded into the background. He seemed happy there, most days. But every now and then, he wanted her to himself, and she was happy to oblige. "Okay, just you. How are you?" Grace settled back on the new bed, Cathy by her side.

"I'm okay. I told Barry you were gone."

Barry was JJ's best friend. He lived with his mother and as far as Grace knew, there was no father. "And what did Barry say?"

"He said –" JJ's voice broke off. Grace heard him clear his throat and she wondered if he was getting a cold. But when his voice came on again, shaky, Grace realized he was clearing away tears. "He said you're not going to come back. He said his dad left just like you did and he never came back. And Mary's dad never came back either." JJ burst into tears, winter coat-muffled tears that couldn't possibly be heard by the others from the back of the closet.

Grace was shocked. "Honey, I'm coming back. I am. I promised you, and I will."

"Barry said…Barry said his dad said that too."

It was hard to fight against a best friend's word, a best friend's experience. So Grace raised her voice. She needed to be heard. "JJ! I'm not Barry's dad! I'm coming back! I would never leave you!"

"But you did," JJ said.

Grace was sucker-punched by his logic. She had to catch her breath. "Honey, you just have to believe me. I'm coming back. Did Barry's dad ever phone him?"

There was a pause and then, "He didn't say. I'll ask him."

"I'm calling you. And I'm sending you pictures. I left you a letter. In writing. That's as real as it gets. I'm coming back, JJ. Really truly."

He sighed and his voice steadied. "Okay. I told him you would."

"And you're right." Home seemed very far away right then, but it still existed just an inch back from the front of Grace's mind. She couldn't imagine leaving her kids forever. She almost couldn't imagine being separated from Nick forever, but if she tried really hard, she could. Her first husband taught her that.

"Where are you now?" JJ asked.

"I'm in a hotel near What Cheer, Iowa. I'm sitting on the bed."

"Wutchair?"

"What Cheer." Grace pronounced each word clearly and separately. "It's in Iowa."

"Iowa," JJ said slowly. "Can you tell me how to spell that Cheer thing? I want to look it up on Google maps and see where you are."

Grace doubted if What Cheer would be shown, but she spelled it carefully. "It's off of I-80," she said, knowing that JJ was a fan of the freeway system.

Sure enough, he said, "I-80!" and his voice warmed in admiration and recognition. "Is it nice there? Is it as nice as here?"

"It's nice." Grace looked around the room. The distant sound of Virgil's shower reminded her of the clocks in the museum that afternoon. This hotel was similar to the one in Illinois, but a definite step up, with a refrigerator and a coffeepot and a microwave. It was nice, in ways Grace couldn't describe to her son whose definition of nice was the old furniture in their living room. "Not as nice as home," she said to him.

"But if it's not as nice as home, why are you there?" His voice grew thin again. Thin with his eternal damnable logic.

Grace didn't know what to say. How do you tell a twelve-year old boy that you just can't stand to be home right now? Home was wonderful, home was Nick and Mary and JJ and TheCat. It was the memories of Paul and her mother. It was everything familiar, where Grace could walk around with her eyes closed and never bump into anything. In St. Charles, Illinois, in What Cheer, Iowa, wherever she and Virgil went, Grace had to turn a light on to keep from hurting herself.

But staying home was hurting her too.

At home, there was that hole threatening to swallow her alive. It was here too, but it was a hole she could carry in her pocket. Her fingers weren't always worrying at it, her hands had other things to do. New things. Like look for dolls. Or brush Cathy's hair. Talk to Virgil.

"Sweetheart," Grace said and her voice broke. "Sweetheart, it's hard for me to explain this to you. I just can't be home right now. It doesn't feel right."

"Because of Paul?" His voice grew so small, Grace pictured him climbing right into the mouthpiece of the phone, then riding the airwaves to her.

"I guess mostly because of Paul." She could hear JJ breathing, little short breaths that made her want to hold him, to calm him down, feel his heart beat from fast to slow against her ribs.

"Mommy?" he said, and those two syllables coming out of a middle school child undid Grace. She could hear just how much he was hurting, how sad he was. "I miss Paul too and sometimes I want to run away. But Mommy, I'm still here."

Grace nodded and hugged herself as tightly as she could. It was all she could do. "Sweetie, I know. I know you're there. And I'll be there too, in just a little while. It won't be too long, I promise." She suddenly wanted to tell JJ that he was a better person than she was. But he would never understand that. She was the one that understood. JJ didn't abandon his family. They were all still there. She was the one that ran.

His voice shrunk to a pinpoint. "Mom. Is it because of what Mary did? I'm sorry I didn't tell you."

And there it was, another chance to make it all right. To tell JJ, if not Mary, that it wasn't Mary's fault. A chance to do the right thing, with this remaining child.

But Mary was what caused she and JJ to become remaining children, wasn't she?

Grace wanted to do the right thing. But it just didn't feel like the right thing. Nothing felt like the right thing. Everything was wrong.

"It's okay, JJ," she said. "It's okay that you didn't tell me. And I guess…I guess it is partly because of what Mary did. I have to just figure all of this out."

"She didn't mean to, Mom," JJ said.

Grace was sure she didn't. There was no intent to bring harm, to kill. But Paul was still dead.

"I saw him climb," JJ said. "I was supposed to be hiding my eyes, but I watched him. I cheated. I knew Paul was in the tree and Mary told him to go there." No longer the size of a pin, JJ's voice sunk into concrete. Each word was separate and carefully spoken. "Maybe I should have told him to stop. Maybe I should have told her not to say that."

"Oh, JJ," Grace said. "You didn't know what was going to happen. And Paul never listened to you anyway." Paul was the big brother. What big brother listens to a little brother?

But Grace wished so hard JJ had said something. And that Paul had listened. Like he listened to his big sister. She wished Paul said no to Mary. Just that once.

There was a sigh and she knew JJ's shoulders just slumped and he was relaxing against the closet wall. Sighing with him, Grace wondered why it was so easy to tell this child that it wasn't his fault, but she couldn't say the same to Mary. Grace thought of the five-legged cow and her two-headed calf. She thought of that acceptance. Did the cow ever have any other calves? Did she love them all exactly the same?

Grace wished it was easy with Mary. She wished it was as easy to let her off the hook as JJ. But Grace could hear her daughter's voice. "Climb the tree, Paul," she said. "He'll never find you there. Climb the tree."

So much of Grace's life was wishes now.

She shook her head. "So are you okay?"

"I'm okay, Mom," he said. And just like that, he was.

"And you know I'll be back? No matter what Barry says? No matter what Barry's dad did? No matter what Mary's dad did?"

"Yes. Those were both fathers. You'll be back because you're the mother. Mothers don't leave." And there was his logic. Grace's shoulders relaxed too.

"JJ, I want to talk to Daddy and Mary. What are we going to do? Dad will be mad if he finds out you lied about this phone call."

"You call back. I'll let someone else get it."

"Then I'll have to talk to you again."

"That's okay, we'll just talk about school and stuff."

"All right. It's a plan. I love you, JJ."

"Love you too. Come home soon!"

Grace heard the phone click and she hung up too. She pictured JJ closing the closet door and bringing the phone back to its cradle. TheCat chased at his heels, hoping to convince JJ that an extra handful of kibble was most necessary. JJ obliged, he always did, and then he walked through the kitchen to the living room, settling in front of the television, if Nick bought a new one, to play video games. Or he might go upstairs to do his homework. Grace looked at the time on her cell phone screen. Seven-thirty. He'd be doing homework.

Grace dialed again. This time, Nick answered. "Hello," he stated.

"Nick, it's me." She pictured his eyes widening and the way he leaned on the counter.

"Grace," he said. Then a pause. "Grace, where are you?"

"I'm in a hotel in Iowa." Grace thought about adding the town name, but decided against it. Iowa was enough for Nick to handle. JJ could fill him in on her exact whereabouts later.

"Iowa!" He was probably slapping his forehead; Grace thought she heard the sound of skin against skin. "Why? Why aren't you on your way home? I told you I wanted you back here yesterday!"

"And I told you no, remember? I'm not ready yet." It was as hard to explain to him as to a twelve-year old boy. Grace tried to remember her words. JJ seemed to get it.

"Look, Grace, I don't know what ready means. You need to come home."

"In a while, Nick." Grace waited, listening to him. His breaths were short and jerky like he just ran up some stairs.

"Grace, I don't know what to do. I don't know how to come and get you.

What am I supposed to do?"

Grace heard a new desperation in his voice. "Just wait, Nick. I'm fine. I'm doing what I needed to do. Okay? You're going to have to trust me in this."

"Trust you?" He laughed and it wasn't happy. "Grace, you spend all day sleeping. You nail the curtains shut. You tell our daughter that it was her fault her brother died. Does that sound like someone who can be trusted?"

Well, no. It didn't. Grace didn't know what to say. She wondered if she felt as flummoxed as Nick did.

But she didn't feel flummoxed with Virgil that afternoon. She didn't feel flummoxed with the two cows, or with the museum full of clocks.

"Nick," she said. "I just have to do this."

There was silence. Maybe the smallest of sighs.

Grace decided to change the subject. "Listen, Nick, has JJ said anything about going to visit Paul's grave? He was talking about getting a pumpkin."

"Yeah, he has one. I took him to a pumpkin patch yesterday." Nick's voice relaxed just a little. Grace knew it was from the familiarity of talking about the kids. It was what they did. It was who they were. "It took him over an hour to pick it out. He wanted one shaped like a rocket ship. Can you imagine a pumpkin shaped like a rocket ship?"

Grace laughed. But she could. She knew pumpkins weren't just round. But she also knew that JJ probably stretched Nick's imagination a bit too far. Poor Nick. His patience was stretched, and now so was his imagination.

"Anyway, we found one. We'll probably bring it out this weekend."

Grace nodded, easing into the familiarity, hoping it would stay. "Would you do me a favor please, Nick? Would you put a baggie of candy corn by his stone? And some of those little candy pumpkins too, you know how he loves those."

And the familiarity blew backwards, falling right into incredulous. "Oh, Christ, are you kidding me? Grace, maybe we should stop this. Maybe it's not healthy. Paul's dead, for God's sake, he's not going to eat the candy!"

The impact of her son's name with the word dead was just as strong as it was on the first day. It was a tall brick wall. And Paul was behind it. "Nick, it's his favorite. He always has them at Halloween. He's never been without."

The sound of a puncture. Air leaving lungs. Nick was hitting a wall too, Grace could see it. "All right," he said softly. "I'll do it. Will you come home then?"

Grace chose to ignore that. "Can I please talk to Mary?" Grace wondered at herself, asking for permission. "I'd like to talk to Mary now," she amended.

A sigh sounded different than a puncture. "All right. But then talk to me some more, okay? No hanging up. I miss you, Grace." The last was said quickly and he was gone before Grace could respond. She heard him yell Mary's name. And then Mary was there, with no introduction. No sound of footsteps, no intake of breath. She was just there.

"Mom," she said.

"Hi, hon. How are you?"

"Fine."

Grace waited, but no other information came. "Are you all right?" she asked.

There was a laugh, she recognized it as Mary's, but it was a broken laugh, a hiccup, sliced off in the middle. And then there was a clunk.

"I'm back," Nick said.

Grace blinked. "Where did Mary go? She didn't say anything."

"She just dropped the phone and went back upstairs." He must have turned away because his voice became distant. "Mary! Don't you want to talk to your mother?" He waited, then said, "She's not coming, Grace. I don't think she wants to talk."

Grace felt hurt and immediately felt completely wrong for doing so. Grace was the one doing the hurting, not Mary.

But Mary told Paul to climb the tree.

Grace closed her eyes. "She won't talk to me?" she whispered.

"Hon, what do you expect?"

Grace didn't know. She just didn't know.

"Grace, are you all right? I mean, with money and everything?"

"I'm fine, Nick." Which was exactly what Mary said. Fine. Was Mary fine?

Virgil came out of the bathroom, toweling his hair. Grace had to admit, for an older man, Virgil had a great head of hair. Silky, it looked like. Silver. That lovely shade that wasn't gray or white.

"Well, how are you...I mean, the motels and stuff. Grace, we don't have that much available on credit."

"I'm okay, Nick," Grace said. "Don't worry. I'm not using any of the cards. Look, I'll explain it all when I get home."

"You're sure you're coming home then?" His voice sounded sad, an echo of JJ's, and Grace was tempted to tell him JJ's logic. Mothers come home.

"Yes, Nick, I'll come home, I promise. Soon. Don't worry. I love you,

Nick." And she did.

"I love you too, Grace. But I want you home. I want to take care of you." The words were an odd thing, given the defeated sound of his voice. She thought of how he said he didn't know how to come and get her. She supposed that was true.

"I'm fine, Nick," she said again. Was Mary?

But Mary told Paul to climb the tree.

"All right. Talk to you soon?"

"Yes, I promise. Very soon." She hung up the phone and immediately realized she hadn't talked to JJ for a second time. She wondered if Nick noticed.

Virgil threw the towel on the bed and began combing his hair. "You okay?" he said into the mirror.

"I don't know what to say to them," she said slowly. "Everything I say sounds wrong. I can't be okay, because then I wouldn't be gone. But if I'm not okay, I should be home. It just keeps adding up to I should be home. But I can't be. I wouldn't be okay there. I'm not okay here either." In that moment, it became overwhelming and Grace covered her face with her hands. She held back the tears. "I miss them, Virgil. But I can't be there."

"And they miss you. But they're all right, right?"

Fine, Mary said. Nobody was all right. Grace knew that. And now she'd made it worse for them. Even as she tried to make it better for her.

A text came in from JJ. "I luv U, Mom," it said. "Talk 2 U next time."

And then another. From Mary. "I'm sorry. I'm sorry. I luv U, Mom."

Grace broke. Again. She couldn't help but picture a crack on her body, a new crack among many others. She was breaking. One piece, one crack at a time.

Virgil didn't wait. He sat beside her and when he opened his arms, Grace leaned into him and started to cry.

****

The next morning, when Grace and Virgil returned to the Home For Wayward Clocks, Cooley was already sitting out on the front stoop, her hands folded and resting between her knees. She waved when they pulled in and then crossed the lawn to Virgil, who rolled down the window. "I thought maybe you changed your mind," Cooley said, glancing at her watch. Grace wondered if it chimed the hours.

"No, we just took a while getting organized this morning. We're not too late, are we?" Virgil asked.

"It'll be okay. I'll take my own car, you follow behind me. That way, if you want to leave before I do, you'll be able to. I tend to make a full morning of it."

What Cheer wasn't big and so it only took about five minutes to get through town and then to the outskirts. Grace wondered how this could be called the outskirts as the town was so small, there really wasn't any transition from in town to out of town. They followed Cooley up a winding drive to a farmhouse surrounded by outbuildings and two barns, one red and one yellow. Cars were parked in a field and Cooley and Virgil each pulled into the next available slots. Grace was surprised there were so many people.

Cooley was stopped at the big double doors of the yellow barn by a man who called her name and then gave her a quick hug. He eyed Virgil and Grace. "Who's this, Cooley?" he asked.

"Frank, these are friends of mine, in from out of state. They came for the flea market and are heading out later today. I thought I'd bring them along."

Frank frowned. "You know this is a local thing. Not for outsiders."

Grace suddenly felt like an alien.

Cooley nodded. "Of course. But what's the harm? They're heading out. They won't tell anyone."

Virgil shook his head, a solemn look on his face, and Grace quickly followed suit. Frank glanced at Cooley and scuffed the dirt a few times. "All right," he said. "Because it's you. But let's not make a habit of this."

Grace and Virgil shook Frank's hand, and then they followed Cooley to a cluster of people, waiting by a velvet rope stanchion. It looked like what used to block off entrances to old theaters and Grace wanted to laugh. It stood independently and you could easily walk around either side of it, but the people waited politely and they didn't seem to think it was odd to find a theater stanchion in an old barn that, despite being swept very clean, and no stalls were apparent, still smelled of cow.

Frank moved behind the velvet rope and the crowd fell silent. "Okay," he called, "you all know the rules."

Virgil and Grace looked at Cooley and she leaned over and whispered, "We all know the rules, but he tells us anyway. Just listen."

Frank continued. "Everything here is from the weekend's flea market and it's all priced to sell. There is no haggling. Hear me? No haggling. You pay what it's marked or you don't pay. Period."

Grace heard Virgil's soft grunt and knew he wasn't happy, but for her, this was a relief. There was nothing simpler than looking at a pricetag and either liking it or not. Virgil liked a challenge. Here, he wouldn't find one.

Frank said, "I'll leave it open today for about four hours, until noon. So you have plenty of time. No need to be crazy, no need to rush. Cash register is set up right outside the doors, so that's easy enough. Oh, and I got that new square thing now for my cell phone. You can even pay with credit card if you want."

A murmur of excitement went up from the crowd. Virgil looked at Grace and rolled his eyes. Grace went from feeling like an alien to feeling like a city slicker.

Frank ceremoniously unhooked one end of the stanchion. Grace was amazed there was no pushing, no shoving. The crowd just neatly filed its way in. Behind her, Cooley said, "There's not really any rhyme or reason to the organization. Frank just unloads, prices and places. So you'll have to look all around. Anything could be anywhere."

Virgil grabbed Grace's hand. "You okay with splitting up like we did in St. Charles?"

Grace nodded. The barn was a lot more compact than the flea market was, so she wasn't worried about getting lost or never finding Virgil again. He'd be right here, within these four walls. So she squeezed his hand and let go.

Cooley was right; there wasn't any rhyme or reason. There weren't any booths. There was just pile after pile of stuff. Appliances next to antiques next to clothing next to toys. Because so many in the crowd seemed to slow and cluster at the opening, Grace moved through and headed for the back of the barn. It was quieter there and she liked that. She no longer saw Cooley or Virgil, but she was fine. She glanced at her cell and saw she was still connected. She could still be reached. She could still reach out.

As she wandered, the sounds around her diminished to a pleasant buzz. Grace picked up things, touched them, dusted them and put them down, much as her mother used to do on their travels through antique stores. A flower vase. A dial phone. Several books. What looked like a sculpture gone wrong…it was clay and it curved and was smooth, but then it was suddenly rough and angled. She pondered that one for a while, but then left it behind. Some things she held on to, though. An old leatherbound book for Mary, Louisa May Alcott's *Under The Lilacs*. Mary read anything you put in front of her, and the leather was soft and regal and lovely. For JJ, she found an amazing apatosaurus, made by a now extinct toy company.

Tucked at the base of a lamp, Grace saw a box that attracted her attention. The colors were bright and on the front was a bare-breasted woman. Her hair flew out behind her in rainbow streams and the look on her face was tranquil and strong. The box was cardboard and a little larger than a deck of cards, and Grace realized that was exactly what it held. Tarot cards.

Her mother used to do Tarot, though she did it in her own way, of course. She never followed the ancient patterns described on the instruction booklets. Her mother laid things out randomly and then she looked full in the face of each card and full in the face of the person looking for predictions and came up with her own interpretations. Grace couldn't remember a single fortune her mother foretold with the cards coming true. Yet people always came back.

There was a crack in the barn boards near where Grace stood, and as she held the box and opened it, she enjoyed the sun coming through, sending a dust-sparkled beam down her shirt and jeans and into the floor, and she enjoyed too the coolness of the air. It was like a little private fan, just for her.

The cards were lovely, with the rainbow-haired woman in different poses, and Grace knew from her mother that all the cards meant something different. The instruction booklet was here too and Grace considered looking at it. She always wondered what the actual explanations said. But Grace loved her mother and never looked.

Now, she thought maybe she would.

After setting down her things, Grace cleared a small table and sorted through the cards. She knew that there were four minor arcana – earth, wind, fire and water. And there were twenty-one major arcana, representations of the divine. Grace's mother always called them The Divine Sisters. Creating her stacks, Grace, like her mother, looked into the face of each bare-breasted woman on the cards and even before she knew that the deck was complete, she decided to buy them. She would have bought them for just one card.

The Divine Sister Yemaya. The picture on the card was rich and dark, but it wasn't a dark that was scary. There was a large blue moon in the background and somehow, the blue shot through the woman's full and curvy form. Grace didn't feel intimidated so much as she felt quieted.

Pulling out the deck's explanation booklet, Grace paged through and found Yemaya's description. Yemaya, it said, was "the ultimate female goddess, the soother of heart troubles, carrying deep unknowable power." Grace smiled and stacked the deck again, leaving Yemaya on top.

The soother of heart troubles. That was just what Grace needed. As for a deep unknowable power, Grace's mother always professed to have that, and she expressed it with her strange spells. Which mostly failed, like the dollars hanging in the attic and chasing evil with a clattering pot. But they always made Grace feel full to bursting with love for her mother, because her mother always managed to turn the spell around from failure to accidental success. And because she knew her mother always performed these spells with the best of intentions, out of love for her family. Grace couldn't recall her mother ever doing a spell to hurt someone.

Cooley suddenly showed up at her elbow. "Those look interesting," she said, laying one finger carefully on the box. "Are you going to buy them?"

"Yes," Grace answered and realized she hadn't even looked at the price. She glanced at the tag – five dollars – and breathed a sigh of relief, which she immediately rebuked herself for, because she could certainly afford them. Then she pulled out Yemaya again and showed her to Cooley. "I told you about my mother. This reminds me of her."

Cooley took the card and studied it closely. "How does it do that?"

Grace explained Yemaya and then said, "Once, my mother was trying to cure me of a cold. I'd been home sick for three days, and my nose was so plugged, closing my mouth brought on a feeling of suffocation. My mother came up with this poultice that was supposed to dry up the mucus. God, I don't even know what all was in it. Mustard, for sure. Chili powder and garlic. Some dried leaves from the back yard, crumpled up and crushed. Pennies and nickels. And something that stunk so badly, I couldn't even put a word to it. It was one of those smells that you could taste, it was so strong. I took one whiff and slammed both hands over my mouth, which caused me to gag because I couldn't breathe, but I had my hands over my mouth, so the forced air went up and plowed through my nose instead. I blew out an incredible load of snot, all down my nightgown and on the blankets…oh, it was a mess." Grace laughed out loud, thinking of the sticky, stinking horror she became in just a matter of seconds. "My mother got me up and into the shower, and by the time I got out, I could breathe just fine. No more clogged nose. But the spell wasn't supposed to work that way." She touched her nose now, remembering the sudden freedom in being able to breathe. How wonderful it felt. "But it fixed the problem. So my mother took the credit and claimed the power."

Cooley studied the card a little longer, then gave it back to Grace. "Sometimes," she said, "things invented for one thing end up being useful in another. Sounds like your mother was an inventor."

"Maybe an accidental one." Grace gathered her things. She saw that Cooley was carrying only one clock. Grace nodded toward it. "You found something?"

Cooley held the clock by its base with one hand, and smoothed the fingers of the other over the clock's rounded top. It was like watching a mother smooth her child's hair. Grace thought of Yemaya, the heart soother. "It's a mantel clock of sorts. Not as big and heavy as the originals, but it has a lovely patina, and it seems like it still works." They started to move toward the front of the barn when Cooley stopped. "Grace?" she said. Cooley turned to Grace with a face so clear, so wide in wonder that it seemed like a young girl stood there. A young girl with a question. "Grace, tell me what it's like to love your mother."

Grace remembered Cooley's question yesterday, and the look of longing that went with it. "Cooley, were you an orphan?"

She shook her head. "No. Not really. I was removed from my home when I was sixteen years old. James, the original owner of the clock museum, raised me from that point on." And with that, Cooley's eyes were no longer wide and childish. They were sad.

Grace held the Tarot cards and the presents for her children and she fully considered Cooley's question. She suddenly wanted to give her the best possible answer. "It's warm, of course," she said. "And it's different from other things. The love for your father or your spouse. It feels like…like a circle, I think."

Cooley frowned. "A circle?" She looked over as Virgil joined them. Virgil was carrying several dolls; Grace counted at least six heads.

"It's like knowing that every bit of love you give to her, you get back. And then you give it to her. And she gives it back." Grace nodded. "A circle. A moving circle."

"What're you talking about?" Virgil asked.

"What it feels like to love your mother."

Virgil looked down at the dolls in his arms. "A circle makes sense. You just know that no matter what, she loves you. No matter what you do. No matter who you are." His arms tightened. "No matter who you become, even if it's not who she thought you would be."

Grace thought of Paul. Of all the things she expected him to be. Of all those things, she never expected him to be dead at the age of fifteen.

But she loved him anyway. Even though it seemed like everyone else wanted her to stop. To let go.

She would never let go. A mother would never let go.

Cooley turned away suddenly and moved toward the doors. Grace and

Virgil followed her. "Looks like you had some luck," Grace whispered.

"There's a few nice ones in here, yes. And some that aren't really much, at least according to collector's standards. But I couldn't just leave them here. Who knows what the next stop would be for them if I didn't bring them home."

Grace thought of Cathy, sitting safely on the bed in their hotel room. Virgil would bathe these dolls, dry them, then wrap them carefully for the trip. He wouldn't leave them behind, even though he likely wouldn't make a profit from them. He just couldn't leave them.

She just couldn't leave Paul. She just couldn't leave her mother.

Grace looked down at the box of cards in her hands. The circle wouldn't be broken, she was sure of it. Even if she broke the biggest rule her mother had.

She was learning how to play with dolls.

****

They said a quiet goodbye to Cooley in her driveway. They offered to take her to lunch at the Tick Tock Quick Stop Diner, but she refused, saying she had to open the museum for business. Grace watched as Cooley walked up the steps to the door. After removing the plastic clock sign that explained when she would be back, Cooley turned and waved, the new mantel clock still held firmly in her other arm. Grace waved back. She thought again about how her mother would have loved this place. She wished she could introduce her mother to Cooley.

They kept the rest of the day low key. Virgil napped after bathing and packing the new dolls. Grace used the hotel's hot tub and nearly fell asleep herself. They decided to just order pizza for dinner instead of going back out.

Grace didn't call home that night and no one called her. She received no texts that day. She wondered about this mutual silent decision, and she wondered if her family at home passed the phone and looked at it and at their cell phones as often as she looked at hers. She set hers aside, and they must have walked by as well. She stowed the book and the apatosaurus in the trunk of the big Chrysler and she brushed Cathy's hair. At bedtime, she pulled out a pair of doll-size pajamas she bought in St. Charles. She set them on the bed next to Cathy and looked at them.

Virgil, who was reading the local newspaper, folded it and looked over. "What are you doing, Grace?" he asked.

She shrugged. "I was thinking about putting Cathy in these pajamas. You know, dressing her for bedtime." She laughed.

"Well, why don't you?" He swung his legs off his own bed and sat on the edge.

"It seems sort of silly, doesn't it?" She picked Cathy up, stood her so that her eyes were open. "I mean, she doesn't really sleep. And in the morning, what do I do? Dress her again, like she's a real person?"

"Yes." Virgil picked up the pajamas and unbuttoned the teeny buttons on the shirt. "That's what you do with dolls, Grace. You play with them. You treat them just like they're real people."

"But they're not." Grace touched Cathy's hair, felt the synthetic threads, the hardness of the plastic skull beneath.

"No, they're not." Virgil reached over and tweaked Grace suddenly on the nose and she startled. He laughed. "They're always the same. They don't grow older. They don't do anything to hurt you. They're just always there." He tugged off Cathy's shoes and socks and set them on the bedside table. "It's like that circle you were talking about to Cooley. You give love to them, they give love to you. It never ends."

Grace fought the tears she knew were right there, right there where they always were. "They don't die."

"No, Grace. They don't die. Some people give them away. Some even throw them away." His mouth quirked. "But they never ever die."

Carefully, Grace undressed Cathy. She left her in her little silk panties and then she pulled on the striped pajama bottoms, the top with the teeny buttons. She struggled with pushing them through the holes, but she managed. There were only three. Then she pulled Cathy's string.

As if on cue, Cathy said, "I'm sleepy."

Pulling back the covers, Grace set Cathy's head on the second pillow, the one closest to the bedside table. Cathy's eyes closed and Grace quietly pretended she was asleep. Just like that. Just like the way her own babies would suddenly loll their heads in the crook of her elbow and they'd be out. Like night and day.

Just like Paul used to do.

Alive one minute. Gone the next. Grace quickly stood Cathy up again and her eyes popped right open. Then she lowered her. Asleep. Awake. Asleep again. Grace tucked the blanket to the doll's chin.

"They don't die," she whispered.

"Good job, Grace," Virgil said, and returned to his paper.

Grace sat alongside Cathy. She kept thinking about the candy corn and candy pumpkins she asked Nick to bring to Paul's grave. For Paul's first trick or treat, Grace dressed him like a ghost. When he was twelve, he trick-or-treated for the last time, dressed in a costume of his own creation. He paraded around the neighborhood as the planet Saturn. He took foam rubber and fashioned it into a ball around his body. Then using dental floss, he hung cardboard rings around his waist. He looked spectacular.

A month after Paul's death, Grace and Nick began the difficult process of sorting through his things. There were memories to consider. There were Mary and JJ to consider. Grace remembered kneeling on the floor in the boys' room and thinking there was her own self to consider. Paul's mother.

It seemed to Grace that night in the hotel room as she sat beside Cathy on the bed that her life was a lot like that odd sculpture she saw at the barn. Curves and smoothness, suddenly turned to rough edges and angles. She wished now that she bought it; maybe studying it would have given her some answers, some explanation as to how to go on. Beyond running away from home.

A lot of Paul's things were boxed and sent to Goodwill. Grace avoided Goodwill for months afterwards, not wanting to see her son's stuff in the racks and shelves. But when she and Nick found that costume, the Saturn costume, Grace sent Nick with it directly to the dump. Grace knew she just couldn't risk opening the door on Halloween night and seeing another child nestled in the rings of Saturn. She couldn't even stand the idea of that child being JJ, wearing his older brother's costume. Made by Paul's very own hands.

Grace held his hands at the bottom of the tree that day. They were cold. Paul's hands were never cold. She could still remember the press of his warm baby palms against her breasts as she nursed him, first the right side, then the left.

Paul loved ghosts and goblins too, but differently than Grace's mother did. Her mother's spiritual world was a mystical and very friendly place. She embraced the spirits, hugging close her antique store orphans, casting simple spells to bring good fortune. Paul was more traditional; he liked to scare himself. He liked ghoulish gory stories, tales from the crypt of hauntings and poltergeists. He and his grandmother just saw the afterlife differently. Grace's mother found peace in good, Grace's son found excitement in evil.

And yet they loved each other. When Paul was a baby, his favorite toy was the crystal ball Grace left behind on Mary's dresser, the one that was to predict the state of Grace's marriage. When Grace's mother came over, she would sit the baby on the floor, sit down herself, join their spread-wide feet together, and then roll the ball to Paul, who would crow and roll it back. Nick tried to offer them a rubber ball, but to no avail. They loved the spark of the crystal as it rolled between them.

Grace couldn't remember if she looked at the crystal ball on the day Paul died. She wondered now if it was black, if there was some warning and she missed it, just like she completely missed the chance to call out to Paul, to tell him not to climb the tree, to hide somewhere safe. After the funeral, Grace threw the crystal ball over and over against the tree that killed her son, but the ball refused to break. Grace left it there, at the base of the tree, but someone brought it back in and returned it to its spot in the curio cabinet. Grace didn't know who. She didn't care. The crystal ball was intact, and from the outside, Grace appeared to be too. But she wasn't. And she knew it.

Was she fragile now? Grace looked at Cathy, her eyes closed in her pretend sleep, and she nodded. She had to be fragile, to do such a thing. To throw a crystal ball. To abandon her family. Maybe even to play with a doll, to dress her in pajamas, pull a string to hear her voice, pretend that she slept in peace. To believe that she would never die.

Maybe even to think about candy corn and orange candy pumpkins. To ask that they be left in baggies at his grave. "He's not going to eat it," Nick said.

Paul especially loved that candy. The day after Halloween, when all the candy went on sale, Grace bought bags and bags of the corn and pumpkins to treat Paul to it year round. He got some in his Christmas stocking and in his Easter basket and usually in his lunch bag at least once a week.

Grace loved that special candy too, especially the pumpkins which were so nice and round and squashed so easily in her mouth. She and Paul used to laugh about the number of pumpkins they could eat.

"Mom ate twelve pumpkins today!" Paul used to announce at the dinner table.

"Me? What about you? You ate sixteen!" And they laughed.

Nick worried about the dentist.

That night in the hotel room, as they shared their pizza, Virgil and Grace talked about Halloween and candy pumpkins. She told him about Saturn and the crystal ball and the Easter baskets. But she didn't mention Paul's death. She couldn't. She didn't want to bring it into the room, though she knew it was there. It was in her skin, in her words, in the way her eyes looked when she combed her hair in the mirror. But she just couldn't talk about Paul yet.

Virgil smiled, shreds of cheese clinging to his teeth. "I know a place in Tennessee," he said. "A little candy factory. It makes the best candy corn in the whole world. I'll take you there. I planned on stopping there anyway, and now we have a whole new reason: so you can have the treat of your life." He winked at her. "There's another place there too, the purpose for my stop. I'm going to leave that as a surprise for you."

Grace put her pizza down and reached for her soda. She wanted to believe Virgil about the candy corn and pumpkins. She wanted to put a candy pumpkin on her tongue and moisten it, then sink her teeth in and feel the sweetness fill her mouth. She wanted not to choke, not to spit it out. Not to cry because it didn't taste sweet anymore. Paul was dead. It was no longer possible for that candy to be sweet. But she wanted so much to believe Virgil. She wanted to like surprises again.

"It's almost Halloween, you know," he said.

Grace nodded. "I know," she whispered. She could feel the cold coming. It crept right outside the door. She could feel it in the air and in her bones.

In his grave, she knew Paul felt it most of all.

CHAPTER SIX
Virgil

Backtracking down I-80 from Iowa to Indiana, Virgil decided to make the trip in one day, even though it was a long drive to catch up to where he wanted to be: Shipshewana, Indiana. The Shipshewana Auction and Flea Market was one of the few places Virgil knew of that operated on weekdays instead of weekends and had been since 1922. Virgil loved this flea market and swore that some of the vendors were the 1922 originals. They stretched out in old lawn chairs and fell into a slack-jawed sleep behind their booths. He often had to wake them up to make a deal. It should have been easy to walk away with their stock, but in Shipshewana, Indiana, respect and honesty were status quo and everyone watched out for everybody. Virgil knew if he saw someone walking off with a treasure, he'd holler, and if he didn't, the younger next-door vendors had their eyes wide open.

Besides the flea market itself, the Miscellaneous and Antique auction and the livestock auction were held every Wednesday too. Virgil loved the auctions, but he had to sacrifice that in order to insert the trip to the barn in What Cheer on Tuesday. All things considered, it was probably just fine, as he didn't think Grace would be able to handle auction hysteria. She still seemed so fragile.

With Wednesday being a travel day, ending in a steady night of sleep at the new hotel, both Virgil and Grace were ready to go early Thursday morning. At the flea market, noise and tables full of quality junk greeted them and Grace brightened immediately. Virgil offered to stay with her this time and he was surprised when she slid her hand into his. He'd always pictured strolling through the aisles and out-buildings with a partner; in the last years, that partner in his dreams was Brad. Brad wasn't really one for flea markets though; he essentially lived in a free flea market. But now, Virgil was with Grace and her hand was warm in his. When he squeezed, she squeezed back.

Even with the world lurching both reluctantly and exuberantly toward acceptance, Virgil knew he would never have this experience with Brad. The two of them would never feel comfortable walking hand in hand out in the real world. The past was far too ingrained. Virgil saw rainbows everywhere; but he still avoided stepping directly into the rays. It was one thing to wear a t-shirt. It was another to be the printed-on logo. Virgil just didn't like the attention. He didn't want his sexuality to be a public triumph, something for other people to applaud.

But with Grace, Virgil relaxed and looked around. This was nice. No one stared. No one nodded in approval and no one pointed in accusation.

They walked in the stop and start fashion that was flea market shopping and the sun was warm and Grace was happy by his side. They didn't talk much; they mostly just picked things up, showed them to each other, and set them down again. Grace looked at a few clocks and a few pieces of jewelry; she bought five more outfits for Cathy. Virgil hoped he would be treated to a fashion show that night, starring Grace's doll. To his surprise, which was beginning to not feel like a surprise at all, he looked forward to it.

When they spotted a box of dolls, Grace fell to her knees in front of it. She dug through, scooping up the dolls and holding them in her lap like a litter of kittens, trying to touch and hug each one. There was nothing of value in the box that Virgil could see. They were mostly just plastic- and soft-bodied dolls, less than ten years old; not of an age yet to be considered collectible.

But Grace looked up at him. "Virgil," she said. "Buy these!" He shook his head and started to walk away, but Grace didn't follow. "Okay," he heard her say. "I'll buy them myself. How much are they?"

Virgil looked back at the grinning vendor. The man clearly knew an easy touch when he saw it. "Thirty-five bucks," he said.

Grace was already reaching into her purse when Virgil stepped back. "Fifteen," he said.

The man nodded toward Grace. "The lady's already accepted thirty-five, buddy," he said.

And that was that. There was nothing Virgil could do. Grace reached for her money, the universal sign of acceptance in a bargain. He watched the bills change hands and then Grace walked away with the box of dolls. They started moving down the dirt aisles again.

"I'm sorry, Virgil," she said. "I know it probably wasn't a really good deal, but that's okay. I don't mind."

Virgil shook his head. "You got taken, Grace. Those're just regular dolls.

They aren't worth what you paid for them."

She stopped dead. "Just regular dolls? How can you say that? Of all people, how can you say that?"

Virgil took her arm and they moved on. "It's just that you paid too much, Grace. It's okay that you wanted them. But you overpaid. You should have tried to talk him down." Her elbow was stiff and Virgil knew she was angry.

She stopped again. "How are these dolls any different than the ones you bought in the barn in Iowa? You said you couldn't leave them behind, even though they weren't worth much."

Virgil started to sift through the box, trying to see if there was anything redeeming in there, but she pulled them away. He sighed. "Those dolls, the ones in Iowa, they were reasonably priced, Grace. They were priced for what they were. If they'd been overpriced, I would have walked away. The rule there was no haggling, remember? But because they were a bargain and not the vendor's steal, I bought them. You got taken, Grace. You shouldn't have paid more than fifteen."

Virgil knew that Grace loved every doll indiscriminately. Every doll was one she wasn't allowed to play with when she was a child, but could play with now. That was their value. Virgil loved dolls too; he loved the dolls in his shop, he loved the special ones he kept in his home. But when he was out on the hunt, he looked at the dolls first, figured their worth, then decided whether to buy or abandon. Looking at Grace now, her arms clenched around the box, Virgil wondered what it would be like to love like that, to not question value at all, but just plunge in and devote his heart.

Just as he had in the beginning. Before he knew about worth at all. Virgil caught his breath.

Grace stepped back. "I wasn't buying them to make money. I just wanted to save them. I would have paid more." But she held the box away from her body while she looked down at the dolls. A frown creased the skin between her eyebrows.

Virgil took her arm again and she didn't fight. "It's okay, Grace, I'll take them. When we get back home, I'll see if I can sell them for you."

She relaxed. "I just want them to have good homes, Virgil," she said.

"Okay." He nodded. "I understand." He thought of those first five dolls he purchased years ago at the rummage sale. He bought them quickly, out of love and out of a desire to give them a home. It wasn't until the lady brought out that collectibles catalogue that Virgil discovered the financial value of dolls, the pleasure of buying for a buck and selling for a bundle.

Grace was in those rummage sales days now. And maybe it was time for Virgil to go back too. Maybe he needed to just sweep dolls up again, without adding and figuring, without going through his client list in his head. Without equating his passion with the payment of his mortgage, his grocery bill, a new jacket, a night out.

Just letting it be his passion.

Virgil still had those first five dolls. But they were in a box, in the back of his bedroom closet. When he returned to Waukesha, he vowed he would take them out and give them their own places in his home.

Virgil bought himself a soda and Grace an iced latte and they settled down at a picnic bench for a break. Grace drank slowly, but her eyes never stopped moving. She watched everyone walking by and her expression changed by the second. She was like a clearwater pond, every emotion rippling the clear surface.

Virgil was thirsty and drained his soda almost in one gulp. While waiting for Grace to finish, he idly dug through her box of dolls. At the bottom, his fingers touched a sharp corner of cardboard and he pulled out the smaller box. When he saw the bright yellow, the swirly red letters, when he saw the doll inside, the blond hair, that broad-mouthed sneer, he knew immediately who it was.

Gay Bob.

"Oh my God, Grace," he said and dropped the box. "Oh my God," he said again. "Grace, do you know who this is?"

She picked up the yellow box. "Gay Bob," she read out loud. And then she looked at Virgil, her cheeks flaming red.

Virgil covered his face with his hands. He thought how just a short time ago, he was walking through the flea market hand in hand with Grace, with a woman, and thinking how he would never be able to do this with Brad. Never. And now, here was Gay Bob. Here was the reason.

Gay Bob was a fashion doll who appeared on the market in the late seventies. He was anatomically correct and came complete with a purse and a change of clothes for cross-dressing. His box was designed as a closet and across the front, in screaming red letters, was the demand, "Come Out of the Closet with Gay Bob!"

At first, the gay community cheered Gay Bob's arrival. He was lauded as the first step in a path toward equality and acceptance where gay dolls could share shelf space with straight toys in toy stores. Where the whole world, even the world of children, could include homosexuality in their daily lives without stigma. It would just be the norm, the way things were, the way they were meant to be. The vision included little girls playing with Gay Bob, setting him in the backseat of Barbie's pink convertible while Real Hair Ken drove Malibu Barbie home from the ball to the Barbie townhouse.

The vision was shattered. Snapped in two and three and more by the very world it wanted to be a part of, to normalize.

Virgil hated Gay Bob. He hated that the doll could be bent into whatever effeminate pose howling college boys at bars could think of. He hated that the doll could be dressed up in women's silk and lace underclothes or forced to wear a skirt and walk with a swish. He hated that giggling schoolchildren could lay him in a big pink canopy bed next to Ken or worse, next to Teen Skipper's friend Todd. He hated the confusion, the blurring of public lines, between homosexuality and transgenders and cross-dressers and pedophilia. Virgil hated the doll, he hated his closet, he hated his clothes, and he hated that "Gay Bob's Friend Steve" was supposed to be released to the public within a year.

It never happened. Gay Bob was banned from shelves within months. Virgil went home during that time, determined that his father would understand that Gay Bob and he were not one and the same, that his dad would see Virgil for who he really was. Virgil tried several times to tell his parents the truth, about who and what he was. Each time, he failed. Virgil choked. But with Gay Bob on the market, blond and lacy and leering, Virgil wanted his father to know the truth. Whatever his father thought, whatever excuses he came up with for Virgil's love of Josephine in his childhood, and his lack of bringing a girl, the right girl, that girl, home to meet his parents now that he was in his mid-twenties, his prolonged bachelorhood and dry dating season, dry only in heterosexuality, not hidden homosexuality, Virgil wanted him to know the truth. He wanted his father to truly know the boy he took to the toy store that day years before and forced him to walk down the aisle of plastic soldiers and cowboys and Indians.

It didn't take long. Virgil never even had a chance. He sat down with his father after supper and he said, "Dad, I need to talk to you."

Virgil's father looked over his newspaper. Front page first, just like always. The other sections draped and waiting over his knees. His father could take hours to read the paper.

Virgil cleared his throat. He needed his voice to be strong. "Dad," he said. "I think you already know this, but I'm telling you anyway. I'm gay."

The paper snapped back up. His father's voice, low and gravelly, rolled from behind it and said in a black headline, "Get out." And as a sidebar, "Don't come back."

"Dad," Virgil said, standing up and trying to see his father's face over the newspaper. "Please."

"Get out," he said. He didn't yell. It was a statement of fact. His truth. His truth stared Virgil's truth full in the face and in the end, Virgil backed down.

So Virgil left, and the only time he saw his father since then was at his mother's funeral. They didn't speak. As he drove back to his apartment that night, Virgil knew that this was all Gay Bob's fault. He knew that the doll somehow got into his father's brain, the advertisements and editorials slitting his eyes and his memories. When Virgil said that word, when he said gay and attached himself to it, he morphed from a young boy who wanted to play with baby dolls, play with them not because he was gay, but because it was fun and he enjoyed being paternal, to a doll himself, a blond bimbo doll in a yellow box shaped like a closet. He carried a purse and wore silk panties and a bra under his jeans and flannel shirt. Gay Bob was his father's truth. And now it was his son as well.

Even though playing with dolls had absolutely nothing to do with Virgil's sexuality. Even though Gay Bob had nothing to do with Virgil at all. Gay Bob wasn't gay. He was a gross representation of a falsehood. Not the truth. Not the truth at all.

But it didn't matter. Virgil's father shoved his son into that yellow closet, encased it in cellophane, and threw it out the door. And Virgil let him.

"Grace," Virgil said now through his fingers, still plastered to his face. "Throw that fucking doll away. Take him out of his box and get rid of him." Virgil knew Gay Bob was worth a small fortune on the market, but he didn't want anyone to have him. He didn't want to make money off this doll, and he didn't want anyone else to either. He sat up. "Wait," he said. "First pull his arms off, take off his head, rip his box into pieces. Kill him."

Grace looked from the box to Virgil to the box again. "Virgil," she said. "This is a doll. Just a doll, remember? You're not like him. You're not like this at all. Not like any part of him."

Not like any part. Not like him. And it wasn't her responsibility to kill Gay Bob. It was Virgil's. "I'm not, Grace," he said. "You're so right. I'm not like that. That's the truth." He picked up the box and shook it. "But this isn't a doll. It's an abomination." Virgil tore the box open and yanked the doll free of the plastic bands that held him upright on the cardboard.

And then he decapitated Gay Bob. He ripped his clothes and tore the cheap vinyl purse. He snapped off the smooth tan legs and arms and bent them into impossible angles so the doll could never be put together again. Then he ran to a booth and bought a cheap lighter and he put the shredded box on the ground and he set it on fire. His heart rose as he watched the yellow and purple cardboard sparkle and go up in flames and then he stomped it into ashes on the ground. People watched, but he didn't care. He reveled in the fact that pieces of Gay Bob were scattered over eight different garbage cans and pounded into ash on the ground. Many pieces. Damaged pieces. Pieces that could never reform and do their own damage again.

Panting, smiling, Virgil turned to Grace. She sat at the picnic table, her hands over her mouth. Tears spilled over her fingers. A strange woman was standing behind her, gently patting her shoulder, but Grace didn't seem to notice. The woman, and the crowd, must have thought Virgil was an enraged husband, protesting and breaking a buy he thought his wife should not have made. Wasting money. Gay Bob was a waste of money.

Virgil realized he just killed a doll in front of possibly the only person in the world who loved dolls more than he did. Who loved dolls indiscriminately. No matter who they were or what they stood for.

Virgil sat down across from Grace and tucked her hands into his. The strange woman frowned at him and turned away. The crowd that gathered to watch wandered off too. "Grace," Virgil said under the noise of the flea market, the noise that suddenly seemed capable of shattering. "Grace, I'm so sorry."

Her tears continued. "No," she said, and her voice was even softer, but Virgil was surprised to not hear any fragility. None at all. "*I'm* sorry. I'm sorry there was a doll like that. There never ever should have been a doll like that."

That was the truth too. Grace saw it. Virgil knew it. Intimately.

"Grace," he said. "Grace, I love you."

She smiled, took her hands back, and wiped her eyes. "And I love you too, Virgil." And then she crossed to the other side of the picnic table and she hugged him. She hugged him like a mother, pressing his face against her breasts, and she swayed.

Virgil didn't care that he found Madame Alexander's precious Dionne Quintuplets. He didn't care that he was sitting in the middle of a flea market in Shipshewana, Indiana, declaring his affection for a woman he knew for only a few days and being hugged by her as his tears soaked her shirt. He didn't care that he was on his way to see the man he loved, his southern man, a gay man, who lived in the middle of a garbage dump in Macon, Georgia, and he had to answer to an ultimatum about committing to their lives together in this world where rainbows sparkled on t-shirts and bumper stickers and on the evening news. Rainbows that sprinkled colors over his life like a circus sideshow that people could cheer and applaud and whistle when all he wanted was to be left alone with the man he loved.

All that mattered right then was that Gay Bob was dead, Virgil killed him, and for the moment, he was the happiest man alive.

****

That night in the hotel room, Virgil tried to find out more about Grace. She moved from the bathroom to the dresser, bathing her cache of dolls. She wanted to try doing it herself, following Virgil's instructions. Because the dolls weren't that old, they also weren't that dirty, so it wasn't a difficult job. He stretched out on his bed, Cathy on Grace's, the Quints lined up beside her, and he watched Grace work. Her voice was a murmur in the bathroom and he knew that she talked to the dolls. She started out stiff and unsure, but then her voice softened and became what he remembered of his own mother, bending over him in the bathtub. Warm. Gentle. Loving.

Grace was lovely in that way women are when they aren't conscious of themselves. Her movements between the dresser and the bathroom were fluid. Her blonde hair, windswept from the flea market, moved with her, swaying gently just above her shoulders. On one of her trips, Grace carried a handful of soapsuds and she blew them at Virgil. The smile on her face and her genuine laugh gave Virgil the real definition of grace; she was graceful all over, and her mother must have noticed it from the beginning. Even if she was clumsy. There was more to grace than fluidity.

"So how long have you been married?" Virgil asked. Grace set up three dolls on the dresser, facing the mirror, and she armed herself with the hairdryer. The other dolls, hairless, she set out next to the box on the bed.

"Sixteen years," she called over the roar.

A long time, Virgil thought. A long time to run away from. "That's quite a while," he said out loud. "How'd you meet?"

Grace concentrated on the doll before her. She held the brush in her right hand, the dryer in her left. The doll, small, tipped over easily and Grace had to keep setting aside the brush to sit her back up again. "We met at a park. I brought my oldest, Mary. She's from my first marriage, and she was just a baby. My first husband had been gone for about six months by then. He left right after she was born. Well, I had Mary in the infant swing on the playground and I was pushing her, you know, trying to be gentle. Nick was over in the grass, throwing boomerangs."

"Boomerangs?"

Grace smiled and moved on to the next doll. She was bigger and easier to handle. "Yes, isn't that weird? He collects them. Anyway, it was our first time at the park, Mary and me. It felt like it had been a long winter, what with having a baby and my husband leaving and all. I gave her a push, I thought it was gentle, but the swing flipped and she fell out. Oh my god. I freaked out." Her hands fell to her sides and Virgil knew she was seeing it all again. "Nick ran over. He just dropped his boomerangs and ran over. I held on to Mary and rocked her while she cried, and he held on to me."

Virgil got up and checked the box the dolls came in. It was clean and so he got out the bubble wrap. "He just held you? A stranger?"

She nodded. "And it was perfect. Honestly. It was just what I needed. When Mary calmed down and it was clear she was all right, he packed up his boomerangs and he took us out to lunch. Well, me. Mary wasn't really eating anything yet." She started on the third doll, the last with hair. "We got married six months later. He held Mary in his arms throughout the entire ceremony."

Virgil took the dolls without hair and wrapped them, then placed them neatly in the box. He knew Grace would require air holes, so he got his pocket knife out and ready. "Does Nick still have boomerangs?"

Grace brought over the three dolls with hair. Then she sat on the bed and pulled Cathy onto her lap. "I think so. I think they're in the attic."

That seemed odd to Virgil, boomerangs in an attic when they were so obviously important to Nick. But there was something on Grace's face that kept him from asking.

"What does Nick look like?" Virgil cut the air holes, then closed the box and set it on the dresser. He pulled back the covers on his bed. Grace did the same with hers. It was getting late.

She scooped up the Quints. Looking around, she found a spare box. "Can I use this?" She blushed. "I want to make a bed for the Quints. Is that all right?"

Virgil smiled at her.

Grace tucked a towel into the box, then lined up the Quints, covering them with another towel. "Nick is…well, he's good-looking, I guess. He has light brown hair and brown eyes. He's not real tall and he's not heavy. He's…average. Just average, I guess." She put the box on the dresser, shoved it all the way back to the mirror, Virgil assumed for the babies' safety. She was getting better at playing.

He looked at her. "Grace. A man who gets married while cradling his stepdaughter is average?"

Grace's eyes misted over and she turned away. Virgil wondered if this was the reason for her trip then, this sudden average rating of her husband. At what point in a marriage, Virgil wondered, does a Prince Charming become Prince EveryDay? He thought of Brad, his hair shining in the early morning sun, his eyes just open and smiling as he lay on the pillow next to Virgil's. He felt again the way Brad's hand stroked his cheek, the way he leaned over and gently kissed his lips, saying, "Good morning, sweetheart. Know what I want for breakfast?" And breakfast always ended up being a warm slow wake-up lovemaking, his body over Virgil's, his breath whispering against Virgil's neck, his ear, his chest.

When would that become average? Could that become average?

"Grace," Virgil said softly. He crossed the room and put his hand on her shoulder. "Tell me what happened. Tell me what came between you and Nick."

She shook her head. "It didn't happen between us, Virgil." Her voice weakened, lost volume until it was just above a whisper. "It happened to us. And I just can't talk about it. Not yet."

Virgil nodded and felt a lump grow in his throat. He needed to know what happened, how boomerangs and a wedding after only six months and a cuddled baby in a stepfather's arms could turn into a stumbling run across country with a talking doll and a gay man. He needed to know if he would ever turn tail and do the same thing. If perfection could turn to imperfection so fast, all the years previous convulsed into dust.

But Grace's tears held Virgil back. He couldn't ask her now. "It'll be all right, Grace," he said.

She turned to Virgil then and leaned against him. "Sometimes I think it will never be okay again, Virgil," she said into his chest. He wrapped his arms around her. He found himself swaying, rocking her, just like she rocked him that afternoon at the flea market, the remains of Gay Bob all around. Just the way Nick must have rocked her by the swingset in the park, the way she rocked the tumbled-out Mary. Virgil hummed under his breath, almost crooning a tune it was impossible to name. When Grace climbed into bed a short while later, he kissed her softly on the forehead and then ever so briefly on her mouth. Her lips were warm and slightly parted. He cupped her face in his hands. "Goodnight, Grace," he said. His voice trembled.

He wanted to make her feel better. And in his head, there was only one way for a man to make a woman feel better. And he wasn't supposed to feel capable of that.

Her eyes closed, as gently as any doll's. "Goodnight, Virgil." Cathy was tucked in by her side. She was in her pajamas.

When Grace slept, Virgil went to bed himself, but he lay on his side and watched her. He remembered growing erect for her on that first night. The desire remained, on his mouth still warm from her kiss. But there was more there now too. While he wanted to climb in bed with her and join with her, to comfort her, to experience her, to make her feel safe, he knew that sex just wouldn't be an adequate expression of what he felt. Making love to Grace would be out of kilter, it would be like saying a speech with all the wrong words. Standing in front of an English-speaking crowd and talking to them in French when he really wanted to speak in Spanish.

But then why the arousal? There'd been no arousal for a woman in such a long time.

Virgil told himself it was because Grace was a beautiful woman, a warm body lying a few feet away, and he hadn't had sex in six months. His body was on overdrive. Of course he was attracted to Grace. It didn't mean that he wasn't in love with Brad. It didn't mean that he wasn't gay. It didn't even mean that he was bisexual.

Virgil lay there for awhile. He thought about the two of them, about Grace and about Brad. Thinking about Grace was like covering himself with a quilt. It was warm and soft.

But Virgil burned for Brad. He burned.

Getting quietly out of bed, Virgil grabbed his cell phone and robe and stepped into the hall. Making sure the door closed and locked behind him, Virgil padded barefoot downstairs, nodded at the young man behind the desk, and then went outside. The concrete was cool on his feet. It wasn't freezing in Indiana in October. But it wasn't the heat of summer either.

Settling on a bench just outside the doors, Virgil called Brad. It was two in the morning. If Brad didn't answer, it would be okay. Virgil could hear his voice anyway, through that miracle called voicemail.

But Brad answered. "Sweetheart?" he said, his voice thick with sleep and southern surprise. "What's the matter? Are you okay?"

"I'm fine," Virgil said. "I just wanted to talk to you. Needed to hear you, I guess."

Brad yawned, the sound hollow through the phone. "I'm right here. Don't know how good I'll sound, I was asleep, but I'm here. What's up, darlin' man?"

"I just…" Virgil wondered how he could say what he wanted to say without bringing Grace into it. It didn't feel like the time to tell Brad that Virgil wasn't traveling alone this year. "I just wanted to tell you I love you. And I can't wait to see you."

There was the low rumble of a laugh. "And I love you too. You know that. I know you won't be here for a bit yet, but every day, I keep my eyes peeled for that big ass car."

Virgil smiled. Brad was forever after him to get a new car, a smaller model, something more fuel-efficient and easy on the environment. But Virgil loved the Chrysler. "Brad…I know you want this to be the last visit. That you want the visits to stop and we move in together permanently."

Brad's voice became more alert. Virgil pictured him sitting up in bed, leaning against the headboard. Maybe he put his spare hand on Virgil's pillow. Virgil's. No one else's. "You know I want that more than anything in the world."

"Well, but can you see us together in…" Virgil thought back to what Grace told him, "sixteen years? Twenty? Do you really see us together forever?"

There was no hesitation, no pause. "I do. I wouldn't ask you to move in here otherwise. I've never asked anyone else. Never."

Virgil rested his elbow on his knee. That was new. He knew that Brad was promiscuous, at least in the past. When he left Brad after that first encounter in the flea market, Brad was open about his other relationships, and his intention to stay available. As they grew serious about each other, Brad still insisted on his availability, because of Virgil's absence. But Virgil wasn't so sure that was still the case. He didn't ask, because Brad might tell him something he didn't want to know. But Brad didn't offer the information anymore either. "Never?"

"I never felt about anyone the way I do about you. I never wanted to be with someone the way I want to be with you. Christ, Virgil, don't you feel that?"

Virgil nodded. "I do." But he thought about Grace. Did Grace feel that way about Nick when she walked up the aisle at her wedding, looked at the man who was to be her husband, looked at her daughter in his arms?

But here she was now. Sleeping in the bed next to Virgil's. She didn't even call her family for the last couple nights.

"I just…it's hard to know what the future will bring. I know you don't want to give up the junkyard and your home to move in with me."

Brad laughed again. "Well, your doll shop is more movable than my junkyard. I've built everything here. Everything has my touch."

That was true. The dolls in The Nursery were chosen and touched by Virgil. But he didn't build the house. He bought it.

But it was home.

And so was Brad. In Georgia.

Virgil closed his eyes. "Brad, would we be able to continue as we are, with the visits, if I decide not to move in? Not to move to Georgia?"

There was a breath and a silence. Virgil opened his eyes, looked into the dark that was an Indiana fall middle-of-the-night, so much like the middles of nights everywhere else, except this one was now thick with an answer Virgil knew he didn't want to hear.

"No, Virgil," Brad said finally. "No, sweetheart. I told you this is the last visit and I mean it. I can't keep going like this. It just gets empty here, in between. Virgil, I said I love you like I've loved no one else. I said I've never wanted to live with anyone else. But…" his voice broke. "I've never known loneliness like this before either. Because I never knew what it was like to miss *you*."

Virgil's voice completely disappeared. He had to wait a while in that new silence, the silence that was now thick with that answer, but also with repeated ultimatum and with an incredible love. Then he whispered, "I understand that. I do. And I'll keep thinking about it, Brad."

"You think about this," Brad said. "I love you, Virgil. And I want to wake up every morning with you. I want to make love with you every morning that the passion hits, and I know it will hit a lot. I want to be out at work and look at the house and see you on the porch. I want you to wave me in to lunch, and I want lunch to start with a kiss that's an invitation and end with a kiss that's a promise. I just…I just want you here. I need you."

"I need you too. God, I love you." But Virgil thought about Grace again. About Grace and Nick. And about Grace and himself, the desire that was gentler, quieter, for Grace than it was for Brad, but was there nonetheless. "I love you, Brad," he said again. "I'm going back to sleep. Goodnight. I'll let you know when I'm close."

"Oh, I'll feel it when you're close, sweetheart. I'll feel it when the heat rises in the air. Goodnight." The phone went dead.

Virgil retraced his steps back to the room. Grace was still sleeping and it didn't look like her blankets were disturbed at all. And then Virgil couldn't help himself; he checked on the Quints and Chatty Cathy too.

This new playground, this new layer of pretend, new for Grace, well, it was affecting him too. He laughed at himself.

Everyone was just fine. Virgil slid into bed. He hoped for sleep.

CHAPTER SEVEN
Grace

A week into the trip, Grace's purse full of money was still holding out well and that made her feel happy and safe. She wondered what her mother thought she would be doing that would require so much money. But then, her mother likely didn't picture Grace going on a cross-country trip with a gay man who collected dolls. Though Virgil was no odder than some of her mother's spells. Maybe Virgil was a spell too.

When Grace married Nick, her second marriage, she thought about her parents a lot. Her mother and father were such odd ducks, such an odd match. They made it work. Grace didn't know how, but they did.

Yet her mother left her this money, should she "ever need to be away." Grace wondered if her mother ever needed to be away, and then she wondered if her mother thought of Grace and Nick as odd ducks, odder than herself and Grace's father, and if she thought Grace might end up all alone again.

But Grace and Nick themselves didn't bring trouble to the marriage. Grace wasn't even sure if there was trouble in the marriage. Though she did walk out on it, she supposed. If their marriage was in trouble, it could be because of that. And Grace walked out because of Paul. Because he died.

Because Mary told him to climb the tree.

Could a child's death bring death to a marriage too? Grace didn't recognize the signs of a child about to die, a child climbing a tree he shouldn't while his mother watched from the kitchen window. While the mother watched and did nothing. Maybe she was missing the signs now too.

But Grace needed to be away.

Her mother's gift, Grace decided, was being used in a way she would have approved of; to finance Grace's escape, buy a few special things, then bring her home again.

Grace never doubted that she would go back home.

When she and Virgil left Shipshewana, they started working their way in a winding path toward the candy corn factory Virgil knew about in Tennessee. They stopped for lunch outside of Indianapolis at a small diner on the side of the road. The place was almost empty and they chose a booth in the sunshine.

"Look at that," Virgil said, nodding toward the back of the restaurant.

There was a booth in a corner with a heavy curtain pulled around it, held by what looked to be a shower curtain rod stuck between flanking high wooden poles. One side of the rod slipped and the curtain was crooked. The gap at the higher side didn't expose anything but the bright red vinyl of the seat and a snippet of the wallpaper, crowded with aged brown teapots. A thin line of smoke drifted toward the ceiling.

"I guess someone wants privacy," Virgil said.

"Maybe it's their smoking section." Grace leaned forward, trying to see who puffed behind the heavy curtain. "Do they even allow those in restaurants anymore?"

Virgil shook his head. "They're not supposed to. But that could be the reason for the curtain. A secret smoking hideaway."

The waitress, bringing the menus, must have noticed their stares. She said, "That's where our fortuneteller works."

"Fortuneteller?" Grace opened her menu and looked over at Virgil. He cocked his eyebrows.

"She started out as a dishwasher, then became a waitress. She started reading people's tea leaves and she read their palms when they paid their bills. Then she switched to predicting their fortunes from what they ordered and what they left on their plates. Customers came back and requested her, saying her forecasts came true. She's real good." The waitress flipped open her pad. "If you want, I'll tell her your order. Then I'll just bring her your plates when you're through."

Virgil shook his head. "I don't want my fortune read," he said. "I like surprises." He scanned the menu. "I'd like a roast beef sandwich, please, heavy on the gravy, and French fries and a salad."

"Dressing?" the waitress asked.

"Surprise me."

The waitress laughed, then turned to Grace.

With her future resting on it, the lunchtime decision suddenly felt very serious. Grace kept looking at the choices and wondering what they could mean. Burger? Sandwich? Salad? Which would bring good luck? And what about the soup of the day?

The waitress tapped the menu with her pencil. "Best thing to do is just order what you're hungry for. Go with your gut."

"BLT," Grace blurted. "With extra bacon. French fries. And a chocolate shake, extra thick." She watched as the waitress took the order to the kitchen, hanging the slip from a clothespin on a roller. Then she went to the curtained booth and stuck her head in the gaping side. When she left, Grace saw movement and a hand pulled the curtain away, just a few inches. A young woman's face looked out, then she snapped the curtain back.

Grace turned back to Virgil when their drinks arrived. The shake was topped with a generous helping of whipped cream and Grace carefully carved it out with her spoon and popped it in her mouth. She always liked her cream separate; her father always stirred his in. Grace used to wonder how he could taste it that way. He said it was richer blended; she thought it was richer to have two separate treats. "Why don't you want your future read, Virgil?" she asked after swallowing.

He took a sip of his soda. "I don't want to know my future," he said, "not until it happens. If there's something bad, I'd rather not be warned. Just let it happen and I'll deal with it then." He stirred his straw, making the ice tinkle against the side of the glass. "When I was thirteen, I went to the county fair. There was a fortuneteller there, a palm reader."

Grace's shake was too thick for the straw so she spooned it into her mouth. That was just the way she liked it. It made it last longer.

"I was worried by then, worried that I might not be normal, which at that time, to me, meant straight. That's what normal meant to most of the world, really. I was afraid that the things I felt weren't right. So when I went to the palmist, I asked if there was going to be a woman in my life. She touched a line on my hand and said no."

The shake was cool, sliding down Grace's throat. She loved the chocolate. She could smell bacon frying. Sitting there, she wondered what it must have been like to be thirteen years old and to hear the truth. Especially a truth you didn't want to hear at all.

"I was so scared, I didn't know what to say next," Virgil said. "I remember having trouble breathing. She said there would be no woman and I knew that already, but I didn't want to be alone. Not for my whole life! I felt that there was another way, but that way seemed so horrible, so unthinkable. My hand was soaked, I could feel the sweat rolling through my fingers, but her skin was dry. She kept pressing her fingernail, sharp, against that single line. I cried out, 'Will

I be lonely? All my life?'"

Grace looked at Virgil. His skin seemed suddenly tightly drawn against his face and his hand clenched around his glass. Out of the corner of her eye, she saw the waitress stacking their food on a tray. Grace stopped eating her shake so she would have some left with the meal.

Virgil shook his hand free of his glass. "The palmist looked at me and said very quietly, 'No. There will be company for you.' And she dropped my hand. I don't know if she dropped it because she was disgusted, or because she was done. I took off, running from her tent, from the fair. I cried for hours."

The waitress set their food on the table. Virgil admired his plate, loaded to the rim with a sandwich swimming in gravy. "I don't want to know my future," he said when the waitress left. "When I die, I want my eyes wide open. I want to see it coming. And I want to feel it hit."

Grace shuddered. She'd seen death coming, she saw it hit, she held death in her lap and she closed her son's eyes. She didn't want to talk about that. "My mother liked to read fortunes," she said, swiveling away from death. "She read the neighbors' all up and down the block. She used tea leaves, palms, the bumps on people's heads. She read feet too, the lines on the soles. And she used Tarot cards, though she never read the instructions. That's why I bought those cards in Iowa. They reminded me of her." Grace pulled three slices of bacon from her sandwich and chewed on them, one at a time. "Sometimes even strangers came. She always took them in. And she never charged anybody. Sometimes we found offerings in our mailbox or on our porch. My mother always donated those somewhere, sometimes to the Humane Society, sometimes to the women's shelter, sometimes to a totally new and different place. She said she had a gift and in order to truly appreciate it, she had to give it away. She couldn't fall to the temptation of making money." The French fries needed salt. Grace showered them.

"I know what she meant," Virgil said. "Sometimes I feel guilty, selling my dolls. Sometimes I'd like to give them away to special people. Like to you." He nodded out the window toward the car, where Cathy waited in the back seat and the Quints slept in their makeshift bed in the trunk. "I wanted to give Cathy to you. But I also like to make ends meet."

Grace looked too and wondered if she remembered to crack the windows. Then she reminded herself that the dolls couldn't breathe. "I understand. And I'm glad you sold me Cathy. Look where it's gotten me." They both looked around the diner. The curtain at the fortuneteller's booth fell into place again.

"Okay, maybe it hasn't gotten me much. But it has gotten me far. I'm really enjoying our trip, Virgil." Grace reached over and patted his hand. "My mother read everyone's fortune," she continued. "She even read her own. I often saw her looking at her palm, touching her head, reading her own tea leaves. Once I saw her sitting cross-legged on the couch, examining the bottoms of her feet. But she never told me what she saw. When I asked, she just said that it was her fortune, not mine."

Grace ate her sandwich until the rest of the bacon disappeared. Then the bread became soggy, loaded with mayo and tomato drippings, so she left the remains on her plate. She finished all but three of her fries, which were cooked a bit more than she liked. After scraping the ice cream from the sides of the shake glass, she tilted it up to dribble the last drops into her throat.

Virgil reached for the fries, but the waitress stormed their booth. "Don't touch," she said sharply. Virgil sat back so quickly, the sound of his shirt hitting the vinyl was like a slap. "The fortuneteller must see it as the client leaves it. Are you ready?"

Grace nodded. The waitress carefully picked up her plate and shake glass and led Grace to the booth. The curtain was pushed aside, the things deposited, and Grace sat down. The rings clattered as the curtain was pulled shut, sending a shiver down her back.

The fortuneteller was barely an adult, not much more than eighteen years old. Her hair hung greasily to her shoulders and into her eyes. These weren't rainbow tresses; this wasn't Yemaya, and Grace felt the sting of disappointment. The girl's gaze settled on what was left of the meal and her lips pursed. She picked up the scraped-clean shake glass. "You have lost…" she said slowly. "You have lost a sweetness in your life. A sweetness is empty now."

Grace swallowed.

"A chocolate shake with whipped cream," the girl murmured. "Extra thick." Grace had to lean forward to hear her. "Whipped cream and chocolate, tossed whipped cream…tousled. A tousled head. Dark hair." Her head snapped up. "A boy."

Grace felt compelled to answer, to confirm. "My son," she said. She teared up.

The fortuneteller nodded. "He's dead," she said slowly. She looked at Grace, her pale eyes filling with tears too. "He's all right, he is at rest. But he misses you."

Grace choked. "I miss him too," she whispered. "Tell him I miss him."

The girl nodded again. Then she looked toward the plate. With a fork, she poked at a half-eaten tomato, smeared with mayonnaise. She lifted it and stared. "Your mother…" she muttered.

With that, Grace startled so hard, the plates rattled and the fortuneteller dropped the fork. Grace heard the creak as Virgil swiftly rose from his seat. "It's okay," she called to him.

The fortuneteller picked up the tomato again. "Your mother is concerned. Concerned about you." She waved the tomato. "Red is the color of anger, but it is tempered with the mayo which is white. She is concerned about you, worried about your safety."

"Can you hear my mother?" Grace asked. "Can you see her?"

"I hear her." She smiled. "I think she's nice." Then she set the tomato down and looked again at the plate. "You didn't finish your meal. You left good food on your plate. You left something behind?"

Grace nodded.

The girl picked up the three French fries. One was large and she pulled it from the others. "A man," she said.

"My husband."

"And two little ones. Children." The fortuneteller sat back. "You have to finish what you set out to do," she said, motioning to the remains of the BLT. "Then you must return and complete your meal…your life." She closed her eyes. "Your son is fine, but he misses you. Your mother is concerned. Finish, then go home."

She seemed to be done, so Grace stood up. She was shaking. "What do I owe you?" she asked.

"It's part of the bill."

Pulling the curtain aside, Grace stepped back into the diner. Virgil stood next to the cash register and Grace quickly joined him there. The waitress didn't say a thing, didn't look up at all. Grace wondered if she'd listened in on the reading. If Virgil did. If so, Grace didn't care.

It felt like Paul hovered close by. She wanted to crawl into that booth with the greasy-haired girl and stay there, if that's where Paul was, right this very minute. If her mother was there too. But her mother said she had to finish, and then go home.

Finish what?

Worry Number Four. What the hell was Grace doing?

She just needed to be away.

Virgil led her to the car, his hand on the small of her back. As they drove away, Grace looked in the windows of the diner. The heavy curtain around the booth was pulled back and the fortuneteller hunched over her meal. Grace wondered what she ordered, what she ate. Did she know what meal to choose to guarantee the best life? But the best life couldn't be sitting in a booth in a roadside diner. So maybe she didn't know everything. Their waitress sprawled on the seat opposite, smoking a cigarette, and watching them drive away.

"Grace," Virgil said, and his voice sounded deeper by an octave. Grace looked at him. His eyes were wet. "Grace, I heard what you said. You lost your *son*?"

That emphasis was there again as Virgil said it, as everyone said it. You lost your *son*? Like they were saying, You lost your arm? Your leg? Your heart?

Yes, Grace lost her heart. Yes, Grace lost her *son*.

She closed her eyes. "I can't talk about it, Virgil. I just can't."

"But Grace…" His voice cracked. "You lost your *son*."

"Virgil, please." He left her alone then, concentrating on his driving. Grace waited for his hum, that hum that accompanied them everywhere they went. It was as familiar to Grace now as the roll of the tires, the bong of her clock.

As familiar as the children's voices in the living room, Nick's hand on the small of her back.

But the hum didn't come. Virgil drove in silence. Grace glanced at him and saw tears on his cheeks. She wondered what he was thinking, what he imagined happened to her boy. There were so many ways a child could die. But she couldn't talk about it just then. Not even to help Virgil. Reaching into the back seat, she slid Cathy out of her seatbelt and held her on her lap. She ran her fingers through the doll's hair, over and over again, and she told herself she should wash Cathy's hair that night when they settled in a hotel. Grace's fingers might still have some grease on them, might still have some salt. She tucked the doll to her chest and then, imagining Virgil's hum and the tapping of his fingers on the wheel, she drifted in and out of a doze.

It was about an hour later when she woke up. She felt better; the familiar thump of the tires and answering low of the clock soothed her nerves. She returned Cathy to the backseat. Slipping off her shoes, she brought her feet to rest on the dashboard. The sun on the vinyl warmed her skin and she stretched her toes toward the windshield. Virgil patted her knee. "Sorry about that," he said. "I didn't mean to be nosy."

"It's okay," she said.

His fingers tapped on the steering wheel. "But, Grace, I really want to talk to you about that fortuneteller."

She slumped back down in her seat, dropping her feet, shoving them back into her shoes.

"I'm sorry if I wasn't supposed to hear what you said, but I couldn't help it. You were just a few feet away."

"It's okay," Grace said again. "I would've listened too, if it was you."

He touched her hand. "Grace, please tell me about your son. It's why you're here, isn't it? That's what this is all about."

Grace looked out of the window. She deliberately hadn't told Virgil about Paul. She wanted to stop talking about Paul, she wanted to be away from his death for a while. She needed to be away, that's what the money was for, that's what her mother intended. But now, there seemed to be no way around it. There was no being away. She couldn't lie to Virgil. She couldn't make anything up. "He was my second child," she said. "But the first from my second marriage. JJ came a few years later. Paul died about six months ago. He was fifteen years old."

Virgil nodded, but was silent, tapping the steering wheel. "Did he look like you?" he asked finally.

Grace considered this. She saw Paul's blond curls, his face, examined his eyes, the slender nose, the way his chin slid gracefully into his neck, his neck into his shoulders, and then the rest of his body just poured out. She used to call him her long drink of water. "Like me," Grace said. "And like Nick too. My mother used to say how much Paul looked like both of us. You know how some kids look so much like one parent, you kind of forget that the other had something to do with it? Paul was obviously a two-person creation." Grace spread her fingers, remembering how Paul's hand fit into hers the day they left the doctor's. The day he surprised her. "He had my hands, Nick's shoulders. My hair, Nick's eyes. My nose, Nick's cheeks. It was like his body was evenly divided between us."

Virgil grabbed her left hand, pulling it from her thigh. "Tell me about the day Paul was born. I like birthday stories." He squeezed her fingers and then they held their hands between them on the seat. Just like at the flea market, Virgil's touch was warm. Grace knew that saying his hand was like a glove was what everyone said; but it was true. And it was the first time she found it to be so. Nick's hand was dry and strong. He slid his fingers between hers, topped her thumb with his own. And the kids; the kids slid their hands into hers, she didn't slide hers into theirs. She was their glove.

And now Virgil was hers.

Grace swallowed painfully. "I guess it would help if you knew Paul alive before you know him dead."

Virgil gave the softest of grunts, but he nodded.

Grace sat up a little higher. She turned away from the window, curving her body toward Virgil. "The day my Paul was born. Well, I was three weeks overdue, as big as I could get. Nick was freaking out, wondering if something was wrong. Nick likes things just so, and Paul just wasn't fitting into the timetable. But the day Paul came…well, he came fast. We didn't even make it into the hospital room. He was born in the hallway. I was in a wheelchair and the nurse whipped off my pants and underpants, knelt down in front of me, put my feet on her shoulders, and caught Paul as he came flying out."

Virgil laughed.

"Nick ran yelling for the doctor and Nick cut the cord, right there, and eventually, they got us into a room and it all calmed down. But all that mattered was that I was holding him. I was holding Paul. I was forty years old…I didn't think I was ever going to have another child besides Mary. But then Nick came along and Paul came along a short time after. And then JJ."

"Boomerangs," Virgil said suddenly.

"What?"

"It all happened because of boomerangs. And Mary falling out of the swing. If she hadn't, and Nick hadn't been there with his boomerangs, you would never have met. And there would be no Paul. And no JJ."

"I suppose so." Grace smiled for a moment, then realized this meant that Mary, who was responsible for Paul's death, was also responsible for his conception. His life.

She shook her head. "I don't know how to explain it, Virgil, but there was something special about Paul right from the start. He was a quiet baby, staring into space and sucking his fist. When I held him, he molded himself into my body. No matter how I carried him, he became a part of me."

Virgil patted Grace's knee and she appreciated it.

"I spent a lot of time watching Paul. I looked at him, at his face, his eyes, his eyebrows. I looked at his body, the curve of his shoulders, the flatness of his hips. I looked at his homework, I watched what he checked out at the library, I listened to him as he learned to read and then I still listened even when he read only to himself. I knew everything about him. Everything." Grace's voice tripped. "And I thought, This boy is special. This boy is going to accomplish something, something huge." She grabbed Virgil's hand and clenched it, so tightly, he cried out, but didn't pull away. "I just didn't know what his special thing would be. I thought it would be space for a while. I thought he would be an astronaut."

"What was it, Grace?" Virgil's voice was soft and she closed her eyes. "What did he do?"

"He died during hide-and-seek." Grace's eyes collected tears behind the lids, making them full and swollen. "I mean, nobody dies playing hide-and-seek, Virgil. For Christ's sake. Only Paul. It was a fucking *game*." Grace released his hand, opened her eyes, and slapped away the tears.

"How did Paul die playing hide-and-seek? How did it happen?" Virgil's voice barely rose above the hum of the tires. Grace thought she felt the words more than heard them.

She turned her face away. It seemed to take great effort. "He climbed a tree. It was his turn to hide and Mary told him to hide in the tree. He got high enough to touch the electrical wires." She closed her eyes again and everything in her wished it was for the last time. She wanted to be with Paul. She wondered if he was still back in that diner booth and if she could convince Virgil to drive her back there. To leave her there. She could order something every day, for every meal, and she could hear each and every time from her son. Or her mother. She could hear from them both. Or maybe she could just convince herself to stop breathing. She didn't want to hurt anymore. She saw the flash again, Paul's flash, the light of his life exploding and going out. "His death was spectacular," she whispered. "It was special. No one dies like that."

Virgil's voice rose. He was above the tires now. "Oh, God, Grace, that was Paul? That was you? I remember reading about it in the paper," he said. "I didn't know he was yours. Oh, Grace. Oh, Grace, I'm so sorry."

Everyone was sorry.

Grace's voice sunk, it fell down her throat and through her chest into her stomach. She wondered if she would ever be able to speak again. And then she realized she didn't want to. She kept her eyes closed. She kept seeing the flash. The light of his life, she thought. The light of mine.

"God, Grace," she heard Virgil say. "You lost your *son*."

She lost her arm. She lost her leg. She lost her *heart*.

****

At a rest stop outside of Bernie, Missouri, Virgil bought the local paper and found an interesting auction advertised for the next day. He said the littlest towns had the best auctions and a lazy Sunday auction was the best. There was something about being in the middle of nowhere that brought out the most secret treasures, the best deals. Although it was only mid-afternoon on Saturday now, they decided to find a motel and attend the auction. It would be Grace's first.

Virgil stretched out on the bed. "Nothing to do until tomorrow," he said.

"I know." Grace felt itchy for movement. She didn't want to just stay in the motel room. At least in the car, there was a forward motion, a feeling of accomplishing something even while sitting absolutely still. Placing Cathy on her lap, Grace began to brush the doll's hair. She wished the motel had a swimming pool. "Do you think Maribel Get Well might be at the auction?"

Virgil shrugged as best he could from a lying position. "Dolls were mentioned in the ad. Usually they're not listed unless they're collectibles." He yawned. "It's just like with everything, Grace. Whether you're walking into a flea market or a rummage sale or a Goodwill or an antique mall, you just never know what you're going to find. It's all a treasure hunt."

Grace admired Cathy's hair and thought about Maribel's picture in the old Sears Christmas catalog. She never saw her outside of those shiny pages. Grace remembered crying over those pictures. Maribel stood in different poses, a leg or an arm or both encased in a cast, or she was covered in measles and chicken pox. She also had some bandages for various cuts and scrapes, cuts and scrapes that were always there, no matter how much healing the doll's mother performed. The child Grace wondered how one little doll could get so sick over and over again. The adult Grace wondered now.

At the height of Maribel's popularity, Grace lucked out and found a Woolworth's ad that included the little poem that came printed on Maribel's box:

MARIBEL, THE DOLL THAT GETS WELL

I need crutches and I must wear a cast
'cause I broke a leg riding pony too fast

I caught chicken pox from my friend Bella
When you have chicken pox your spots are yellow

I broke my arm when I stumbled and fell
Now I wear a cast to make it well.

I have the measles and my spots are red
But I'll soon be well if I stay in bed

Look Mommy – I'm Well Again!!

The child Grace so wanted to hold Maribel in her arms, to take her temperature and put cool cloths on her forehead. Grace wanted to make her better, to have her throw up her arms and shout, "Look, Mommy, I'm well again!!" and to stay that way forever. Somehow, Grace knew she was the only person who could do it. She could break the endless cycle of crutches and casts and dots and bandages.

As usual, the doll requests on her Christmas list were ignored that year. Grace sobbed under the Christmas tree, surrounded by new games, building logs and an electric train that her father picked out himself. There was even a cuckoo clock of her very own to hang in her room and sing out the hours above her bed. It was the third and final clock to come into Grace's room. Her mother felt its spirit and knew it was friendly to young growing girls. Grace cried because among all of these new wonders, there wasn't the one thing she really wanted and she cried because she knew out there somewhere, Maribel was crying too. Maribel would never get well. Grace grieved the doll whose home was in a catalog, the doll no one wanted. Except for Grace. And Grace wasn't allowed to have her, for a reason that was never explained.

"All little girls should have dolls," Virgil said. Grace believed that too.

Years later, when Grace was an adult and a mother, Mary fell ill for the first time with her first real cold. Not just the sniffles, but a fever and a red throat and jam-packed sinuses. Nick was in their lives by then, but they weren't married yet, and Grace barred him from her apartment so he wouldn't catch the cold too. As Mary lay in her crib, breathing noisily through her mouth, Grace busily checked her temperature every two hours, fed her acetaminophen every four hours, along with an infant decongestant, and made sure her humidifier misted effectively. She tilted the head of Mary's mattress to ease her breathing and she covered her lightly with a soft blanket fresh from the dryer. Mary threw aside the cold compresses Grace put on her forehead, but Grace kept trying anyway. She read Mary innumerable stories and sang her songs and watched her sleep, breathing every breath with her. Grace didn't call her mother, who she knew would have a poultice or a spell to place over her granddaughter. Grace remembered well that poultice that blew all of the mucus out of her own small head. But Grace wanted to do this herself; Grace wanted to make her daughter better. She was Mary's mother.

So she took care of that child. She took care of her and made her well.

Look Mommy - I'm well again!!

Forty-eight hours later, Mary was out of the crib and taking her first steps. Grace was deathly ill and moved from bed to couch to bed, trying to keep up with her daughter. But Grace didn't care. She made Mary well, she was there when Mary needed her. Nothing was ever so satisfying.

But she wasn't there when Paul needed her. She didn't stop his climb.

In the Missouri motel room, Grace's grip on the brush loosened and she dropped it to the bed. Virgil picked up the remote control and searched the channels on the television until he found a show with lots of shouting and chases. Propping his head on two pillows, he seemed to settle more deeply into his bed.

Grace knew Virgil wanted to ask more about Paul. The first conversation was enough for her; she couldn't handle anything else right then. If she stayed in the room and got comfortable, if Virgil was comfortable and he sensed hers, that conversation would start up again. Grace glanced out the window. It was sunny and clear. She needed to get out for a while. "I'm going for a walk," she told Virgil.

He looked at her and started to get up. "Want me to come along? Think you'll get lost?"

"In Bernie, Missouri? Please. But if I do, I'll just sit until you find me. I know you will. I wouldn't even have to call."

He smiled and returned to the television.

Grace left the motel room, shutting the door quietly. It was one of those whose doors led immediately to the outside and she breathed in the air of Bernie, Missouri. In October, it was still reasonably warm and she didn't need a jacket. She stood for a minute and let the sun soak into her scalp, her shoulders. It felt good to be outside. Looking to the left and the right, she decided to go to the left. The motel was in the middle of Bernie and she wandered down the street, knowing it was an unfamiliar place, yet it felt familiar all the same.

Grace stopped by a school yard. It was dark and quiet on a Saturday afternoon and Grace imagined the building gathering its breath for the return of students on Monday. She wondered if at her children's schools, Mary was speaking to a girl named Amber and if Amber was ever punished. She wondered if JJ chewed his fingernails all the way down again and if Nick knew where the medication was to take the pain away, to help the nails grow back.

She wondered if there was candy corn at Paul's grave.

It was time for a phone call home. She sent each child a fast text, just saying, "I love you. Thinking of you." She sent one to Nick too, asking if everything was all right. Then she tucked her phone in her jeans pocket, knowing that she would hear it when it rang and feel it when it vibrated, hopefully with answers.

As Grace moved on, walking past the blacktopped playground, she saw a painted-on foursquare game. She loved foursquare when she was a child, and she loved jumping rope too. Did kids still jump rope? Grace was in second grade when she came home from school, crying because at recess, she couldn't join in with the girls jumping rope. She knew how to do it with her own rope, but leaping in while two other girls turned the ends had her mystified. It was a complex ballet and her feet just weren't coordinated; Grace's lack of grace again.

She told her mother her story over a snack of Oreos and milk. Then her mother led her outside. They found some clothesline in the garage. After closing the big garage door, Grace's mother tied one end to the door's handle and then she held the other.

"You'll learn," she said to Grace. "I'll help."

Grace stood in the middle and her mother swung the rope over Grace's head again and again until Grace learned to watch the swing of her mother's wrist and jump at the right time. She was delighted.

Except "But Mom," she said, "the girls don't start in the middle. They run in. They watch the rope go round and round and they just run in from the side and they begin to jump. It's really cool."

They kept practicing until Grace's father drove in. Seeing them there, he parked the car in the street and then walked up the driveway. Grace's mother called him over. "Take this," she said, handing him her end of the rope. "And turn."

Still in his suit, Grace's father didn't even question. He just began to turn the rope. He smiled at Grace and she couldn't help herself; she giggled. Then her mother stood to the side of the turning rope.

"Watch," she said. "See how when the rope passes you and starts to swing away, you have a moment before it comes back? That's when you run in." She and Grace studied the rope, their heads nodding with the effort. Then Grace's mother ran in and she began to jump.

Grace stood there, both hands over her mouth in wonder, as her father turned the rope and her mother jumped, laughing. Then her mother ran out the other side. "Now you try," she said to Grace, coming back to her.

It took a few tries, a few smacks of the rope against Grace's ankles. But she did it.

And then her mother joined her and they jumped in tandem while beaming at Grace's father, who smiled back.

From that afternoon, all the way to this afternoon, standing on a street in Bernie, Missouri, Grace remembered that moment. Her father, turning a jump rope, his business suit ridiculous, smiling in front of her, and behind her, her mother, jumping in exact rhythm with Grace. In that moment, it didn't matter that Grace couldn't play with dolls. It didn't matter that her parents were complete opposites who sometimes didn't get along and left Grace feeling like a magnet between two poles. At that moment, they were just all there, jumping rope. Helping her learn to do something so she could join in with others at the playground.

Grace blinked and the image was gone. She thought of her own kids. She didn't remember ever teaching Mary to jump rope; she didn't know if Mary even knew how, or if she wanted to. The boys never asked. Grabbing her phone, she checked it and found no messages. Then she texted Mary. "Do you know how to jump rope?" Then she walked away.

This school was surrounded by neighborhoods, of course, and Grace moved through them, admiring the neatly kept houses. The trees here were still in the green of summertime and with the green and the sun and the warmth, Grace felt like the clock and the calendar were moving backwards. Which made her wonder if she could keep moving down the sidewalk to spring and then find a house where a boy climbed a tree and she could stop him before he fell.

She told herself she was being as ridiculous as wearing a business suit to turn a jump rope. The jump rope was gone. The business suit was gone. So were her parents. And so was her son.

Grace remembered a summer afternoon, climbing a tree with Sarah Ann, her childhood friend with all the dolls from across the street. Sarah Ann had a large tree in her backyard, with low hanging branches for wonderful climbing. It was almost like a staircase into the leaves. The last time they climbed, they were quite high, almost as high as Paul was when Grace saw his hand stretching out of the branches. Sarah Ann's mother came running out of the house.

"Sarah Ann!" she shrieked. Anything louder than Grace's mother's voice was a shriek to Grace then. "You both come down from that tree this instant! Sarah Ann, you know your father told you to stay down from there. You're going to fall and break your neck! Grace, you get yourself down too, I see you up there!"

Sarah Ann's mother knew. Sarah Ann's mother stopped them. They didn't break their necks. There was no flash of light.

Why didn't Grace know? Why didn't she run out and stop it all before it happened?

There was no use in either Grace or Sarah Ann cowering that day. When they climbed down, Sarah Ann was banished to her room with all those dolls for the rest of the day. Grace envied her the punishment. She went into her own backyard and looked up into one of the trees. The branches weren't as low, but it looked climbable. She dragged over a lawn chair and boosted herself up.

The limbs seemed to reach out, to catch her arms and legs and help her higher. Grace stopped when she found a wide fat branch that was just made for sitting. Putting her back against the trunk, she looked up into the leaves and reveled in the patches of blue popping through the green. The sun lit through luminescent. The air was fresher up here and the branches framed her house and the sky into a picture fit for hanging in the living room. The bark was rough and Grace hugged it tightly between her knees.

Her mother came out of the house and looked up. Grace wondered how she knew where to look; it was Grace's first time climbing and she thought it would be the last place her mother would expect to find her. She braced herself for the shriek, the banishment, though to a doll-less room. Across the street, she learned how mothers were supposed to behave when their children climbed trees. But instead, her mother leaned against the trunk. She stroked its bark and she smiled up at Grace.

"Don't just play in the tree, Gracie," she said. "Feel it, pat it, put your face against it. Find out why it grows, why it's here, how it feels to have a hundred arms. Find out what it's like to be so tall and to go down so deep." She patted the tree and Grace could hear the thump beneath her mother's fingers and Grace imagined that she felt the tree purr and rub against her. "Trees are so much more than playthings, Grace," her mother said and then she returned to the house.

Her mother was never like any of her friends' mothers. And her mother knew that day that Grace wasn't going to hurt herself.

Grace thought of Sarah Ann's mother, saving the girls from harm, and her own mother, knowing that no harm was coming. And she thought of herself, watching Paul, thinking no harm was coming and then it did anyway.

What kind of mother was she?

In her pocket, her phone chimed. Grace pulled it out and looked at it. A text from JJ. "Love you too, Mom. Call tonight?" Grace answered yes.

And then a text from Mary. "Of course I know how to jump rope. I'm not a baby. Love you too."

When did Mary learn? From who? And what kind of mother was Grace?

But from both remaining children: "Love you too."

There was nothing from Nick. Grace pocketed her phone and moved on.

Grace thought of the tree in her back yard, the tree she couldn't avoid seeing through the window of her kitchen. The tree held Paul up, just like the tree in her old back yard held her up. And both trees had a hundred arms. Grace didn't want to know how it felt to hold a boy in her arms, to feel that boy stretch out toward danger, but not have the mobility to stop him. She didn't want to know how it felt when the boy fell away.

Except, she realized, she did know. She stood at the window. She saw his hand. She couldn't move.

It seemed she was in partnership with the tree. They had a kinship. Maybe a tree, that tree, of all things, could understand more about how she felt than anyone else. It was the last thing to touch Paul alive. She was the first. And then she was the first thing to touch him dead.

Grace tucked her head, determined not to look at any more houses, not at any more trees, and began to walk quickly. She left the neighborhood and found a small grocery store. She restocked their chips, popcorn, cookies and soda. On a whim, she added crackers, fancy crackers, usually served at parties. In the deli, she picked up a package of sausage and cheese and then she went into the liquor department for a bottle of wine, a special treat for her and Virgil that night. A grown-up treat for two people who played with dolls.

She found her way back to the motel, even though she stared down at the sidewalk all the way. She counted the cracks, careful not to step on them, even though she no longer had a mother. She never stepped on cracks when she was a little girl either. Never. Not even when the dolls from her Christmas and birthday lists failed to appear again and again and again.

Letting herself in the motel room, she found Virgil snoring in front of the television.

Grace put the groceries away, waking Virgil without meaning to. He asked how her afternoon was, what the town was like. Grace told him it was lovely. She showed him their treat and he exclaimed over the wine. He asked if she bought a corkscrew and she immediately wanted to cry. He promised they would stop somewhere and buy one after they went out to eat.

Virgil was in the bathroom when the text came through from Nick. She read, "Everything is fine. Talk tonight? Love you too."

And Grace clutched the phone to her heart.

****

That evening was warmed by the wine and the rich taste of cheese and sausage on buttery crackers. Grace and Virgil moved outside, ignoring the television, and they watched the stars come out. They sipped their wine in plastic glasses. The motel had a wide sidewalk running around its length and there were plastic lawn chairs and a small table outside of every door. Grace felt more like an adult than a runaway child for the first time since leaving home. Despite the fact that a doll sat on the table next to her. Grace and Virgil didn't speak much, just small comments here and there, and Grace thought about how comfortable she felt. She could sit in the muted outdoor light of the motel, listen to the buzz of passing traffic and the call of a night bird, swat at the occasional late mosquito, and not feel like she had to make conversation. She could be quiet with Virgil. There was so seldom quiet in her house.

Her mother loved the quiet. When her father was away on business trips, Grace and her mother often sat on the front porch of the house like this until long after dark, even on school nights, not saying a word. They watched fireflies or snowflakes, crisp stars or iridescent and welcome raindrops. Grace always felt the treasure of her mother's quiet, sometimes broken with a hand squeeze or a pat on the knee. When she was told to go to bed, she did so reluctantly. She knew her mother remained outside for hours after.

And now she reluctantly left Virgil in the quiet so she could call home. She wasn't reluctant to call her children; she still felt the pang of loneliness from her vigil outside the silent school that afternoon. But the quiet and the wine, the sharp taste of cheese and sausage, was so nice. "I'll be right back," she said to Virgil.

He nodded. "I'll give you your privacy. Cathy and I will be right here." He patted the doll on the knee, just the way he patted Grace's. Just the way her mother patted her back on those special nights on that front porch.

Inside, Grace sat on the bed and pulled out her cell phone. She wished that Virgil had come inside with her. He provided a comfort, and it was comfort she needed right now. But she set it aside and called home. She knew others needed comfort too.

She hoped that one of the kids would answer. She timed it so that the phone would ring when they were likely in the kitchen, scrounging for a snack before bed. It always amazed her how kids could get hungry right before sleep. But it was Nick who answered.

"Hi, Nick, it's me," Grace said. The wine kept her voice from shaking.

"Hi." He didn't use her name and he sounded uncertain, unsteady. She could hear the kids in the background. "It's been a few days."

"I'm sorry," Grace said. "I just thought, after our last conversation, that maybe you could use a break from me for a little bit."

"Grace," he said and his voice cracked. "Grace, I don't want a break from you. I want you home."

Grace's heart leapt.

"I'm going to put you on speaker phone, so we can all hear you at once. Kids, it's Mom."

Grace heard JJ cheer. Mary's voice was absent. Grace was happy to speak to all of them at once, but she knew she was going to miss the intimacy of hearing each of them in the singular, one on one conversations between mother and daughter, mother and son, husband and wife. At home, the only time she ever got to speak to the kids individually, or even to Nick, really, was at bedtime as she said goodnight to each. But this was okay. This would do. She laughed as she heard JJ's and Nick's voices collide like runaway cars.

"Mom?" JJ's voice rose to a new height and shoved his father away. "You're laughing! Does that mean you're feeling better?"

"I am feeling better, honey." She told them about the barn in Iowa, the dinosaur and the book, the box of dolls in Indiana. She told them how she thought of them that day as she stood outside of the school in Missouri.

"Missouri!" she heard Nick exclaim, and she knew he was calculating the miles. He must have realized she was further away, not closer. Not coming home yet.

"It sounds like you're having fun," Mary said. It was the first Grace heard from her.

There was something in her daughter's voice that kept Grace from answering. Her kitchen, so far away, fell to odd and awkward quiet. She didn't hear the clunk of a glass of milk being set down or the rustle of cookie packages. "Well, it's not fun, exactly," she said finally.

"It sounds like fun," Mary said. "Kinda like a vacation."

She heard the accusation then. An accusation from her oldest child. Mothers weren't supposed to have fun when they ran away from home. They weren't supposed to run away from home at all.

Grace did run away, and she was having fun, that was true. But there was so much more to it than that. "I'm sorry," she said into that strange silence. "I suppose it does sound like a vacation. But there's a lot more going on too. I'm…doing a lot of thinking."

"About Paul?" Mary cut in. "About what happened?"

Her daughter was always so blunt, so flat-outspoken. "Sure. But about other things too. About all of you. And about me too." Trying to explain the unexplainable made Grace sweat. She wished again that Virgil was in the room.

"I think…" Nick said. There was a scrape as he sat down at the table. "I think Mom is trying to think of a way to think about Paul without thinking so much that it hurts all the time. Is that it, Grace?"

Grace breathed out. "Yes, that's almost it. It's like…well, Dad said once, and so did your principal, that we have to let Paul go. But it's like I need to figure out how to let Paul go without letting him go at all. Which is like thinking about him without thinking about him."

The room was quiet again, until Mary said, "Mom, that doesn't make any sense."

Grace nodded, even though she knew the kids couldn't see her. "Paul dying doesn't make any sense, honey. And that's why this is so hard," she said and her voice broke.

JJ grew alarmed. "Mom, don't cry!" he said. "That's what you're trying not to do. You were laughing before. Go back to laughing."

"She will," Nick said, and Grace felt a flutter of annoyance. *It's time, Grace.*

"Mom," Mary said, "I'm sorry. I'm so sorry." And then her voice, which Grace had grown used to with its new adolescent snarl and sneer, seemed to fling off years and she began to cry. I'm not a baby, she'd texted that afternoon, but the tears Grace heard were five years old. Grace wasn't sure when the last time was that she heard Mary cry. She wondered if that last time was under the tree, while Grace held her son and listened to the wail of the coming ambulance, the wail of her children. Her remaining children.

And so they were back there again. Mary saying she was sorry, Grace at a time when she should console, when she should say it's all right, when she should explain that it wasn't Mary's fault. *It's time, Grace.*

But Mary told Paul to climb the tree.

Grace couldn't say a word. She just cried alongside her daughter. And then she heard the scrape of a chair and footsteps and she knew Mary was gone.

"Mom," JJ said with a quiet a twelve-year old boy shouldn't know. "I don't want to let Paul go."

"I know, sweetheart. Neither do I. Which is why I have to think of something else we can do. Not let him go, but learn how to keep on walking even though he's not in the house anymore. I have to think of a way for us to walk around his absence, but still have him beside us in a new way." Grace turned so she could see out the motel window. The back of Virgil's head was there. So was Cathy's. She was wearing her blue corduroy hat.

"That's going to take a lot of thinking, Mom," JJ said, his voice resolute. "You're not ever coming home."

"I am!" The pain that seared through Grace then was almost as heavy as Paul's death. "I am! I promised you that. Honey, I would never ever leave you for good. I will be home."

As soon as she said it, she knew what JJ was going to say. Her logical son, her even-keeled son. She knew.

"Paul left for good." And then JJ sobbed. He grew muffled. Nick must have been hugging him. "Nick?" Grace walked to the window, put her hand on it. Her fingers splayed around Virgil's hair.

"It's all right, Grace." There was such tightness in his voice, Grace pictured his tongue like a tightrope, pulled from the back of his throat to his words.

Nick was holding everyone together while she fell apart. When she was home, he tried to hold her together while she held the kids together. She wondered if he worried that he was going to fail, just like he failed with her. He would see it as his failure. She'd been failing too.

Grace knew he was worried.

"I will be coming home, okay?" she said, and she said it as much to Nick as she did to JJ, and to Mary, who wasn't even there to hear. "And I'm going to call more often. Right, Nick? That's okay?"

"Yes," Nick said. "I think you should call home every night." Grace waited for and heard his exhale. It wasn't exasperated. Just settled.

"I love you guys. I'll call again soon, okay? Tomorrow?"

"Yes." JJ was back and he was definitive. "Tomorrow. Every night."

Grace told them again that she loved them, she asked that Mary be told too, and she heard their love in return. Then she hung up the phone. She went into the bathroom and washed her face and took a couple breaths before returning outside to Virgil.

"Okay?" he asked. His head nodded just a bit. They'd knocked off the whole bottle of wine between them. Well, Virgil finished it while she was inside.

Grace reached for another piece of sausage. "I think so."

She nibbled some more as Virgil stumbled into the room to take a shower. She waited for the impact of emotion, the slam of guilt and worry that knocked her to her knees whenever she called home. Whenever she thought about her own selfishness at running away. Abandoning two children. Well, two children and a grave. Her remaining children and the one taken away. And a husband. And a cat.

She thought of the fortuneteller, the message from her mother. Finish what you're doing. Then go home.

When she was at home, when Paul was still alive, she often felt stabbed with this same guilt if she spent one more minute with one child than the others. If she helped Paul with his homework, then she would take extra time admiring Mary's art or reading JJ a story. "Equal time!" always ran through her head. "Love your children equally! Be with them equally!" Her children were a pie of equal slices.

But sometimes, one child just needed more. Particular attention. Abundant attention.

Grace sat up with a start.

That's what this was. Paul needed her particular attention. How could you grieve for someone if you were constantly worried about someone else? Worrying about the survivors. The remaining children. She wasn't running away from Paul's death. She was running toward it as the world threatened to erase it.

Paul was the one who died. The kids lost their brother. Grace and Nick lost their son. But Paul lost all of them. He lost his life.

She thought of the grave she never visited once Paul was lowered into it.

Grace had to grieve. She had to grieve her son as if he was the only child she had. Just as he was the only child who was lost to her. She had to give him her undivided attention.

She just couldn't be equal right now. One child needed her more. And she needed that one child.

CHAPTER EIGHT
Virgil

Two days after learning about Paul's death, Virgil woke up the morning after the wine and cheese and realized that so much suddenly made sense now. Grace made sense; her movements made sense. Her slow walk, her stooped shoulders weren't signs of a doomed romance with her husband, as he'd thought. They were signs of grief, a grief so big, Virgil couldn't even begin to imagine it.

When Virgil's mother died, he walked like that for a few weeks. But it gradually lifted, the grief went to some corner of his heart where it only emerged a few times a year; Mother's Day, his mother's birthday, Christmas, the anniversary of her death. Being estranged from his father caused that posture for a while too, but then anger replaced it and he walked tall, with a stiff spine and thrown-back shoulders, clenched fists.

But Grace moved like the ground was sucking at her feet.

Virgil saw a look on her face sometimes, as she looked out the window of the big Chrysler, or as she lay on her bed and stared at the ceiling. He'd taken it as loneliness, that she was missing her husband, she was missing her kids. And she was, but she was missing one in particular, and she was missing him in a very different way. He wouldn't be there when she went back home. He would never be there again.

She lost her *son*.

Virgil only had dolls to lose. And dolls could be replaced, although he didn't like the thought of that. He knew that if he lost one of his special dolls, Baby Boo or Baby First Step, Tippee Toes, Pixie or Poor Pitiful Pearl, he'd be able to find another, that there were hundreds and thousands made from the mold of every individual doll. He would be sad, but the spot wouldn't be empty for long. He'd find another at a flea market, an auction, eBay or CraigsList. He might have to pay a fortune. But Grace couldn't pay any amount and get her son back.

He glanced over at Grace and saw she wasn't awake yet. Chatty Cathy lay on the pillow beside her. He'd yet to find Grace asleep with the doll in her arms, but every night now, she was brushing Cathy's hair, changing her into pajamas, and putting her to bed next to her, giving the doll her own pillow. This made Virgil smile. But that sleeping embrace wasn't there. Not yet.

Virgil sent his gaze to the ceiling. He thought of Brad and tried to picture what it would be like to lose him, the way Grace lost Paul, not the way he thought she lost her husband. Death. What would it be like to lose Brad now, the way things were and had been, and what would it be like to lose him after living with him, being a partner to him, maybe even marrying him. In Virgil's mind, he watched Brad wither, saw his southern golden color drain away, the skin hang loosely from his bones. He saw Brad's eyes close for that last time, and a pain sliced through Virgil that made him gasp.

Would the ground suck at him too? He didn't want to feel that. He looked back at Grace, her breaths even, her face relaxed, and he desperately didn't ever want to be like her. If only she hadn't met Nick, hadn't had Paul. If only she could have fast-forwarded through that part, kept Nick, kept Mary and JJ, and skipped right over Paul, her life would still be intact now. There would be no loss.

That loss colored her face like the tattoo of a funeral veil. For Virgil to have Brad, only to lose him, suddenly seemed too big a risk. He didn't want to have to survive that. How could anyone survive that? Though he knew, of course, that they did. Even Grace was surviving. Somehow, through this trip, she was.

There was just so much to consider, to weigh and balance, to decide. Virgil wished, not for the first time, that all he had to do was love Brad, that the rest of his life wouldn't interfere. He wished that there wasn't an ultimatum. But at the same time, he understood it. The years were growing shorter and the loneliness was getting stronger.

But for now, Virgil shook free of his thoughts. There was the auction. He got out of bed and rousted Grace too because the viewing for the auction started at ten. There was barely enough time for showers and a breakfast of hotel room coffee and whatever they could scrounge from their supplies. Grace grumbled, but when Virgil reminded her of Maribel Get Well, she rallied.

When they arrived at the grounds, they wandered. Beautiful things were set up on rows of tables under the trees. The sun broke through the leaves and sent sparkles over the dullest of pots and pans and Virgil watched Grace's eyes light up as well. There was furniture, heavy ornate brass beds, dressers with lion's feet.

Leather-bound books and solemn clocks. Grace stopped by a table loaded with clocks and Virgil stayed with her, though he tried to inconspicuously crane his neck to see what was up ahead.

"You go on," Grace said, patting his arm. "I want to look at these. I'll catch up to you later."

So Virgil strolled the rows, his hands in his pockets, trying to look relaxed and unhurried. It was the bargainer's walk. You couldn't look too eager or the auctioneers would spot you from a mile away and know they could milk your heartstrings. Bargainers spot the eager ones too and then you had to hope that they weren't bidding on the same items as you were, because eager ones would pay just about anything to get what they wanted. Virgil joined the slow-walkers and worked his way through the tables, noticing everything, but touching nothing.

Against the barn, under yet another table, he saw a laundry basket. From the blonde hair sticking out of the woven plastic sides, he figured there were dolls in it. He wandered by, cocking his head and scratching his ear, and managed to get a good look. The dolls were dirty and mostly naked, though a few wore clothes. He recognized the Vogue Baby Dear and his own Baby Boo, the doll who cried incessantly when her plastic pacifier was yanked from her mouth. Passing by again, he estimated that there were at least fifteen dolls in the laundry basket. From their condition and lack of presentation, he hoped that the organizers didn't know their real worth.

Suddenly, Grace was by his side and her eyes followed his to the basket. "Is Maribel there?" she whispered.

"I don't know," he whispered back. "I haven't looked through them. I —"

Grace started forward and Virgil quickly grabbed her by the elbow and tugged her away.

Grace rubbed her arm and looked over her shoulder. "Geez, Virgil," she said. "I just wanted to see the dolls."

"I know." He felt a bolt of shame and he patted her on the back. "I know, sweetheart, I'm sorry. But look around you. Look at the way everyone else is behaving." It was the first time he used an endearment with Grace, but it was out of his mouth before he knew he said it. He wondered if she noticed, but her expression didn't change. Instead, she riveted her eyes on the crowd.

There were a lot of people now, walking the grounds. Some of the women wore dresses and walked on heels that sank into the grass. They spoke in high chattering voices and their hands flapped and pointed. They likely just came from church. Other visitors looked more like Grace and Virgil, with jeans and flannel shirts and hoodies. They walked slowly and carelessly, not following any particular path. They often looked like they stared at the ground or off into the trees. But Virgil knew their eyes constantly moved, darting from table to table. Like his were when he discovered the laundry basket.

He took Grace's hand and nodded toward the slow-walkers. "They're the bargainers," he said. "Like you and me. We know what to expect, how to dress for an outdoor auction. No pretense, no image. Just business. We also keep our faces blank. We don't want to tip off the auctioneer if he has something that might be valuable. We want to get it for the lowest price possible."

Grace nodded and studied Virgil's face. He tried to make it blank, but it was impossible with her nearby. He burst out into a grin and she laughed. "These others," Virgil continued, "these fancy ladies and gentlemen, they're just here to shop. To find a treasure, that's all. And they'll pay for it. The auctioneers will make sure to start the price high on anything they're interested in."

Grace looked at her clothes. "I'm dressed like a bargainer," she said. "But I think I feel more like the shoppers. I'm excited, like I'm looking for buried treasure. Maribel might be here somewhere."

"I guess you're the middle ground then," Virgil said. "You're looking for treasure, but a specific treasure. You know what you're after. You're a bargainer too." He made sure Grace's arm was looped through his, preventing her from charging any other tables. "So did you find anything? Something you want to bid on?"

"I think so. You'll have to show me how it's done." She led Virgil over to the table she stopped at before, loaded with clocks and other household ornaments.

There were anniversary clocks, cuckoo clocks and mantel clocks. Grace nodded to a miniature grandfather clock perched on a corner. Virgil made a slow perusal of the table, rocking back and forth on his heels. He turned his head like he was looking at everything, but he kept his eyes pinpointed on Grace's clock. Then he moved around the table, all while glancing at the tables around them, and he was able to get a look at the clock's four sides.

He returned to Grace. "Okay, I'm going to pick a few up, look at them, and put them down. I'm also going to push a few pendulums, including the clock you've chosen. That way, we can see if it still works, without alerting the auctioneers which one we're really interested in. You move on to the next table over, and talk to me about anything, like we're not even really discussing this. We're not interested, remember. We're not interested."

Grace nodded and moved over a table. Virgil picked up clocks, put them down, started pushing pendulums. He found a key on the little grandfather's back and so he gave the movement a couple quick cranks. The clock had a real pendulum and when he pushed it, it swung in a slow concave arc. The tick was deep and ponderous. He opened the glass over the small face and moved the minute hand until it reached the top of the hour. The chime was light and tinny, especially compared to the serious tick. Virgil liked the incongruity and he thought of Cooley, of the clock museum back in Iowa.

Grace called over, "So did you like the wine we had last night? We can get some more."

When Virgil looked over, she glanced quickly at the clock and waggled her eyebrows. Virgil realized she was talking in code and he wanted to laugh. "I liked it a lot." Out of the corner of his eye, he saw a man in a red apron watching them. It was time to move away.

But when he joined Grace at the next table, she slipped a smooth round object into his hand. Opening his fingers, Virgil found the smallest crystal ball he ever saw. It was about the size of a golf ball and he could easily close his fingers entirely over it. In the sun, light glinted through the crystal, sending rainbows into the air.

"Feel how warm," Grace whispered. "My mother would say the spirits are friendly."

The ball did feel heated. It glowed against his skin.

The man in the red apron moved closer. "Careful," he joked, his voice light. "Don't scare all the spirits and hobgoblins away."

Grace rolled her eyes. "Spirits don't scare that easily," she said. "And there's no such thing as hobgoblins."

Virgil laughed at the man's expression, then led Grace quickly away. Somewhere, a church bell chimed the half-hour. Virgil looked at his watch – the bidding would start at noon, thirty minutes away.

"I'm getting hungry," Grace said.

Virgil was too; their hotel room breakfast was wearing off quickly in the fresh air and sunlight. "I'm not sure there's anything here that we can get to eat," he said. "I don't think there's time to go back to town. That clock and the crystal ball are small, so they'll probably be sold near the beginning of the bidding. The dolls won't be too far behind. They usually save the big item stuff, like the furniture, for last." He looked around. "Let's go see if we can find a refreshment table. I thought I smelled coffee before."

They scouted out a table with free coffee and fifty-cent doughnuts. Just as they picked up their coffee cups, the PA system came to life, announcing the bidding was just twenty minutes away. Balancing their coffee and doughnuts, they made their way with the crowd to the auction site, set up in a flat section of the field. There were rows of folding chairs and a portable stage with a table and a podium with a microphone. They found seats in the third row.

Virgil sat back and looked around. This last stretch before the bidding was always the most nerve-wracking. He wanted to get going, to bid on his items, score, and get out of there. The energy was an undertoned hum. Some people sat with their heads bowed, looking at their fingers, while others leaned forward eagerly, stretching their necks toward the podium, watching for the first movement to begin. Bargainers and shoppers, Virgil thought and nodded. Grace turned and wiped her lips with sugar-whitened fingers.

"So what do we do now?" she asked.

"We wait for our items to come up. After the auctioneer sets the starting bid, you'll raise your hand, signaling that you're interested and you're willing to pay the price. Hopefully, nobody else will want your things."

By the time the auction started, every seat was full and people stood in the grass along the back and sides of the staging area. There were a number of people on cell phones and Virgil knew these folks represented the really serious collector, the ones who didn't even come themselves, but sent agents. Even if he was well to do and could afford it, he couldn't imagine sending someone in his place. He enjoyed this.

He and Grace sat quietly and watched through the first sales. Virgil could tell by the way Grace leaned forward, her elbows on her knees and her mouth just slightly open, that she was fascinated by the auctioneer's fast tongue and the bidders' subtle moves. Virgil remembered his first auction, one he attended soon after buying his first collectibles catalog. He went home with a case of tennis neck from trying to watch too many things at once.

Things moved along swiftly and items were held up, praised, sold, and sent on their way to their new homes. The auctioneer told charming stories about the estate and its owners. The couple, he said, had no children. Their children were their things, and when the husband died, and then the wife, their house was filled with orphans. The proceeds from the auction, he said, were going to a favorite charity. Virgil saw Grace's mouth turn down at the corners and he knew she was picturing all the items suddenly without a home, without a family that loved them. That was the auctioneer's exact goal – make the buyers think that not only were they buying a treasure, they were giving an orphan a home, plus supporting a charity. There was much applause and light laughter, held breath and deep sighs. When the auctioneer started on the clocks, Grace sat up straight. Virgil put his hand on the back of her neck, hoping to keep her calm.

The miniature grandfather appeared, brought to the auctioneer by the same red-aproned man that spoke to them about the crystal ball. The tendons in Grace's neck tensed and she held her breath as the auctioneer held the clock up. It looked even smaller in his beefy red hands. Virgil wanted to snatch it away, to present it to Grace himself, settling it in the cradle of her lap. He shook his head. Not only was he being affected by the auctioneer's sad story, he was being affected by Grace's too. He wanted to make her feel better.

"We'll start the bidding at twenty-five," the auctioneer said.

"Forty!" Grace yelled, waving her empty coffee cup.

Virgil groaned. The auctioneer and the other bidders laughed. There was no other bid. "Sold!" the auctioneer said, nodding in Grace's direction. "Have a wonderful time with your clock, ma'am." He handed it back to the red-aproned man who carried it over to the cash-out table. Grace relaxed in her seat.

When the auctioneer moved on to the next item, Virgil patted Grace's knee. "Next time," he said, "start with the opening bid and work your way up. You don't want to pay more than you have to. Remember what I said about the dolls in Shipshewana. You don't want to be taken. The object is to get the item, but to get it as cheaply as you can."

Grace glanced at him, her gaze straight, her eyes wide. "But Virgil," she said evenly, "that box of dolls had Gay Bob in it. You said yourself that doll would have gone for hundreds. So what I paid was worth it, in the end." Then her eyes returned to the front, where china figurines were marching one by one across the podium.

Virgil wanted to argue, but he couldn't. Grace was right. There was a valuable treasure in that box that she only paid twenty-five dollars for. There was also an immeasurable value in what happened after she bought it. If Virgil had known Gay Bob was there, buried deep, he would have paid for the box himself, and he would have paid more. Not everything of value was to be taken home.

Soon, the crystal ball was held up. The bidding started at ten dollars. Grace cocked an eyebrow at Virgil, then scrunched down in her chair and nonchalantly raised her hand. She got the crystal ball for fifteen.

Rugs were sold, followed by draperies, quilts, lamps, glassware and Christmas tree ornaments. Then finally, after a series of antique Fisher Price toys, the laundry basket was held up. Virgil could see the eyes of the dolls peering out between the slats. Baby Dear looked pathetic, so sad and scared. Baby Boo's eyes were tightly closed and Virgil knew if someone pulled her pacifier, her wails would be heard through the crowd.

"We'll try the whole batch first," the auctioneer said. "If there's interest. Otherwise, we'll sell the dolls one at a time. Starting bid, twenty-five."

Virgil raised his hand. So did another man.

"Thirty," the auctioneer said. "I have thirty, can I have thirty-five, thirty-five, thirty-five?"

Virgil raised his hand again.

"Forty, forty, forty?"

The man raised his.

Grace's face started to shine with a fine sweat. Her attention was sealed on the basket and Virgil knew the dolls stared at her, crying a silent plea, making her squirm in her seat. But he wasn't sure if the dolls were worth forty-five dollars. He sat quietly, but jogged his knee.

He thought of the dolls in Shipshewana.

He thought of the dolls in the barn in Iowa.

Where would these dolls end up, if he didn't buy them?

And more importantly, Virgil realized, even more important than that, what would Grace think if he let these babies go to a stranger?

"Forty-five, forty-five, forty-five?"

Virgil raised his hand. The other man, thankfully, stayed still.

"Going once!" the auctioneer said. Grace gripped the edges of her seat and so did Virgil. "Twice! Three times, sold for forty-five dollars!" Grace laughed out loud and Virgil relished her joy, even as he hoped he got a good deal.

They walked over to the cashier and paid for their items. Grace reached right into the laundry basket and stroked the dolls' heads. "We get to keep the basket too?" she asked.

"Sure, it's part of the package," the cashier said. "Here's your forty-dollar clock." The man grinned as he handed Grace her tissue-wrapped prize. By the look on her face, Virgil knew it was forty dollars well spent.

He took the basket. "Now when we do our laundry, we'll have something to carry it in." He tenderly nestled the clock among the dolls. Grace took the crystal ball and carried it in her cupped hands.

"Let's go get something to eat," she said. "Real food this time."

Virgil nodded. "What would you like?"

"Something warm." They fell into step. "Chili. I want chili. Something that sounds cold, but tastes warm. Warm with spirits and spices. But no hobgoblins." She laughed quietly. "Then we can go back and dig through these dolls, clean them up."

They walked to the Chrysler together, the basket banging against Virgil's thighs in buoyant rhythm, the crystal ball rolling in Grace's hands. "Did your mother ever teach you how to use one of those things?" he asked.

She shrugged. "There's nothing to learn, really. I never saw my mother do anything like you see in the old movies, like in the Wizard of Oz, where the witch looks in and visions appear. My mother looked for colors. I do too." She looked down at the ball.

Virgil did as well, but saw only the soft pink of Grace's palms. "Does the color matter?" he asked. "Does it mean anything?"

Grace rolled the ball one more time, like a potter rolling clay, and then she tucked the ball into her jacket pocket. "They mean pretty much what you would expect. You don't want to see black." She bumped gently against him. "I don't think we will."

Virgil hoped not.

****

When he woke up the next morning, Virgil felt odd. He was jumpy, nervous, looking over his shoulder. He couldn't put a name to his unease. He wasn't someone that had premonitions, gut level reactions, nor did he have aching joints or headaches that foretold rain or snow or a drop in barometric pressure. Grace didn't seem to feel it; she was fine, her usual half-self that he saw every morning; she was half-awake, her eyes were half-shut, her mouth half-open. Their belongings were all there and the car was parked right outside, so whatever was wrong wasn't with them in the room. But somewhere in the atmosphere of Bernie, Missouri, there was a ripple. Virgil felt cold and he pulled on a heavy sweatshirt. Maybe, he thought, it's just that it's time to get on the road.

Grace seemed to notice his sweatshirt and so she pulled on a long-sleeved shirt as well, and then tugged Cathy in her coat. She'd given up on the hat, which refused to stay on Cathy's head. Virgil noticed she was getting better at dressing the doll, her fingers no longer stumbling quite so much over the little buttons. He smiled, a bit of warmth working its way to his skin. Then Grace looked at him expectantly. "Where to, Virgil?" she asked.

There were a few antique places in town and Virgil had planned to browse before hitting the road. But with the bite in the air and the tension between his shoulder blades, he just wanted to leave this place behind and continue their trek to Macon. And to Brad. Virgil knew that by this point, Brad was pausing to look out a window, glance out his door, to see if the Chrysler was pulling into the drive. Virgil liked it to be a surprise when he showed up. There was a difference between seeing someone burst out of the door to greet you when he had no idea when you'd be there, and a man who prepared for your arrival down to the minute. This way, Virgil could see if there was still spontaneous joy on Brad's face, or if the joy there was carefully placed, carefully planned. Prepared, like a welcome home dinner. With the ultimatum acting as the welcome mat between them, Virgil just wasn't sure what to expect.

"I think we should move on today," Virgil said and scooped up the bed-box with the Quints in one arm and his suitcase in the other. Grace was used to the routine by now and she quietly fell in beside him as they loaded the car. The trunk was filling up nicely with their purchases, but there was still room for more. With a '69 Chrysler Newport, another foot of space could always be squeezed out by turning a box horizontally instead of vertically, or setting a basket on its side.

Virgil loved his car.

Grace slid into her seat, but Virgil stood for a moment and looked around. The clouds were low and the tang of rain was in the air. Maybe that was the disturbance he felt in his head and shoulders. But even before he buckled his seatbelt, he reminded himself he was never bothered by the weather and so he disqualified that.

"Are we going to stop for breakfast right away?" Grace asked. She still looked sleepy and Virgil had no doubt she'd drop right off if he drove for a bit.

"No, it's time to get out of here. We'll go for a while, and then we'll stop." He patted her knee. Virgil's stomach was already growling and he hoped she didn't hear. Despite his hunger, he just needed to go.

She nodded and settled back. He drove toward the downtown area and looked forward to the open road beyond and the first decent diner.

But before leaving the city limits, they came across a crowd gathered outside the courthouse and Virgil's shoulders instantly hunched. Grace leaned forward. "What do you think is going on?" she asked.

"It looks like a demonstration of some sort." Virgil slowed the car as they got closer. He squinted to read the signs people braced on their shoulders. GAY RIGHTS, Virgil read. PROUD AND LOUD. IT'S A LARK TO BE LESBIAN. DON'T FLY STRAIGHT, FLY LIKE A FAIRY.

A gay pride demonstration in Missouri. No wonder he felt a sense of danger. Grace turned toward him, her eyebrows a question mark. Virgil started to drive by, slumped down behind his wheel as if his sexual preference could be recognized by just glancing at him through the window of his car, when a man turned in the crowd. He looked straight at Virgil. His eyes were like a raised gun. Virgil's foot moved on its own accord and he slammed on the brakes.

He rolled down his window as the man glanced at the Chrysler's license plates. He motioned to a parking space with his hand. "Join us, brother," he said.

Virgil wondered how he knew. Did he know? Virgil was in the car with a woman. But why issue the invitation? Why call him brother? Despite the muscles bunching in his back and the headache starting to hammer behind his eyes, Virgil parked the car. It somehow felt wrong to ignore a specific call for action.

"Virgil?" Grace asked. "What are we doing? I thought we were leaving. I thought we were getting breakfast."

He'd never before been in any kind of protest, any kind of demonstration. He watched all the events on the news, read the headlines, cheered the 99%, believed that black lives matter, believed that women had the right to choose, booed and boycotted Hobby Lobby, followed which state allowed gay marriage and which didn't, cringed over the bible-thumpers. He did all of that alone in his home. All the times he spent with Brad, they never spoke of it. It might have been their generation, it might have been Georgia, it might have been Wisconsin. It might have been that when they were together, the rest of the world ceased to matter. He thought again of Brad, of being unable to walk with him hand in hand. It was something he would never have considered doing. He very much wanted to see equal treatment and acceptance in his lifetime – he just didn't know if he would ever be able to step out of his own lifelong shadow to celebrate it. And he still didn't believe it was anyone's business but his own who he slept with. Why should he be looked at and immediately defined by his sexual preference? Why couldn't that information be private? For all people?

But walking hand in hand with Grace felt so good. He wanted to be able to do it again, to walk hand in hand, to put his arm around Brad's shoulders, around his waist, maybe even tuck his fingers into Brad's back pocket.

Maybe the Gay Bob discovery and decapitation in Shipshewana led him here, to this march, to this man who called him brother. Virgil wanted his privacy. But he also wanted his freedom.

Despite the discomfort in Virgil's body, despite the unease in the air and the fact that he was a stranger to this area and whatever happened here wasn't likely to affect him in Wisconsin or in the middle of a junkyard in Georgia, Virgil knew that joining the demonstration was the right thing to do. "Let's go, Grace," he said.

It was her turn to slump in her seat. "Virgil, I don't belong here," she said. "I think maybe I'll just wait in the car until you're done. I can watch our things. Don't these demonstrations get kind of crazy sometimes?"

They did. Virgil knew that, from observing the news on television. But he didn't want to leave Grace alone in the big car. He thought she was safer with him, in a crowd, rather than a single sitting duck in a car. "Grace, I think you should probably come with."

"But I'm not gay, Virgil." She shook her head.

Virgil smiled at her. "I don't think you have to be gay to be in one of these marches. Some people are just here to show their support." Though in Bernie, Missouri, he wondered how many straight people would be included, or if this group was totally supported by its own kind.

When Grace looked at Virgil, he could see the fear in her eyes. He wasn't sure where it came from, if it was the newness of being in a demonstration or if it was being seen with a group of gay people, possibly being branded as a lesbian herself. "Grace," he said. "These people don't know us. We'll never see them again after today. I'd just feel better if you were with me."

She pressed her lips together, but she got out of the car. He reached into the backseat for Cathy, preparing to put her in the trunk for safekeeping. But when he raised the lid, Grace snatched the doll away.

"No!" Grace hugged Cathy, a full hug, like a mother protecting her child. "She's coming with me. If it's not safe, I'm not leaving her here."

"Oh, Grace, put her in the trunk. No one will see her there." He reached again, but Grace twisted away with the agility of a headstrong child.

"If I'm going, then she's going, Virgil. You'll feel better if I'm with you, I'll feel better if she's with me. I've seen pictures of demonstrations, just like I'm sure you have. Cars go up in flames sometimes." She tucked the doll inside of her jacket, with only the top of Cathy's head peeking over the zipper.

Virgil sighed and gave in. There was just going to be a grown woman carrying a Chatty Cathy doll in a gay pride march in Bernie, Missouri. He supposed stranger things happened, though he couldn't think of one just then. Unless a Gay Bob decapitation in the middle of a flea market in Shipshewana, Indiana counted.

He figured it did. He wondered what color Grace's crystal ball was now.

The man who waved them out of the car was waiting at the edge of the crowd. Virgil shook his hand. "My name is Virgil," he said. "This is Grace."

"I'm Bob," he said and Virgil nearly fainted. Bob eyed Grace and the blonde synthetic hair poking out from her jacket. "We'll be marching down the main street, from the courthouse here to the city hall at the other end of downtown. We've got people down there already, setting up information booths and refreshments. Here's a sign for you."

Virgil shouldered the sign. It boasted a tame slogan, just the words, "GAY IS GOOD!" with an intensely smiling yellow happy face below it. Grace stuck to his side, putting her hand through his free arm.

"I'm not going to kid you," Bob said. "This isn't a pep rally. It could get ugly."

Virgil nodded. "This is Missouri."

Bob pursed his lips then and glanced back at the car. "I doubt if it's much different in Wisconsin, Virgil," he said.

Grace squeezed his arm.

They moved into the crowd. Virgil wasn't sure, but he thought being in the middle was likely safer than being on the edges, where observers could easily push, shove or worse. His heart was pounding. He couldn't tell if it was from excitement or fear. But this still felt right, even if he held the arm of a straight woman carrying a doll.

Before long, they started off. The group wasn't large; Virgil thought there were about fifty or so walking all around him. At first, it was pleasant, like a warm stroll in the sunshine. There wasn't any sun, the clouds were still low, but the air steamed with humidity and anticipation. People around them began to sing softly and then louder and louder, songs Virgil didn't know about equality and the right to love. He hummed along, not knowing the words, but feeling the rhythms sink into his marching feet. Grace seemed to look everywhere at once, but she was silent. Virgil was still hungry and he looked forward to the refreshment table at the end.

Then the crowds began to form on either side of the street, the protesters protesting the protest. Shouts rang out, rich with curses and slurs. Someone threw a tomato, then a bottle. Virgil switched the sign to his other shoulder and tucked Grace and Cathy on the inside of the marchers, further away from the closest curb, trying to protect her from any other missiles. But he knew she saw the faces, just as he did, those faces red with righteousness, the eyes bulging with hate. Those marching around them cowered just a little, their voices not so sure, their postures not so straight. They seemed quickly outnumbered; the little group seemed even smaller once they were flanked by those shouting from the curbs.

Grace's fear became palpable. She walked in fast skittering skips, taking three or four steps to Virgil's one. Her head swiveled as she watched wall-eyed for danger. She tucked Cathy further down into her jacket.

Bob stepped into the lead and began singing in a loud and beautiful tenor. Everyone else seemed to rescue their own voices then, straightened their sagging signs and walked tall. Virgil did too. He felt a surge of strength, of solidarity, and he sang out even though he didn't know the words, the melody, he just followed a beat behind. He was delighted as unmasked, unafraid laughter rolled around him, drowning out the threatening shouts.

But then there was Grace. She shrunk even more, tucking her face into Virgil's shoulder and blindly following, led by Virgil's arm. He wanted to shake her. "Grace," he hissed. "You're not going to an execution. Stand up. Look around!"

When she did, he saw her face was white. She looked at him like she didn't know who he was. She said something, he couldn't catch it, but in her eyes, Virgil saw the goodbye. In a breath, she broke away and disappeared into the crowd. "Grace!" he yelled. He tried to follow her, but the marchers swept him along. Bob dropped back into Grace's place by Virgil's side.

"I guess she wasn't as supportive as you thought," he said.

And Virgil wondered, tripping over his own feet. Bob took Virgil's arm and steadied him. He heard Grace's words again, telling him in Shipshewana that he wasn't like that, he wasn't like Gay Bob. But what was he like? Who did she think he was? What did she think he did in the privacy of his own home? And why did it matter?

He carried his sign to the end of the march. Then he threw it on the pile and turned to go. There was a crowd milling here too and without the marching lines, the singing voices, Virgil no longer knew who was friendly and who wasn't.

"You're welcome to have something to eat," Bob said.

Virgil shook his head. "No, thank you," he said. "I need to go."

Bob put his hand on Virgil's arm. "There's nothing to be afraid of. Come on, let's get a beer and a burger."

Virgil stood there uncertainly. He needed to find Grace, to make sure she was safe and in one piece. He needed to know what she truly thought of him. Was he okay to her as long as he was quietly gay and not loudly gay? As long as they didn't talk about it? Just like he and Brad didn't talk about it. But he also wanted to be right where he was, this new place of action and declaration, to be with others who knew intimately who he was and who accepted it, lived it themselves every single day.

In the middle of that crowd, Bob embraced him. Virgil turned his face to Bob's and found himself being kissed. Right there, in the middle of the street, in front of everyone, friendly and unfriendly. Virgil heard cheers. Bob kissed him deeply and Virgil drowned in his own desire. The warmth of being held, of being kissed just the way he liked, flooded his brain and his knees went weak. With Virgil's eyes shut, Bob became his absent lover, he became Brad, and Virgil felt Brad around him, his arms tight, his mouth at once strong and soft. Virgil smelled Brad's sweat, smelled their sex, and he moaned with the need to be in Georgia. Tucked in a bed, tucked in a bedroom, a house, filled with things found and restored in a junkyard. Virgil would be restored with Brad.

But when Virgil opened his eyes, when he broke away, it was a stranger's face smiling at him. Bob took Virgil's hand. "Come on, Virgil," he said.

Virgil started to trail after him, but then he felt it. The tension between his shoulder blades returned with a roar. Being with Bob, a stranger, kissing him, being aroused by him, was as wrong as a gay doll with cross-dressing clothes. He needed to be with Brad, with the man he loved and who loved him. And he needed to find Grace.

Breaking away, Virgil rolled into a flat-out run. He hadn't run in years and it felt good, his legs pumping, his breath coming quickly hard in gasps. "Look at that fag go!" he heard a man's voice crow. And then a woman's hiss, "Jim, we don't know that's a fag. He looks just fine. And he's going the wrong way."

Virgil ran back up the street, watching for any sign of Grace, for a flash of her hair or the bright blue-green of Cathy's corduroy coat. But he didn't find her until he was breathless and all the way back to where he left the Chrysler.

She was there, sobbing, crouched against the courthouse side of the car. There were only a few passersby, the world returned to a normal Monday late morning. No one paid a bit of attention to the crying woman on the curb.

It didn't take long to see why Grace was crying. Cathy was no longer tucked inside Grace's jacket, but clutched against her chest. A hunk of the doll's hair was suddenly short, falling raggedly against her head. Her coat was missing and her dress was torn.

Virgil reached down to touch Grace, to pull her to her feet, but she squalled and scuttled away on three limbs, like an injured crab, Cathy clutched in one arm. He tried again and her voice choked. She fell face down on the pavement, Cathy tucked under her body. "Grace!" he said sharply, and then more softly, "Grace. Honey, it's me, it's Virgil. Let me see you, let me see Cathy, I need to know you're all right."

She raised her face from the pavement, her cheeks streaked with black and tears. She didn't say anything, but Virgil saw her mouth his name. He touched her, stroking her hair away from her face, and she continued crying, but silently, her mouth open in a useless wail. He helped her to her feet, then reached for the doll.

Grace's fingers tightened. If Cathy was alive, she would have shouted in pain.

"Sweetheart," Virgil said. "Let me see her." He got the doll, but Grace kept one hand on her, circling Cathy's arm. Cathy's hair was a mess, hanging in ripped strands down her back. But her limbs were all there and they moved smoothly. Her eyes still opened and closed, her teeth were still in her mouth. Virgil turned her just a bit, and tugged at her string.

Cathy, looking directly at Grace, said, "I hurt myself."

And there, right in front of him, Virgil saw Grace's heart break. Again. Another piece shattered.

"She'll be okay," he said softly. "We can fix her. Let's go, let's get out of town and find another place to stay."

He guided Grace into the car. She trembled as he buckled her in. She wouldn't let go of Cathy and he didn't try to take her away, but rotated the doll's legs into a sitting position on Grace's lap. As they took back roads out of Bernie, he wondered if Grace would ever speak again. He wondered if he broke her. If his decision to stay in that town, to be called, cajoled, seduced into a march when he'd never marched, to declare himself in a way he never declared himself, left her in pieces. And he cursed himself. She would have been safer in the car, where she wanted to stay all along.

The sound of the tires and the close comfort of the Chrysler seemed to soothe Grace. Her eyes closed and so Virgil drove for a couple hours. At first, his direction was aimless, but as his mind cleared and relaxed along with Grace's, he remembered where they were headed. The candy corn factory. And the surprise he planned for Grace. In Crump, Tennessee.

Just outside of Crump, he made another decision when he saw a hotel suddenly looming on the side of the road. It was an all-suite hotel, a definite step up from the places where they'd been staying. They deserved it. No, they needed it. He glanced over at Grace, who seemed to be sound asleep. He pulled in. It was late afternoon and they never had breakfast or lunch, but he would get Grace settled first. Talking. Safe. Then dinner. Another bottle of wine.

While Virgil checked in, he worried that Grace would wake and bolt while he was away from the car. But she was still there, curled against the door, when he got back. He woke her and brought her to the suite.

He didn't know what to do. He needed to make her better. He looked at Cathy, still clutched in her arms. Making Cathy better would make Grace better. He needed to restore the doll. She wasn't dead. This wasn't like Paul. This wasn't like Grace's mother. Cathy was just different, changed, but still Grace's first doll, the one she wanted above all the others. The one who could still speak to her. He needed to make Grace see that. "C'mon, sweetheart," Virgil said. "Let's fix Cathy."

He led them both into the bathroom. It was huge, with a Jacuzzi tub big enough for two and a standalone shower. Grace didn't seem to notice. Virgil put the lid of the toilet down, then sat Grace on it. He filled the sink with water just high enough to reach Cathy's waist, well below the speaker holes for her voice. For a little extra protection, he pulled saran wrap he brought along especially for speaking dolls from his suitcase and wrapped her back and chest, so the holes were covered. He would wash all around, and then later, spot wash what was covered by the clear plastic. He added bubbles, special lavender-scented bubbles that he washed all the new dolls in, and the sweetness and steam filled the bathroom. Virgil always told himself he used the lavender for the customers, to make the buyers smell freshness and sweetness in their prospective purchases. But Virgil knew. He knew he did it for the dolls, for their comfort and resurrection.

Virgil sudsed the ragged remains of Cathy's hair and washed the grime from her body. The doll's smile was sweet and he made sure her teeth were clean, as well as her long black eyelashes. He was just beginning to rinse when Grace suddenly joined him at the sink. Virgil held Cathy steady and watched as Grace cupped her hands and poured the warm water over her doll. Virgil placed his hand over the saran wrap, over the holes, adding yet another layer of protection to Cathy's most precious voice.

When she was fully rinsed, Virgil plucked Cathy out of the water, pulled off the saran wrap and tucked her in a towel. Cradling her in his arms, he pulled her string.

"I'm sleepy," she said. Her voice was clear and strong. There were no gurgles or skips.

Virgil looked at the doll and he looked at Grace and at her too quiet face, her still silent voice, and the blankness in her eyes that he recognized from when she talked of Paul. It couldn't be there for Cathy. It just couldn't.

So Virgil decided to play. He was going to play with this doll, in a way that Grace was never allowed to. He was going to play and teach Grace how, pull her into it, into a land of pretend where her doll was real and needed care, needed her. Where Grace could see that she had the power to make her doll all right. "You can sleep soon, Cathy," he said. "But first, I have to take care of your hair. Your mom can help. We'll play salon. You're going to be gorgeous." He touched Grace on her shoulder. "I'll cut it, honey," he said. "And we'll give Cathy a new style."

She nodded.

The suite had a special area for the beds, partitioned off from the living area with a half wall and pillars. There was a vanity with a brightly lit mirror and Virgil set Cathy there, putting her legs into a sit. Grace trailed behind and sat on the edge of the bed. When Virgil looked at her in the mirror's reflection, he saw a fatigue that left Grace lifeless. "Grace," he said. "Go take a shower. I think it will help. By the time you come back out, I'll be well on my way with Cathy."

Grace stood up, but before returning to the bathroom, she ran her fingers through the doll's choppy uneven hair. The corners of her mouth turned down, and Virgil was almost happy to see it. It was the first real expression he saw cross her face since he got her in the car. Carefully, trying to ignore the flinch that ran through her body, he turned Grace and gave her a gentle nudge toward the bathroom. The door closed and he was relieved when he heard the water start to run. He hoped the amazing bathroom could do magic.

What in the world could have happened? How did Cathy get like this, and how did Grace get like that? Why would anyone in that crowd go after a woman with a doll?

Trying to be soothed by the steady percussion of the shower, Virgil set to work on Cathy. Armed with a blowdryer, a brush and a pair of sharp scissors, he sculpted her hair until it fell in a soft pageboy at her chin. She was different than all other Chatty Cathys now; she could not be replaced with another plastic doll on eBay, in a flea market, at an auction. Virgil thought she looked wonderful. Digging through Grace's things, he found Cathy's flannel pajamas and he dressed her, just as he knew Grace would.

Then he held Cathy in his lap and sat on his bed and waited for Grace to emerge from the bathroom. He didn't want to knock on the door, didn't want to poke his head in to see if she was all right. He thought that the steam, the heat, the scent of the lavender, would all help, and then, when she saw her doll, still intact, still lovely, Grace would be okay. She wasn't broken, he hadn't hurt her. His thoughts flitted briefly to Grace's family; would they expect a phone call? Should he call them? Maybe they were calling her. Virgil wasn't sure where Grace's cell phone was. And he wasn't sure it was his place to talk to her husband. He munched on chips and a candy bar, drank a soda. He was so hungry, but he didn't want to leave Grace alone while he went out to find some dinner. He and Cathy just sat and waited. When the shower turned off, the silence was overwhelming.

When the door opened, Grace was wrapped in a towel. Her curls, drenched, seemed to hang almost straight and water streamed down her shoulders. And then she saw Cathy.

Her face flew wide open. Grace, sodden, was suddenly there.

"Virgil," she said softly. "She looks lovely. You fixed her!" She held out her arms.

He put Cathy in them, noticing how Grace's elbows seemed to bend naturally around the curves in the doll's body. So different than the first time he handed Cathy to her, when she grasped the doll by her waist and dangled her at arm's length. They fit together now.

And then the weirdest phrase crossed his mind. *What's good for the goose is good for the gander.* He pulled out the padded stool for the vanity. "Grace," he said, "sit down."

She was busy examining Cathy, exclaiming over her hair, and she sat without question.

Virgil took his brush and he took his hairdryer and stood behind her. And then he dried her hair. Her eyes opened huge in surprise and then closed in pleasure. Virgil delighted in watching the dark wet strands coil back into blonde springs, stretched out like loose corkscrews, lovely. In the mirror, he could see Grace's eyelashes curved dark against her cheeks. When her hair was dry, he kept at it for a little longer, just to keep things moving forward, to keep them returning to this new normal, to making things all right again. Then he turned off the blowdryer and told Grace to go get dressed.

When she came out of the bathroom for a second time, all put together again, he felt his face must be doing exactly what hers did when she saw Cathy. "Are you all right?" he asked. He smiled, to hide his anxiety. "Did I fix you too?"

She looked at him and for a moment, her eyes threatened to overflow again. But she fought back the tears. "They tried to take her from me, Virgil," she said. "That crowd. Somebody grabbed her hair where it stuck out of my jacket and he just pulled her from me. They tossed her back and forth like a game of keep-away and I tried to get her. I had her by the feet and this guy had her by the hair and I was afraid her head was going to come off. He took out a knife and he sawed her hair off and he waved it like a flag, like a prize. When I ran, someone else grabbed Cathy's arm and got her coat. Her dress tore."

A knife. A knife at a peaceful demonstration. Virgil was horrified. "Thank God," he breathed. "Thank God he didn't get you, Grace."

Grace's lower lip trembled. "But he got Cathy."

"I know." He gave her back the doll and she embraced Cathy in a way that knocked away all the years between her childhood and now. She hugged Cathy the way she would have hugged her if the doll was under the tree at Christmas, or sitting by a birthday cake decorated with any number of candles. She just hugged her. There was no stiffness. "She's fine," Virgil said. "You're fine. I fixed her hair, and we can find another coat and another dress. It'll be okay."

Grace nodded and tilted Cathy back until her eyes slowly closed. She cradled her like a baby.

"Grace," Virgil whispered, as if he was trying to not wake the doll. He was still playing. He would play forever, if it meant Grace would be okay. "Why did you run away?"

She shuddered, a movement that rolled the length of her body, shook her in memory. "I didn't belong there, Virgil," she said. "Not with you and the others. But those people on the sides of the road, I didn't belong there either. They scared me, I saw the way they looked at me. The way they looked at you. They hated us, they hated every single person in that march." She took Virgil's hand

and squeezed it so tightly, he felt his fingers go white. "It didn't matter who I was anymore. Or what I did or what I believed. They just hated."

Virgil thought of his father and nodded. "It's like that, Grace. Being gay. With some people, it's like you cease to be human, you cease being a person. All you are is who you sleep with, and in their eyes, you'd better be sleeping with the right person."

Grace pursed her lips. "I don't care who people sleep with," she said. "I don't care if they sleep with sheep, it's none of my business."

Startled, Virgil laughed out loud and the sound brought Grace's smile back. "With sheep?" He laughed all over again, but not just because of the sheep.

"Well, it doesn't matter, does it? Why do I have to know who you sleep with? Why does it matter who I sleep with? You're just Virgil, that's all. I'm just Grace. Everything else is…private."

Virgil nodded. "You're right. You're exactly right. It's funny, isn't it, how some of us have to fight for the right to that privacy." He sat back, thinking about how it felt to march with the group, join his voice to theirs. "I'm sorry, Grace, I should have let you stay in the car when you told me you were uncomfortable with the march."

Her shrug was barely there. "They even hated Cathy, Virgil, and she doesn't sleep with anybody. Not that way."

Virgil's throat tightened. He knew how Grace felt about Cathy. He thought about his own dolls at home, about his sister's doll that he kept hidden under his childhood bed. "Some people hate anything that's different, Grace."

She hugged Cathy again and Virgil could see the protection in her action. He could see the mother who would do anything to protect her child.

What would it do to a mother if her child died just out of her reach? If the willingness to do anything at all ended up not meaning a damn thing?

Virgil couldn't think of it. He was just so sorry. He'd nearly brought another grief down on her head. While she was still running away from another. From her son's death. And from her mother's, too. "Grace," he said. "Please forgive me. Please…just don't hate me."

She frowned and then said, "Why would I hate you? I love you, Virgil. You're just my best friend. Which is so weird, because we've known each other for only ten days. But it's true." She nodded, her nod as definite as any declaration. "You're my best friend."

And she was his.

"What time is it?" she asked. She looked around. "Virgil, I'm starving. And where are we?"

Virgil was never so happy to laugh.

****

That night, after a comforting meal of fried chicken, cole slaw, fresh corn and peach pie, Virgil took a shower while Grace called home, giving her the privacy he felt she needed, and he noticed the redness of her eyes when he returned. She was already in bed and she blinked at him and then she was out, just like that. Cathy was beside her, and Virgil noticed that while she didn't hug the doll, she did have an arm thrown over her, drawing her close. Virgil turned out the last of the lights and slid into bed. He didn't set an alarm; Virgil intended to let them each sleep. They weren't on a schedule; they didn't need to be anywhere at any time, although his own clock ticked steadily toward Brad. He looked at Grace, seeing her shape in the shadows, hearing the softness of her breath. He thought of the sound of her voice, her laughter, which still came too infrequently. But when it did, it was honest and he knew she was truly happy. Looking at her in the dark, he loved her with all his heart.

She was his best friend.

And there was no arousal. Virgil noticed that, noticed that there was no stirring, no yearning. There was only a deep warmth, a desire to keep Grace close, to protect her and get her home safely. To see her fully happy again, to see her smile the way he knew she could, without unhappiness tethering the corners of her mouth. He wanted to see her throw back her head and laugh, as loudly and as long as her voice and lungs would allow.

Virgil considered his decision that night, as he lowered himself to sleep, to bring Grace here to the candy corn factory. He thought of Grace and her dead son, eating candy pumpkins and brightly colored candy corn in the middle of March, in the middle of July, bringing the warmth of fall to the dead of winter, the cool of fall to the heat of summer. It was important somehow, that Grace eat the bright orange candy again, that she take it in and smile, savor the sweetness, laugh at the memories, then look at the day around her. Just as the warm bath and haircut healed Cathy, Virgil knew the candy corn, once inside of Grace's body, bringing the sweetness of the past and the present together in the flow of oxygen and blood, memory and freshness, would heal her. Or if not heal her exactly, then send her down the path.

And then he had to get to Brad. He had to face the ultimatum and decide what he was going to do.

He wished his decision was made. He wished his hands on the steering wheel were sending him in a predetermined direction. But while he knew full well where he was going, he just wasn't sure what he was going to do when he got there.

He thought of the kiss with Bob in the middle of the street. Then he shook it away. He remembered the upsurge of love he felt for Brad, the rightness of being with him. He loved Brad. That was never in question.

But to give up everything else? His home, his store, the life he'd built for himself in Waukesha. And now Grace was a part of that too. Though he didn't think Brad would take too kindly to Grace being a part of his consideration.

And there was the big question. Would it last? Would it last to the point of loss? And what kind of loss? Maybe Virgil would run away, the way Grace was running now. Maybe Brad would die and Virgil would have to face the grief that Grace was now facing.

Though even if Brad died right now, on this night, Virgil would face grief.

Virgil sighed and rolled over. He faced the wall, away from Grace. Away from the window which looked out over the road that would lead him to Brad. He faced away from all of it.

And then he closed his eyes.

CHAPTER NINE
Grace

That first night in Crump, Tennessee, after Virgil cut Cathy's hair and dried Grace's, after she began to feel a bit steady again, Grace called home. She wanted to keep it short; she felt stretched past her limit and she just wanted to give in to sleep.

Grace waited until she heard Virgil start his shower and then she sat on the couch. A couch! It would be the first time she called home while sitting on a couch and not a bed.

Actually, it was a while since she even sat on a couch. Gingerly, she lowered herself onto the cushions and felt the back and the arm of the couch support her. She sighed and put her feet up on the coffee table. It all felt so familiar, yet it was a luxury as well. She wondered if home would feel like a luxury, when she got there. It hadn't felt like home for so long before she left.

Nick answered this time. There was a hesitancy in his voice, a held-breath hope, and she knew he'd be glad it was her. She held hope too, hope that the glad would be there without the undertone of anger. She was going to have to tell him she was further away again. She'd already decided not to talk about the march. "Hi, hon," she said.

"Grace!" She heard the quick movement of his feet and a door slam. Nick must have locked himself in the coat closet, just like JJ. Grace nearly laughed out loud in surprise. "Grace, where are you now?" he whispered. Grace wanted to tell him that there was no need. That closet seemed to be the best insulated room in the house.

"I'm in Tennessee," she said. "Virgil is taking me to a candy corn factory. He says if I eat candy corn and pumpkins again, I'll feel better."

Nick's breath escaped loudly and Grace's hidden laughter of surprise changed to a feeling of dread. She felt his exhale extinguish her hope. "Grace, honey, that's ridiculous," he said. She heard a strain in his voice and she wondered if he was trying not to yell. "You know that's ridiculous. How can candy corn fix anything? You can eat candy corn here. Come home. Now. I mean it."

The strain wasn't anger; it was desperation. That was new, and Grace wasn't sure how to respond to it. She was the one who was supposed to feel desperate…desperate enough to run away. She hadn't thought about his being desperate for her to come home. "I know you do, Nick. But I'm not done yet. Soon, though."

"Any idea when soon is? Thanksgiving? Christmas? New Year's?" Plaintive. But there was a little river of anger there now too. Grace braced herself against it. "God, you've already missed —"

Grace cut in. "I've only been gone ten days, Nick."

There was a rustle, a rustle she knew well. Nick was crossing his arms, which meant that he was getting, in his own word, "serious." An ultimatum might be on the way. "Grace, look. I've been really patient, and I'm trying to stay that way. I'm here all alone with the kids. I'm trying to take care of them, the house, and my work. I'm worried about you." Nick's voice drew tight as a guitar string. "Look where you are. Look at you!"

Grace looked. She was in a very nice hotel suite in Tennessee, albeit after being attacked in a gay march in Bernie, Missouri. "I see, Nick," she said. "I'm fine."

Nick pounced. "Then come home."

Grace sighed. "No. I'm not fine at home. Not yet."

They sat in silence for a moment. Then she asked to talk to the kids.

"No." It was as flat as that, like a dull nickel on a tabletop.

Grace sat stone still. So they were back to that. The returned cruelty sunk over her shoulders like wet cement. "Nick, come on. I've had a hard day. Don't do this again. Please let me speak to them. We just told them two nights ago that I would call home every night."

Nick barked; it couldn't be called a laugh. "You've had a hard day? I said no, Grace. It's my decision to make, Grace, and I'm making it. I'm here alone with them and I have to choose what is good for them. I am their only parent."

"No, you're not!" She stood up and started pacing. "I'm their mother!"

"Then act like it and come home." And he hung up.

Grace stared at her cell, not believing that there was only silence, a blank screen. What could have happened that caused this sudden switch back to being locked out? He started to say she missed something; what was it? Apparently, his day was hard too. A hard day at work, a hard day with the kids? Both? She knew days like that, she remembered them from before Paul's death, from when she still worked, when she was up to her neck in frustration and then came home and found arguing children and a cat that barfed and supper still frozen in the freezer because she'd forgotten to take it out. Nick would walk in too and they'd look at each other and he would see that she was neck-high. He'd toss his briefcase on the counter and yell for the kids. "We're going out," he'd say. And then he'd kiss her cheek and add, "We'll bring some back for you. Go take a bath or a nap or something."

Maybe it was a day like that. But there was no one there for Nick.

The guilt returned. And again, she had to remind herself: if she was home, there'd be no one there for him either. He'd likely be the one taking the kids out. She'd already be in bed. And she wouldn't have been at work.

Everything was different now. Different before she left, still different after she left.

She needed to talk to her kids. They needed to talk to her. She was their mother. Mothers were allowed to take breaks, weren't they? When there was nothing left to do but take a break or break down?

She speed-dialed home again. Nick said, "Hello." His voice was tired; he knew it was her.

"Let me talk to the kids, Nick," Grace said. Her voice was solid. "I've lost one child. Do you really want to take the others away too?"

She expected his voice to come back like a slap, but he sighed. "You can't keep hiding behind that, Grace. I lost Paul too."

Grace was stunned. "Hiding? You think I'm hiding? I am not hiding, Nick. I had to do this. It was do this, or just…just…"

Nick's voice dropped low. "Or just what, Grace? What would you have done if you stayed here?"

Grace thought of the nailed-shut Priscillas. The painting somewhere in her daughter's room of a dancing skeleton wearing a blue backpack. That tree. That tree that couldn't be blamed, but was a daily reminder of everything she'd lost. Even though she didn't visit his grave, Paul's deathspot was in her vision every single day. "I would have disintegrated, Nick," she whispered. "I already was. I just wouldn't have made it any longer."

Nick breathed, then spoke more softly. "Which is why I'm worried. I don't see how this is helping you. I know it's not helping me or the kids. Look, Grace,

I told you –"

In the background, Grace suddenly heard JJ. "Dad! Is that Mom? You said Grace!"

"JJ, it's not –" Nick said and then Grace leaped.

At the top of her lungs, not caring who heard, Grace yelled, "JJ! JJ! It is Mom! It's me! Tell Dad to give you the phone!"

The suite rang with her voice. Grace could imagine the people in adjoining rooms looking at each other, wondering what was going on. She could imagine Nick and JJ eyeing each other, squaring off. Her little boy. Her youngest, her second surprise. Her boy was strong enough to do this.

"Dad." JJ's voice was deep and steady, not whiny. "Dad, that's Mom. She wants to talk to me, can't you hear her?"

Nothing. And then another sigh, defeated, a sigh that would have pulled wind out of the sails rather than billowed them. "Yes, JJ, I hear her. Do you want to speak with her?"

"Yes, Dad, please." The phone was turned over and JJ's sweet voice filled Grace's ear. "Mom, are you there?"

Grace burst into tears. She hated herself for it, but they were there without control. She knew they would scare her son and she tried to stop.

"Mom, is that you? Are you okay?"

"Yes, JJ," Grace managed. "Hang on. I just…I just thought I might not get to talk to you and it made me sad. I'm okay now." She swallowed her tears and forced her voice to brighten. "How are you, sweetheart?"

"Good. I mean, it's…I miss you, but I'm good. Where are you tonight?" JJ spoke softly and evenly. Grace felt herself soothed. She described her suite to him, described the view out her window. She didn't mention the candy corn. She didn't want to think about it. By the end of their conversation, Grace was breathing evenly again. Her son brought her there.

She wished he didn't have to. She wished she didn't have to rely on a twelve-year old. It wasn't his place. "I love you," she said and knew it wasn't even close to being enough.

"And I love you too. Mary's here."

Grace sat up. "Oh, good. She'll talk to me?" Mary had only said hello and goodbye the night before; nothing else was offered.

For an answer, Grace heard a shuffle and then Mary greeted her. It was low, but the "Hi, Mom," was definitely there. They shared how are you's and then sat in silence.

Grace eked forward on the couch. "Sweetie, can I ask you something?"

Mary took a breath before saying, "Sure. But I might not answer."

Grace could have predicted that. "Do you hate me?"

This time, the silence stretched on forever and Grace wondered if Mary truly was going to not answer. Grace hugged herself.

Then, "Of course not, Mom. I don't hate you." Mary's voice sounded crinkly, like it might crack, but it didn't. Grace waited for the "I love you" that she hoped would follow, but didn't receive it.

Instead, in the new silence, Grace felt herself fall into Mary's train of thought. She saw the tunnel it dove into and she thought, Oh, no.

"Mom," Mary said slowly. "Mom, actually, it's me that wonders. About hate, you know. Do you hate me? For what I did to Paul? Is that why…is that why you're not here today?"

And there it was. Again. Another chance. Again. How many chances would she get?

"Mary," Grace said. "Mary, I love you with all my heart. I could never hate you. Never ever. No matter what." And in her own head, she coached herself to say, *And it wasn't your fault.* But still, her voice refused to cooperate. Stubbornly, her mind back-talked like Mary herself, *She told Paul to climb the tree. And then he died.* The hate Grace asked Mary about, the hate Mary asked Grace about, spun around and around and spread through Grace's body like a textured reflection. If Grace hated anyone, it was herself. And actually, there was no if about it. Grace wished there was some way to show Nick this, to cover him with this feeling. Then he would understand, like she did, that she couldn't go home yet.

Grace and Mary breathed together for a few more moments, both of them waiting for the words that refused to come. Then Mary spoke, in the smallest voice Grace ever heard from her child. "I love you too, Mom. Please come home. I don't belong to them, you know. I belong to you. It should have been me who died. Then you could have your happy and whole family, all of you related to each other."

And she was gone.

"Mary!" Grace called. "Mary, come back! We're not done!"

"She is." Nick was back and his voice was even more tired. "And that's what I'm dealing with. She won't call me Dad anymore. She calls me Nick, and even that isn't said often. JJ told me that she thinks if you blame her, then I must blame her more, because she's not really my daughter."

"Oh my god." Grace's head spun. Nick was the only father Mary ever had.

"It's just one more thing, I guess, Grace. One more bit of fallout. It's like this never ends. We won't ever go back to normal."

Grace knew that already. Now Nick knew it too. One more thing. All the weight of those one more things came across in his words and in the tone and lack of lilt in his voice. All the one more things. Taking care of the kids. Taking care of the house. Balancing work, which paid the bills, with the work at home, which nourished the children. A dead son. A runaway wife. And now a daughter who felt she wasn't a daughter. A daughter who couldn't call her stepdad Dad and whose mother couldn't tell her she wasn't at fault for killing her brother. Her half-brother. Her stepfather's son.

Grace knew she should go home. She knew it. But she couldn't. Not yet.

"I don't know what to do, Nick," Grace said slowly. She felt her tears start again, effortless. She thought she heard an echo over the phone. Nick was crying too? "I'm trying to figure out how to go on."

His voice broke. "So are we, Grace. And now it's like we've lost you too."

Grace gasped. There was the slap. "I'm right here." She listened to the silence, creased with shaking breaths. "Nick, do you hate me?" Please, she thought. Just answer. "Nick? Do you hate me?"

"No, Grace," he whispered finally. "I love you."

"I love you too," she whispered back. Then the phone was dead.

Grace threw it on the coffee table. She was tired of death. She wanted only to crawl into bed and sleep.

****

The next morning, when Grace woke up, the first thing she saw was the space of the suite and she couldn't get over it. The space! There was a small living room with a couch and a coffee table and a big television on its own stand. There was a kitchenette with a tiny refrigerator, a tinier stovetop, and a microwave. The bedroom held two king-sized beds and Cathy almost disappeared in all the pillows.

In the bathroom, Grace admired the amazing bathtub she barely noticed yesterday and hugged herself. The tub had jets and the idea of being sunk up to her chin in hot burbling water, water churned only for her comfort and relaxation, seemed the ultimate in luxury. The suite was like a mini-mansion, all boxed up into its own space among many mini-mansions.

210

When she came back out of the bathroom, Virgil was just hanging up his phone and frowning. "Hell," he said, looking at her. "Since it's no longer summer, the candy corn factory is on its off-season schedule. During the week, there's only one tour a day and today's is already full. I had to book us for tomorrow. So we'll just be hanging around today."

Grace was getting discombobulated with the passing of time. "What about my other surprise? The thing that you said was the purpose for the stop?"

Virgil shook his head. "I want to wait on that. Let's do the candy corn first. I think it's important."

Grace shrugged, puzzled over what her surprise could be. "What day is it today anyway?" she asked.

"Tuesday." Virgil went into the kitchen. "Yesterday was Halloween."

"Yesterday was Halloween?" Grace sat down hard on the couch. Paul's favorite holiday. Her mother's too. Nobody said a word last night on the phone when she called home. Instead, so much more was said.

But they did say something, didn't they. Nick said she already missed something, right after he asked if she'd be home by Thanksgiving, Christmas, New Year's. JJ comforted her, instead of finishing the sentence he started. And Mary asked if Grace wasn't there that day because of what happened with Paul.

They did try to tell her.

Paul would have never let her forget. But Paul wasn't there to remind her, even though she was reminded of him every single day. She was supposed to forget him. Instead, she forgot Halloween.

Grace wanted to put her head between her knees, things were spinning so badly.

Virgil opened and closed the microwave. "Yep. I forgot too." He opened the cabinets and inspected the pots. "I was hoping to make you a home-cooked meal," he said. "But how can I do that with only a microwave and burners? Why isn't there an oven?"

Grace took a deep breath, struggled to pull herself out of her spin. "I've never understood kitchenettes in hotel rooms anyway. Seems to me when you're out in a hotel, you probably want to eat out as well. Though I admit, home-cooked does sound good." Halloween. Did Nick remember to buy candy? This was the first year, she remembered, that JJ was going to stay home, not go out trick or treating. He said it was because he was twelve. Grace wondered if it was because of Paul.

Virgil looked at his watch. "Maybe I'll go out and pick up some spaghetti fixings. I can make that on the burners. And a nice fresh salad too. Warm Italian bread, dripping with butter and dusted with garlic." He grabbed his jacket. "The hotel has a free continental breakfast and it's still being served. Why don't you head downstairs and get something and I'll go take care of our supper. After breakfast, we can go down to the pool if you'd like, just relax, then go out for lunch since we're having dinner here." He waved and was gone. Grace's stomach growled and she hoped he'd remember dessert. Cannolis would be perfect. She texted him and received a thumb's up back.

It wasn't odd to spend more than a night at the same hotel, but it was odd to not have anything doll-related to do. No estate sales, no flea markets. Grace went downstairs and made her own waffle in the hotel's wafflemaker. She burned it, just like she always did at home. And then she made a second and allowed herself extra syrup, poured herself more coffee. She and Virgil paddled in the pool and she fell asleep in the still-warm Tennessee sun. There was a laundromat in the hotel and Virgil washed their clothes.

Through it all, Halloween was over. Paul's favorite holiday was over, and she hadn't even thought about it.

Grace felt guilty. She remembered telling Mary she wasn't on vacation, but here she was, eating waffles and soaking in the sun.

And having a man cook for her.

And losing track of time. And Halloween. How could she forget it was Halloween?

After dinner, while Virgil was soaking in the jacuzzi tub, Grace sat on the couch to call home again. She had to. She was supposed to call every night. And yesterday was Halloween. She had to say something. Someone had to say something.

Halloween was always special, to Grace's mother, to Paul, and so to Grace too. From the time he was a little boy, Paul spent the week before Halloween recording himself telling and reading scary stories on an old cassette recorder. On Halloween night, after trick or treating was over, he and Mary and JJ huddled in the boys' room with a single candle and shrieked while listening to Paul's bodyless voice. Shrieked and laughed, but shrieked and shrieked. Grace and Nick crept outside the closed door and listened too, laughing about it later in the privacy of their bedroom, in the haven of their bed. One by one, the kids dropped away from trick or treating; Mary first, Paul second, and this year, JJ. But the recording remained, a new one each year, and they listened to the old ones too. Halloween was one of those moments where, despite their increasing age and drawing away from each other, the kids still came together. Tradition over hormones and growth spurts and distracted and varied interests.

But this year…no Paul. And JJ wasn't going trick or treating. And Grace wasn't at home.

Grace and her mother always had tradition too. After the children were asleep on Halloween night, Grace went over to her mother's house. They sat in the living room and Grace's mother told and retold stories about her own childhood Halloweens, before the town built up and while houses were still spaced far apart. Grace's mother always chose to dress as a witch, she said, but she never looked scary. She wore all white; a gown made from a king-size pillowcase, and her peaked hat was made from heavily taped tissue paper. She wore no makeup, but carried a crystal ball in one hand and her treat bag in the other. After trick or treating, and after her parents fell asleep, Grace's mother snuck out of the house and ran to the cemetery. She said she could always feel the spirits rising in celebration on Halloween night and she danced around the graveyard, looking for them. Some years, she found them and they held her hands and joined her dance in the darkness. Other years, the spirits sat quietly and she sat with them in a circle and still held their hands. Those years, she said, the spirits were just too sad to play. Too sad, because they were dead. Some spirits, her mother said, hated to be dead. Others were happy and some were never alive at all so they didn't know what they were missing. After a few hours in the cemetery, her mother always fell asleep, curled against a carefully chosen headstone, a different one every year, always selected for its newness. She wanted to offer comfort to those that weren't used to their new surroundings yet. Grace's grandfather found her there the next morning, year after year, and he carried her home and tucked her into bed. Her parents wondered sometimes, her mother said, if she was "touched in the head". Grace always smiled at that phrase. Her mother was touched in the head, but in the most wonderful way.

Grace wondered if her mother and Paul were among those who were sad at being dead. She wondered if her mother offered comfort to Paul. If they leaned against each other.

Her mother always had a cold during the first two weeks of November, even as an adult. Each and every year that Grace lived at home and each and every year after she moved out, Grace checked on her mother the morning after Halloween. Grace was always afraid her mother still visited the cemetery on Halloween night and she was also afraid her mother wouldn't find her way back.

She always did. Until, of course, she moved to the cemetery permanently.

Even then, Grace knew where to find her. There, and also in the bank vault. And now, carefully tucked away in dollars in a suitcase, in an Easter Island pendant, with Grace on this journey.

So Grace called home on this special day-after-Halloween night. Her kids had to know their mother could find her way back too.

Nick answered again. "Where are you now?" he asked, his voice still flat and tired. There was no patience left, Grace could hear its lack, and so she answered carefully.

"I'm still in Tennessee. We're going to the candy corn factory tomorrow. Nick, yesterday was Halloween. I forgot. Did you and JJ put candy corn on Paul's grave?"

"No."

That firm and steady "I'm the only parent" voice again. The only parent who decided that Paul's grave should be blank and empty on Halloween, his first Halloween away from home. "Why not? I asked you to!"

"I think we need to stop that kind of thing."

Those words were so cold, so bare. Leaving Paul alone, leaving him behind. No longer a part of them, of his mom and dad, his brother and stepsister, as if his death amputated him from his family. "Why? Why would you take that away?"

The gusty sigh. The impatient sigh. The I'm-at-the-end-of-my-rope sigh. "Because it's time, Grace. I've told the kids they can visit the grave and bring flowers, they can do that as often as they want, but they can't bring anything else. Nothing that a living person could use. None of us are going to do that anymore." Nick's voice was matter of fact, rule-setting, and Grace knew that this was how he sounded when he told the kids about the giftless visits to Paul. Mary probably didn't care, she wasn't bringing anything to the grave anyway, but what did JJ think? He had plans for around the year.

Grace thought about her own visit to the flower shop right before she ran away. She thought of the birdbaths, and how she considered leaving one at Paul's grave.

Only flowers?

It was time, Nick said. But it wasn't Grace's time. In your time, Gracie, her mother would say. "Nick," she said. "I don't think that's a good idea."

His response was obvious. Grace should have seen it coming. "I'm here alone, Grace," Nick said. "I'm a single parent, remember, at least until you decide to come home. I have to make the decisions on my own and I'm going with what I think is right."

The voice of reason.

So Grace swallowed it. What else could she do? She was in Tennessee, sitting on a strange bed with her doll, and there was a gay doll salesman in her bathroom. She realized that right then, right at that moment, she didn't feel like a mother. Maybe Nick was a single parent. Maybe it wasn't Paul that was amputated from the family. Maybe it was Grace. And maybe she did it to herself, taking the scalpel to her own skin to sever her body from her kids, her husband, her responsibilities. Maybe she was just a dead limb.

Was Paul a dead limb? Was she dead too?

She looked at her hands and noticed how empty they were. Her voice shook when she asked to speak to Mary.

Nick paused and Grace wondered if he was surprised that she wasn't giving him an argument. Then he said, "Okay, hold on." When he called Mary's name, Grace heard a steady step and then a quick intake of breath.

"Hello, Mom," she said. "How are you?"

Grace was taken aback. She knew this was her daughter, but she was using another new voice. There was no snark. There was no sneer. And the quiet and sad voice she heard last night, the smaller than small voice, was gone. "I'm fine, sweetheart," Grace said slowly. "I forgot to say Happy Halloween yesterday."

"Happy Halloween to you too." She sounded so grown up and for a moment, Grace swirled into disorientation. She put a hand on Cathy's knee.

"Mary, Dad told me about what he decided," Grace said. "About how you can only bring flowers to Paul's grave. Are you okay with that? Is JJ? I'm sorry." The last two words slipped through before Grace knew she was saying them. Right then, Grace couldn't have said what she was sorry for. Not being home? The ban on bringing things to the grave? Allowing that practice in the first place? For not stopping Paul a second before he touched that live wire?

For blaming Mary? For not telling her Paul's death wasn't her fault?

Grace was just sorry. For all of it.

There was another quick intake of breath and then Mary's voice burst suddenly into full life. "Mom," she said. "Mom, we listened to a tape last night, me and JJ. When Paul died and you guys threw his stuff away, I went through his desk before you did and I got the last tape he made. The last Halloween one. I hid it, because I didn't want you to get rid of it too. JJ and I listened to it, up in the boys' room with a candle, just like we're supposed to. Like we always do. We had to, we had to, I mean, there was no candy pumpkins and Paul wasn't here and you weren't here and JJ didn't go trick or treating. It felt wrong. So wrong. So I got the tape out last night—"

Her voice broke and Grace could only gasp into the phone as she pictured the two of them, her remaining children, sitting by a tape recorder, listening to Paul's voice. Listening to the one who was missing. Who was taken away. At that moment, Grace wanted to be with them more than anywhere else in the world, but she didn't want to be there to offer comfort. She wanted to be there because Paul's voice was there. She wanted to hear him, just one more time. She wanted to hear him trying to be scary, his voice deep as he attempted to be a ghoul. Deeper than his natural voice would ever have the chance to be. "Mary, you did? You still have it?"

"It's here, Mom, it's here! I hid it again. But it made JJ cry. It made…it made me cry. And then it seemed like you forgot. And after you called, JJ and me, well, we just couldn't stop crying. We cried in my room after Dad went to bed."

There was a sound and Grace wondered if Nick was listening.

"Mom, really, I didn't mean to, I guess it wasn't a good idea, I'm sorry, I didn't think. I'm so sorry." Mary began to cry, loud sobs that weren't at all like the Mary who used to cry, but like the Mary now, this new Mary, the angry, sullen teenager whose sullenness went beyond the typical adolescent, whose sullenness was born of a grief she should never have had to face. "I just thought with you and Paul gone, it would be nice to do something normal. Something we always do."

Something normal, when nothing would ever be normal again. Grace cried with her daughter and their sobs were in harmony. "I know, honey," Grace said. "I know you just wanted to hear him. I'm glad you kept that tape, I'm glad."

"I just wanted a normal day!" Mary wailed and her voice echoed every day of Grace's life since Paul fell out of that tree.

Then she heard Nick's voice, the calm voice, that damned voice of reason. "I found the tape," Grace heard him say to Mary. "Your brother just showed me where it was. I threw it away. And I broke it too, so don't even think about pulling it out of the garbage."

Mary shrieked, a shriek so different from the ones Grace used to hear through the doorway of Paul's bedroom. This shriek was horror and grief all rolled up into one long and sorrowful shaky note. Grace's voice rang with hers. She'd already been thinking how she could listen to that tape when she got home, how she could hear her boy again, reciting his favorite stories, trying to scare his brother and sister and even himself. Mary did such a smart thing and it would have been the best gift to return home to. And now it was gone. Paul's voice, restored for a few moments, was gone again. Mary dropped the phone and over the clatter, Grace heard her screaming to her room and slamming the door. Nick ran after her, calling her name, begging her to stop.

There was a click and the phone was picked up. "Hi, Mom," JJ said. His voice was soft and Grace knew he was rubbing his left ear, a habit he fell into whenever he was tired or stressed.

"Hello, sweetheart," Grace said. "Are you okay?"

"We shouldn't have done it," JJ said. "We shouldn't have listened. I should have told Mary no. I didn't know Dad would break the tape, that it would be gone too. I didn't know." For a moment, his voice wavered in such a way that Grace thought he might wail too, that one long and expressive note, just like his sister's. JJ, the most practical of her three children, never wailed. Sometimes, as an infant, JJ cried so quietly that Grace wouldn't even notice it until it was over, until she checked on her baby and found him red-cheeked and tear-streaked, but sound asleep in his crib. She felt so useless then.

She felt useless now.

"JJ, you didn't do anything wrong. You didn't! You just listened to your brother, that's all. It's okay, sweetie."

"No," he said flatly. "It isn't okay. It isn't okay at all." He sounded amazingly like his father. "Mom, I've got to go. I'm sure Mary is mad at me."

When his voice was gone, they would be away from her again. Her children, her little boy and girl. The remaining ones. Only Paul could have given Mary and JJ that title, that classification. "Okay, honey, but don't hang up. Dad might want to talk to me yet. I love you, JJ."

"Love you too, Mom." There was a thud as he set the phone on the counter and Grace wondered how much longer he would be able to put a good spin on things. Her practical, good-natured peacemaker boy.

She was waiting for Nick to come back, when she heard a snuffling over the phone. It puzzled her for a moment, then she realized it must be TheCat. "TheCat's on the counter!" she yelled out of habit, the counter being strictly off-limits to a certain cat. The snuffling stopped and then she caught a faint purring. "Hello, kitty," Grace said, her voice softening. "How are you?"

To hell with rules. What were the rules about anyway? There weren't any more rules. In a life where a child could die, could climb a tree on a glorious day and end up with no breath, no life, no play, no candy, how could there be any rules at all?

Footsteps, and then Nick muttering, "Get down!" and a sweep and a thump as TheCat hit the floor. "Still there?" Nick asked.

"Still here. Everything okay?"

"Of course not." His voice was more than quiet, it was lifeless.

"Nick, why did you break the tape? I could have listened to it when I got home." Her voice cracked and she told herself not to shriek. "Why did you do that?"

"Grace, you can't hear him," Nick said. "You can't. He's dead, okay? The kids shouldn't be hearing him. You should be home. We should be moving on. If the tape was here, you'd be listening to it all the time. All the time. You can't listen to him, Grace." He paused. "Grace, please come home." His voice changed. Grace felt a shock as she realized how much he wanted to shriek too and then just rest his head on her shoulder.

He cried when Paul died. But mostly he held Grace as she wept. Not once had he leaned on her, putting his weight against her, his tears joining hers. Now, she could hear that lean in his voice, she could hear the strain of holding it all together. Holding himself, holding the kids, holding his wife. She so much wanted to catch him as he fell. She wanted to steady him as he stumbled. At that moment, she wanted to say, "Yes, Nick." She wanted to get on a plane and be home in only a couple hours.

But she just wasn't ready. It would be a mistake. "I can't believe you broke the tape," she said, her voice trembling. "I can't believe you destroyed his voice. Didn't you want to hear him?" And then, quietly, she hung up. Nick's voice and the sounds of home were gone, just like that.

Just like Paul's.

****

It was a short drive to the candy corn factory the next day. The closer they got, the heavier the air became. Sugar. Sweetness. Grace expected to see the clouds in the sky stiffen into meringue and the trees turn into fat candy pumpkins with green tops. At first, she thought she was going to be sick. Paul and candy corn were everywhere, she couldn't get away from the smell and the invasion of memory even if she plugged her nose. She wanted to stop breathing.

"I don't want to go, Virgil," Grace said. She stared at her knees. There were billboards now, announcing the factory, exclaiming the distance as it grew smaller and smaller and she knew she's soon be in the parking lot.

"I know. But you've got to, Grace." Virgil drummed his fingers on the wheel. "I think it's important. I want you to realize that some things don't have to change. The taste of candy corn, for example."

But Virgil hadn't lost a child. Everything changed when you lost a child.

Time to move on. It's time, Grace. But it wasn't Grace's time. Sometimes, she felt that Nick wanted her to stop loving Paul, wanted her to forget about him, just like she forgot about Halloween. If she was able to forget Halloween, could she forget her own son?

Sometimes, if Grace held her breath long enough, if she quieted herself long enough to think it, she could hear her own secret. Sometimes, she wished Paul never existed at all. It would be so much easier if she didn't love him so.

How awful.

Grace closed her eyes, pretended to sleep. Maybe if she slept, Virgil wouldn't wake her, would just let her stay in the car. She didn't want to do this. She was in the car with someone who wouldn't understand, who never lost anyone, as far as she knew. He never said. He may have lost a parent or a friend. But not a child.

Not a child.

Grace should have died first. Her father died. Her mother died. It was Grace's turn, not Paul's. That was it, plain and simple. *All in good time,* her mother would say. *In Grace's time.* But Paul's time was cut short, and suddenly, Grace's time was interminable.

Her son's name didn't belong on a gravestone. There wasn't supposed to be a gap in the generations.

It was all out of balance.

Shuddering, Grace cast aside her plan to play possum and opened her eyes. They were pulling into the parking lot of the candy factory. "Virgil, I don't want to go on the tour," she said. When he began to protest, she snapped, "Let's just go straight into the store. Let's just get this over with. Will that make you happy?"

She saw the sheen of hurt cross his face. But then he nodded. "All right, if that's how you want to do it," he said. "If you think it'll be easier that way."

"The only thing that will make it easier is if Paul himself comes running out that door with a bag full of candy pumpkins and candy corn for me to buy for him." The harshness of her own voice caused Grace to take a breath. "Nothing will make it easier," she said. "I don't want a crowd of people staring at me if I fall apart in a candy factory. Nobody falls apart in a candy factory, Virgil. Just like nobody ever dies playing hide and seek."

Although the car was stopped, Virgil rested his hands on the steering wheel. He looked out the windshield and Grace wondered if he was going to start the car, if they were going to drive away and she was going to be spared this sweet trip she didn't want to take. "If you start to fall apart, Grace," he said, "if it really gets to be that hard, we'll just leave. I promise. I'm not doing this to hurt you." He dropped his hands into his lap. "I want to help."

She nodded. But she couldn't say thank you. She couldn't say that it was all right, that it would help, and she was ready. Her voice balked again, but this time, she really didn't even try to force it. She just reached for the door handle. "Let's go then."

They walked slowly into the store. The sugary smell intensified and pressed down on Grace's shoulders as soon as the door swung shut behind her. She was trapped. She could see the candy corn and pumpkins, front and center for the holiday display, stored loose in great bushel baskets, and she quickly turned away. The factory made other candy as well, jelly beans and the little molded chewy animals sold at Easter, circus peanuts, licorice whips of all colors. Grace never knew there were other options in licorice than red and black. She moved toward those.

"Before you pick out your purchase," a woman called from the register, "you can sample from each of the treat cups. That way, you'll know which you like best."

Grace smiled thinly at the woman as Virgil whispered, "What if we like them all?" He laughed quietly and poked her in the ribs, clearly trying to raise their mood.

"Then we go broke and get fat," she said, joining in. She picked out a green licorice nib, popped it in her mouth and struggled to taste the unlikely sour apple mixed with the rubbery texture. They worked their way around the room, Virgil sampling and exclaiming over everything while she chewed on a select few. Her senses were abandoned by the baskets of candy corn and pumpkins. Despite her chewing and swallowing, nothing had a taste.

Eventually, she found herself again in front of those Halloween and harvest baskets. She gazed at the mounds of orange and yellow and white. The pumpkins were an especially deep orange, a burnt orange, and they were topped with bright green stems. Grace always ate her pumpkins whole. Paul always bit the stem off first, letting it flicker around his mouth before he tossed in the rest of the pumpkin. He often threw it in the air like a miniature basketball and his gaping mouth became the net. Grace always laughed, even as she cautioned that he could choke. Why didn't she caution him instead about climbing trees? About electric wires? She wondered why she warned him against something he loved, rather than the things that killed him.

She stayed silently in front of the baskets and Virgil placed his hand on her shoulder. Grace expected her heartrate to race, but it slowed. It slowed to the point she had to remind herself to breathe.

"Go on and try one," the woman said, walking over to join them. "They're our specialty, they made us famous." She scooped her fat fingers into the pumpkins and rained them back into the barrel. All but one, which she held out to Grace. "Here!" she said. It was a gift, specially selected just for her.

Grace turned her palm up and the woman dropped the pumpkin into her hand. Grace felt the candy, round and smooth, and she saw the way its color reflected onto her skin. Carefully rolling it, until it was between her thumb and forefinger, she raised it to her mouth.

And she bit off the stem.

She could hear Paul's crow. "Mom ate a whole pumpkin! Mom ate eight pumpkins today! Mom ate twenty-three!"

Oh, the sweetness of that stem.

Tears rolled down Grace's cheeks as she tossed the rest of it into the air, then angled her open mouth beneath it. She tried to smile reassuringly at the woman who gaped. Grace turned to Virgil. "Buy me some," she said and then she bolted from the store.

Leaning against the car, Grace allowed her body to shudder and cry. That pumpkin tasted delicious and it raised the old lust in her for more and more pumpkins and candy corn. The lust she shared with her son, with her boy who tried to control it by eating just the stem first, then the whole pumpkin, but still matched her, pumpkin for pumpkin, in quantity. The taste on this day, this first Halloween without Paul, only made Grace sad, not sick. She didn't hate the candy. It didn't taste like death. It tasted like memory.

She dropped into her seat, clutching her shirt and the Easter Island face of her mother's pendant. Her mother was there with her. Paul was there with her. She ran her tongue around her teeth, seeking out every last fleck of sugar. She wanted to buy bushels of candy pumpkins. She wanted to go back to the hotel, retrieve the suitcase with the cash, and offer it all to the lady behind the register.

Grace laughed out loud. And she cried.

Virgil came out eventually and placed several bags of candy in the back seat. Sliding behind the wheel, he dropped one large, lone bag into Grace's lap. A bag of candy corn and pumpkins. More pumpkins than corn. Just like Paul would have picked out.

"See?" Virgil said softly. "Not everything has to change, Grace." He rocked her and she nestled into his rhythm, clutching her bag of candy. "Some things go on. The taste of candy corn." He stopped and thought. "The love for a child." He looked at Grace and his face was as open as a spring window. "No matter what."

"Even when I can't hold him, Virgil?" she said, her voice breaking. "Even when I can't hear him? Even when he's not here anymore?"

"Even then," Virgil said. He reached into the bag and pulled out a candy pumpkin. She opened her mouth and he laid it on her tongue like a communion wafer. "You'll always love Paul, Grace. He's your boy."

As Grace chewed, the salt of her tears mixed with the sugar. With one hand, she held the black Easter Island face. With the other hand, she clutched the bag of candy. She held it to her heart. And she thought of Paul.

Her mother would never want her to stop loving Paul. Stop loving her son. Even if he was a spirit. Her mother would know that the best thing, the best possible thing for both Grace and Paul, was for Paul to live. To be a boy, then a man, to tower over his own mother, to take a wife, have children, and then to grieve the loss of his mother just as Grace grieved her mother. That was how it was supposed to be. That was the natural order of things. But even though that wasn't to be, Grace would always love her son.

That was the natural order of things too.

CHAPTER TEN
Virgil

When Virgil came out from taking a shower, the morning after the candy corn factory, Grace was on her bed, brushing Cathy's hair. She brushed it a lot since the haircut; there was no more "fixing it", putting in braids or ponytails, but she still brushed it, giving Cathy's hair a high sheen that looked almost human. Grace looked up expectantly and he knew what she was going to ask.

"Is the surprise today, Virgil?"

He smiled. "It is!" Sitting down across from her, he admired the way the doll looked. It seemed like years since the morning he set Cathy among the gourds and autumn leaves in The Nursery's window. Chatty Cathy was just a doll then, one of the orphans looking for a new home. Now, there was something else about her. Her cheeks actually seemed rosy, her smile wider, the blue eyes a deeper shade. Which, of course, was impossible, but Virgil admired her anyway. "There's a doll shop and hospital in town. It's run by a friend of mine, Hannah. I met her one fall soon after I opened The Nursery and started making these trips every year. Her shop is so much bigger than mine."

Hannah became a presence in Virgil's life even before Brad did. Virgil pictured Hannah all those years ago, sitting behind her cash register, one doll in her lap, another doll on the counter, both of them glowing under Hannah's ministrations. As Virgil's trips expanded and rattled helter skelter around the entire United States, he made Hannah's shop a stop no matter which region he was heading toward. Now, of course, his final destination was always Georgia. "I buy many of my own personal dolls from Hannah," he said. "And sometimes she gives me a deal or two if I find something there that I want for a customer."

Grace straightened Cathy's outfit, something new, a plaid jumper over a plain white shirt, a flea market find from Shipshewana. The clothes weren't specifically made for the Chatty Cathy doll, but Grace didn't care. She wasn't a purist. She just wanted her doll to be well-dressed. Just like any mom. "You don't think of the dolls in The Nursery as yours?" she asked.

Virgil reached for Cathy and for a moment, Grace hesitated, but then let her go. He studied Cathy's face, trying to find the source of that new human glow. "They're mine," he said. "But they're transients. Just passing through. I'm not planning on keeping them. Upstairs in my apartment, that's where my own dolls are. The ones that are like Cathy is for you."

Grace turned toward the mirror, fussing with her own hair. Virgil wanted to tell her to leave it alone, that her best look was that bed-tousled mop, but she always fussed with it, sticking in barrettes to keep it under dubious control. "Who do you have?" she asked.

Virgil noticed the "who". As he called off his dolls' names, a roll call of his family, he could see them, waiting in his darkened apartment for him to come home. Baby Boo, Baby First Step, Tippee Toes, and Pixie. And on the bed, Poor Pitiful Pearl, his Josephine substitute.

"I remember Poor Pitiful Pearl!" Grace cried out. She leaned toward him. "I used to stare at her in the Sears Christmas catalog. She affected me like Maribel Get Well…I needed to make Maribel well, and I needed to lift Pearl out of poverty."

They moved into the living area and Virgil set Cathy on the couch. The Quints were already there, lined up against the cushions. Grace, he noticed, had the television set to children's programming. He smiled. "I'll show her to you when we get home. She's the closest I've come to a doll I played with when I was a kid. She was my sister's. I loved her."

Grace's eyes wandered away and Virgil thought she might be thinking of The Nursery, filled with dolls of every kind. Or she might be thinking of all the dolls she never had. The dolls she was never given the opportunity to love. Once again, he wondered at Grace's mother. "You'll like Hannah's place," he said, standing up. "There are four floors. Four solid floors of dolls, all the brands, all the types. All in beloved condition, dressed, hair brushed, gorgeous."

Grace glanced at the television. "Maribel Get Well?" she asked. "Maybe?"

Virgil nodded. "Could be. I've seen her there before."

Hannah's shop was within walking distance of the hotel, so they left the Chrysler where it was. Walking down the sidewalk with Grace at his side was like walking with her at the flea market, at the auction. She was right beside Virgil, her elbow bumping his, and so he took her hand. Her palm was warm, her fingers flexible and he ran his thumb gently over the curve of her knuckle. He pointed out different shops and they made plans to eat lunch at this diner, supper at that restaurant, stop for coffee in that coffee shop. He watched ahead for inconsistencies in the sidewalk that could trip her up.

He was protecting her. And Virgil found he liked protecting Grace. He liked knowing he was capable of doing so.

Going around a corner, Hannah's shop, a tall old Victorian rooming house with a wide front porch, came immediately into view. The four floors of windows were already lit with Christmas lights, even in the daytime. A wooden sign spelling out, "Hannah's Hopefuls," swung and creaked from the soffit, waving visitors up the steps and into the tall and ornate front door. Virgil pointed out the showcase window, something Hannah designed herself, and Grace gaped. On a specially built set of bleachers, over thirty dolls stood, looking out at the world. Each one raised a hand, mostly righties, but a few lefties too, and they waved at passersby who couldn't help but wave back. Grace and Virgil certainly couldn't. They both raised their hands.

"Hannah's Hopefuls?" Grace asked as they climbed the steps.

Virgil nodded. "She says these dolls are like her foster children. She takes care of them, but they all hope to go home someday. Like my transients." He knew how Hannah felt. Whenever he saved a doll, cleaned it, dressed it, and set it up for sale, he swore he saw disappointment shade its face. He imagined each doll hoped for a home when he bought it. And when they found they were only in another waiting place, although a comfortable and warm and safe waiting place, they were sad. He often found himself treating the new dolls in a special way, keeping them close by the counter or setting them in displays where they had the company of many similar dolls. Placing them in a pose, he might hold their hand a little bit longer than usual or brush their hair more slowly. He laughed at himself every time, but a part of him believed that the dolls held feelings deep inside their plastic or cloth bodies, and he wanted them to know there was nothing to be afraid of. They could stay with him until a home was found. No more attics or garbage bags for them.

Just like he was protecting Grace now. Just like he held her hand.

As soon as they walked in the shop, Hannah saw Virgil. "Virgil!" she bellowed and she rumbled out from behind her counter. All three hundred or so pounds of her. Grace took a step back, but then she laughed out loud. Hannah beamed from ear to ear and there was obviously no threat there. She engulfed Virgil in a hug so deep, it took his breath away. But it was breath-stealing that he welcomed; he waited for it every year on his trip. He imagined it when he was home. He missed it on nights when he was the most lonely.

"I've been waiting for you, I knew you'd turn up any day now!" Hannah stepped away, but kept a hand on his arm. She looked toward Grace.

"Hannah, this is my friend, Grace," Virgil said. "She came with me on the trip this year."

Hannah cocked an eyebrow. "But I thought you were…"

Virgil smiled. "I am. Grace is truly a friend, not a girlfriend."

She sighed. "Well, one can always hope." She stepped toward Grace and Virgil braced himself to catch Grace after the force of Hannah's greeting. But Hannah seemed to know to be gentle. Virgil delighted in her intuition. "It's nice to meet you, Grace," she said softly. She put an arm around Grace's waist and drew her toward the counter. "Virgil taking good care of you?"

"Wonderful." Grace followed along willingly, but her head swiveled in every direction. "I've never seen so many dolls, Hannah," she said. "How many do you think you have?"

Hannah laughed, not the guffaw she usually affected, but a quiet, careful chuckle. "I haven't the foggiest idea. There's four floors here, all full to the brim with dolls. Every time I sell some, I get more in, so there's never a vacant spot." Hannah sat back down on her chair and picked up a doll, a pristine Mary Hartline in a bright green dress, the skirt decorated with the trademark music notes. Hannah vigorously brushed the doll's hair.

"Hannah," Virgil said, "what a gorgeous doll! That's Mary Hartline, and just look at that green dress!"

Hannah nodded, lifted her hand for a high five. "Everything he knows, I taught him," she said to Grace.

Grace frowned and reached out to touch the doll's dress. "Mary Hartline?" she asked. "I don't remember her."

Hannah set the doll to standing on the counter, facing Grace. It was an introduction. "She's probably a bit before your time, sweetie," Hannah said. "This doll was made by Ideal in the early 1950's. I bet you weren't even thought of yet."

"I was born in 1960," Grace said. She played with the doll's drum major boots. "She's lovely."

Virgil cleared his throat. He felt if he didn't insert himself into this conversation, Grace might forget all about him in the presence of this charismatic doll-queen. "Mary Hartline was a real person, a television star on a show called Super Circus," he said.

"That's right, Virgil." Hannah looked around the room. "I just got this one in, though there are others here. This is the first one that came in a green dress though. It's rare. That's why he was making a fuss over it." Hannah's gaze came to rest on Grace and she smiled, the most maternal smile Virgil ever saw from this boisterous woman.

"I'm going to look around," he said, and that brought Grace to his side.

"Wait for me, I'm coming," she said. "Hannah, do you have Maribel Get Well?"

Hannah frowned and Virgil knew that in her mind, she searched her rooms, going into every nook and cranny where a doll could hide. "I don't think so," she said. "I'm sorry, sweetie. I know I had one, but I just sold it two weeks ago."

Grace gasped at how close she came to her doll.

Virgil reclaimed Grace's hand and led her away. Maribel or not, there was still plenty to see. He already had that Mary Hartline earmarked as his own; she would join the rest of his family in his apartment. He and Grace walked slowly through each of the four floors. They found more Chatty Cathys and Grace hovered over each one, comparing it to her own. But only hers had the cut and styled hair, and only hers was real to her, though Virgil knew she offered a wish over each of the others, that they would go to a good home. They found a corduroy coat to replace the one that was stolen and another original party dress as well.

"I can't get over how many dolls I don't know," Grace said.

Virgil poked his hand cautiously into a shelf, trying not to disturb the rows of dolls, but wanting to see who might be hiding in the back. "Did you think the first doll was created when you were born? They've been around forever, Grace. Little girls have always wanted babies."

She shrugged. "I guess I just think of them all as dolls I was never allowed to have. So I keep it in my lifetime." She looked away. "I don't like to think about what I didn't have. Not when it comes to my mother."

A mother who wouldn't let you play with what you most wanted, Virgil wanted to say. He just didn't understand it. But he let it go.

It was on the third floor that Virgil found treasure. And he saw it purely by chance. They were on their way back down after searching the fourth floor and he thought they'd seen it all. But as he came around the corner of the stairwell, some sunlight fell in and lit up a blonde head standing on a windowsill. The breeze puffed her, making her a pale and lovely dandelion wish.

Hair so blonde, it was almost white and soft as snow. That downturned mouth and a clear teardrop falling just below her left eye. And what a set of eyes, big brown eyes as big as half-dollars. Throughout his childhood, those eyes stared at Virgil from his cradled arms, under his bed, or the top shelf of his closet. Until she disappeared. Until his father stole her away. Killed her forever from his life.

"Josephine," Virgil breathed. He dropped Grace's hand and fell to his knees in front of the doll. She wore the burlap dress he remembered so well, the one he tried to copy with Poor Pitiful Pearl's rags. "Josephine," he said again and he took her enormous stretched-out hand, begging for a penny. The hand was not proportionate to the rest of the doll. It begged in its hugeness to be held. It begged to be cared for.

He held her in his arms, held her the way he did in his bedroom so long ago, stroking the impossibly soft hair, drinking in the love he found in those saucer eyes. His doll. The duplicate reject his sister never wanted. His wonderful, dearest, contraband doll.

"Virgil?" Grace knelt on the floor beside him. "Who is she? Josephine?"

Virgil wasn't surprised to find tears on his cheeks and when Grace reached out to touch the doll, he moved her away. "She's mine, Grace," he said softly. "I can't share."

And he couldn't. Not right then. Not even with Grace.

Grace seemed to understand. She wasn't offended or hurt, but leaned her cheek against his shoulder and just looked at Josephine. "She's beautiful, Virgil," she said finally. "But why is she so sad?"

"I don't know. Maybe she missed me too." He laughed at his own foolishness. "Oh God, Grace, I'm sorry. This is the doll I told you about, from my own childhood. She was my sister's, really, but she was a duplicate, my sister already had one and so the duplicate became mine. In secret. I loved her. She was…You remember what I said a while ago, about all little girls wanting babies?"

Grace nodded.

"Well, this little boy wanted one too. And Josephine was my baby." He stood up. "My dad hated her, he hated that I wanted to play with dolls, so I kept her hidden under my bed. When I left for college, I was afraid the other guys would laugh at me for bringing a doll, so I hid her deep in my closet. My dad found her anyway and he got rid of her."

Grace sighed deeply and tried to touch the doll again. Virgil let her stroke Josephine's hair. "Sounds like your father should have been married to my mother," she said. For a moment, Grace's mouth grew just as downturned as

Josephine's and Virgil expected a single teardrop to appear under her left eye. But then she smiled, a sad smile, but a deep one he knew came right from her heart, or even deeper than her heart. It came from whatever made Grace Grace. "I need to say that differently," she said. "I loved my mother."

"And your mother loved you. Even if she didn't let you play with dolls." Virgil tucked Josephine under his chin and wrapped both arms around her as tightly as he could. "I can't say that about my father. I don't think he liked me very much, and I didn't like him either. I envy your love."

They went downstairs then, all the way to Hannah. She already had the order for Mary Hartline written up and the doll waited on the counter, standing patiently with her baton in the air.

"How did you know he wanted Mary Hartline?" Grace asked.

"I know this boy," Hannah said. She reached out for Josephine, but Virgil couldn't let her go. Not yet. Hannah looked at him sharply. "Virgil, you set yourself down for a moment," she said. "You look like you need a rest."

"Hannah, who is this?" Virgil asked. He turned Josephine's face toward Hannah, then sat obediently down on the stool she hauled out from behind her counter. "I never knew her real name."

Hannah laughed, not holding back the guffaw this time. "That's because she doesn't have one," she said. "She was called Little Miss No Name."

Virgil set the doll on his lap, keeping hold of her hand. "She has a name then," he said firmly. "Her name is Josephine and she is the love of my life."

Neither Hannah nor Grace laughed. In any other room, in any other place, Virgil knew he would have been laughed to a ball on the floor, buried under a harsh and teasing mirth that would make him bury his head, and himself, under his arms. But not here.

He wondered if Brad would laugh.

Hannah sat down in her chair and Grace, looking around and seeing no other seat, sank down on the floor between the two of them.

"No doll for you?" Hannah asked Grace. She put her hand on Grace's head and rolled her fingers through the curls. Grace could have been one of her dolls.

Grace shook her head. "No. I need Maribel Get Well. But I'm getting these things for my Chatty Cathy." She held up the coat and dress.

They sat quietly that way for a minute or two, Virgil clutching Josephine, Grace and Hannah just keeping watch. Eventually, he let his arms go a little bit slack. Josephine seemed to relax too and he knew she was his. No one was going to take her from him anymore.

"So what have you been up to, boy?" Hannah asked.

Virgil shrugged. "Not much. Selling Chatty Cathy to Grace here. But that's about it." He smiled at Grace who stroked the corduroy coat. He knew she was already picturing buttoning Cathy into it. At home, the days were getting chilly.

"You headin' south to see that too-loose lover of yours?" Hannah rolled her eyes.

Grace's eyebrows shot up.

"We're sort of heading that way, yes, Hannah," Virgil said carefully. "And please don't call him that. Things are different this year." He shook his head, wondering how much to say, how much to let her in, and how much to keep from Grace. "I have a decision to make." But he wondered if he really had a choice at all. Everything in him yanked him toward that junkyard in Macon. Whether it was to commit to Brad or if it was to say goodbye forever, Virgil needed to see him. But as much as he loved Hannah, as much as she understood Virgil and his dolls, he didn't want her opinion on this. She wanted nothing more than to see Virgil settled down with a nice girl. His father would want the same, though he was sure that his father would have been happy with any girl, nice or not. It was different with Hannah…he knew that Hannah would still love him, would still talk with him, no matter what he decided. Even if she couldn't fully support him in his lifestyle, in more than his lifestyle, but in his life, she would still always be there.

As far as he knew, Gay Bob never stood among the dolls in Hannah's shop. He never saw that doll here, lurking in any corner, on any shelf, or in a dollhouse. Virgil never asked Hannah about it either; to him, it was enough that the doll was never present. It could be that Hannah just didn't approve of homosexuality, he knew that. He heard that in her reference to looseness, to promiscuity. But he also saw acceptance in her love for him. And so Gay Bob's absence felt like a like mind. A blessing.

Virgil wanted to tell Hannah more, but he didn't want Grace to know all about Brad just yet either. He didn't want her to know that the junkyard was where they were heading and why. The vision of Grace running away through that hateful crowd was still just too fresh. He didn't want her to run away ever again. She was already running away from her family. He didn't want to be left behind too.

Hannah snorted. "Don't know why you stay with that guy. Him sleepin' with everything that stops by when you're not there."

Grace looked at Virgil, questioning.

"I don't own him, Hannah. How can I tell him what to do when I'm not there? I don't want him telling me what to do either." Virgil wondered if Hannah talked to him the way his mother would, if his mother was alive, if his mother could just have found her tongue. Though he didn't know if his mother talking would have made it any easier. If he could be straight just to make other people happy, he would have done it long ago. He looked at Josephine, touched her outstretched fingers. If it was that easy, Josephine would never have hidden under his bed. She would never have left his sister's room. "I'll be fine, Hannah. I'll be okay."

"You better hope so, Virgil boy," Hannah said. "You just better hope so. That kind, it doesn't settle down even after making a commitment. That kind thinks with their crotch first."

Virgil flinched. Was that the only way Brad thought of Virgil? But there was Brad's kindness, the way he moved around Virgil, touching his shoulder as he went by. Year-round, he found junkyard dolls for Virgil, and tucked them safely away, not letting them get soaked in the rain or covered with other garbage. And there was his face when he saw Virgil, his face the first moment Virgil woke up, Brad looking down on him, smiling, his hand stroking Virgil's cheek. And the early-morning lovemaking…

So they thought with their crotches sometime. Didn't every couple? Virgil thought of Brad, asleep, their hands still curved together, how Brad's fingers clenched every time Virgil went to move away.

"We're not like that," Virgil said to Hannah. She cut her eyes at him. "He's not like that, Hannah, and neither am I. Believe me."

Hannah sighed so hard, her hair blew up from her forehead, but Virgil saw Grace nod. She knew. She understood. Virgil relaxed. "You know I love you, boy," Hannah said.

"I know that. And you wouldn't love me any more if I was straight."

"Wouldn't love you less, though." Hannah laughed, the deep chuckles worked in between sharp wheezes and intakes of breath. Each year, Virgil wondered if he would find her here, still loving and selling her dolls.

"We'd better be going, Hannah," Virgil said and stood up. He could let go of Josephine now, just for a second, while Hannah looked at the pricetag and rang her up. But then the doll was back in his arms again, back where she needed to be.

After their items were paid for, they stood at the doorway, Virgil with a doll in each arm. Hannah packaged Mary Hartline for travel, but Josephine was unwrapped, tucked up close against his chest, her face pressed into his coat. Grace looked around one more time.

"This place is incredible, Hannah," she said.

Hannah nodded. "Thank you. They're all loved, you know. I like to think of it as a rescue shelter, like one for dogs and cats. Or even a shelter for women. A place where people and creatures go that haven't been treated so well." She patted her chest. "I treat them well."

Grace smiled. "That makes me so happy."

Hannah hugged Virgil and then Grace. And then they were out the door.

On the way back, Virgil handed Mary Hartline's box to Grace and he walked with Josephine tilted away from his body. He wanted to see her face. While he knew a Little Miss No Name with an intact tear was more valuable than one without, he began to scrub at that expensive teardrop. He wanted so much to make Josephine stop crying, to make her as happy as he was right now, that the tear, brittle with age, broke right off. He dropped it on the sidewalk, a bit of plastic that people would step over, would kick away without even knowing it, and he pulled Josephine back into his chest again. He swore he felt that doll inhale deeply and then breathe easy against him. He felt her reach out that gigantic asking hand and press it against him. They were together again and there was a circle completed. He had his doll back.

The first member of his family.

His father, damn him, might be sitting right now in his easy chair in the house in the heart of Chicago, in the home Virgil left behind, the home he still dreamed of. But Virgil's family was back, the family he always wanted. And it grew. Besides Josephine, there were the other dolls. And there was Brad. And there was The Nursery. What was he going to do about The Nursery? What was he going to do about Brad?

And now there was Grace too.

Grace held Virgil's hand all the way to a small coffee shop where they had lunch and lattes. Josephine sat beside them. Then Grace led them all back to their suite in the hotel. This time, she was the one watching out for danger, protecting Virgil on the uneven sidewalks of a small town. And Virgil trusted her to keep him safe, to keep Josephine safe and Mary Hartline too, as he stared into the eyes of a doll that left a hole big enough in his heart years ago to drive the Chrysler through. But now she was back.

****

Virgil expected to fall instantly asleep that night, but he didn't. He and Grace celebrated the arrival of Josephine by sharing another bottle of wine, and chips and salsa. As they were preparing for sleep, Virgil put Josephine on the table between the two beds, just under the lampshade. The light glowed down on her, casting a halo over her hair. And her perpetually open hand. A hand that seemed, to Virgil, to be impossibly empty.

Grace put the Quints in their cradle box and then, yawning, she got into bed with Cathy. Virgil kept waiting for Grace to ask him about Brad, to ask about where they were going and why. But she didn't. She was quiet though. She'd stepped outside earlier to call her family and it was a short call; she was back within five minutes. She said the kids were busy with homework, Nick busy doing whatever it was that husbands do. She hadn't offered any details other than that.

But Virgil wasn't offering any details either and he was grateful for Grace's continued silence on the subject of Brad. He didn't know what details to offer. He just didn't feel like he knew what he was doing.

They spent the evening watching television and enjoying their treat, toasting their dolls. By the time Grace climbed into bed with Cathy, her voice was thick with slumber and wine as she said goodnight. She frowned at Josephine, placed a finger in the doll's outstretched hand, but then slid down beneath the covers. Virgil turned the light off. And then he stared at the ceiling.

He turned on his side and switched his gaze to Josephine. The curtain at the window let in a stripe of light that caught the edges of the doll's profile. She wasn't in his sister's room. She wasn't under his bed or in his closet. She was right there, next to him, just like he always wanted her to be. She was out in the open.

He wanted to be out in the open.

Virgil thought of Brad and about Georgia and the junkyard. He thought about leaving The Nursery and Wisconsin behind. It would be so different to live with Brad, so different than just seeing him twice or so a year. Two men, two buddies, having a little visit, that was one thing. But two men living together. Well, that was another. That was being out in the open too, wasn't it. Just like Josephine now, her profile lit in white gold. People, though Virgil couldn't identify who exactly, would want to look through their walls and see if they shared a bed or if they had their own rooms. Virgil could feel these unidentifiable people. Sometimes it seemed like he'd known them all his life.

And now there was the possibility of marriage. Not just being two buddies having a visit, two buddies that happened to live together. Marriage let the world know there was more to it than that. Marriage let people know what was happening on the other side of the walls. Virgil accepted long ago that marriage wasn't in his future. But now it was the present and he could be married. It was possible. But it wasn't as easy as that. Men and women who got married didn't have to worry about those unidentifiable people fretting over what went on behind closed doors. But gay couples did. It was a dangerous invasion of privacy. At least, that was how Virgil saw it.

He returned to staring at the ceiling.

Out in the open. But not alone.

Virgil was alone right now, in that bed by himself. Alone, despite Grace breathing soft a table-length away. Despite Chatty Cathy. Despite the Quints on the dresser. Despite Josephine, beside him on the table. Not under the bed at all.

Out in the open.

But it still didn't feel right.

Virgil was still alone in the bed. In his room in his own house, he didn't want to be alone. Back further, back in his father's house, he didn't want to be alone in that bed either. He didn't ever want to be alone.

"For Christ's sake," he said softly now, so as not to wake Grace, but so he could hear himself speak. "You're sixty-five years old. Old men don't sleep with dolls."

But old men don't want to sleep alone either.

Virgil took Josephine's outstretched hand. He lifted her, straightened her legs, then tucked her under the covers beside him in the bed. Her head, tiny, rested on its own pillow.

Virgil held her enormous hand. He filled her palm with his index finger. And then he fell asleep.

CHAPTER ELEVEN
Grace

It was amazing to see Virgil with that doll. Grace saw him with other dolls, of course, with her own Cathy, the Quints, and all of the dolls he purchased on the trip. But he was so different with this one, this Little Miss No Name who now had a name. Josephine. He held her as if she would break, he talked to her, he stroked her hair and let it stream through his fingers. When Grace woke up the next morning, he was sleeping with Josephine, and the sight of a grown man sleeping with a doll, something that should have made Grace laugh, made her want to cry instead. She felt like she was seeing the real Virgil for the first time, with his face, open in his sleep, with his hand placed just so over Josephine's. This wasn't the doll salesman, not the gay man, but Virgil himself. Grace saw what made him tick, what made him love, what made him so angry. His father.

When Virgil got out of bed that morning, he left Josephine tucked under the covers. Grace wanted so much to touch her, to hold her and brush her hair, but she knew better. This was Virgil's doll. To lift her out of bed, to hold her tight, would be like taking someone else's child. Virgil's child, the one he always wanted and wasn't allowed to have. Just like she wasn't allowed to have the dolls she so yearned to play with.

Grace knew what it was like to be kept from something you wanted more than anything else in the world. And she knew what it was like to have your child snatched away. She would never do that to anyone else.

Grace thought about Paul. She wondered about her mother.

The water ran in the bathroom and Grace sat on her bed and waited for the concert to start. Virgil always sang in the shower, not his hum, but a full-voiced array of songs, most of which Grace didn't recognize. It reminded her of Nick, who also sang in the shower. Until Paul died. Now his showers were silent.

Grace wondered when it would be time for Nick to sing again. When would it be his time? He kept saying it was hers. *It's time, Grace.*

When Virgil came out of the shower, he beat Grace to her question. "Time to move on, Grace," he said.

She stepped into the bathroom, ready to brush her teeth. "Okay. Where are we going?" She thought she knew. She wanted to ask. But yesterday, with the finding of Josephine, Grace felt it just wasn't time to bring that up. It wasn't time.

So much time. Apparently, there was a time for everything.

Virgil sat down on his bed and began putting on his shoes. "I thought we'd swing down through Alabama, then maybe into Georgia, then start working our way back up."

Alabama and Georgia. When Hannah referred to the "loose lover" the day before, she said down south. Is that where they were headed? To this man that Hannah didn't like? But then Grace registered the last words Virgil spoke and she froze. "Back up?"

"Sure. Kentucky, Indiana, Illinois. And then home." He didn't look at Grace. Instead, he reached behind him and pulled Josephine from her sleep.

"Home." Grace couldn't quite see herself; there was a layer of fog on the mirror from Virgil's shower. "When do you think we'll be getting back?"

"A few weeks or so. Maybe less, maybe more." Grace could feel Virgil's stillness. Ordinarily, on days when they traveled, he prowled the room, touching things, deciding where to put them in the Chrysler. "I thought you'd want to be home by Thanksgiving."

Grace hadn't thought much about Thanksgiving, the first without Paul, the second without her mother. "I guess you're right," she said. She closed the bathroom door and backed against it. Licking her teeth, she could still taste the candy in the air, even mixed with steam and shampoo and soap. She could still taste the candy corn and pumpkins she ate with her wine and chips and salsa the night before.

Grace pulled her nightshirt over her head. Straightening, she caught sight of her naked reflection running with droplets in the foggy mirror. She stared, then swiped the mirror with both palms.

Maybe, she thought, maybe I should go back to the candy factory and buy more pumpkins. Maybe I should bring the pumpkins and candy corn to Paul myself.

It's time, Grace.

****

Back at the candy factory, Grace bought a huge bag of pumpkins, mixed with some candy corn, for Paul. She got JJ his favorites, the little heart-shaped Valentine's candies imprinted with special messages, like "U R CUTE!" and "Text me." For Mary, there was jelly beans in a myriad of flavors. Grace bought herself more pumpkins and then she picked out a selection of molded Easter candy. She got Nick circus peanuts, the only candy he ate, though not very often. He was afraid of tooth decay and the dentist. He had the whitest teeth of anyone she ever knew.

Virgil made his purchases at their first visit, so he didn't buy any more. However, he made his way through the samples again while Grace was shopping. After grabbing a handful of candy to keep in the front seat, Grace put her packages in the back next to Cathy. Grace ate a yellow chick as they pulled away.

"Let's go to the next town for breakfast," Virgil said. "I want to eat away from this sweet air."

They drove in silence for a while. Grace watched Tennessee roll by and she wondered when the next state line would come up. She thought about asking Virgil more about where they were going, who they were going to see. But there was something guarded about that information; she didn't feel like it was something he would want to talk about. Just like she originally didn't want to tell him about Paul.

But they weren't going to see Paul.

"You don't talk about your father much, Grace," Virgil said suddenly. "Didn't you like him?"

Grace considered this. It wasn't something she really thought about before. He was her father, after all. With parents, you just don't think about these things. They're a given. "He was different than my mother," she said.

And he was. When Grace's mother was alive, and even in Grace's memories now, her edges seemed to be blurred. Soft. Her father was clear and solid. But being clear and solid wasn't necessarily warm. A brick was solid. Her father was like a brick. Her mother was like a favorite blanket, frayed at the edges, threads floating to the ground.

Grace's father always brought Grace surprises from the depths of his coat pockets. Little toys and candy when she was a child and simple pieces of jewelry when she was older. He insisted that Grace have her ears pierced on her twelfth birthday. To him, it was a rite of passage; with earrings in her ears, Grace would be well on her way to becoming a sophisticated woman.

Grace didn't want to have it done, she was scared of needles and she was scared it would hurt. Her mother promised that they would find a fine pair of dangly gypsy earrings. That didn't make her father happy at all, he promised Grace tiny diamond studs. But when he saw the junk jewelry piquing Grace's interest and wearing down her resistance, he agreed.

Grace's mother never gave her those gypsy earrings. Her father did, bringing them home after work in a crushed velvet box on her birthday. The earrings hung down to Grace's shoulders and had gold discs and balls that rattled and clanged together whenever she moved her head. The noise just about drove her crazy. She wore them for an hour.

Tucked with the gypsy earrings in that velvet box was a pair of tiny diamond studs. Grace remembered putting them on for the first time and looking in a mirror as stars flashed in her ears. She wore them at both of her weddings. She wore them at her father's funeral. And at her mother's. And at Paul's. She looked at those little stars that day and thought about how Paul loved space. She wore the stars for him. Paul never met his grandfather, but his grandfather offered Paul the stars that day, and comforted Grace as well.

She turned to Virgil. "I loved my father," she said. "In flashes." She nodded. "Brilliant solid purposeful flashes. My mother could be flashes too, like fireworks, but her light was constant as well. My father was like a flashlight."

Virgil smiled.

Pulling Cathy from her seatbelt, Grace settled the doll into her lap. "One Christmas, I heard my father trying to convince my mother to let me have a doll. I wanted Baby Boo that year, I couldn't stand to hear her crying in all the commercials and I wanted to rock her and give her the pacifier and make her quiet. My father said, 'Let Grace have the doll, she wants a doll, let her have it. Soon she'll be too old.'" Grace remembered lying on the floor with her ear pressed flat on the heating grate, listening to their voices.

"What did your mother say?" Virgil reached over and rustled one of the candy pumpkins out of the bag. Grace slapped his wrist lightly and he grinned.

"She said that she would never let me have a doll. She kept saying no, she wouldn't allow it. And she said, 'I can't, you know I can't,' which I never understood. Why was it so hard to give me, her little girl, a doll? Then my father said she was being ridiculous and he was going to give me a doll anyway, maybe more, maybe one of every doll I ever wanted." Grace remembered sliding off the floor at that point and sneaking one foot at a time down the stairs, just far enough to hear them more clearly. She sat down on the fifth step from the top, the step she knew was safest for hidden listening and peeking. Her hands clutched at her throat and her heart swelled at the thought of so many dolls, every one she ever wanted! "But then my mother said if he gave me any doll, even just one, she would pull it from me, from my arms, and take it directly to the dump, before I even had a chance to hug it. She said something about having to keep a promise." Grace pressed Cathy against her chest. "I ran to my room after that. There were no dolls that Christmas, nor any Christmas. I've just never understood it. What did she promise? Who did she promise and why was that person more important than me?"

Virgil shook his head. "I don't get it either, Grace," he said. "What did she have against dolls?"

"I don't know." Grace held Cathy and thought about the Quints and Josephine and Mary Hartline. She wondered how her mother could hate dolls so much. Did she think Grace would love the dolls more than she loved her mother? Grace loved Cathy, at times loved her in a way she supposed was senseless, but not more than her children. Not more than her husband. Certainly not more than her mother.

Yet there Grace was in the car, holding Cathy on her lap, on a quest for Maribel Get Well. And her children were at home alone. Well, alone with their father. But without their mother.

Shaking her head, she tried to shove the image of her lonely children, an image that suddenly made them bear a striking resemblance to Little Miss No Name, to Josephine, with the saucer sad eyes, to the back of her mind. For now, she thought, I don't care. I need to do this. I am doing this. "I'm hungry," she said to Virgil.

"We're almost to the next town."

Grace put Cathy back in her seatbelt. "What about your father, Virgil?" she asked.

Virgil shrugged. "What about him?"

Grace looked at him then, sitting straight, staring at the road. "You said you hate him."

"I haven't talked to my father in over thirty years," Virgil said. "He hates that I'm gay, he says I'm an atrocity. He told me to get out of his life and so I did."

"Oh." Grace studied the landscape. Virgil began to hum his usual tuneless tune, so different than his shower concerts. "Virgil," she said, interrupting him.

"Does your father know where you are?"

He shook his head. "Probably not. I've moved a few times since I saw him last, though I've been at The Nursery for almost twenty years." He puffed his chest out. "Imagine a doll shop and hospital staying in business for twenty years, Grace. Pretty damn good, I'd say."

"It is good. Any business that stays around that long is really impressive." Grace couldn't believe The Nursery was twenty years old. That meant she resisted it, walked by it, drove by it, saw it lit with the sparkle of Christmas lights and snowflakes, saw the picture window filled with doll after doll after doll, for twenty years too. She resisted because of her mother, of course. And now her mother was gone a year and Grace owned a doll from The Nursery. And she was sitting in a car full of dolls. "Virgil," she said. "What if your father has changed his mind? How could he tell you to come back?"

Virgil stopped humming and his mouth opened and closed a few times. Finally, he said, "It's not easy to stay hidden these days. He could have found me through the internet."

Grace thought of her mother. She never used the internet. Grace couldn't even get her to use a cell phone. It was a major triumph when her mother upgraded to a cordless phone in the house. And Virgil was nine years older than Grace, so his father was likely older than Grace's mother. "Do you think he'd really use the internet?"

Virgil thought a bit, then gave a short laugh. "Probably not. He didn't even like the phone book." Then Virgil just drove, but Grace thought she saw his eyes glimmer.

She thought about fathers and sons, fathers and daughters. Mothers and sons. Grace's father, a brick, who put stars in his daughter's ears and gave her gypsy earrings. Her mother, who gave Grace everything, but the one thing she really wanted. Virgil's father, hating that Virgil was gay, and Virgil hating his father's hatred.

And Grace and Paul. Paul's death. Grace's inability to tell her daughter that it wasn't her fault.

"Sometimes," Grace said softly. "Sometimes I hate Paul's atrocity too."

Virgil looked over. He took Grace's hand and held it against his knee. "Atrocity, Grace?" he asked.

"His death was atrocious."

Virgil sighed. "He didn't die on purpose, sweetheart."

"Just like you aren't gay on purpose. You just are."

Virgil squeezed Grace's hand, then briefly pressed it to his lips. Reaching into her candy bag, he pulled out a pumpkin and popped it into her mouth. Then he began to hum again.

As Grace chewed, she thought again of those words Virgil used. Back up. Going back up to Wisconsin. Going home.

To her kids. To her husband. To the bank vault. But also to that tree and the unvisited grave. To her house with the unfillable absence.

Grace didn't know if she was ready. She didn't know if she would ever be. How can you ever be ready to accept that your child is gone?

But she was eating candy pumpkins. Something she couldn't have done a couple days ago. She was bringing them home for Paul.

She thought of Virgil's words. Not everything had to change. The taste of candy corn. The love for a child.

Grace loved Paul. And she missed him. The thought of going back up scared the hell out of her. But she would go. She promised.

"When we get to the hotel tonight," she said to Virgil, and to herself, "I'm going to call Nick and the kids. I want to tell them that I'll probably be home by Thanksgiving. That we'll be swinging up soon. Nick will be happy to have a…definite date." She nearly said deadline. But the use of the word dead just didn't seem appropriate. The deadline already passed. Her son passed.

"Good." Virgil nodded slowly. "That's so good, Grace."

She hoped so.

****

Sitting on the latest bed, in a hotel in Gadsden, Alabama, Grace clasped her cell phone tightly in her hand and watched as Virgil fiddled with the television set. It looked like snow on the screen and suddenly she was homesick for Christmas. Cold air, icicles, steam rising from smiles on the street. Grace always loved Christmas, though this would be the first holiday season without Paul. She barely made it through last Christmas, the first without her mother. She was tired of every holiday ushering in a season of firsts.

Grace sighed suddenly and Virgil looked up from the television. "What is it?" he asked.

She looked at her cell. "Just getting ready."

Virgil nodded. "Do you want me to leave?"

"No, of course not." Grace sat up straight, putting both of her feet flat on the floor. Instead of hitting speed dial, she very deliberately pressed out the whole number, the number that now seemed so strange, like it was no longer hers, like it belonged to another world.

JJ answered. Grace felt herself instantly light up. "Hi, honey, it's me."

"Mom! Where are you now?"

"Uh…Alabama, I think." She looked over at Virgil, who held his thumbs up. "It's still warm here. How about by you?"

"It's cold. Dad's already got out our winter jackets. He aired them outside, I told him you do that every year so they don't stink of back-of-the-closet."

Grace was delighted with his voice, chattering away like any normal child. He didn't sound desolate and abandoned at all.

"Mom? Thanksgiving is soon."

"I know, just a few weeks."

"Will you be home?" He stopped and Grace knew he was holding his breath, crossing his fingers. His toes too, if he could move them in his shoes.

Grace took the breath he was holding. "I'll be home, sweetie."

"Mom." There was the exhale, her name slipping out of his mouth in a whisper.

Grace smiled and she knew he was too.

"Do you want to talk to Mary? She's here."

"Yes, please. And Dad too. I love you, JJ."

"Love you too."

There was a scrabble as the phone exchanged hands. Then Mary was on. "Mom? You'll be home?"

"Yes, honey. For Thanksgiving."

She sighed and Grace heard her say, just barely, "Thank you."

"Is everything okay?"

"I'm all right. I miss you though." An admission that Grace never expected. Not from her adolescent so deep in snarl. With an extra allotment of grief and guilt thrown in. Her daughter's voice softened and Grace felt her insides soften too. It had been so long since Mary was soft. So long since their relationship was soft. "So do you think you've had enough time on your own yet? Are you better?"

"Almost." Grace hoped that was true.

Grace sat in the whisper of her daughter's breath. She wondered if she was truly almost better. She wondered if better was possible.

But there were two remaining children. It was time.

"Mom? I love you."

Grace was startled with the strength in Mary's voice. The belief and the commitment. She loved Grace despite everything. She loved Grace anyway. "And I love you too." Grace realized her voice was strong as well. Of course she loved her daughter. Anyway.

"Dad's here now." And the phone was passed.

"Hello, Grace," Nick said.

"Hi, Nick. How are you?" Grace lifted her chin.

"I'm fine. Did I hear the kids say you're coming home?"

"Soon." She winced at the word and moved quickly on before he could snap at her for using it again. "By Thanksgiving. We'll be swinging back up."

"That's still weeks away."

"Just three. It's all the time I will allow myself to have." It didn't feel like something she allowed at first. It didn't feel like a choice. It was a decision inflicted by Virgil. And that's exactly how it felt earlier that day…inflicted. But now, hearing her children's voices gain strength with the joy of their mother's definite homecoming, it became a due date. An end note. Or even just an X at the end of the map.

"All right then. I'm glad to hear it." He paused and it felt thick. "When you get back, I'll probably be moving out for a little while. I've begun looking at apartments."

Grace blinked. "Move out? Why? What are you talking about?"

"Well, I've been thinking along the lines of a separation, maybe." His voice guttered to a stop. Grace wanted to jump in, but her breath disappeared. She wondered if the children were close by, if they were hearing this. "With all this stuff going on…you know. I've just been thinking."

Grace grabbed her breath and her voice came out, louder than she expected. Her teeth were no longer biting the words back. "Nick, I don't want a separation! I just wanted some time, a chance to think things over. To grieve more than anything. That's all."

Nick cleared his throat. Grace heard it as a cue, Nick always cleared his throat before launching into a rehearsed speech. "I didn't say you wanted a separation, Grace. I was talking about me. You left me here with two kids and a house to run. You didn't tell me where you were going or how long you'd be gone. You even left with somebody else. I think I could have accepted all that if you just came back when I asked. Begged, really. But you didn't."

He sounded so reasonable. Nick was always reasonable. But the unreasonable part in Grace shrieked to be heard. Sometimes, being unreasonable was absolutely necessary, and she knew it was necessary for her. "Nick, I'm sorry, this was just something I had to do. And I have to finish it. Please, I need you to understand. Let's talk when I get home, don't make any decisions about us until then, until I can talk to you and explain all of this to you. Nick, it had nothing to do with our marriage. I just needed some time."

"Maybe I need some time now too, Grace. Maybe it's my turn. Wouldn't that be fair?"

Reasonable. Nick needed time. He said it was time to move on, he said it was time to let Paul go. But this was supposed to be Grace's time. In your time, Gracie, her mother would have said.

Grace started to cry and Virgil held out a tissue from the always-present hotel box. "All right, that is fair, maybe you do. I can't argue with you on that, I know this has been hard on you. I just hope we're still together. I'm sorry I did this to you, but Nick, I really haven't done anything. I haven't done anything wrong." She heard him laugh softly. "All right, you think I did something wrong. But to me, there was no other way. You haven't mentioned this to the kids, have you?"

"Of course not." He cleared his throat again and Grace clenched her fists. "I've had to deal with so much, Grace. So much more than just grief. I had to deal with it all. I had to deal with you. With who you were and how you were acting before you left. And with you becoming someone who could leave."

Just grief? Grief to Grace came with a capital G. Never ever was it just grief. It was something that tucked itself in her body and then sat next to her wherever she went. And wasn't she dealing with it all too? Wasn't she dealing with herself and who she was becoming too?

"Nick," she said. "Nick, are you singing in the shower?"

She heard the click in his throat as his voice caught, capturing the answer he had ready, but she knew he just got a question he wasn't expecting. "What?" he said finally.

"You used to sing in the shower all the time. Before Paul died. You haven't since. Are you singing in the shower again?"

He gasped. Then, in a voice as quiet as Mary's uncharacteristic whisper, he said, "I cry in the shower, Grace."

And she whispered too. "What?"

"I cry in the shower."

Grace rattled for words, rattled to form them into questions. "Why…why didn't you tell me? Why didn't you cry with me?"

"Because." Throughout that single word, his voice began to grow and then it was a roar so loud, Grace had to hold her phone away from her ear. "Because one of us had to hold it together!"

He hung up.

Slowly, Grace tucked her phone into her jeans pocket. She looked at Virgil. He sat, watching her, remote control in hand, television on mute. "I don't know if I could have survived without this trip, Virgil," Grace said. "I was sinking so fast, I was losing so much. I needed to go. I know I have a family, I know I'm a wife and mother, and I know I was only thinking about myself. But I had to this time. I never thought Nick would decide to leave, that I might lose my marriage. Not another one." The tears started again, but with new reason. "Not this one. Not Nick. Oh, Virgil, I can't lose him."

Virgil handed over another tissue and then he leaned away. "It's something I've wondered about, Grace," he said softly. "You love Nick, you say you can't lose him…but then how could you leave him?"

Grace didn't know how to answer his question. She struggled with her thoughts, with discovering an explanation. On this night, everyone wanted an explanation, and Grace wasn't prepared to suddenly have to understand what she had to explain.

"I always thought if you really loved somebody, you'd never want to leave," Virgil said.

Grace swallowed. "I don't want to leave Nick. I guess I never saw this as really leaving him. It wasn't leaving, it was getting away. For a time. Not forever."

Virgil nodded. "But this is hardly a trip to the mall for an afternoon, Grace. Or even a weekend retreat. You just walked out."

In Virgil's face, Grace could see how Nick must feel. She saw the confusion and the hurt and how both Virgil and Nick wanted there to be an answer. A right and a wrong. Nick was big on rights and wrongs, he lived his life out of shoebox compartments. Everything safely tucked away in its place. It would be hard to tuck away a runaway wife into the right shoebox.

"Sometimes big things come along," Grace said slowly. "I mean, big things. Like the death of a child, like Paul. And it feels bigger than anything, bigger than your job, your marriage, your kids…it becomes your whole world." She thought how everything in her life became divided by a big black line. Before Paul's death. After Paul's death. Paul died on a Wednesday and Wednesdays were now days filled with darkness, even if the sun shone brightly. The calendar no longer said June, July, or August. It said two days since Paul died. A week. Two weeks. Six.

And now, seven months.

She turned back to Virgil. His chin was cupped in his palm. "I love Nick. I've always loved Nick. I've loved him since the day I met him. But when Paul died, it was like everything telescoped. To that bright spot I couldn't look at, but I couldn't look away either. Paul was all I could think about. Well, the negative, really. All I could think about was the empty space where Paul used to be. The others were there, Nick, Mary, JJ, but all I wanted was Paul." She shrugged.

"So…" Virgil sat up straighter and he frowned. "Your love for Nick couldn't overcome your grief. Isn't love supposed to solve everything?"

Grace laughed. She couldn't help it, even when she saw the look of hurt on Virgil's face. "Virgil, you sound like you're about fifteen years old. Like you've been reading too many romances. My love for Nick can't overcome my grief for Paul, how could it? They're two separate things, two separate people. Nick, Paul. Life, death. Nick loves me, but he can't bring Paul back. I love Nick, but that doesn't stop me from being sad about losing Paul." She stopped and thought for a minute. "It's like my relationship with Nick went into hibernation for a while. My relationship with everything and everybody went into hibernation. I went into hibernation."

"But it's still there? You still love him?"

"Yes." She was surprised at how simple that answer was. Of course she still loved her husband. "I just hope he still loves me."

Virgil stood up and paced the length of the room. It wasn't big. "Maybe he needs some time, Grace," Virgil said. "Like you did. Nick's been through a lot too, you both have. He lost a mother-in-law. He lost his son. Maybe his style of grieving is to help someone, to be stronger than someone, like he tried to take care of you."

I cry in the shower, Grace.

"When you left, he was alone. Well, with two kids. That must have been really hard on him."

"Yes, I'm sure it was." She thought of Nick's voice on the phone. The range of volume. "I know it was." She sank to the floor. And just like that, her body and mind decided to veer away, into a sudden left curve. It was as if body and mind together decided this was just enough for now. She became overwhelmed with hunger. "Virgil, do we have anything substantial to eat around here?"

Virgil followed her around the curve. Grace knew he would. He looked around the room, as if a waiter would appear. "Like what?"

"Something besides candy and chips. I'd like…a bagel. A toasted bagel soaked through with melted butter. A cinnamon and raisin bagel and a cup of really good coffee."

"Let's go look." Virgil retrieved their coats. "It's not too late, and there's always a bagel and coffee place."

Outside, it was cool with the sun down. Grace sniffed the air, recognized its briskness and felt more at home. Putting her arm through Virgil's, she decided to let herself smile. Despite everything. Despite all of it. Anyway.

"Grace, your father is dead too, isn't he?" Virgil asked.

Grace nodded. "He died over five years ago. He had a heart attack, a sudden one. Though my mother didn't seem surprised. She told me later that when my father left for work that morning, she glanced at the crystal ball in her room and it was black. She called his office to try and warn him and convince him to come home, but he died on his way to work." She kicked at some leaves. "She called me too, that morning. She said, 'Gracie, I think something bad is going to happen.'"

"Did you grieve when he died?"

The question surprised her. Grieve for her father? Of course she did. But, "Not like this. I loved my father, I really did, but in a different way than my mother. My relationship with her was more…intimate. She was everywhere, in my hair, my walk, my reflection. And Paul was in my body. There wasn't one part of me that didn't flow through him during our pregnancy, like my mother flowed through me. But my father was more on the outskirts, I guess. He's here, in me." She pressed her hand to her chest. "But he only left a niche, not a hole."

"It was a comfortable death, for both you and your father. You were as sad as you expected to be."

"Yes. My mother too, really. I knew her dying would devastate me and I was prepared for it, even though it was still hard. I knew it was coming and I knew I would survive it." She pressed that spot on her chest a bit harder. She felt the ache. "I miss both my parents, Virgil. But it's the natural order of things, you know? They were supposed to die before I did. They were supposed to leave me behind."

They turned down a street and Virgil pointed out the lit marquee of a coffee shop. Then he wrapped his arm around her shoulder. "And Paul?"

Grace shook her head. "My God, Virgil. How could I expect anything like that? How could anyone? And how can I survive it?"

Virgil stopped. "This trip. You said back in the hotel room that you didn't think you would have survived it without this trip."

Grace's eyes filled.

"Do you know you'll survive it now?"

Grace thought of the grief that sat beside her wherever she went. That huddled inside her now, coming out in dribs and drabs and sometimes in a whole fabric of misery. But then she smiled that night, as they left the room in search of a cinnamon and raisin bagel and a good cup of coffee.

She was breathing.

"Yes," she said as the tears streamed down her face. "Yes."

****

They were quiet in the darkness of the hotel room that night when suddenly, Virgil rolled over. "Grace, are you still awake?" he whispered.

"Yeah." She sat up and turned on the lamp between their beds. "I can't sleep. I guess I've got too many thoughts in my head."

Virgil sat up too. "Honey, I have to ask you something."

In her ears, Grace could hear him asking again how she could leave Nick. She didn't know; how could she know the answer to that? How could you give a reason for leaving somebody when you didn't think you did? Grace didn't leave Nick. She didn't leave her children. Literally, she did. But did she? Really? No. This just wasn't about leaving them. "What is it?"

Virgil scooted up until he was leaning against his headboard. He picked up Josephine and set her on his lap. He seemed to be looking into her eyes. "Grace, if you knew what was going to happen, and if you could choose, would you go back in time and not have Paul? If you knew you were going to lose him?"

"Of course," she started to say, but then she stopped. She thought about it. A life with just herself and Nick and Mary and JJ. A life like now, but without unfathomable loss. No Paul to lose. She would still be at home, still be happy. There would be no gap in the generations. They would be intact. Grace would be intact.

But there was Paul.

Grace saw him again as a baby, snuggled in her mother's arms, reaching out for the ridiculous grandfather clock she bequeathed to him when he was born.

Her mother gave all the children something upon their births; Mary had an old Singer sewing machine, JJ a stand-up console radio. For Paul, a grandfather clock. The clock sat now in the entryway to their house, but it watched over Paul throughout his too-short life. Paul couldn't walk by that clock without giving it an affectionate pat, without saying from time to time to his brother and sister, "This is really my clock, you know. Grandma gave it to me." Grace remembered overhearing him once saying to a friend who was over for the afternoon, "This clock will go with me wherever I go."

But it didn't. Paul was gone. The clock was still here. Whose clock was it now?

Grace saw Paul reading his ghost stories, looking through his telescope on warm dark nights, looking up from his snack to give her his own smile. The day before he died, he draped himself over her shoulders as she stood, looking out the back window before the view out the back window became something she couldn't stand to see. Paul was always a huggy child, he never hit that "don't touch me" teenager phase. Now he never would. He whispered, "Bye, Mommy," and kissed her on the cheek, on his way out the door to whatever he had to do. He always whispered Mommy to Grace; he called her Mom any other time. But when it was just the two of them, when only he and she could hear, she was still Mommy, and she loved it.

To miss all that, to relieve herself of the pain now?

She turned to Virgil. "No," she said. "No, I wouldn't change it so I wouldn't have Paul. I'd do anything to have that boy. And I would do anything now to get him back. I'd die myself, if it meant having him back for only a minute."

Something happened to Virgil's face then that she just couldn't read. It opened up somehow, it gained a light. Grace saw the skin loosen up and smooth out around his eyes, around the corners of his mouth. "Thank you," he said.

Grace had no idea what he was thanking her for, but she felt that she wasn't supposed to ask anything more, so she just said, "You're welcome." She turned out the light. All that was left was to curve down into the covers and fall asleep.

Virgil did just that, but Grace stayed awake and thought about what it would be like if Nick moved out of the house. If he separated from her, if there was a divorce. There was no separation in her first marriage; that husband just walked out the door and stayed away. The marriage was, then it wasn't. She still remembered the huge ache inside of her after Steven left. She and Nick had almost seventeen years together. She couldn't begin to imagine the size this ache would be.

Grace hugged Cathy and looked over at Virgil, his breathing even in sleep. Josephine was on the pillow next to him and he had the sweetest smile on his face. Nick also slept with a smile. And now, apparently, he cried in the shower.

Nick really did try to help her after Paul died. He tried to take over, tried to help her along. He didn't deserve to be up and left.

But Grace didn't deserve to stay. To see that tree every day, to hear Paul in each room, see him just a shadow ahead, always out of reach. Bits and pieces of Paul existed in Mary and JJ and there were times when they said something a certain way, when their eyebrows cocked up one at a time, when their laughter reached a certain trill, that Paul was there, and then he wasn't, and she ached and ached and ached. It was so hard to carry that hurt around, day after day, and then there was the extra weight of caring for two kids, the two remaining children, caring for a house and a husband, even trying to feed TheCat, clean the litterbox. Grace remembered that figure from mythology, Atlas or some such name, who went around with the entire world on his shoulders. Grace knew how he felt.

She also knew she was right to leave. She had to.

She was a good wife. She was a good mother. She knew that. Nick knew that, their kids knew it.

But as she lay there that night, thinking about two marriages dissolved, thinking about three kids with two different fathers, one who chose to leave, one who was considering it, she wasn't so sure.

She was a woman carrying a doll, running across the country with a gay doll salesman. But she was also a woman who lost the first treasure she ever had, her mother, and then one of the biggest treasures of her life. One of three treasures. Her son. Her wonderful sweet-faced fifteen-year old son. Her boy.

"Sometimes," Grace whispered to Cathy, "people have to break. You have to let it happen. There's no other way." She pulled the doll's string.

"I love you," Cathy said.

"Thank you," Grace whispered back.

Virgil stirred. "Grace?" he muttered.

"It's okay, go back to sleep." She watched him shift and shimmy, groan and roll over, his arm swinging over the small doll at his side. And she thought, I've found a treasure all over again.

There were treasures still at home too. Mary. JJ.

Nick.

When Grace cried into Cathy's hair that night, they were new tears of a new grief. A loss that hadn't happened, but very well could. Grace didn't think she could withstand any more.

****

But there was, of course, more to withstand. The next day, in the car, Virgil suddenly interrupted his humming to ask, "Grace, if you went home right now, right this second, what would be the hardest thing? Would it be facing Nick?"

Grace, who had been staring out the window, found herself immediately shaking her head. She didn't even have to think about it. "No. That's going to be hard, of course. But the hardest thing will be facing Mary."

Virgil frowned. "Mary? Your daughter? Why?"

Grace turned in her seat, hooking her leg up so she sat sideways, facing Virgil. "A few days before you and I left, Mary told me that it was her fault Paul died."

"Her fault?" Virgil glanced at her. "How could it be her fault?"

"She told Paul to climb the tree. She told him where to hide." She watched Virgil's facial expression, waiting for any change. Any sign that like her, he could agree with her daughter. It was Mary's fault Paul died.

But Virgil just nodded. "I get that. What did you tell her?"

Grace was ashamed to say. Here was where Virgil could suddenly side with Nick. She ducked her head. "I said, 'Let's go to McDonald's,' and then I took her out to lunch."

Virgil laughed softly. "Do you blame her, Grace? Do you think Paul's death is her fault?"

"She's just a kid, Virgil," she said automatically and protectively. It was the right answer, the one she was supposed to say, even if she couldn't say it herself to Mary.

"Yes, I know, and I'm sure she knows that too. But do you blame her? Is it her fault?"

Grace folded her hands. She tried to form words that would tell the truth, but not make Virgil hate her. She didn't want Virgil to hate her. Then she sighed and decided to plunge into it. "Yes, Virgil. It is her fault. If she didn't tell him to climb that tree, he would have hidden someplace else. He wasn't the type of kid to climb trees. He wouldn't have died. God!" She grabbed one of Virgil's hands and held it tightly between her own. "I must be the worst mother in the world, to say that about my own daughter. But it's the way it happened, it's the way I feel. Nick wanted me to tell her it wasn't her fault, to tell her it was okay. But it is her fault and it will never be okay again."

"Have you said anything else to her, other than inviting her to McDonald's?" Virgil laughed again. "Now you've put me in mind of it. We should stop there for lunch today."

Grace hadn't been there since that awful lunch with Mary. "Not really. But Nick keeps telling her it's not her fault because she didn't mean it. It wasn't intentional."

Virgil snorted. "Of course she didn't mean it! She didn't send Paul up that tree with the purpose of killing him. But it did happen. Maybe what Mary needs is for you to acknowledge that it did happen that way, and that you forgive her."

Grace blinked. "What?"

"Look." Virgil shook his hand free of Grace's and conducted the air as he made his points. "What she's been told, that it wasn't her fault, makes it seem like it never happened, or like it happened in a way that she knows it didn't. Like everyone else but Mary refuses to believe that such a thing occurred. She knows, she knows that she told him to go up a tree, he did, and he died. If she didn't tell him, he would've hidden someplace else. She just needs someone else to admit it and to forgive her." Virgil picked up Grace's hand again and squeezed it. "You're the only one that hasn't said that it wasn't her fault. She hears that. She knows you know, that you agree with her. She doesn't need to hear that it's not her fault, Grace. She needs to hear that you forgive her."

Grace shook her head. "That isn't what Nick says," she told him. "And she does seem to be doing better now." But Grace thought of all the times that Mary apologized over the phone.

"Sure. She's being a good girl, trying to earn your forgiveness." Virgil sighed. "Grace, when I told my father I was gay, he wouldn't accept it. He wouldn't admit it, that it was true and he knew about it as long as I did. He stopped talking to me, he threw me out, I ceased to exist. Which has made it so hard to get on with anything. It's hard to feel real when you know you've disappeared from someone's life, you're invisible. But if he just said, okay, son, I know it too, and I forgive you, well, then I could have moved on. We could have continued. Even though what I did wasn't intentional. It's just what is. And it's something my father needed to forgive me for." Virgil yanked the car to the side of the road, threw it in park and then turned toward Grace. "Grace, you can't let who Mary is not exist. She's the girl who told her brother to climb a tree and he died. The Mary who did this needs to exist, and she needs to be forgiven. Everything else is going to feel like a fraud to her."

Grace hesitated. This was crazy. But it was what she'd been feeling all along, wasn't it? Maybe Mary felt it too.

Virgil touched her cheek, her shoulder. He rested his hands on her knees. "Can you do it? Are you able to forgive her, Grace? Because she'll know if it's just words."

Grace shuddered, a whole-body tremor that left her shivering. "I don't know, Virgil. I mean, she's my daughter and I love her! But to tell her it's all right when it's not all right, I don't know if I can do that. How can it be all right that Paul's dead? How can that ever be?"

Virgil shook his head. "You don't have to say it's all right, Grace. Because it's not, and you're right, it's not anything that can ever be fixed. Your son is dead, and how can that ever be a good thing, the right thing? But you can let Mary know that you understand how it happened and you forgive her. You can move on."

Move on. Let it go. It's time, Grace. In your time, Gracie. This was moving on, but in a different way. A different path. In her time? It was what Nick wanted her to do, what everyone seemed to want her to do, but in a new direction. Grace began to cry and both she and Virgil let the tears fall. "I don't know yet, Virgil. I'm trying."

He nodded. "That's all you can do, isn't it." He pulled the car back onto the road.

Grace wiped her eyes and nose. "If it helps you, Virgil, you exist. You exist a lot. Maybe not to your father, but to me."

He smiled. "Thank you, Grace." Then he pointed to a sign on the side of the road. "Look, we're in Georgia! I think we should probably stop soon."

Georgia. Grace wondered if she should say something. Virgil was there during the conversation with Hannah, he knew that she knew. "Virgil?" Grace asked. "Is Georgia where that guy lives? You know…the guy Hannah talked about? The one she didn't seem to like very much."

Virgil jerked and the Chrysler veered. After swearing profusely, Virgil steadied the car. Then he said, staring straight ahead, "He lives here, yes. His name is Brad. And…" He glanced at Grace, then held out his hand. She took it. "And I'm out of my head in love with him." He smiled and it was like his face caught fire. The pink of love and excitement caught at his neck and flamed upward, soon washing him in red. But not an embarrassed red. A joyous red beyond the red of Christmas presents and chocolates on Valentine's Day. "Brad is my lover. He's been my lover for ten years. And now he's asked me to move in with him. To marry him." Virgil laughed, full-throated, but there was an edge of worry to it too. "No one has ever asked me to marry him before, Grace. And I'm sixty-five."

There was another moment and Grace waited.

"And I don't know what to do. What do you do when an absolute impossibility becomes a possibility? What do you do when you've never allowed yourself to want something because it's not yours to want, and then suddenly, there it is? And you haven't shaped or planned your life around that? Because it could never happen, but now it could?" He laughed, but it wasn't happy. "I don't know what to do. And I don't know how to do it."

Virgil was looking at the maybe of marriage for the first time. And Grace was wondering if her second marriage was about to go the way of the first. Out the door without looking back.

Grace held Virgil's hand. She savored the warmth.

This was crazy.

CHAPTER TWELVE
Virgil

The Georgia border reeled Virgil in. That state line just curled itself like a whip, lashed out and got him around the ankle, and then dragged him the rest of the way. Though that was too negative; he was more than willing to be dragged. If he could have, he would have grabbed the whip, looped it around his elbows and shot himself like a slingshot toward the house, and to Brad. When he saw that sign, "Welcome to Georgia!" the nose of the Chrysler turned like a hound dog's toward Macon. Macon was Georgia to Virgil. And Macon was Brad, the man he loved. He just declared his love for Brad, out loud, to Grace in the car. Hearing his voice say it, and say it to a third person, made it feel real. It was real. It was real in a way that he could have never imagined, and that he never expected.

As each mile passed, Virgil's stomach and shoulders tightened with apprehension and his heart beat faster with anticipation. He had to tell Grace that this was more than a pit stop. They were staying. There wasn't going to be a hotel on that night. Or for several nights. This was the final stop before turning back up.

"Grace," he said.

Grace had been napping since their lunch at McDonald's. But she lolled her head against her headrest and looked at him with half-open eyes.

And Virgil lost his nerve. It was one thing to have her accept that he was gay. It was another to have her stay in a house while he slept with a man in another room. Though sleep, he knew, would be a long way away that night, the first night he and Brad had together in months. Virgil wondered if even that would be affected, stymied, with a woman just down the hall.

How was Brad going to be with an unexpected guest? Especially when the guest was a woman, and a straight woman at that. But Virgil couldn't drop Grace off at a hotel by herself. Not because he didn't want her to be alone; he didn't want to be without her. He wanted to share Georgia with Grace. He wanted to have Brad and Grace both, under the same roof.

Because of their distance apart, Virgil and Brad never had to share each other's company when they were together before. But if they lived together permanently, Virgil reasoned, they would be sharing their lives outside of themselves. They wouldn't always be private, away from the world's eyes.

Though bringing a runaway woman to Brad's house, and to their annual liaison, and a particular liaison where decisions had to be made, was one hell of a way to pull back the curtain.

Virgil sighed and shuddered and the mighty car shook just a little beneath his hands. Grace patted his leg.

"Are you all right?" she asked.

"I'm fine." Virgil decided to just concentrate on driving, on getting there in one piece. When he turned into the long drive leading into the junkyard, his knees shook. He needed to see Brad. He needed to be with him now. Brad was so close, Virgil could taste him in the air.

But for the first time ever, his arrival had him shaking in fear too. He'd never been afraid to see Brad before. But now, there was Brad's ultimatum. And there was Grace. Virgil knew very well that Grace could be uncomfortable and ask to leave. And he knew that Brad could see her as an interloper.

"Good lord, Virgil," Grace said. "Where are we?"

On either side of the dirt road were piles and piles of two- and three-legged furniture, couches, chairs, tables, old washing machines, and refrigerators with no doors. Cars. Heaps of dollhouses with no roofs, bikes with no tires or handlebars. Junk. Miles and miles of junk.

Grace cleared her throat. "I know you said this guy lives in Georgia, Virgil," she said. "But where? What is this place?"

Virgil laughed. No, he giggled, and Grace stared. "Isn't it great? It's a junkyard, Brad owns his own private junkyard. Sometimes I picture myself here, spending my days digging and looking, marveling over the stuff people throw away. It's like archeology, modern archeology." He waved his hand out the window. "Brad says it's like a kingdom."

"But where does he live?"

"In the middle of all this. He built himself a house, inside and out, mostly out of the stuff people throw away here. It's actually quite nice. He's got two bedrooms and two and a half baths. Great kitchen, large living room. And a big Southern-style verandah for surveying his grounds." Virgil nodded, bobbing his head like a felt dog on a dashboard. "He's found dozens of rocking chairs and porch swings and he sets them up on the verandah or on the little bit of a yard. He sits and he swings and he watches the cars coming and going with their junk. He does most of his treasure-hunting in the morning, since most people don't dump then. They come in the afternoon, if it's not too hot, and even more come in the evening or overnight when they think that no one can see them." Virgil felt Grace staring at him and he kept his eyes on the dirt path.

Grace sank into her seat. "I suppose he has a junkyard dog."

"No, actually. He has a skunk."

She sat back up. "Oh, terrific. A skunk. A skunk in the middle of a junkyard, living in a house with a junkman named Brad. Virgil, what are you up to? Are you making this all up?"

Virgil shook his head. "Brad says a skunk scares an intruder faster than a dog. Most dogs just wag their tails or bark a little. But skunks are armed. They shoot for bear."

"It's descented though, right?"

"No, he's completely au natural. He started hanging around the house and Brad fed him. Eventually, the skunk became tame and he doesn't squirt unless he's alarmed. Look, you can just barely see the house now."

The road widened and around a mountain of garbage, they could see the edge of a roof. Virgil drove around the corner and the road ended in a green glade. A very green glade. Grace's jaw dropped open and she sat straight up in her seat.

The house rose up two stories and it was blinding white in the sun. The porch ran around the front and sides and it was freshly swept and painted. The promised chairs and swings, all painted bright colors, sassy purples and reds and yellows, were scattered around the porch and lawn. They leaned toward each other as if engaged in conversation. The lawn that ran in an even square around the house was greener than green; it looked spray-painted, the way it shone and bent in the breeze.

"My God," Grace breathed. "It's HG-TV stuck in the middle of a junkyard!"

"If the G stands for garbage," Virgil agreed. "I told you." He parked the car and honked lightly, though every part of him wanted to leap out, lunge into the house, and grab Brad in a bearhug so tight, he wouldn't escape for weeks. From the porch, a black and white rug unrolled itself and strolled down the steps. Virgil pointed the skunk out to Grace. "Don't get out of the car yet," he said.

"Brad will come out and let Percy know we're okay." He leaned out of the window. "Hey, boy, how are you?"

The skunk stopped two feet away from the car. He arched his back and raised his tail.

"Percy?" Grace said.

"Percy." Virgil watched the house's door. It swung open, without a creak or a bang, and whispered shut again. The man that came out wore bright blue and white striped overalls and no shirt at all. His skin glowed with a construction worker's bronze. His hair was blond and neatly trimmed and combed. He raised his hand to his eyes and then he grinned.

Brad.

"It's okay, Percy, it's okay!" he shouted and ran down the steps. In one motion, Virgil was out of the car and in his arms. They kissed and Virgil was drawn in so deep, he didn't think he would ever breathe again.

Virgil broke away, but kept his arm around Brad's waist, bare above the band of the overalls. Virgil turned breathless toward the Chrysler. Halfway out of her seat, Grace was frozen with one leg on the ground and the other still in the car. Her mouth was open.

"Grace," Virgil said and Brad stiffened beside him. "Grace, this is Brad, my…well, my lover. The man I love. Brad, this is my friend, Grace. She came along with me this year."

Grace seemed to shake herself and she got the rest of the way out of the car. Slowly, she came up to Brad and held out her hand. "Hello, Brad," she said. Her voice was soft with shyness. They shook hands and Virgil watched where their hands joined, watched the way their fingers seemed unable to bend, the knuckles barely creased. Then Grace stepped away. "This is unbelievable," she said. "The house, I mean. It's beautiful."

Brad smiled, that slow warm Southern smile that melted Virgil's heart. "Thanks, I like it. Come on up on the porch. I'll get y'all some sweet tea. Just made it this morning." He looked sideways at Virgil. "There was something in the air…I knew you were coming."

Virgil and Grace followed him up the steps, Brad sneaking peeks at Grace over his shoulder. Grace chose a pink rocker. It moved smoothly, without a sound. Percy jumped into her lap and she startled, both hands flying to her face. "Just pat him nice," Brad said. "He likes his back rubbed."

Grace quickly began rubbing Percy's back. Virgil sat down in a porch swing and soon Brad bustled out again with a tray of glasses and a pitcher. He set these on a table and handed out the drinks. When he joined Virgil on the swing, he pressed his thigh to Virgil's and Virgil pressed back. Virgil felt Brad's muscle, tense and tight, and he knew what Brad was thinking. Normally, they'd be in the house by now, and they wouldn't even make it to the bedroom. The hallway, the stairs, wherever they ended up was comfort enough. But now, with Grace here, there had to be Southern hospitality. There was sweet tea. Passion would have to wait.

They talked generalities, the trip, the dolls Virgil found. Brad asked Grace if she was a collector. She shook her head.

Virgil smiled at her, trying to encourage her into joining the conversation. "I met Grace when she bought Chatty Cathy from me. It was a doll she always wanted, but never had."

Brad and Grace watched each other, unblinking. It was like they were sizing each other up.

Brad turned to Virgil. "Got a good crop of dolls this year, Virgil. At least thirty."

Virgil whistled. "We'll take a look later tonight, or maybe in the morning after the search." Grace's chair creaked, something Brad's chairs never did, and when Virgil looked at her, she was leaning way forward. Percy dug into her lap and hung on for dear life.

"Are we staying here, Virgil?" She swallowed audibly and leaned back, Percy bumping against her stomach. "I mean, here? In this house?"

Virgil nodded, coming face to face with his decision not to tell her earlier. He took Brad's hand. "Sure, Grace. Brad has a great guestroom, you'll be more comfortable than you've been since we left home. I thought we'd stay here until the end of next week, and then start our trek back up to Wisconsin."

Her eyes filled with tears and Virgil frantically tried to figure out why. It wasn't an easy fit, working himself into Grace's state of mind. He saw a woman who was going to spend the night in a room completely alone for the first time since she ran away from her family. Virgil was always with her, on every other night. But tonight, he wouldn't be in the bed right next to hers. He'd be across the hall. With someone else.

"Grace, sweetheart," he said, and with that, the tears spilled over. He squeezed Brad's fingers, then went to kneel next to Grace. Her hands nestled in Percy's rich black fur and Virgil put his fingers over hers. Her skin was cold. "Honey, I'll just be across the hall. We're still together, we're still in the same place."

"That's not it," she cried, and it was a different sort of cry than Virgil was used to. This wasn't coming from some place deep inside, but on the surface. These tears were about right here and right now, about him, and about him and Brad. "I just feel so out of place. I feel like I'm extra. It's like I'm not...not..."

"Wanted? Important?" Virgil prompted. "Of course you're important. I still love you, nothing changes that."

"You love her?" Brad said, and there was no disguising the hurt and anger in his voice. "You love her?" he repeated.

This wasn't working out so well. Virgil stood up and held onto one of Grace's hands while he reached and grabbed one of Brad's. He stood there between the two of them, stretched out like a clothesline, them hanging on either end like poles, one in tears, the other with bright spots of red on his cheeks. "Look," Virgil said. "Let's slow this all down, let's figure this all out. I'm in love with Brad, I have been for years. He means everything to me, I traveled this far to be with him, to see him. I love you, Brad," he said and watched the coals quiet on his lover's face. "And I love Grace too. Not like that, but in a deep way that hasn't happened to me in a while. A friend. She needed me. It's been a long time since anyone needed me." In answer, Grace's fingers formed a death grip on his.

"I need you," Brad said, the anger gone, but the touch of hurt still there. "I've always needed you."

Sweeter words were never spoken. "Not like this, Brad. This is different." Virgil pulled his hands free and returned to Brad's side. "I'd like us to stay here until the end of next week, Grace. Then we'll get you home."

Grace and Brad looked at each other again, Brad's eyes narrowed, Grace's still wet. But then Brad moved toward the door.

"Let me show you your room, Grace," he said. "Not too many people have stayed there. You'll have your own bath, I've added a bath since last year, Virgil, remember? Just a sink and a john and a tub. A clawfoot tub, the genuine article. It's real nice."

Grace looked down at Percy. "Will he let me move?"

Brad snorted. "He hasn't stopped you yet, has he? Just wiggle around a bit, he'll get the message." He turned back to Virgil. "I was going to have steak tonight, I'll get a couple more out of the freezer. If I nuke them, they'll be ready for the grill."

Grace shifted and Percy unrolled and ambled away to his rug. Virgil took her elbow and they followed Brad inside and up the stairs to the guest bedroom.

"What do you think?" Brad asked, spreading his arms.

The sun poured in through large windows. Outside, over and between heaps and heaps of garbage, the town peeped at them. A door opened to a small elegant bathroom, its tile gleaming with lack of use. "It's very pretty," Grace said. Virgil agreed; it was. Everything Brad did was always high class.

"It's perfect, Brad," Virgil said and hugged him again. "Why don't you and I go get the stuff from the car while Grace settles in?"

"Just a minute. Look at this, Grace." Brad moved toward the bathroom. "Here's something you don't find in hotels anymore." He motioned them both in.

They stood in crowded wonder around a gloriously pink claw-footed bathtub. Grace, shoving her sniffles aside, laughed out loud. "It's beautiful, Brad, did you find this too?"

He beamed in pride. "Yep, that was a real banner day. I couldn't believe someone left it behind." He touched the tub the way Virgil touched dolls' heads. "Why don't you have yourself a long hot bath before dinner? Bet you haven't had a real bath since you left home. In this thing, you can soak up to your neck. I've got bubbles in the vanity. Virgil and I will get your stuff and then we'll cook, so you can come down to a great dinner."

Grace agreed and Virgil shut the door, leaving her behind. He and Brad went down the stairs. They were only four steps down when Brad's hand wrapped itself in Virgil's, entwining their fingers, each one a match for the other. Virgil hated the term, especially since he was in Georgia, but he wanted to swoon. By the front door, Brad grabbed Virgil suddenly and pulled him onto the couch. Flattened beneath, Virgil found himself kissed breathless.

"God, I've missed you," Brad said, his hands in Virgil's hair, drifting down his face, his neck. "I love you so much, Virgil, I couldn't wait for you to get here."

Virgil could hear the water running upstairs. "I love you too," he said and grabbed Brad in a kiss again. Brad's hips clenched in Virgil's hands felt delicious. "And I've missed you too." He rolled his eyes toward the ceiling. "Though I bet that bathtub has seen some action."

Brad groaned and he buried his face in Virgil's neck. Brad's hands worked their way down Virgil's chest. "There's been nobody, Virgil," he whispered. "Nobody for years. Only you, there's only you."

Virgil's breath caught. Then he shoved Brad away and sat up, as much as he hated to break the maddening movement of his hands. "What do you mean?

Why did you tell me there were others?" He thought of Hannah's calling Brad loose and Virgil found himself surprised that his defense of Brad was correct.

Brad bit his lip, ran his hand through his hair. "To get you here. It's stupid, I know, but I thought if you thought there was someone else, you'd be here in a minute. It didn't work out that way."

Virgil closed his eyes. He wondered how many men Brad told him about over the ten years they'd been together. Six? A dozen? And each time, he ached in his own loneliness and misery. He couldn't stop Brad, he wouldn't ask him to stop, but now it turned out there was nothing to stop at all, at least for a while.

If Brad was telling the truth. What was he supposed to believe?

The water quieted upstairs and Virgil heard a splash as Grace settled herself in. Brad put his hands on both sides of Virgil's face and shook him gently.

"I love you, Virgil," he said. "I want to spend the rest of my life with you. I want you to move in here with me. I want to get married. This needs to be our last visit."

And there it was again. The ultimatum, face to face. Virgil opened his eyes and Brad's gaze bored in, their lips met, and they kissed for a long time, their eyes open, taking each other in. Then Virgil said, "I love you too, Brad. I've been doing a lot of thinking…"

Brad sat back hard, his back banging against the armrest. "This is about that woman upstairs, isn't it? You've been sleeping with her." He turned away and Virgil heard his voice break. "All this time," he whispered. "There's been nobody but you. Nobody but you, Virgil. And now you have her. Not only that, but you bring her here, you wave her right in front of me." He looked at Virgil and his face was a mask of grief. "What were you thinking?"

Virgil's mouth dropped open. What could he say? He couldn't deny that he had thoughts about Grace those first nights in the hotel room. Those thoughts were there, and Virgil's physical reaction was there too. But he wasn't in love with Grace, he didn't come here to flaunt her, as if he suddenly found the key to being straight. Because he didn't. He was still himself. And he didn't even want to find that key anymore. "Brad," he said slowly. "Would I have even come here if I was involved with a woman? Why would I do that to you?" Virgil was amazed to see Brad's eyes fill and overflow.

"To get your dolls?"

There was nothing to do but blink.

"Well, that did sound stupid, didn't it?" Brad's face relaxed and he released the soft tenor of his chuckle. "I know you wouldn't do that."

Virgil tentatively nodded, not sure if he should agree or not, but yes, it did sound stupid. To get the dolls? Brad had to know him better than that. Just like the way Virgil knew him.

But then Virgil would know that Brad wouldn't see anyone else.

He thought of his words to Hannah. His easy defense.

He did know. At some level, he knew all along.

Brad took Virgil's hand. "You were saying?" he said, and Virgil's mind went blank. "You said you'd been thinking."

Virgil had done a lot of thinking. He filed through all the thoughts, all the pros and cons, his vision of the sick Brad, the dying Brad, his life suddenly alone again, but he just couldn't do it. Those thoughts were gone. There was only Brad now, there was only the feeling of being here with him right this very minute. Throwing his thoughts out into the air of this immaculately clean house in the middle of a junkyard, Virgil said, "I love you too, Brad. And I want to spend the rest of my life with you."

And that was that. The commitment was made, the ultimatum met. Virgil wondered at how easily, at how quickly it emerged and flew into the room. His whole life suddenly changed. And he was scared to death.

But it didn't stop him. On the couch, Virgil and Brad made the quietest love they'd ever had while Grace splashed from time to time upstairs.

When Brad rolled away and sat up to kiss Virgil, his lips still warm and salty, Virgil felt the last part of himself that held back break away and disappear. This was where he belonged. He needed to be with Brad, Brad needed to be with him. Virgil would move here. He and all of his dolls. And he would marry Brad. He'd be a married man. An impossible thing.

Brad stuck out his hand. "Men always shake on a deal," he said. "I don't think we get down on our knees for this kind of proposal." He winked. "But I'll have you on your knees later."

Virgil grabbed his hand and pumped it and they laughed. Their voices joined and blended and their fingers intertwined again. Brad kissed Virgil delicately, running his tongue around Virgil's lips. Virgil never wished more that later could be now. Then they walked out to the car for the suitcases.

****

While Virgil and Brad prepared the steaks, they could hear the water turn on and off as Grace refreshed the heat. When the coals were ready to cook, Virgil sensed Brad's impatience to get on with the dinner, so Virgil went up after her. He knocked quickly before going into the bathroom. Grace was buried in bubbles up to her neck.

"You look like a Calgon commercial," Virgil said.

"That's exactly how I feel."

Virgil sank down to the floor next to the tub. Resting his head on the rim, he soon felt Grace's damp hair leaning against him. "You don't mind, not really, do you, Grace? Being here? I really needed to see Brad."

"I know." Her voice was a sigh. "I just feel like the one too many. Maybe you should put me in a hotel and stay here by yourself. You can pick me up later, when it's time to go home. I'm in the way here."

"I don't want you to be alone and I wanted you to see this place." Virgil sat up suddenly and Grace's head clunked against the tub. "Sorry. But isn't this place wonderful?"

Virgil knew he looked eager and Grace rolled her eyes. "I guess wonderful is the word for it. I love this tub."

Virgil poked at the bubbles and smelled them. Lavender, Brad's favorite scent, and the same scent Virgil used on his dolls. He blew the suds at Grace.

She brought her fingers up in a soapy teepee by her chin. "You said something in the car…something about picturing yourself here when you retire. Do you really think you'll do that? It's hard for me to imagine you living in the middle of junk."

"It's not junk, Grace. It's opportunity!" Virgil crowed the way he heard Brad crow, but then, at Grace's cynical look, he wilted a bit. "Well, okay, some of it's junk. But look at all he's found! It's what we've talked about, how he wants it, my settling out here. It's easier for me to move my shop to Georgia than for him to move his dump to Wisconsin. I can always do all my business online. It's a way that we can both get what we want. I know it'll be different. But I could maybe open a small shop here."

Grace nearly sat up, but then remembered where she was and sank back down. "But you already have The Nursery! At home!"

"I know." Virgil turned around and rested his back against the wall. He marveled at their ease with each other. She was naked; he knew it; it didn't matter. "And I'm not sure what I'll do about that. But it doesn't really matter, Grace. What matters is that I'm here with him."

"Then why weren't you here ten years ago? Five years ago? Last year? Why haven't you stayed?"

The bluntness of her questions made Virgil's fingers curl. "Actually, that's kind of what I want to ask you about. You've done it. Twice. Made that commitment, I mean. You married both your husbands, thinking you'd be with them for the rest of your life, right?"

She nodded. "I was wrong with Steven. And it looks like I might be wrong with Nick. I guess I'm not very good at this." She closed her eyes. "Though it was Steven that ended the first marriage. This time…well, this time, I guess it's my fault."

Virgil leaned forward. "But you've felt it. You've wanted to do it. I've never made a commitment like this to anyone before. And Brad's been wanting me to for a long time. I want to too, I guess, in fact, I told him I would, but it's just so…"

"Big?" Grace said. "Yeah, it's one of those big things, isn't it." Then more quietly, she said, "You told him you would?"

Virgil nodded. "Just a little bit ago. It was…sort of the heat of the moment. But more too." He reached out, held his hand open until she took it. "So how did you know? How did you say yes?"

Her fingers were wet and soapy. Warm. But she managed to hang on to him without slipping. "It was different both times. Steven felt like he'd stepped out of the pages of a fairy tale book. He wanted to take care of me and he had the means to do so. When he put his arm around me, I felt safe and protected. He kissed me and I felt giddy. When I thought about it, I could picture us together, in the future. Him in a three-piece suit, me waving at him from the doorway while our children hollered for breakfast in the kitchen. It was that image that convinced me. I could see myself with him."

Virgil closed his eyes. He saw himself getting up with Brad every morning, fixing him breakfast. Then they put on orange coveralls and they searched the grounds for treasure. Afternoons, he saw himself puttering on his own, maybe making the shed in the back into his doll workshop, or maybe he'd be reading a good book, looking out the window every now and then to see what Brad was up to. And evenings, they curled up together, on the porch swings, the couch, in bed. It all fit. "Grace," Virgil whispered. "I can see it."

Grace tugged her hand away. "Okay, you can see it. But look what happened to me and Steven."

"Well, what about Nick? Could you see it with Nick? I mean, after Steven just left you, how could you…"

Her face softened. "Oh, I saw it. But there was more. I felt it. When Nick kissed me, I wasn't giddy. I was just gone. Just…" She lifted her hands, then raised them to the ceiling for a minute, bubbles falling iridescent from her fingers. "I don't know how to describe it."

Virgil smiled. "You just did." He thought about kissing Brad and felt his heartrate rise in his chest, just like Grace's hands. "Grace, I feel that too."

She looked at the bath water. "So what are you waiting for then? You've already said you would, so why are you questioning it now? Has it even been an hour?"

That was the question and Virgil thought of that commitment he just made downstairs, the deal sealed with a handshake and the promise of more. "It's a lot of change, Grace. A lot. Moving, giving up The Nursery, all of it. And there's something else too." He reached into the tub and splashed around until he found her hand again. He held it. He needed to hold it, to hold her. "Grace, what if he gets sick? What if he dies?"

She looked away. "You mean like Paul did."

Virgil nodded. "I've seen, you know, what something like that can do. To you. To everyone in your family. But especially to you."

They sat like that in silence and Virgil could feel the wheels turning in her brain. There was a shift, a pulling back of her shoulders, and he knew their roles just switched. She wasn't leaning on Virgil right then. He was leaning on her, looking to her for the answers.

"You asked me a while ago if I would do it all again, if I knew things would end up this way. Paul, dead. Maybe my marriage too. I said yes when you asked me. I'm saying yes now. It's worth it, Virgil," she said simply. "It's just worth it. Even if you lose it all." She squeezed his hand.

Virgil clenched. "When I'm here," he said slowly, "it seems like the right thing. Whenever I'm with him, it is the right thing."

She wrapped her arms around herself. The bubbles were fading. "Then I guess you've answered your own question, huh?" She crossed her legs. "Every time I held Paul while he was alive, from the moment he was born until that last day, I knew he was the right thing. That it was right that I had him, that he belonged to me and to this world. I knew it then and I know it now." She sighed, a small and sad sigh as wet as the bubbles. "Even if it means that his death, and what I've done, causes me to lose Nick." She swished the water. "Even if it meant losing Paul and having to live with his absence."

Virgil moved up the side of the tub and kissed her forehead. "Look, it's time to throw the steaks on the grill. You come on down. Be happy for me."

She looked up, her blue eyes as wide as a doll's. Shiny half-dollar eyes, like Josephine's. "I wish you didn't have to move." Then she gave Virgil a bit-lip smile. "I'll be right down," she said.

Virgil pulled himself slowly to his feet. He knew, at his age, he shouldn't be sitting on a floor, especially a tiled one, but he didn't regret it. It was worth every ache and pain to be that close to Grace. He moved to the doorway, then stopped to look at her again. That mop of hair fell in damp ringlets over the edge of the tub and she was soft pink curves and warmth. For the moment, those eyes were closed and her eyelashes curled against her cheek. Her face was peaceful and she looked happy. Relaxed and happy and close to him.

Virgil wanted to remember her like that forever.

****

Virgil was the first to wake the next morning. Brad's shades were only half-down, and the glorious Georgia sun tumbled into the room and lit the floor and the base of the bed. Brad was asleep with the sheets tossed aside. He looked like he threw himself into sleep, his arms and legs widespread, his stomach rising and falling with his breath. Virgil sat up carefully and looked around the room. The master bedroom. It was Brad's, but soon it would be his too. Virgil pictured where his own things would go, where his chair or dresser would fit, which furniture he would bring and what would have to be sold.

And his dolls. This would be their home too. They could sit in rockers on the porch or relax in the living room. Josephine was already here, sitting in a captain's chair near the bedroom door. When she and Virgil came back for good, along with all the other dolls, she alone would stay in this room with them. She alone would be witness to the fullness of their pairing. Having Brad, having Josephine, somehow made this all real. It was a dream made real. A connection between the past and the present and what was going to be their future.

"Hey." Brad looked up, blinking slowly. "Oh, hey. You don't know how many times I've woken up, hoping you would be here."

"I'm here," Virgil said and nestled down next to him. "I'm right here."

They lay there, arms and legs entwined. "As soon as I get Grace home, I'll be back," Virgil said. "I'll close down the shop, and be here as fast as I can."

Brad touched Virgil's cheek. "I'll come help," he said. "I'll come along with you."

Virgil shook his head gently. "Come after I get her home. When there's time for only us, Brad. Just us."

Brad started to protest, but then he stopped. "I love you, Virgil," he said. "But I just don't get what's between you and this girl."

"And I love you. And I don't get it either. But she's something special, Brad." Virgil wanted to tell Brad that Grace was a large part of why he was able to commit to Brad now. Somehow, watching Grace, seeing her go through all the grief she experienced with losing her mother and with losing Paul, yet still wanting to go back to her husband and kids, to be in their lives, to have them in hers, made Virgil realize that Grace's reassurance that it was all worth it was absolutely true. Grace was finishing up a dark time, but look at the bright times that came before. If she hadn't married Steven, there would be no Mary, and if Steven hadn't left, she wouldn't have met Nick and there wouldn't have been Paul, there would be no JJ. The grief was there, the loss was beyond huge. But the love for Nick was there as well. And the love for Mary and JJ. There were bright times to come.

But he didn't tell Brad any of this. Remembering the way Brad looked at Grace, Virgil knew Brad couldn't accept that. For now. Brad needed reassurances, that he was first in Virgil's life, that when Virgil said he loved Grace, it had nothing to do with his love for Brad. Virgil closed his eyes and pictured all the mornings he would wake up here, in Brad's arms, in this house. It was like his past fell away, fell into a space in his own personal attic where he could look at it if he wanted to. If he chose. But until then, it was locked away, safely and dark.

Virgil's dark time was coming to an end too. It was. He was sure of it.

CHAPTER THIRTEEN
Grace

The first morning Grace awoke at Brad's house, she was amazed to find herself well-rested. The night had been filled with junkyard silence. This threw Grace at first, trying to sleep in the profound dark without parking lot lights, and causing her to concentrate on the ticking of her clocks on the dresser, the big clock and the little grandfather. She held her breath until they struck the half-hour, the hour, filling her room with welcome and familiar sound. She'd grown so used to the noises and lights of hotels and motels; cars going by, people talking and watching television, and Virgil rustling around the room. Eventually, she fell asleep anyway, and when she did, she tumbled so deep into the still, she didn't reopen her eyes until the morning filled her room with light.

Mornings at a junkyard, she discovered as she stretched and walked to the window, were as raucous as the night was silent. Birds descended, scavengers, she figured, from everywhere. Crows, seagulls, things that might have been buzzards. The noise was like a party about to go out of control. And the out of control felt subtly violent – she could picture the birds on the ground or circling in the sky, their necks arched, beaks open, suddenly breaking into bloodthirsty battle over whatever treasure they could find.

Different than what she would consider treasure, for sure. Different than what Virgil considered. She wondered if Brad got along with the birds.

The golden boy, she thought, the silky southerner, and she shoved her thoughts deliberately away from picturing him with Virgil. He could seduce anything, she decided. She thought of Hannah, accusing Brad of being loose. And then she remonstrated herself; she didn't know Brad. And Virgil loved him. That should be enough.

Virgil wasn't hers. Although he felt like hers, felt like her own treasured discovery, he wasn't. When she returned home, it would be to her family. Virgil wouldn't be moving in; she wouldn't be moving across town to The Nursery.

Their lives would go back to normal.

A new normal, she hoped.

She smelled bacon and eggs and that certain sweetness of pancakes. The men's voices were below her, Brad's in a set spot under the bed, Virgil's winding around the room. Virgil had to be the one cooking, in his glory, crafting an extravagant breakfast. Grace crawled back into bed, hugging Cathy, and she listened to Virgil and Brad. She couldn't make out their words, but she could hear the smile in Virgil's voice. He sing-songed as he puttered and he punctuated with laughter.

Grace was worried, the night before, that she would be able to hear them…together. Hear them in the master bedroom across the hall. Even her room, the guest room, Brad called it repeatedly, let her know she didn't really belong there. She loved Virgil, but it wasn't her place to hear their intimate reunion. That was private and it was none of Grace's business. She was prepared to pull the pillow over her head, her blankets too. She knew how noisy sex could be, even though it was years now that quiet children-in-the-house sex ruled her experience. She'd never had boisterous shouting sex with Nick; Mary was with them throughout their relationship. But there was Steven. She remembered Steven.

Now she wondered if there ever would be empty house sex with Nick. If they would stand together when JJ drove off to college, Mary already graduated and out of the house, and if they would look at each other and head toward their bedroom. Or their kitchen. Or their living room. If they would gape with newfound freedom.

And, she realized there in that bedroom in the middle of a junkyard, miles and states from her home, she was thinking about sex for the first time in seven months. Considering it as if it was a reality in her life. When, in reality, it might be exiting out the bedroom door, out any door that might have been possible before.

But she was thinking of it.

Getting out of bed, she dressed carefully. She realized she wanted to impress Brad, though she couldn't understand why. She chose fresh jeans, purchased on the road, and a clean white button-down shirt, neatly tucked in. A leather belt hugged her waist. She thoroughly brushed her hair and tucked it neatly back with the barrettes Virgil hated. Virgil might like wild loose curls, but Grace's feeling, after seeing this house, was that Brad liked things tidy, like she did. She unbuttoned the blouse enough that the black wooden pendant peeked out just above her cleavage. For the first time in almost three weeks, she made a bed and placed Cathy in the center, propping her against the pillow. She did the doll's hair as well, working it into a smooth pageboy that curled under her ears. Breakfast's aroma was growing stronger and Grace could smell coffee now and so she hurried downstairs.

Grace felt shiny, somehow civilized, as she walked into that sunny kitchen. She was in a house, she made the bed, her clothes were clean. The scent from the bubble bath still clung to her skin. "Good morning," she said to the men. They looked up, Brad sitting, as she thought, at the table. Virgil was by the oven, reigning over skillets of bacon, eggs, and pancakes.

"Morning, Grace," Brad said and motioned to a chair.

"Breakfast is almost ready," Virgil said, bringing her a cup of coffee. "Isn't this great, Grace? No restaurant, but fresh-cooked. God, I've missed cooking."

"I haven't," Grace said. "But it does smell good, Virgil." She took a sip of coffee and faced Brad. "So what are we doing this morning? Looking at the dolls you've found?"

He leaned back. "Well, it depends on what y'all wanna do. I go on a dig every morning, checking out any new stuff that showed up overnight. You two could come with me, if you'd like. You can look at the dolls this afternoon, when I do the sorting and burning."

Grace frowned. "Burning?"

He nodded. "Part of my job is to figure out what can be recycled, what can be resold, and what just needs to be destroyed. I sort for monthly trips to the recycling facility, and then I bring stuff back to the mini-barn to clean up and photograph and list on my eBay store; Virgil helped me with that. Some of it, things that could be fixed or harvested for parts, but really can't be sold, I leave out there. Sometimes we get folks who are looking for things. The rest of it…well, the rest of it gets burned."

Virgil joined them at the table. "Come on the dig with us, Grace," he said. "Brad's got some extra coveralls. You'll be amazed at what we find."

Brad cleared his throat. "Well, not every day's a banner day. Some days, there's just junk. But others…" He waggled his eyebrows.

Grace just shrugged. She was feeling so clean, so put together, that the thought of digging in garbage like one of those scavenger birds really didn't appeal to her. But she knew Virgil would be disappointed if she didn't go.

After breakfast, Grace helped Virgil clear the dishes while Brad sat over another cup of coffee. He offered to help, but they both protested. It felt good to help and she took the washrag out of Virgil's hands to wipe down the counters. Grace remembered the last few months at home, how hard the dishes were to do. How hard anything was. Nick will be glad, she thought. My energy is back. She thought of his message in the dust.

She turned and found that Brad was gone, his cup still on the table. This noiseless, well-oiled house let him escape without a sound. She picked up the cup and gave it to Virgil. He looked over at the table. "Must have gone to find our coveralls," he said. He placed the cup tenderly in the dishwasher and then firmly closed the door.

Brad returned with the coveralls and they climbed into them. Grace felt like a mechanic, wearing a blaze-orange one-piece jumpsuit that covered her from her neck to the bottoms of her feet. It was too big, bunching around her waist, knees and elbows, and she walked like the abominable snowman. Virgil laughed at her, but he didn't look much better. Orange was definitely not his color. It was Brad's. The orange set off his rich blond hair, that deep tan. Brad reminded Grace of Malibu Ken, one of the many versions of Barbie's boyfriend. He was tan too, and golden-haired, and his sculpted body looked great in orange swim trunks.

The child Grace never wanted any of the Barbie collection. She didn't want to play with adults. She already had adults.

They followed Brad outside. "Most of the time," he said, "people drop stuff off at one of the entrances. There's four of them, all at opposite ends of the yard. I use the truck to check those out." He climbed into the cab of the truck and she could see there wasn't room for three up there.

"Grace, you ride up front, I'll climb into the bed," Virgil said.

Grace didn't give herself time to see Brad's face. She knew what his expression would be. She shook her head. "No, you go up front." She walked to the back of the truck; the tailgate was already down. "Just help me up, Virgil. I've always wanted to ride in the back of a pick-up." She lied.

Virgil entwined his fingers and bent down, offering a stirrup. Grace stepped up, then climbed aboard. Crawling to the cab, she sat down and braced her back. Brad opened the little sliding window behind his and Virgil's heads so they could still talk.

They drove cross-country over mounds and mounds of garbage. Grace wondered how the truck's tires managed to stay together. There was no road, Brad just drove straight over things. She heard glass breaking and things bending and she imagined her mother crying out in protest as these items' spirits were all but mashed out of them.

At the first two gates, there wasn't anything worthwhile. Virgil and Brad scrounged around some, but Grace stayed in the truck and watched. At the third gate, there were twelve large garbage bags, all lined up neatly in a row. She climbed down to help search through these.

They each opened a bag and held up a piece of glassware. Grace lifted a plate, Virgil a bowl, and Brad a glass. All the bags were filled with glassware and delicate knick-knacks. Whoever brought the bags must have set them down gently as not a thing was broken.

In the eighth bag, Grace found a small plate, a collectible plate, the type that gets hung on the wall rather than eaten from. "Virgil," she called. "Look at this." She showed him the plate, etched with a drawing of a little girl from behind. They could see over her shoulder, and she was cradling a doll. The little girl's hair was blonde and curled, spinning down her back. By the way she held the doll, the soft cradle of her hands, the tilt of her neck as she bent toward it, Grace knew she loved this doll more than anything in the world. If she'd had Cathy when she was a little girl, if she'd had any doll when she was a little girl, this was how she'd have looked at it. Grace felt a stab of loss. For the first time in a long time, it wasn't about Paul, but what she could have had. What she should have had. Those blonde curls could have been Grace's own corkscrews.

For a moment, fleeting as a scavenger feather in the air, Grace felt anger at her mother. But then it was gone. It was always that way.

"It's pretty," Virgil said and Brad joined them. He looked in the bag and found many more collectible plates. But this was the only one with a little girl and her doll.

"Can I keep it, Brad?" Grace asked.

"Sure," he said.

She stayed in the truck the rest of the time, admiring the plate, wondering how it felt to be so young and to love something so completely. To have it be yours and nobody else's, your own special baby, a toy that you loved and cared for and never wanted to put down.

Grace wondered again if that was what her mother was really afraid of. If she thought Grace would love a doll more than she loved her own mother. Grace thought of Mary and Pinky, the ragdoll that was forever crushed to Mary's face in her sleep. JJ had a teddy bear named Bruno, Paul had a stuffed devil named Hot Stuff. Grace knew the completeness of her children's love for these toys. But she also knew they loved her.

But Grace wasn't her mother. And Grace was her mother's only child. Was that it?

Reaching through the coverall and through her shirt, Grace grasped the black wooden face.

But this still didn't feel right. That just couldn't be the reason for the no-dolls rule. Her mother must have recognized Grace's love, just as Grace recognized hers. It was always so there, a force that was almost palpable between them. From Grace's embrace, from her voice calling for "Mommy!" then "Mom," from the way Grace held her hand, from the way they talked. Grace knew her mother loved her, and she knew her mother felt the love returned.

That couldn't be it. But why would any mother keep a little girl from having dolls?

That feather anger again. Then gone.

"Did you say something, Grace?" Virgil called.

"No," she said. She brought the pendant briefly to her lips, then tucked it away.

When they returned to the house, Grace and Virgil took off the coveralls. Brad stayed in his and walked off to check things out closer to his yard. Sometimes, he said, people brought special things and left them near his house, making sure that he found them. Grace put her little plate on the kitchen table before she and Virgil wandered into the back yard.

At the very edge of the green grass, tucked into different corners, were two wooden sheds. One was fairly large and painted and shaped to look like a red barn. Grace figured this was Brad's mini-barn, his eBay store. The other building was small and yellow, with a white door and shutters and window boxes filled with geraniums. It reminded Grace of a playhouse. Virgil slid the doors open and they went inside. Near the back, under a window, were four boxes filled to the brim with dirty dolls.

Virgil wrapped an arm around Grace's shoulders and squeezed. "He does that deliberately, Grace," he said. "He knows I want the dolls to see the light of day. So he puts them by the window."

Grace felt a flicker of appreciation for Brad. He loved Virgil. And he did things for him. She thought of Nick, of the warm brownies and hot chocolate on a tray tucked between them in bed. Maybe then, there was more to Brad than Malibu Ken.

And maybe she needed to be more aware of what she had in Nick.

While Virgil dug through the boxes, muttering exclamations, Grace sat on a nearby barrel. She watched Virgil admiring each doll as he lifted them one by one, pushing back their hair, examining their eyes, their clothes, their teeth exposed in smiles. The gentleness in those big hands still surprised Grace and she swore she could see each doll shudder with pleasure as they were finally touched by someone who cared.

Then Virgil froze, elbow-deep in the box of dolls.

"What?" she asked, leaning forward. She wondered, and hoped against, another Gay Bob.

He pulled a doll from the bottom of the box. The light shining in from the door hit her full in the face.

And there she was.

Grace recognized the fevered cheeks and the pouty mouth, even though she was hidden under several layers of dirt. Sliding off the barrel, Grace wordlessly held out her arms.

Virgil gave her Maribel Get Well.

Hugging the doll to her heart, Grace ran from the shed, into the house, and up the steps to the guest bathroom. She placed the doll carefully on the closed toilet seat and then filled the sink to doll level. She poured in bubblebath and then stripped the filthy clothes from Maribel's body.

"Go easy," Virgil said as he walked in. "The clothes might be delicate. Let me have them. And be careful of her joints. They might be stiff."

Grace handed over the clothes and then placed Maribel in the water. Unlike Cathy, there weren't any voicebox holes to worry about. Maribel could soak with the same luxury as humans. Gently, Grace shampooed her hair, three times sudsing and rinsing. She emptied and refilled the sink each time. The doll's pink body emerged and began to gleam and her hair finally squeaked.

"I've got ammonia for her eyes," Virgil said and handed Grace the bottle and some cotton balls.

Carefully, Grace folded Maribel's eyelids back and swabbed on the ammonia. The white flaked away and Grace saw the silvery blue eyes looking up, sadly up, toward her. Grace told herself recognition grew in those eyes, lighting them fully, and that Maribel realized she was now where she was intended to be all along.

She lifted the doll from the sink and wrapped her in a towel. While Grace cradled her, she softly chanted Maribel's poem, memorized years ago when Grace could barely read, still in her mind now, verses intact, and helping Grace to remind Maribel that she promised she would get well.

I need crutches and I must wear a cast
'cause I broke a leg riding pony too fast

I caught chicken-pox from my friend Bella
When you have the chicken-pox your spots are yellow

I broke my arm when I stumbled and fell
Now I wear a cast to make it well

I have the measles and my spots are red
But I'll soon be well if I stay in bed

Look Mommy – I'm Well Again !!

How well Grace knew those words. How she recited them over and over again in her bed at night while she clutched a contraband torn-out page of dolls from the Sears Christmas catalog. Little Grace hoped and prayed that, with or without her, Maribel would get better. And now, here she was. Safe in Grace's arms, clean and shiny, and she would never be unloved again.

Brad walked in. His coveralls were gone, and from his slicked-back hair, Grace assumed he was fresh from a shower. He smelled good, in a way she'd never expect a junkyard man to smell. "You got a find?" he asked.

Virgil nodded. "A doll that Grace looked for this whole trip. Not even Hannah had her." He dunked the doll's clothes and things from a bag into the sink and the leftover suds.

Grace and Maribel went to the bed and Grace settled her on her lap. She found Virgil's hairdryer on the bedside table, already plugged in, and she turned it on low and borrowed Cathy's brush. Maribel had a cap of caramel curls and they twisted and turned in Grace's fingers as she blew the warm air over her head. When Maribel was completely dry, Grace nestled her against the pillow next to Cathy.

Virgil came out of the bathroom. "Her clothes won't be dry for a while, Grace," he said. "I'm going to hang them out on the line. They're not her originals, but a set of pajamas that came out about a year after she was released. We'll have to keep an eye out for her original outfit. It was a pink satin romper."

"Pajamas are better anyway," Grace murmured. "She's sick, she needs to rest." Grace got out Cathy's nightgown and pulled it over Maribel's thin body. It was too big, Cathy was much taller than Maribel, but at least she was covered and looked whole again.

Virgil patted something with a towel and then he poured it out on the bed. "Look," he said.

It was all of Maribel's things. Her casts, one for her leg, one for her arm. A set of crutches. A cloth bandage. Even her spots were there, red and yellow, on a strip of sticky paper. Grace knew better than to touch those, they would never stick again after a few applications, but she picked up the casts and clipped them onto the doll. Her right arm was broken from a fall and her left leg was broken from riding a pony. Grace propped the crutches under the doll's armpits and wrapped the bandage around her head. Somewhere, between the pony and the fall, Grace figured the accident-prone Maribel must have bumped her head. Then Grace cradled her, casts, crutches and all, rocked her deep within her arms. Maribel couldn't talk like Cathy, but she needed care and care was what she would get after all these years.

Grace looked up at Virgil. "I can't believe we found her!" she said.

He smiled. "It's not hard to find something when someone leaves it in a bag at the dump, just for you," he said.

Grace instantly thought of her mother.

"I'll leave you two alone for a while," Virgil said. "Brad has to run into town and I'm going with him. See you at lunch." He waved and Grace thought how happy he looked, running out the door. She heard his footsteps going down the stairs, and then his voice and Brad's blended together. She never heard the slam of a door, but then the truck started and she listened as the sound of the engine and crunch of the tires drifted away.

Grace looked down at Maribel. Carefully, she brushed the hair away from her forehead. Then she held her palm against Maribel's skin, as if she was checking for a fever. She adjusted Maribel's bandage and her casts. She looked at the doll and she thought about what you do with a sick child.

You give a sick child medicine. You give a sick child care.

This was a doll.

But if she'd had the doll while she was a little girl…like the little girl in the collector's plate…

Grace reached her hand into the air. She grasped an invisible medicine bottle, opened it, and then poured it into an invisible spoon. She held it to Maribel's lips, and while the lips stayed closed, there in front of Grace's eyes, she saw them open, she saw the pink of that little girl's tongue as she poured the medicine on it, and she saw Maribel's face scrunch from the taste. Just like Paul's used to. And Mary's. And JJ's. Then Grace put Maribel down for a nap on the bed, tucking the blanket up to her nose and propping her crutches close by in case she needed them.

Grace played. She played and played. She lost herself in a world where dolls were real. Where they breathed and cried. Where she could help. Where children never ever die.

Sitting on that bed, Grace was a little girl again, but she became the little girl she always wanted to be. She dressed Cathy in her party dress and then Grace and Cathy sat around Maribel, singing her songs, lulling her to sleep. Grace was a little girl playing with dolls in her bedroom. Her mother loved her, her father was at work, the crystal ball was bright, the clocks ticked, and Grace didn't even know yet of a young boy that would climb a tree, touch an electric wire, and forever break her heart.

Grace basked in that bedroom. There was no other word for it. She basked in dolls and love and sunshine and warmth, the leftover scent of a bath of lavender, the leftover scent of cologne and a clean man, the leftover aroma of bacon and good coffee. She knew her lunch would be prepared for her and set on the table with loving hands. She knew she would take a nap, with Cathy and Maribel on either side of her, through much of the warm southern afternoon. In the middle of an improbable junkyard, filled with treasure and scavenger birds, policed and tended by an orange-suited man and his skunk. Named Percy.

And then, after supper, and after a dozen days capped with deep nights' sleep, Grace knew she would grow up and go home. But for now, she was a little girl with her dolls, and the world of pretend made every happiness possible.

****

Several evenings later, after a full and satisfying southern supper of barbecued ribs, Grace sat on a swing on the porch, with Cathy on one side and Maribel on the other. Percy was in her lap. The skunk decided to like Grace and crawled on her whenever he had a chance. When she took a walk through the junkyard that afternoon, Percy walked along, close to Grace's heels, obedient as any dog. She reached down now and scratched his back and heard the peculiar happy skunk sounds he made.

Cathy wore her corduroy coat and Maribel was wrapped in a warm blanket. Each afternoon since Grace found her, they napped together, the sheets pulled up, sleeping deep in a way Grace could only barely remember from her childhood. On this night, she deemed Maribel healthy enough for a little fresh air and so they sat on the porch and swung.

The sun was already down, but the setting colors were still in the sky. The men were inside. Virgil was cleaning up the kitchen again, with a glee Grace envied. Brad sat at the table and watched him. Their conversation was slow and comfortable and Grace knew in a while, they would go upstairs, climb in bed, and sleep wrapped together in a deep blue blanket.

That was always the best part of belonging to somebody. When Grace was little, her mother came into her room at night and cuddled for a few minutes. The warmth of her body always stayed behind in the sheets. With Steven, and then later with Nick, Grace found that same comfort, knowing that in the dark, someone was just a touch away, and if she needed it or wanted it, arms could be wrapped tightly around her. There was a special kind of warmth to being in bed with somebody. And Grace missed it.

She missed Nick. And she missed Mary and JJ. She missed Paul too, of course. But the others…the others were still here. It was still possible to have them back. With Paul, missing him was the only possibility. There was no cure, no solution.

Virgil stepped out on the porch. "We're going to head upstairs, Grace," he said. "Is there anything you need?"

"I've got two dolls and a skunk. What else is there?" She smiled at him and he kissed her on the forehead, as gentle a touch as she ever felt.

"Goodnight then." He patted Percy and went inside.

"Goodnight, Grace!" she heard Brad call. "Help yourself to a snack if you want. There's still ribs left over."

In the south, there was always something left over that in the middle of the night, in a dark kitchen, tasted like heaven itself. "Thanks. Goodnight," Grace said. She listened to their steps and then, on the front lawn, a square of light appeared. A lamp was on in their bedroom.

Grace thought about calling Nick, about talking to the kids. But she didn't move. This was too perfect, these thoughts of them and the soft push toward home against her back. She only called them once since arriving at the junkyard. Nick was cordial, and the kids entranced by the idea of living surrounded by trash. She told the kids her cell phone reception was choppy and she would call them when she left Georgia and was on her way home. For this week, she stuck to that. For this week, she pushed reality away and immersed herself in the healing world of imagination.

Grace was playing. And for that week and five days, that was all she wanted to do and feel. She didn't want to hear Nick talk about separating. On this night, as she raised her head from her own imagination, turned on sharp the way it should have been in childhood, she just wanted to think of her family. She thought of being at home, Nick in the kitchen, reading the paper and drinking coffee while the dishwasher rumbled. The kids in the living room, JJ playing video games, Mary pretending not to watch, while Grace sat in her chair, reading with TheCat on her lap.

There would still be a voice missing. There would always be a voice missing. But next to Grace on the end table would be a bowl filled to the brim with bright orange candy pumpkins and candy corn. When Grace felt that empty voice, she could grab a pumpkin, press it gently between her teeth, and be awash in sweetness and memory.

Grace sat on Brad's porch for a long time, remembering the day she and Nick met, their first date, the first time they made love. Introducing Nick to Grace's mother. The wedding. Grace remembered the kids' births, their first steps, first words. Grace sat there and dreamed until the square of light in the yard flashed out.

It was time to go home. It settled on Grace with the sureness of nightfall, with the bright of the stars all around.

Grace tucked Percy onto his rug and then she carried her dolls up to bed.

****

The morning they left the junkyard, Brad stood on the porch, holding Percy and waving. Percy had followed Grace forlornly as they loaded up the car. The sounds he made were almost like mews. On the porch, Brad took one of his little black paws and waved it, but the skunk only looked sadder.

In the backseat, Cathy, Maribel and Josephine were strapped in. The Quints and Mary Hartline were in the trunk, with all of the others. Grace settled herself in her own seat and watched the mountains of garbage and waited for them to break up and bring them into a clearing. The sun was bright and Virgil shielded his eyes with his hand as well as his visor. Grace just squinted. "It sure doesn't look like fall around here," she said.

"No. Imagine having Thanksgiving in the summertime." He hummed. "At home, the leaves must be all turned and mostly fallen by now. It's getting cold, furnaces are switching on, storm windows up, plants hauled inside. Lawnmowers put away and snowblowers serviced."

Grace thought of winter, of the snow and ice. Nagging her children into boots, hats and mittens. Shoveling and salting. And the joy of going back inside, TheCat warm on her lap, a cup of coffee and a fresh muffin on the endtable.

Though fall was her favorite season, Grace's mother liked winter as well. Grace remembered her mother's gloved hands cupped around a snowball as she held it over the sink and instructed Grace to watch it melt. It dripped through the leather of her fingers and it got smaller and smaller and transparent. Then suddenly it was gone, drips going down the drain, a water stain on her mother's palms.

"See how things change, Gracie," she'd said.

Grace's mother liked to watch Grace play in the snow. Her mother stood, hugging herself, and called out directions as Grace built snowmen, snowforts, or fell to the ground to make angels. Grace's mother always found just the right accessories for Grace's snowpeople.

Once, Grace built a little girl. Her mother brought out an old string mop, fallen from its wooden handle. They braided the strings and gave the snowgirl some hair. Grace's old art-smock went around her middle and Grace gave her red lips with some Red Hots candy she saved from Halloween. They admired their work.

"She still needs something," the young Grace said. "Her arms don't look right."

"A purse?" her mother suggested. "A lunch box? School books?"

"No." Grace cradled her own empty arms. "A doll. Little girls should hold dolls."

Her mother turned and went inside. It was the first snow sculpture Grace had to finish by herself, without her mother's direction. She got a towel from the house and rolled snow inside of it, making a papoose. After balancing it carefully in the snowgirl's stick arms, Grace thought it looked like a doll baby, wrapped in a blanket.

The next day, when Grace looked out at the snowgirl, she was holding a lunchbox and some of Grace's old school books. The towel was draped across a chair near the stove, drying.

"The snowgirl looks better now," Grace's mother told her.

"Not better," Grace said. "Just busy." Later that afternoon, she kicked the little girl over, put her out of her misery, trampling her until she blended in with the rest of the snow. Then Grace fell on her back and made an angel.

The Georgia junkyard wasn't the first place Grace felt that feathered anger.

"The little girl died of loneliness," Grace told her mother, passing her on the way inside. "She's an angel in heaven now." Grace didn't stay to see what her mother would do. Grace wondered now if her mother looked out the window at the angel-stamped snow. If she stayed there for a while. If she ever had any doubts at all.

Was there ever a mother on this earth who didn't have doubts? Who didn't wonder if she should change something, stop something? If there was something she could have prevented, just by calling out, just by reaching out a hand?

Grace turned toward Virgil. "I like snow," she said. "I can't imagine living here with no snow, no winter."

Virgil nodded. "I know what you mean. Brad says it gets cold, so that's something, I guess. For when I come to live here, I mean." He thumped the wheel. "I love snow too, but sometimes you have to give up one thing for another. I'm giving up snow for sunshine. I'm giving up snow for Brad."

They drove quietly for a while. When Virgil came to a clearing, he turned left, and within minutes, it was like there'd been no junkyard at all.

Virgil patted her knee. "Grace, what are you going to do when you get home?"

She shrugged. "I don't really know. Try to pick things up where I left off, I guess. If Nick will let me."

"Do you think he will?"

Grace folded her arms and thought about the look on Virgil's face when he saw Brad bounding down the steps on the day they arrived at the junkyard. "I think we just have to see each other," Grace said slowly. "Then things will be okay."

"I hope so. I don't want any more bad to happen to you, Grace."

Grace settled back in her seat. "My mother thought there was a way to break a streak of bad things happening. She poured melted butter over spiders."

Virgil snorted. "Excuse me?"

Grace smiled. "Soon after my father died, my mother learned a new spell, one that was supposed to make bad fortune slip away. Or maybe she made it up...I was never sure with her. She was afraid my father's sudden death was the start of a bad streak and she wanted to cleanse the household and herself of any misfortune. This spell said you had to butter a spider. The spider represented evil and the butter allowed it to slip away."

Virgil chuckled.

"I know, it sounds weird. But my mother liked that kind of thing. She trapped a spider in a bowl and brought it into the kitchen. We tried to butter the spider, but we were worried we'd squash it or accidentally stab it with the knife. So she had to think of another way."

"Why didn't she just drop the spider into a tub of butter?"

"There wasn't a tub, she only had sticks. My mother didn't believe in tubs."

Virgil glanced sideways. "Of course she didn't."

"And besides," Grace continued, "we didn't think of it at the time. My mother decided to melt butter and pour it on the spider. Unfortunately, he drowned."

They both laughed. Grace could still see the look on her mother's face, hanging over the bowl, as she realized the spider could not plant his feet and escape. By the time they spooned the poor thing out, it was dead. After a few moments of panic, Grace's mother convinced herself that the spider's death symbolized the death of her bad fortune. She didn't just convince evil to slip away; she killed it.

Grace was still thinking about spiders and butter when Virgil changed the subject. "I've been thinking about my doll shop, Grace," he said. "What to do with it once I move down here with Brad. I don't think I should have to close The Nursery, just because I'm in Georgia."

"No," she said. "You could move the business down here. Open a new shop. I'm sure the town is nice, you could find a place to rent. You wouldn't have to stay in the junkyard all the time."

"I think I want to, though." Virgil rested his hand on her knee. "Brad and I missed a lot, since we just visited twice a year. I'd like to make up for that."

Grace set some candy on the dashboard, making a pattern. Pumpkin, corn, pumpkin, corn. Then she ate it.

"I could keep The Nursery open. You could run it for me, Grace."

Grace nearly choked. "What?" She pictured The Nursery, with Virgil behind the counter. Virgil was always behind the counter. She tried to push him out the door, put herself in the shop, tried to picture herself surrounded by all of the dolls. Combing their hair, changing their outfits, finding them new good homes. Just like Virgil. Just like Hannah.

Heaven.

"You could do it, Grace. I know you could do it."

She could.

Grace thought about visiting her mother at the bank. She wouldn't have to tell her about The Nursery. Or she could tell her, and let her know that Grace was all right. That it was okay to be surrounded with dolls. She wondered again how her mother, who could find spirits in anything from clocks to trinket boxes, didn't feel the spirits in dolls. Cathy and Maribel and Josephine had spirits. So did the Quints and Mary Hartline. All the dolls in Hannah's Hopefuls, in The Nursery, in boxes and bags all over flea markets, or abandoned in a junkyard in Georgia, had spirits that begged to be loved and cradled.

Then Grace saw her mother again as she looked out the kitchen window at the smashed snowgirl. Did she ever wonder about letting it all go, letting that one incomprehensible rule go? Did she ever think she made the wrong choice in barring dolls from her daughter's life?

Every mother wonders. Maybe Grace's mother did too.

Grace could do this. She could make it right.

She looked at Virgil then and squeezed his arm. "I could run The Nursery," she said slowly. "Maybe sometimes, the kids would help."

Virgil nodded. "You love dolls, Grace," he said. "That's all you need to know in this business."

Grace thought of the little collector's plate she found at the junkyard and the way her mother's pendant glowed warm in her hands. She thought of the melting snowball in her mother's hands, saw it again as it dripped through her gloved fingers and down the drain. Grace hugged her knees.

"See how things change, Virgil?" she said. "Isn't it amazing how things change."

****

They made it into Kentucky that day. Grace marveled at the grass which was truly a bluer shade of green. There were horses and more horses and miles and miles of white fences. They ate Kentucky Fried Chicken in their motel room that night. Grace expected it to taste better in its home state and it did, fresher, as if the chickens were fried right out of the coop. She was on her third piece when Virgil began to moan about his home-cooked meals left behind in Georgia. "It was so good, wasn't it?" he said. "That steak we had the first night? And breakfast every morning…I think everything tastes delicious in Georgia."

He wiped the grease from his chin and reached for another biscuit.

"I don't think it's just the food that makes you like Georgia so much, Virgil," Grace said. She batted her eyelashes at Virgil, then looked coyly away.

He smiled. "Maybe not. I miss him already."

Grace put down her chicken. "I don't want you to move to Georgia, Virgil. You know that." He nodded and a moment later, she did too. "But that's where you belong, I guess."

After dinner, they cleaned up the way one does in motel rooms – they threw everything in the garbage.

"Grace, do you remember telling me about when you and Mary met Nick in the park? About the boomerangs?"

Grace wrapped her arms around Cathy's shoulders. "Sure." She smiled. "I remember when Paul got big enough, Nick told him they were like spaceships and so they played together a lot. It was something they shared."

"You said that Nick doesn't play with the boomerangs anymore, right?"

"No. They're all in the attic, I think." Grace remembered the day they disappeared. She heard noises coming from the garage all morning. It was one of the first days that she felt a little human after Paul's death. It was a Sunday and she got up that morning and made cinnamon rolls for breakfast, just like she always did, but for the first time in over a month. Paul died, and so did the cinnamon roll breakfasts, until that day. Mary and JJ sat at the table, all goggle-eyed at first and looking a little sick, but then they gobbled the rolls up. Grace relished their faces, sticky with white frosting. She stood and watched them, her hand on the back of Paul's empty chair. Later, Grace heard Mary and JJ laughing in the living room. Laughing, a sound she thought she would never hear again.

But she did. And it was okay. It was cinnamon rolls for breakfast. It was children laughing. Even though she was too tired then to do anything more, worn out by bringing a little familiar into their Sunday, it was still something.

But then there were bangs from the garage. Nick never came in for breakfast. When he did come in, he brought three large cardboard boxes, strapped shut with tape. He started to walk past, but Grace stopped him with a hand on his shoulder. "What're those?" she asked.

He stood there for a moment, looking straight ahead. Grace felt a chill and she stepped away. "Boomerangs," he whispered suddenly. "They're all my boomerangs. I was going to bring them to the dump, but I just couldn't. I can't stand to see them on their shelves either. So I'm putting them in the attic."

Grace watched him walk away and it was like the cinnamon rolls and the laughter never happened. It stopped, just like that. There were only the boomerangs in the attic and the phenomenal fatigue Grace felt beyond her bones. Beyond breathing, beyond her skin, beyond her thoughts. She went upstairs and climbed into bed and didn't get up until Monday afternoon when the house had been quiet for hours. Nick took over again.

Grace wondered what would have happened if she joined him in the attic. If she packed the boomerangs with him, placing them gently in their boxes, strapping them in to a dark that might be permanent. She wondered if Nick cried upstairs in the attic, all by himself. Just the way he cried in the shower where he used to sing. She didn't know, because her world closed in and she was suffocating in her own grief, buried under blankets in the bedroom.

Grace looked at Virgil. "Nick was grieving, wasn't he? Packing away the boomerangs. Crying in the shower."

Virgil stopped moving, holding a chicken leg midway to his mouth. "He was Paul's father, Grace."

Grace nodded and closed her eyes.

"People grieve differently, I guess. For Nick, boomerangs and showers, and he tried to take care of you. That's how he handled it. But he lost a son too."

Grace opened her eyes and stared at the ceiling. The feeling of needing to be home hit her in the chest first, then roiled through her body, into every pore, every cell. She missed her kids, she missed her husband. She missed TheCat. She missed her mother and Paul with such a dreadful intensity, it was almost solid in her veins. But this new missing, the missing of the living, was new. The feeling was ferocious.

And they were missing her. Their mother. His wife. Grace.

"Virgil," Grace whispered. "I want to go home."

"That's where we're going," he said.

****

A day and a half later, they drove into Waukesha in mid-afternoon. Grace unbuckled Cathy and Maribel and held them tightly in her lap. The leaves were fallen and thin lines of smoke trailed from the chimneys. Furnaces were on. Winter's chill was re-introducing itself.

The trip home passed quickly. Virgil said it was because they had a goal, where before they were just wandering around. Grace asked Virgil if he could drop her off at her house. Since it was the middle of the afternoon, she knew no one would be home yet. As soon as they pulled into the driveway, she saw the gap in the sky. Before the car stopped moving, she threw open the door and ran into the back yard.

Paul's tree was a stump. Nick must have had it cut it down.

Grace knelt on the grass and placed her hands palms down on the stump. She saw the rings, brown and full, and she knew the tree was old; it lived a full life. Stroking the wood, she felt a loss, a sadness that pulled at her shoulders. She'd hated this tree. Or not the tree exactly. She hated the fact that Paul died in it. There were all the days since Paul's death when she couldn't tear her eyes away from this tree, from the back yard. And there were the days when she couldn't stand to look. She remembered the priscillas, hammered to the windowsill in the kitchen. The priscillas that were now gone, like the tree. Like Paul.

This was the last thing his living hands touched. She touched the tree stump now, her fingers following the labyrinth of rings, following the tree's life.

Virgil came up behind her, carrying her dolls, one in each arm. "This was the tree," she told him. "Nick must have had it cut down."

Virgil nodded. "That's good, isn't it?"

She stood and took the dolls. "I don't know. It wasn't the tree's fault. Not really."

"It's okay, Grace." He touched her arm. "You don't need props to remember Paul."

Grace nodded and walked to the door. Virgil went to collect her things from the car. Inside, she set Cathy and Maribel on chairs at the kitchen table. The kitchen was neat, there were no dishes on the counter and the table was washed and shiny. She opened the basement door and found no stiff towels on the banister. All of this reminded her of something, but she couldn't think of what. Wondering, she moved into the living room and opened the front door for Virgil. Then she realized.

This was how the house used to look. This was how normal looked. It looked normal without Paul here now. And it must have looked normal without her here too.

As Grace let Virgil in, she heard a short squeak. She turned to see TheCat slipping out from under a chair. He arched his back and yawned widely before sitting down to consider her.

"Hey, TheCat!" she said and squatted down.

He waited for a moment, giving her a thorough feline once-over. Then he climbed onto her thighs and pressed into her chest, purring loudly. She hugged him and stood up.

This was what Grace needed. A hug to welcome her home. Despite anger. Despite feeling abandoned. This normal included love for Grace, even if Grace had been missing.

"Where should we put these things, Grace?" Virgil asked.

Grace looked around. She didn't want to clutter up the living room. That wasn't the kind of homecoming she wanted, a disruption of this new normal, yet there didn't seem to be anything else to do. "I guess we can tuck it all in the corner there, by the couch. I'll sort through it later." She watched Virgil, carefully stacking her things, and thought about how he would not be nearby that night. That night, she would be in her own bed, next to her husband. TheCat at her feet, the kids down the hall. And Virgil would be across town. Soon, he would be in Georgia.

She felt a new loss slipping over her like a woolen winter jacket. She didn't know what to say. He faced her, putting his hands in his pockets and rocking on his heels. "Well, sweetheart," he said.

"Oh, Virgil." She put TheCat down and stepped into Virgil's embrace. Burying her face in his sweater, she memorized his smell, the sound of his breath, the strength in his arms. She wanted to soak him in, to make him a part of her.

"It'll be all right," he said. "You're back where you belong. Things need to be picked up where you left off, even if everything feels different." He smiled. "See how things change, Grace. Isn't it amazing how things change?"

"I know," she said into his sweater.

"So I should be going." He put his hands on her shoulders and gently pushed her away. "Give it two days. Just two days. Forty-eight hours. Get used to being home again. Then come see me. Bring the dolls."

"Okay." TheCat was winding around Grace's legs so she picked him back up and squeezed him tightly as Virgil walked out of door. She heard the Chrysler start up and then move down her street. Then there was just the purring of TheCat against her chest.

Grace went into the kitchen and wrote a note to her family. She told them she was home and she had errands to run, but she would be back for supper. She looked in the refrigerator and saw pork chops thawing. So even supper was planned.

Though she saw there were three pork chops. Not four. Not five.

She decided to stop at the grocery store and pick up one more. For herself.

After moving the dolls into the living room, perching them on top of her suitcase, she dug out the bag with Paul's candy corn and pumpkins. Then she went to her car in the garage. It started immediately. It was a good feeling, thinking of Nick sitting out there every now and then, running her car, making sure it still worked. It was a feeling of security, of being thought of. She drove, smiling, to the bank.

When Grace passed The Nursery, the big Chrysler was parked in front and there were lights on in the apartment upstairs. It was all she could do to stop herself from running into the shop. But she remembered what Virgil said about giving it two days, and she kept to their plan.

Sheri the bank teller was in her place when Grace walked in. Instead of giving Grace a blank stare, Sheri's eyes widened. "Hello, Grace," she said in a hushed voice.

Grace was startled. "Hello, Sheri, how are you?" she said uncertainly. Without waiting for an answer, Grace held up her key. "I'd like to see box number eighty-one, please."

Sheri nodded. They walked into the vault while she kept glancing back at Grace. "The last time I saw you, you showed up twice in the same week. That was unusual."

Grace was surprised Sheri noticed. They stopped in front of the row of boxes. Grace's mother's was still there, number eighty-one. Still the same, no different from the others, on the outside anyway.

"I know," Sheri said suddenly. "I know who you are. You lost your son. I saw it in the paper."

Grace startled and stepped sideways, away from her.

"I lost a son too." Sheri looked at the keys in her hand. "He was thirteen. He was at a friend's house, riding one of those ATV's. I never liked those things, I wouldn't let him have one of his own, but I couldn't stop him from going over to his friend's, could I? He fell and hit his head. No helmet." She shook the keys, letting them ring together. "They're like big motorized trikes, nobody wore a helmet." She raised her eyes. "I was told he died instantly."

Grace looked at her, at the brown suit and ruler-straight nametag, at the glasses, and through them into her eyes. "Paul too," Grace said. "Died instantly, they told me."

Sheri's lips trembled. "For years, I felt guilty because I wished he didn't die right away. Even if there was pain. I just wanted the chance to see him and hold him. It wasn't the same, holding his body. There wasn't anyone in it."

Grace remembered cradling Paul, his body still warm, under that tree. It was like holding a shell. "I know," she said. "I understand. I'd give about anything to have him back, even for a second."

Sheri's eyes met Grace's again. This time, there was real recognition. Recognition, Grace realized, that used to be hidden. Camaraderie that nobody ever wanted.

Grace took Sheri into her arms. They hugged and cried on each other's shoulders. Grace felt Sheri's body shake and Grace's shuddered with hers. It hurt and yet it was a moment of such shared pain, connecting with someone who truly knew what Grace felt, she thought she would never let Sheri go.

But she did. They took their turns with the keys and then Grace held the box in her hands. Sheri wiped her eyes and nose with a tissue before walking away. Grace went into one of the privacy rooms and set the box on the table.

Her left-behind junk was still inside. She made two piles, one to throw away and one to keep. It was as good a time as any to clean out her purse. When the box was empty, she returned the remaining money, stacking it neatly. There was still quite a bit left.

"I'm going to tell Nick about this money, Mother," Grace said. "I've used what I needed. Now I'm going to use the rest to put things back together. Nick should know about it. The money will belong to both of us." She touched the black wooden pendant resting on her sweater. "I'm going to keep this with me now. It didn't belong to me before, it was yours. But now it's mine. Thank you for giving it to me." At that moment, like a long released exhale, Grace felt that her mother was no longer at the bank. Grace closed the box and returned it without saying another word. She would talk to her mother at her grave from now on.

As Grace walked out of the bank, she saw Sheri sitting at her desk, drinking from a mug. Grace imagined it was tea. She raised her mug in salute and Grace waved back. The florist was the next stop, just a short drive across town, and Grace shivered at the familiar sound of the bell when she opened the shop door. Ann looked up. "Hi, Grace," she said. "I knew it was about time."

"Hi, Ann." Grace looked around. Everything was the same.

There were baskets of roses in the glass-doored refrigerators, deep handsome burgundies, and Grace stepped closer to look at them. "Oh, Ann, those are beautiful!"

"I'll make you up a small bouquet right away. Anything else?" She touched one of the doors. "Carnations are on special."

"No thanks, Ann, make that two small bouquets of the roses please." Grace nodded at the question on the florist's face. For once, Grace's father would have an extravagance. Just like the gypsy earrings he once gave his daughter, when all he wanted to give her was diamond studs. Then she walked around the small shop as Ann worked.

The flowers were all lovely and the plants were so green and fresh, it was hard to believe it was November in Wisconsin. Grace looked at the various baskets and touched the soft petals. "Ann, I need some advice," she said.

The rustling behind her stopped. "What is it, Grace?"

"What do mothers bring to children's graves?" Grace heard Ann's quick step and soon they were standing side by side. Ann slipped her arm through Grace's and squeezed.

"What kind of flower did he like?" she asked.

Grace tried to think. She couldn't remember any flower. He was a little boy interested in space and stars and the universe. "He never brought me flowers," she said suddenly. "Not even dandelions. He brought me autumn leaves. He loved leaves." They looked at each other and laughed. "Really, Ann, what do mothers bring? I want to bring something and I want it to be right."

Ann waved vaguely at the refrigerators. "Well, most mothers bring a simple flower. Like baskets of daisies or carnations. They might put it in a special holder though, a pot or a basket. Something the child would like."

Grace remembered seeing a lot of orange in a clearance section near the back of the shop. She walked over there. All of the Halloween decorations were marked down. In the middle was a big fat orange wicker pumpkin. It had a ghoulish smile. "Something like this? Could I use this?"

Ann nodded. "Sure. What should we put in it?"

Grace looked back at the carnations on special. They were bright, all blues and yellows and greens with white trim around the edges. They looked a little like stars. "Use the carnations," Grace said. "Two dozen of them. A mix of all of the colors."

As Ann tucked the pretty blooms into the basket, Grace touched them, their silky petals, and she could smell their soft scent. But there was still something missing. "In between the carnations, Ann," Grace said slowly, "put in some baby's breath."

Ann nodded and settled into her work. Soon Grace was pushing her way out the door, her arms filled with the two bouquets and the basket. She stopped at the car for the bag of candy pumpkins and then she stumbled across the street to the cemetery.

The grounds were raked clean and the grass was golden and brown. Grace missed the leaves and she knew Paul would too. She wished she brought some with her to sprinkle on the grass. Without them, there wasn't any sound, no cheerful crunching to accompany her as she made her way to her parents. Kneeling, she stroked their stones. "I'm back," she said quietly. "I've come back home." Carefully, she pulled the dried and dead flowers from the holders and replaced them with the roses. Then she turned to her mother. "You told me to finish what I started. That's what I'm here to do."

Grace traced her mother's name and felt the warmth in the letters. "I'm going to work in Virgil's doll shop, Mother. It's the perfect place for me. Virgil's going to move to Georgia to be with Brad. I can't tell you how much I'm going to miss him." Grace knelt in front of the stone and pressed her forehead against it, just like she used to press herself into her mother's chest. "I don't know how the kids are, I haven't seen them yet, but I'm sure they're okay. And I'm okay too. I'm going to visit Paul in just a minute. I'm bringing him these carnations." She put the basket in front of her mother's stone. "I don't know if they're right, but I wanted to bring something." She set the sack of candy next to the basket. Resting one hand on her mother's stone and one hand on her father's, she braced herself, then pulled herself up, as she must have done when she was a little girl, hanging on to both of her parents' hands. She stood between them and looked toward the top of the hill. Grace knew Paul was waiting for her, over the hill, three rows over.

"Oh, Mother, I wish you could go with me!" she cried out. "I don't want to go alone!"

But then she gathered up her basket of carnations and her candy and her courage and she climbed the hill.

Paul's grave was grass-covered, just like the kids said it was. It flowed into the land around it, as if it was always there, like there was never a bunk above JJ's bed, but this was always where Paul slept. The grave felt plain to Grace, with no flowers resting at its headstone. It looked neglected. And Grace's mother always told her that a neglected grave was a shameful thing.

Grace felt ashamed.

She sank down on her knees and wrapped her arms around the stone. She felt the warmth, felt it flow into her, greeting her, welcoming her, making her whole with the rest of the world again. She wrapped herself into this warmth, knowing it came from her son; it was her boy. She hugged that hard rock for as long as she could, until her arms ached and her chest felt flattened. Then she fell back and clasped her hands on her lap.

"Oh, Paul," she said. "Your grandmother was right. I am so sorry." She traced his name as she traced her mother's, and she remembered giving it to him. Paul. It was a strong one-syllable name, solid, an anchor to keep the child on this earth and beside her. It failed to do that, but her son brought her back to her place now. "Paul, I just couldn't get you out of my head and into this grave. Yet here you are. And I've kept you waiting." Grace started to cry then, certainly not for the first time nor the last, but the tears were beginning to feel good. Like she was cleansing herself, scrubbing her soul. "Dad cut down the tree, Paul. I feel sorry for the tree, but I guess it's a good thing." She reached for the basket. "I brought you something. Some flowers. And a basket, a basket shaped like a Halloween pumpkin, because I knew you would like it." She placed it in front of the stone, smoothing the grass around it.

"I love you, Paul. More than I can ever say, more than I can ever tell you. And I miss you so much. I promise you I'll be back." She touched her lips with her fingertips, and then touched his stone before reaching for the candy. Opening the bag, she scattered the pumpkins and candy corn like seeds in the grass. Paul's plot, already bright with the carnations, began to sparkle with yellow and orange. Then Grace turned and ran from the cemetery.

At the gates, Grace stopped and leaned against the wall. She took deep breaths and saw the air steam in front of her. It was fall and the sun was setting early and she really needed to get home. Her children would be there by now. Her remaining children. And Nick too. The pork chops would be simmering in the oven. She still had to stop and pick up one more. Just for her.

Grace faced the dead. It was time to face the living.

****

Grace didn't even have time to close the door before JJ tackled her. She couldn't see his face, he pressed into her so hard that she was pushed against a wall. He was twelve years old, but he sometimes forgot that and right now, she was glad he did. She wrapped herself around him and stretched her arms until it felt like she added twelve inches from her elbows to her wrists. They swayed and for a moment, it was like they were never apart.

Mary stood just a few feet away. Propping her head on JJ's skull, Grace looked at her daughter. She felt that they were both waiting for an opening. But then Grace gave it. She opened an arm and Mary ran in to the embrace.

JJ broke away first, gasping for breath. And then Mary. She stepped back and looked directly at Grace. In that moment, Grace saw it all in her girl's eyes. Saw her watching her brothers, pretending not to, then telling Paul to climb the tree. She felt the directive come out of Mary's mouth. And then she saw, through Mary's eyes, Paul touching that wire. Grace saw it all. And she heard Virgil's words.

"Mary," Grace said, leaning into her daughter, brushing her lips against her ear. "Mary, I love you. I will always love you, no matter what. And I forgive you. I forgive you."

Mary's mouth opened, but nothing came out. Her eyes filled with tears and then she fell against Grace and it was all Grace could do to hold her up. But Grace heard Mary take a sigh so deep, it must have been buried in her ribcage and her lungs for months. Many months.

Seven months.

Taking the kids' hands, Grace led them to the couch. She breathed them in, she could smell their shampoo, the laundry soap, felt tip markers and classroom dust. And beneath it all, she could smell them, their skin, and every part of Grace fell into place. It was like feeling her back crack, a vertebrae snap into line. Suddenly, she was taller. And she was intact in her own body.

Though there was still one left to talk to. The next that could leave a hole so deep, she wondered if she could crawl out.

"I have to say hello to your dad," she whispered. "Is he in the kitchen?"

They nodded and sat back. Grace got up for her long walk to Nick.

He had his back to her and he was staring out the window that had no curtains. Grace smelled pork chops and so did TheCat, winding in and out of Nick's legs. Nick had a fresh haircut, she saw the tender skin at the base of his neck, usually hidden by dark curls. She came to a stop behind him.

"Nick," Grace said. "I'm home. And I brought a pork chop. So I could eat with you guys too."

He turned and there were tears streaming down his face. Grace stepped on TheCat's tail in her haste to get to her husband and they both jumped at the shriek. But then she had him and she held him so tightly, she wasn't sure what would break first, her arms or his ribs. He leaned against her and she leaned into him and he cried and so did she and she held him. Then his arms came around

Grace and she knew it was all right.

"Grace," he said. "The kids called me and read me your note. I stopped at the store on the way home." He stepped away for a moment, keeping a hand on her shoulder, and he opened the oven door. Four pork chops baked in a pan. And then he embraced her again.

She was home.

CHAPTER FOURTEEN
Virgil

When Grace walked into The Nursery two days later, she looked tired. But then she looked up and smiled and Virgil saw it. He saw the light, saw the spirit that was Grace, and she was all there. She was tired, but she was there. Maybe, he thought, happily ever after takes a while.

She folded into Virgil's arms as easily as a favorite sweater. "I've been there, Virgil," she said. "I went to see Paul."

Virgil nodded, then rested his head on top of hers. "And Nick? The kids?"

"We're okay. Nick is staying. We're okay."

They stood there and swayed. Virgil noticed the way the dolls' heads all seemed to turn toward them, especially to Grace. She belonged there.

Virgil belonged in Georgia.

"Brad's already on his way," he said, stroking Grace's hair. "He should be here sometime today."

Grace stepped away and looked around. "So you're really going."

"You knew that." Virgil went behind the counter and pulled out an envelope with Grace's name on it. "I made you your own set of keys," he said. "And here's the bank account for the shop. I've added your name to everything. Make the mortgage payment each month and pay the utilities. The rest, you can keep for yourself. I've got an ad in the paper for the apartment upstairs. See if you can rent it out to someone nice." Virgil was glad to hear that Nick was staying. If the marriage was headed for divorce, he'd been prepared to offer the apartment to Grace. Now, there would need to be someone else.

"But what about you?" She stepped in front of the counter, the same place she stood the day she bought Cathy.

It seemed strange, telling her these details. Virgil wanted to hold her, to kiss her forehead and tell her how much he loved her, how much she meant to him. But business came first. "I guess..." Virgil started, then cleared his throat.

"Well, I'll be dealing with the online stores, supplying those with the dolls I find in the junkyard, though I'll be sending some to you here. You will be dealing with The Nursery. So you keep the profit here, I'll keep the profit from the online stores."

She nodded. "That's fair." She stood there and looked at him and he saw her again on that first day, looking in the window, her nose pressed flat, her hand upraised as if to grasp Cathy's fingers. Her arms were empty now.

"Where are the dolls?" he asked.

She startled. "You know what? I forgot them. They're sitting on my bed."

Grace without her dolls. Yet she looked complete and whole. Virgil stepped around the counter. "Grace," he began.

"Virgil, I love you," she said and returned to his arms.

Holding her, Virgil wished he could pack her up and take her with him. She could sit among the dolls in Brad's house, the sun shining off her hair, her smile warming the entire place. "We'll see each other," Virgil said. "You can be my twice a year visit now."

She nodded against his chest. "I'll come visit you in Georgia. I'll bring the kids."

"And I'll come here. Brad and I will come for Christmas. I'm going to need some snow."

Grace looked up. "I'll take care of the dolls, Virgil," she said. "I'll find them good homes. Just like you and Hannah."

"I know you will." Virgil kissed her one last time and then released her. She walked unsteadily toward the door, her hand reaching out and touching first this doll, then that. She twisted the doorknob, then looked back.

"I love you, Virgil," she said again. "Please be happy."

"I love you too," he said. "And I want you to be happy as well."

She beamed at him then, the full Grace smile that he waited for during those weeks on the road. Her smile lit her eyes and she tossed back those wild corkscrews. Then she turned and was gone, the door whispering her absence. As soon, it would whisper her in to stay.

Virgil sat down behind his counter and waited for whatever came next.

****

On the way back to the junkyard, Virgil's things packed in a trailer behind Brad's truck, Virgil and Brad stopped in Chicago at Virgil's childhood home.

Brad stood behind Virgil when he rang the doorbell. His father answered, and for a moment, Virgil didn't recognize him with eighty-some years curling his body, wrinkling his face and hands. But then in an instant, Virgil saw it. The joy, the recognition between a father and a son, the father that wanted the best for his boy and brought him on a special trip to a toystore in the middle of the week. But then his father looked over Virgil's shoulder, he saw Brad, and the cloud of judgement descended, his expression went black, and he slammed the door. And Virgil fell backwards.

But this time, Brad was there to catch him.

Virgil started writing long letters to his father, telling all about his life. He began with Josephine, the original Josephine, and he went over everything, from the first day he could remember. So far, his father hadn't answered, but there weren't envelopes in Virgil's mailbox saying Return To Sender either, so maybe, Virgil hoped, his father was reading them. Or maybe he was burning them. Virgil didn't know, but he could hope. It felt good to write the letters, to sit at Brad's kitchen table in the early afternoon sun, and put a pen to paper. Virgil didn't type them, he didn't email them. He bought some decent stock stationary, a nice pen, and he wrote. It was a method he grew up with; it was something his father would appreciate. And Virgil liked the effort it took.

Virgil's father wasn't dead yet, and neither was he. Virgil planned on sending the next letter in a box, filled to the brim with the candy Virgil remembered his father loving best. Gumdrops. Virgil knew a little sweetness never hurt anybody. He knew that sometimes, it could help. It could show the things you haven't lost. The love for a little boy. The respect for a father.

See how things change. Isn't it amazing how things change.

CHAPTER FIFTEEN
Grace

It took a year after Grace's coming home for Mary to ask the question. And the question came right after an announcement that Grace never expected from her daughter.

Grace was working at The Nursery when Mary came in. Now eighteen years old, Mary was home from college for Thanksgiving. Grace wasn't expecting to see her; she figured Mary was at home, buried in books, keeping up with her studies even when she was supposed to be on a break. But there she was.

In the middle of this unexpected visit, in the middle of this unexpected afternoon, Mary asked the question.

"Mom? You know when you ran away last year?"

Neither JJ nor Mary ever talked much about that time. They exclaimed over the gifts Grace brought them, and they listened to the stories she told of the two-headed calf, the five-legged cow, the fortune-teller, the amazing candy factory. But when she was done, they treated it just like that…a story. The End. It was over.

Now, Grace sat down on her stool. "Sure, I remember."

"Mom, why did you leave? I mean, I know you were sad about Paul. We were all sad about Paul. But how could you leave us behind?" Mary touched a doll on the counter, smoothing its hair. Grace knew that these words of her daughter's actually translated to, "How could you leave *me*?" And she knew that her words, Grace's words, the next words out of her own mouth had to be the truth.

She took a breath. And then she said it. "I don't know."

Mary jerked her head up and both she and Grace listened to that lack of knowledge, lack of understanding. Daughters were supposed to have questions and mothers were supposed to have the answers. But Grace just didn't.

She folded her hands on the counter and looked at them. Her fingers rested on top of each other. She expected her hands to start shaking, but they didn't. "I don't know how I could have left you behind, sweetheart. I think of it now, and I don't know how I did it. But I did. At the time, it seemed like the right thing to do." Then she shook her head. "No, it seemed like the only thing I could do. So I did it. And it has nothing to do with "at the time". It was the right thing to do."

Mary's hands weren't shaking either when she rested them on the doll's shoulders. It was another Mary Hartline, but wearing a different dress than Virgil's. "Do you think you'll ever do it again?"

Grace started to say no. She wanted to say no. But then she stopped. She knew that if someone asked her a few years before if she thought she would ever run away from her family, she would have laughed. And she would have been insulted. Grace, back then, would never have done such a thing. But that was before her mother died. That was before her son died. That was before it all.

"I don't know," she said again. "I don't think so. But I learned that sometimes, you just can't predict anything. You can't know everything." She smiled at her daughter. Like why my mother wouldn't let me play with dolls, she thought. I'll never know about that.

But she still wondered. Even as dolls became an everyday thing in her life, she wondered.

Now, she wondered something new. "Mary," she said, and her question echoed what Mary most needed to hear that year before, "do you think you can forgive me? For leaving you then? Even if I don't know how I could? Even if I can't explain it? Is it okay that I can't explain everything?"

Mary considered, and the silence grew long.

Grace thought about the words she learned from Virgil. She thought about hugging Mary on her return home last year, whispering, "I forgive you," in Mary's ear, "I forgive you," for something that the world wanted her to soothe away, wanted her to convince her daughter wasn't her fault. It wasn't, but sometimes, forgiveness was necessary for things that didn't need to be forgiven. And now, Grace hoped that forgiveness would come for the unforgivable.

Mary nodded and stepped away from the doll. "It's okay," she said, leveling a gaze on Grace that was all at once adult and a sign of the woman she would become. "And yes, Mom, I forgive you."

It was an hour or so later, when Mary had gone ahead toward home, to put the casserole in the oven that Grace left in the fridge, that Grace cried. She closed The Nursery for the night, turned off the lights, and stood at her counter and cried. From the streetlight outside, the dolls' eyes gleamed with hers.

So much was changing.

Virgil was in Georgia. He sent a shipment of found dolls to The Nursery at least once a month, dolls that were special requests and dolls that he felt just belonged in Grace's care. He was writing to his father. And he was, despite all of Grace's doubts, happy with Brad. Brad was resolute in his faithfulness.

Grace was surrounded by the one thing she wasn't allowed to have her entire life. The one thing she truly wanted as a child. The one thing her mother said no to.

Grace would never know why. It was an answer that was buried away.

Looking around at the dolls, their eyes watching her, Grace's own streaming with tears, Grace said those wonderful words again, directing them at her mother. "I don't know," she said. "I'll never know. But I forgive you. I love you."

In the midst of it all, she heard Virgil again. Everything was changing, but some things didn't have to. The taste of candy corn. The love for a child.

And the love for a mother as well.

The ability to forgive. Even the unexplainable. Even the unforgivable.

See how things change. Isn't it amazing how things change.

Grace dried her eyes, said goodnight to the dolls, and then she locked the door of The Nursery. She started for home.

CHAPTER SIXTEEN
What Grace Forgave,
But Will Never Know
Diana McFarren, 1958

Diana never expected that an entire life could happen in the miles between What Cheer, Iowa and Waukesha, Wisconsin. At twenty-one years of age, she was of the mindset that life extended in front of her like a gilded pathway, a filigree of bricks that led to all good things, and whose length went well beyond the horizon. Instead, a five hour and change drive extended to an overnight, and in the hours that followed, Diana extended from a painfully young runaway lover, to an unwed mother, to a committed single parent, to a woman in grief.

Diana's life should have taken years, it should have covered at least some of the length of that gilded path. But it took hours. And that life affected her life until she truly reached the horizon.

In the middle of the darkest Iowa summer night, Diana McFarren crept away from the man she loved. She hauled with her like a bag over her shoulder the reasons she should stay: James loved her; she loved James; they had a good life. She truly believed there wasn't anyone else like James on the face of the planet. She loved his home, an ancient Victorian turned into a museum of clocks. She loved the town; how could you not love a town called What Cheer? How could you not love such an unusual life? At twenty-one, you want life to be unusual, a miasma of sensations and colors and the intermingling of possible dreams and solid reality and you want it to be yours alone. Diana met James when she was nineteen, she moved in with him when she was twenty, and at twenty-one, that unusual life was hers.

But in that bag of reasons to stay, Diana also hauled a very heavy reason to go. James, the one who owned the clock museum, who started it, who built it out of nothing in the middle of nowhere, Iowa, and made it a tourist destination disrupting the horrible monotony of cornfields on either side of I-80, James would never love Diana more than he loved the clocks. Clocks would always come first. If there was ever a fire in the old museum, Diana had no doubt that James wouldn't shove the clocks aside to save her. Instead, he'd grab her hand and yell, "Grab the clocks! Save the clocks!" Diana could be on fire and he would only douse her in order to have two more hands saving his lifelong love.

His clocks. Not Diana.

At twenty-one years of age, Diana was a renegade, a rebel, a thoroughly unconventional young woman who was living unmarried with a man at a time when that just wasn't done. She told herself she wasn't a romantic, but in her heart of hearts, she wanted to be a lifelong love. She didn't want to be next in line. After two years with James, Diana felt she never moved up a step. In fact, she fell back as more and more clocks were added to the collection and as the business took off. The clocks and the tourists all jostled each other, waving their arms, demanding James' attention.

That night, the dark night, as Diana crept down the stairs and toward the front door, the clocks whispered to her from shelves and tables, walls and mantels. The cuckoo clocks and the birdcage clock, the schoolhouse clock and the skeleton clocks all urged her to go. They reassured her she had no place, she had no home, she had no reason to be there. But the mantel clocks, grandfather clocks and the anniversary clocks told her to stay. Their solidity and longevity, their permanence and ticking of years indicated that she had a place, even if it wasn't the place she most wanted. It was still hers and hers alone. There were many clocks in James' life; she was the only woman. That counted for something. That was better than no place at all.

But still she felt outnumbered. Overlooked.

Diana stopped in front of the stolid grandmother clock, a mahogany sentinel at the bottom of the stairs. Diana knew that James considered this clock the wisest of all and Diana waited to see what she would say. But she didn't say anything; her pendulum swung as silent as James' loving maintenance could make it. The time was between the quarter and half; there was no chime, and Diana didn't want to wait. She felt she waited long enough. In the end, she knew it was her own decision; she had to decide what she wanted. She had to decide what was enough.

She wasn't a romantic. She was a renegade. But not being first wasn't enough.

Diana was young.

So she left. She cried as she got into her car and left the Victorian, the clocks, and James behind. She cried as she pulled onto the divisive I-80 toward home.

Home was in Waukesha, Wisconsin. Her parents were there. They would take her in until she figured out what to do next. They were never crazy about the clock guy anyway. They were good parents, and as good parents, they wanted the best for their young and rebellious daughter. James was older than Diana; he'd never been married; he lived in Iowa, five hours and change away; he made a living with clocks. In her parents' opinion, this did not add up to Diana's best choice.

But Diana loved him. In conversations with her parents, she argued that you didn't choose who you fell in love with. She wasn't a romantic, she was a rebel, and she'd fallen in love with a man who loved clocks. Her parents, good parents, held their tongues. They maintained her bedroom in the back of the house.

Diana made it as far as the Amana Colonies before exhaustion caused her to reconsider the drama of a middle of the night escape. Decision-making, she discovered, took energy, and she'd been making up her mind for weeks. She'd been fatigued and nauseous with a new level of tired for weeks. She found a hotel, crawled into clean, cold sheets, and fell asleep.

In the morning, Diana threw up. Again. She'd been throwing up since she started fighting herself with making a decision and she was sure that on this morning, decision made, it would stop. She would wake up rested and solid-stomached. But no. And that morning, Diana suddenly wiped her mouth and sat straight back on her heels. She began to count. Backwards.

"Oh my god," she said out loud in the hotel room.

In every small town, there is a doctor, and to every doctor in the 1950s, a young woman would come, wanting to know if she was pregnant, and wanting to know right now. Sometimes, these women wore plain gold bands on the ring finger of their left hand, and every doctor knew these plain gold bands were sold at the five and dime for about a buck. After checking out of the hotel, Diana found the five and dime and she found the doctor and she asked her question. The test would take time, of course, more time than Diana wanted to take, but the doctor, examining her, said he was very certain that she was indeed with child.

Runaway lover to unwed mother, just like that.

The decision that plagued Diana for weeks, that kept her, she thought, constantly tired and queasy, no longer appeared so large as the decision that needed to be made now.

Diana told the doctor she would call back for the test results (she wouldn't) and she staggered from his small office. In every downtown, there was also a diner, and Diana went there so she could have a place to sit and try to think. To use the booth for that purpose, she needed to order something, and so she chose the breakfast special; two scrambled eggs, a side of hash browns, and two slices of bacon, with an English muffin and her choice of jam or jelly. An entire pot of coffee was placed on her table. Diana was delighted to find herself hungry when the food was delivered. She didn't expect to be; she thought this new decision would put her off her food even more than she already was.

Instead, she found herself thinking about eating for two. She found herself thinking of a little one, reaching up for her with open arms and an open mouth. An open mouth that smiled. Eyes that glittered with the blue she loved so in James'.

Diana held her fork in front of her own mouth. "Here you go, Little Dolly," she whispered. "I hope you like eggs. I like eggs. I hope you like the same things I do." She whispered before every bite.

Afterwards, she stood by her car and tried to settle her future on the map. If she turned back to What Cheer, to James, she wouldn't be an unwed mother. If she continued toward home, she would be, and she'd have to tell her parents. Who weren't crazy about the clock guy. But who loved her and kept her room intact and ready for her, should she need it.

She might need it. And a whole lot more.

Diana looked down at her beltline. "What do we do, Little Dolly?" she asked. "You have a father. You have grandparents. Where should we go?"

If she wasn't first in James' life now, when they'd known each other for two years and shared the same bed for most of that time, Diana reasoned, she likely wouldn't ever be, even if she presented him with a child. Worse, the clocks would come before the baby as well. And Diana knew from her own good parents that nothing should come before the baby.

Diana decided, quietly, that she'd be willing to be second in James' line if the first in line was their child. But the child wouldn't be first in line. There would be the parade of clocks, there would be the tourists, then the child, then Diana.

In that imagined fire, would James run to save the child first? Or would he yell to Diana to do it? Or would he grab both Diana and the child, yelling, "Save the clocks!" even if his own flesh and blood were in flames?

Diana thought she knew the answer to that. She knew James. She knew him better than anybody. She wasn't a romantic, she was a renegade, but she loved him. And now, suddenly, she loved this child. So she patted her tummy and then pointed the nose of her car toward Wisconsin.

Runaway lover to unwed mother to committed single parent. From What Cheer, Iowa, to the Amana Colonies, on the way to Waukesha, Wisconsin. In well under twenty-four hours. As Diana drove, she drove in a way she never had before. Right hand at two o'clock. Left hand not on a clock at all, but resting on her stomach, seeking out the heartbeat she was sure was beneath her own skin, and the skin of one other.

"How's it going, Little Dolly?" she asked. And she began to describe everything she saw out the window to her baby, the little one with the open arms, smiling mouth, and blue eyes like her father's.

But Diana also began to describe everything inside. What she felt for the child's father. How every mile she drove seemed to drive a deeper ache into her body. Diana wasn't a romantic; she was a renegade, a rebel, and she was prepared to enter the 1960's as a fully evolved woman and she already believed that no woman needed a man. But she wanted a man. She wanted that man. The ache plowed through her body and rammed into her heart.

Diana loved James. She wanted to tell him about the baby. She wanted to place the flat of his hand on her tummy and wake him up to what was inside her, to what she was telling their daughter right now, in this car with her hand at two o'clock and the other on a new heart. There wasn't just the surprise of Little Dolly inside of her. There was her abounding love for him.

But Diana knew who James was. On the steering wheel, her fingers clenched. On her tummy, her fingers flexed, but then smoothed. Supported.

Between Cedar Rapids and Dubuque, Diana came across a flea market. It was in a big red barn and the barn had two eyes and a smile painted on it, and Diana just couldn't resist. She wasn't in a hurry and she loved flea markets. So did James. She pulled over.

Wandering through the aisles and stalls, Diana found what looked like a miniature sleeping bag. It had a white quilted background and was covered with green rabbits and yellow ducks. When she held it up, she couldn't imagine any child using it for a sleepover. It was too small; a child wouldn't be able to get in more than up to her knees.

A woman passing by said, "It's for a baby. Instead of stuffing your child into a snowsuit, you zip them into the bag. Works really well with a carbed." She smiled and kept on going. Diana wondered if the woman knew. If she guessed. If somehow, Little Dolly wasn't so secret.

Diana held the baby sleeping bag. She pictured her baby inside it, snug and warm, and Diana hugged it. Through the rest of her exploration of the barn, she cradled it in her arms. And along the way to the cash register, she picked up a doll too.

A doll with no hair, and with a soft body. Her eyes (in Diana's eyes, the genderless doll was a she) opened and closed. Open, they were marble blue. Like James. Closed, they had thick black lashes. Like James. The lips pouted, around a nipple, Diana supposed.

Like James. For a moment, Diana forgot her own situation and smiled the way she knew she only smiled at that man.

Diana held the doll to her stomach. She turned her back to the center aisle of the barn, so that no one could see. "I'll hold this doll, Little Dolly, until I can hold you. I'll put her in the sleeping bag and keep her warm. I'll practice. I've never even babysat before. I need to be ready. When you're born, you can go in the bag, and you can hold the doll. And we'll figure out just what a carbed is. We'll figure it out together." Diana found herself teary-eyed as she went to pay for her things.

In a few hours' time, she'd fallen in love with her baby that she didn't even know she carried. She didn't even know that she and James conceived. Little Dolly seemed the hidden center of her body and the sudden center of her universe. James was now second in her own line.

Diana slid the doll into the sleeping bag and then laid them both carefully onto the passenger seat. She wondered how much a carbed would cost and how it worked. How much cribs and high chairs and diapers and bottles would cost.

How much would Little Dolly cost? What was Diana going to do?

Little Dolly had a father. She had grandparents. Diana's parents loved Diana, kept her room intact and ready for her. They would help. Diana knew this without a doubt. And…she would ask James for help. She imagined calling him, telling him about the baby, and maybe, just maybe, his voice would choke. Maybe he would ask her to come back.

And maybe she would.

But with this, Diana had doubts.

Diana tried to keep the doll's head poking out of the sleeping bag, but she kept sliding in. Diana wondered how good of a mother she would be. "I'll try, Little Dolly," she said. "I'll practice." She pointed the car again toward Waukesha. She settled her hand on her stomach.

Diana drove through Dubuque and then over the great bridge that crossed the Mississippi River and dropped her back into Wisconsin. She described to Little Dolly this lovely green state with hills and lakes and towns and valleys. She told her about the gold-capped state capitol and about cows, and about fields rustling gold with winter wheat and sunflowers. She talked about state fairs and county fairs and about playing outside until the night was lit blue by fireflies. "I don't know if you'll be born here, Little Dolly," she said. "But I was."

Diana was driving over the rolling hills when she felt a pang. And then she felt another one. The pang was familiar, but strong and she found herself wanting to double over, to gasp.

At the first gas station she came to, Diana parked and then ran for the restroom, both of her hands plastered to her abdomen. After locking the door, she lowered her jeans and found her panties coated with blood.

Just like a period. But different. Thicker, Diana thought. More complex. She pictured the blue of James' eyes, his dark eyelashes. The way his lips would pout around her nipple. The way this child's should have.

Diana leaned her head against the wall and cried.

She cleaned up as best she could, using the sink and wet paper towels. She bought a Kotex from the machine hanging on the wall. Then she settled herself, newly alone, in her car.

Tears still streaming, she considered the question again. To James? To her parents? The decision wasn't over. And this time, there was the new weight of an empty womb. A womb that only she knew was recently occupied.

From runaway lover to unwed mother to committed single parent to mother grieving the loss of a child. In less than twenty-four hours. In a year when life was young and seemed to stretch endless and filigree beyond the horizon. From the middle of nowhere, Iowa, to the middle of nowhere, Wisconsin.

Diana felt in the middle of nowhere. She was only twenty-one years old.

She was young.

Next to her, on the passenger seat, the now useless sleeping bag and doll.

Diana wept.

She stopped at a park near Mineral Point. Wandering into the woods, she came across a tree that she felt looked wise, as wise as the grandmother clock that stood at the foot of the stairs in the clock museum and said nothing to Diana as she left. Dropping to her knees, Diana dug a grave with her hands in the soft dirt around the great tree's roots. When it was deep enough, she wrapped the doll completely in the sleeping bag and buried it there.

"Goodbye, Little Dolly," Diana said, her dirty hands pressed against her stomach, filled with a child for a few hours and then gone. Filled with and emptied of a child Diana didn't even know she wanted that she wanted with her whole heart. A baby that might have created a great bridge to the love of her life who didn't see her as the love of his. A baby that might have created a great bridge from Iowa to Wisconsin, from lover to parents, present to past, home to home, from here to there.

A whole life lived in a few hours. A whole life changed and ended.

"Goodbye, Little Dolly," Diana said again and cried. "I wish I'd known what to do. I don't even know what a carbed is. I will never buy another sleeping bag. I will never buy another doll. Never again. It was only for you. And now…never again. There won't ever be another Little Dolly." She thought a minute and then added, "I'm so sorry." She wasn't sure what she was sorry for. She wondered what kind of mother she would be. Would have been. Would ever be.

Diana couldn't help but wonder if things would have turned out differently if she hadn't crept away. If she'd stayed in the warm bed she shared with James. If she was okay with being next in line. If she hadn't been struggling with a decision.

But Diana wanted to be a lifelong love. She wasn't a romantic; she was a renegade. But you didn't have to be a romantic to want love. To be first in line. To be lifelong.

Now there would be no lifelong. There would be no line at all.

Diana started for home. She took with her her bag of reasons, to stay and to leave, the whispers of clocks, the wisdom of silence, the love of parents, the pout of a special man's mouth, her own special smile. And her newly stated vow. She left behind a doll, and every doll, sleeping forever warm between the roots of a wise old tree.

THE END

ABOUT THE AUTHOR

Kathie Giorgio is the critically acclaimed author of four novels, two story collections and a poetry chapbook. Giorgio's stories and poems have appeared in countless literary magazines and anthologies. She's been nominated for the Pushcart Prize, the Write Well Award, the Million Writer Award, and for the Best of the Net Anthology. Giorgio's teaching career spans 21 years. She is the director/founder of AllWriters' Workplace & Workshop, an international creative writing studio in Waukesha, Wisconsin.

View other Black Rose Writing titles at <u>www.blackrosewriting.com/books</u> and use promo code **PRINT** to receive a **20% discount** when purchasing.

BLACK ROSE

writing™